Alex Lago

Alex Lago has worked as a word monkey on three continents. *Francesca* is the first of a series of novels he wrote in his teens and twenties when he was neither sober enough to contemplate sending them to publishers nor overly convinced his words were worth a lot more than his life. He's decided to self-publish his early novels because life has taught him only one lesson: be kind to yourself. These days, after years spent in Africa, London, and Manhattan, he lives on the shores of Lake Zürich, Switzerland.

For Francesca, and the friends we left behind.
'Al couer se comanda no'.

Published by LxMartini,Inc
Francesca © copyright 2024 Alex Lago
Cover Art: Jason Ong
Cover Image: Ahmet Buğra Avcılar on Unsplash

10 9 8 7 6 5 4 3 2 1

All rights are strictly reserved. For rights enquiries contact:
lxmartiniwrites@proton.me

Set in Odile Book: 9.5/12

ISBN: 979-8-9908791-0-2 (Print Version)
ISBN: 979-8-9908791-1-9 (eBook Version)

ITALODISCO, FRANCESCA & SOME BAD HABITS

This novel was written in a couple of weeks on a Lettera 32 typewriter in 1987. I was back at my parents' apartment in Yeoville, Johannesburg, after being rescued from Italy. I was eighteen years old. This was my first novel.

Milan, by 1989, was the druggy capital of Europe. The heroin wave that had first rolled through Italy in the '70s had just gotten worse through the '80s, and by October of 1989, the *New York Times*[1] was confident enough to report that, "The rapid rise of heroin use in Italy has left the country with the largest number of drug-related deaths in Western Europe. In 1988, the Government said, 809 people died from heroin overdoses, almost three times the number in 1986. Health officials say that with people widely sharing needles, more than half the country's estimated 300,000 heroin users have been infected with AIDS."

Heroin being made legal for personal use was part of the problem. Still a teenager and in Italy studying for a law degree, I'd fallen in love with a girl from Parma one hot, breathless summer night in a nightclub in Rimini. A girl who, like so many other kids back then, would find herself on a one-way trip to a full-scale addiction. Years and decades on, I've come to think of those days as a time of innocent addiction. Just a bunch of kids having a lot of fun, and with no idea what was waiting on the other side.

Those were the fading days of ItaloDisco and those spectacular nightclubs around Italy dripping in beats, sex, and heroin. Really, there was so much heroin running around back then that practically everyone was on the stuff: guys working in the banks and girls at the university and everyone in-between would blissfully shoot-up at lunch alongside shots of espresso.

I was lucky because I found a way out when things got ugly. My girl and I, we fell off the planet for a while back then, and did things that feel, now, as if the memories belong to another person. From another life. Though the scars are reminders that, while the memories may belong to another, the body was mine. Mine and—well—sure.

You get the picture.

---

[1] https://www.nytimes.com/1989/10/08/world/rising-heroin-use-and-addict-deaths-alarm-italy-where-drug-is-legal.html

I was lucky, as I said, that my mom flew in from South Africa and rescued me from that squat in Parma where we'd been steadily digging out our own veins and graves, my girl and I. A week later, I was on an Alitalia flight headed home.

And there, in my childhood bedroom, I wrote this novel.

Make of it as you will. It was inspired by what I saw, and those softcover Ludlum novels I carried around with me. It's a weird novel, I guess, but really, you had to be in Italy in the late-'80s to understand the sheer crazy of it all: the politics, the drugs, the music, the street culture. Mad, intoxicating days.

This novel was never sent to a publisher. It would, of course, never have been published anyway. And so, almost—can it really be?—forty years later, it's self-published here as it was written then, very much warts and all. Violent, obsessive, remorseless, gritty, restless, and with just some cosmetic edits (including the chapter titles).

At its core is the voice of an eighteen-year-old boy. I hope you'll forgive him that.

And if you're wondering what ever happened to the girl I met and fell in love with, the answer is—I never did find out what happened to her. There was no social media back then. No email. No WhatsApp. People simply vanished. I've always hoped she got off the H and found a way back to college to continue her art degree. But it's just as likely that she was found in a café or some backroom squat in Milan or Parma in that killer year, 1989.

So, wherever you are, this one's for you, Francesca. It's not great—but it's who we were, back then. We were works in progress. We always will be. And despite all the darkness, that summer of 1987, in your little green Fiat 500, driving full throttle on the autostrada to Lake Garda, riding that brown horse we loved so much, laughing all the while, windows open and long hair soaring, Righeira's '*L'estate sta finendo*' on the Pioneer stereo, those were some of the very best days of my life.

I survived and made a life writing words. It really happened, just as you said it would.

Zürich, Switzerland, May 29, 2024

Every chapter is the name of an ItaloDisco track. You can listen along on *Spotify: Profile: Alex Martini. Playlist: Francesca*

FRANCESCA

ALEX LAGO

PART ONE

1. Dharma: 'Plastic Doll'

A girl is sitting cross-legged on a wooden floor, her ribs cutting shadows below her tiny, naked boobs. Her wrists lie reversed on her folded knees, bubbling plasma and blood that spills down over her feet and into a pool that collects glossy below a metal-barred window.

Survival now is suicide.

She feels no pain, just a comfortable numbing of senses. Surely there must be pain in death? The thin, deep gashes on her wrists are oddly white, like semen below the flowing crimson fluid. A clot begins to form. She runs a palm over the gashes, scraping off the oozing plasma. It feels like paint, clinging to her fingers. Paint, she thinks. She bleeds paint!

She'd been close to death before. Too many times. With Sandro, last night, when he'd attacked her. Jesus. Where is he? Why is he not here? She wants him to return, to kick open the door to see her naked and dying below the window, hoist her up and drag her to the hospital, whispering encouragement in her ear. Tell her how much he cares. And what she's done—is doing—is brave, beautiful. Please, Sandro, come home. Because she is scared and cold.

Now, with the forming morning and pale light bleeding over her body, she's trying hard not to think of reasons for life. Regardless, they flood in, destroying her calm. There's Sandro to live for; he'll be back. Sandro loves her. Staring at the constant stream of blood dripping on the wood from her wrists, she finds this easy to believe.

Is her arm numbing? She lifts it carefully, not wanting to spill perhaps. It's dead-weight. She flips her wrist. Blood gushes over her thighs. She glances away, her arm dropping instinctively. Time is closing in. Her heart is racing, breath escaping in fitful gasps. Her body shivers, she has never felt so cold, never felt this chill in the winter. So cold despite the sun. Is her arm blue?

She has an urge to stand. This is not where she wants to die. This is where she worked and survived—this is where she suffered. In death, the girl feels like maybe she deserves more. There's a place she wants to return to—in the park, up the road. A special place only Sandro had seen. So green, so serene. She'd found it one night when—her arm is numb. Everything has gone numb—her lips jabbed by a billion pricks, heavy her eyelids. Time has ceased. Not even fear exists now.

Her swollen face falls forward, bowed to the crimson fluid of her life escaping before her. Ever so slowly, her thin body tilts forward before gravity slaps her face into the pool of slime, legs still crossed.

Death is white like the morning sunlight bursting in through the window.

2. Silver Pozzoli: 'Around My Dream'

The grey fingers of dawn drip in from the French windows and over the woman lying below a chequered duvet spread over a double bed. Her fear slowly passes with the reassurance of an awakening day. The nightmares that have kept her awake are just that— distant faded memories—of her daddy and the pistol pointing at his face.

Her hands creep below the duvet, finding the man sleeping beside her. He stirs, gradually forcing open his lids and blinking at her with watery eyes. He smiles, throwing his arm at the bed-side table and the wristwatch ticking beside a photo of the woman and the man standing before an ocean background.

'It's just gone six,' she says.

He groans, gives her a stare before shaking his head and shutting his eyes and slumping his head down onto the head-print on his pillow. 'You havin' nightmares again, Robi?'

She swallows, releasing his body.

'Your old man?'

'Yes.' She rolls onto him, resting her face on his hard chest, her eyes watching the world turn orange. 'I guess it's just my mind, you know, trying to deal with—with things.' His hand strokes her dreadlocked hair, his breathing steady beneath her face. 'Just trying to sort out—this whole. *This* ...'

He draws his body upwards, forcing her off him, and reaches for the table. His groping fingers find a pack of Camels and twirling two in his mouth, he plays fireman with an ivory Zippo, yachts imprinted in the yellow chunk of tusk. He hands one to her, his eyes invading her face.

'When you learn to accept what happened, Robi, when you're able to relieve yourself of this guilt-trip you're putting yourself through,' he shrugs, having said what he means. 'You'll never forget,' he says, 'but you can bury it so deep you'll hardly ever think about it.'

She drags hard on the cigarette and expels a thick stream of smoke like the rear-end of a scud-missile. Starts to say something, hesitates with her mouth forming the first word, shuts up and then, after another drag of poison, 'I'm scared, Wayne.'

'I'm here, baby,' he smiles at her. 'You're so young, Robi—time is on your side. You can put this behind you—all of it. Find something for yourself—escape.'

An astray tear trickles down her cheek. She flips it away irritably, turning her face from him and watching the sunrise beyond the veranda. Tugging a last drag from her smoke, she leans over him, reaching for the ashtray on the table and stubs out the smoke with too much vigour, upsetting gravity and some imperceptible balance that sends the ashtray crashing onto the carpeted floor.

'Shit!' She crawls out naked from below the duvet, rounds the bed with her body silhouetted in the dim light and lowers herself to her knees. She scoops up butts feeling like a whore—a whore, she thinks, to her own guilt. She returns the butts into the ashtray distastefully before blowing the ash around, forming patterns in the kindling radiance. The man motions with his cigarette and on her knees, Robi offers him the ashtray in the palm of her hand, allowing him to kill his smoke. He tosses the duvet off his tanned body, glorious as the warm morning filters over his hardness.

'I was thinking ... Wayne, I just need to get away from this— this *city* for a while, you know?'

'Where?' He glances at the woman standing above him. 'Like the coast, or,' he shakes his head, 'where?'

'I don't know.' She stares at him from the foot of the bed. 'I don't know anything no more—it's like ... I can't decide on anything—I don't fucking *know* anymore! I just don't ...'

Wayne stands and stretches without looking at her. She watches his broad buttocks shuffle through the bathroom door. When the shower begin dripping, she grabs a shirt from the carpet and buttons it up over her breasts. The house is dim on the way down the staircase and into the kitchen with her bare feet clapping on the cold tiles. She pulls ajar the refrigerator door to draw out a jar of honey and a carton of milk with sketches of missing girls. HAVE YOU SEEN *THIS* GIRL? We're all lost, she thinks, and rests the carton on her lips and gulps the white fluid that dribbles out from her mouth and over her chin to drip on the floor. She wipes it clean with her feet.

A bird is chipping outside, joined by another and yet another in a resonating cacophony. Robi steps to the blinded window, lifts the shutters and peers out at the garden, the lawn caressed in the softness of dawn.

'Are you serious about leaving?'

She wields, alarmed, her wide eyes staring at Wayne as he sits on the kitchen table with his hand rubbing a towel through his matted blond hair.

'What?'

'I was thinking.' He tilts his head down at the floor and un-clogs his ear-hole. 'You've been—I think you're headed for a breakdown or something, sweetheart. You know, death is always difficult the first-time round.'

'It gets easier?'

He meets her eyes and says nothing. She steps to him, placing the carton on the table and tracing his lips with her index finger.

'So what about Italy?' he says.

'What about Italy?'

'I have friends there—they'll be happy to put you up, you know, for a while. Show you around.'

'Italy?'

'Sure—the cradle of culture.'

'Yeah. I'll just draw out a million bucks from my private account in Sweden and shuttle right-on over.' She grabs the milk bottle and throws it back into the refrigerator rack before slamming the white door. 'I haven't got that kinda money.'

'I can borrow you twenty thou' or something—'

'Twenty *grand*?' She frowns. 'On what condition?'

'Condition?' He smiles. 'On condition you come back to me.'

'You're all I have, Wayne.' She paddles to him, noting his rise with every nearing step to his naked body. 'I love you. But this—this isn't necessary.' She kneels and licks her palm. She touches his cock before shutting her eyes and accepting it in her mouth.

'I love you, Robi,' he whispers, staring down at the action, an extension now, a sheath, and with his hand he tries to grip the table and swipes the honey off the counter and onto the floor where it smashes by her knees.

3. Steel Mind: 'Bad Passion'

She's gone. Beautiful, kind ... dead Francesca.

A man on the naked mattress lies motionless, eyes blinking up at a peeling ceiling. He reaches beside him on the stained floor to find a crumpled pack of Marlboro. He rips the pack open, disembowelling it, and stares within its foiled interiors. Empty. He crushes it and launches it across the room at a crucifix hanging from a flimsy nail. Sitting up, he crawls to the foot of the bed and lifts an ashtray, his fingers searching within the butts until he finds a smokeable *anshie.* Lighting a match, he squints down at the roach, cringing as he singes his nostril growth.

He stands on unsteady legs, takes a tentative step, and his foot stubs into an empty bottle of J&B. He watches it roll away from him, plunging into the wall and exploding in jagged, green splinters.

His clothes are abandoned in a dirty bathtub. He dresses wearily after having relieved himself, the splitting pain still present. Clothed now, he shuffles his face before a cracked mirror, attempting to get a complete view of his face. He looks like death. Running a hand through his thick, long hair, he wonders why he even bothers. He hasn't left the apartment in a week. What has he done? He can't remember doing anything besides drinking and breathing and doping. Purple rings stretch far below his black eyes. His lips are cracked, chapped, and he welcomes the exquisite pain when he forces a smile to slice and dice 'em. Blinking away his own hypnotic stare, he strides away from the mirror. Get out of here. His boots are beside the bed, and he slips them on before taking a last glance at the room and banging the door shut behind him.

Blinding white light stings his eyes immediately on stepping from the squat apartment block, forcing him to peer between cringing lids at the road. Milan is all but deserted on this August morning. Shops are shut, *CHIUSO* written on the bolted doors and chained metal gates. Traffic has been reduced to the occasional car storming through the suburbs.

A soft breeze bathes his perspiring body as he strolls toward the scattering of tall concrete looming ahead. He gets the subway and comes out near the Duomo and the public works at the under-construction Missori metro station. If he didn't know better, he'd probably believe a holocaust has taken place during his exile in the Via Nervesa apartment. But the only holocaust would have been the mass migration by the city folk to the southern reaches of Italy beginning August first, the national month of vacations. The world can forget about Italy for a month or so.

There's an open *tabaccaio* ahead, near the cathedral basking spectral white beneath the noonday sky. He enters the shop with congealing perspiration making him shudder. An elderly man is watching a portable television set, a rerun of Mike Bongiorno, and he glances up at the young man approaching him.

'Pack of Marlboro.'

'Tre mille lire.'

Sandro searches his torn jeans, suddenly realising he has no money. He frantically turns his pockets inside out. With a sigh, he meets the man's eyes and forces the blush to his cheeks. 'I've left my wallet at home,' he says and turns to leave disconsolately, then as an afterthought, 'are you open all day?'

The man shakes his head. 'Sorry, *figliolo*, I'm closing at one. I'm going on vacation. To Calabria.'

Sandro nods like this isn't a surprise. 'My form. I search the whole morning for an open tobacconist, and when I finally find one,' he shrugs. 'Are there any others that'll be open this afternoon?'

'*Boh.*'

'Okay. *Grazie.*'

Sandro's at the door when the old man shouts. *'Prendi!'*

Sandro wields to watch a pack of cigarettes float through the air toward him. He fumbles the catch, stoops to retrieve the fallen pack from the floor. *'Grazie mille,'* he says, headrushing hard.

'Va bon.'

The Marlboro tastes good as it etches his throat, biting his lungs. He crosses through the piazza *dei droggati*, two naked women standing tall with hands entwined and water belching from their wide mouths into a lily- and syringe-filled pond. Water trickles unnoticed on the shoulders of a boy sleeping with rags covering his body and a needle still stuck in his throat. On the granite stairs leading up to him lie more junkies—beautiful children seeking acceptance amongst one another with minds rushed to mush. They just sit there, day and night, glassy eyes glaring with something less than curiosity—now surveying the world about them with furtive apprehension. Sitting there with baggy clothes and slumped shoulders, sharing cigarettes and confusion. And always present the gentle splashing water glistening below the summer sky. Why, Francesca. Just why?

Sandro pauses above a girl with a gaunt face staring down in her lap where she burns a bottle-top with a lighter dissolving her dreams. 'Ciao, Rina.'

The girl glances up at him, soapy eyes taking him in. 'Sandro? I—we heard … about Francesca.'

'Yeah,' he nods down at her bald head, at the sleepers in her nose. 'That's really cool. You do it yourself?'

'Fuck you, Sandro.'

He wants to ask, for a share of her fix. But it's not like it used to be—before, when they'd shared their dreams and their dope. Now he watches her rid a bloody syringe of air before sucking up her concoction. 'I'll see you around, Rina. Where's Katia?'

'With her Russians.'

'Say hi for me.'

Her mind is otherwise occupied, and he walks away, leaving the girl to search her wafer-thin body for a vein that hasn't yet collapsed.

He hasn't consciously determined his destination until he stands below the concrete, mushroom-shaped Torre Velasca in all its brutal, golden malice. The doorman ignores him as he strides through the revolving doors into a cool, Formica-tiled lobby. He summons one of the elevators, glancing about him at the familiar surroundings; the old couch that stood near the security desk has vanished, but the tainted mirrors are still hanging in the elevator as it slides ajar before him with his pale face beckoning him in.

He rides it up to the top floor, playing with his hair, before emerging in a sun-drenched hallway. He steps to a set of oak doors directly before him. Wrapping on the wood, he focuses his eyes down on his boots. The door whispers open to unveil a semi-naked girl staring out at him furtively, long black hair cascading over pouting boobs. Her lips are puffy, swollen, and her words are filtered without a trace of movement. 'Yes? You delivering?' she asks.

'Zoran around?'

'Who wants to—'

She doesn't have the chance to complete her sentence 'cause Sandro pushes her aside and steps into the penthouse. The lounge is devoid of furniture but for an ashtray growing from the thick carpet beside a large man lying on his back with his propped-up head staring right at him.

'Jesus, look what the garbage truck brought in,' says the man, sitting up laboriously, potbelly swirling like it's alive. 'You look like microwaved shit, Sandro.'

'Appetising then,' Sandro says, and steps closer. 'I need to talk to you, Zoran.' He glances at the girl shutting the door. She senses his look and stares at him diffidently, then at Zoran.

'Sure—I heard about Francesca. Terrible. Fucking terrible, man.' He looks at the girl. 'Get dressed, *cara*.'

'Zoran, you promised—'

'Are you deaf?'

'Zoran—'

'I said *get dressed*!' His hands turn to fists on the carpet, his eyes darkening. 'You wanna feel it, huh?' As if pain is a concrete object. 'You wanna *feel* it?'

The girl shakes her head, she obviously knows what it feels like, and with pouting lips brushes past Sandro as if this is his fault. He watches her vanish into the pink bathroom and then squats beside the fat man, lighting a smoke and offering the pack.

'Relax, Sandro.' Zoran waits for the smoke to be lit. 'You look like you're about to pounce on me.' He slaps his belly pensively, sounding like a drum. 'So tell me what happened.'

'With Francesca? Nothing much—bad ride, I guess—slit her wrists.' He tugs on his smoke.

'You hard up, buddy?'

'Yes.' His answer in instinctive, and he realises why he'd left the apartment, his grief-lodging. His stash had run out last night. A sense of disgust returns in a flood of blood-smeared memories.

'How much d'you want?'

'I've got no fucking money.'

Zoran tips ash into the tall 'tray, rolling the cherry into a point, like a miniature strawberry. 'So then what? The usual story?'

'Sure.'

'Tonight?'

'Whenever.'

Zoran smiles. Yellow teeth. 'I'm glad you've come back. I was just talking about you to Giovanni.' He cranes his head toward the kitchen. 'Giova', get your fucking ass here!' Then he returns his pale, lizard eyes on Sandro. 'I met Azmi the other day—he asked about you, so I figured—' he turns his attention to a tall, silver-haired man in a black suit stepping toward him from the kitchen, 'Giova', look what crawled out of the sewer. You remember the other day when we ran into Azmi—'

'I believe you,' mutters Sandro.

'—and I said he'd be back?'

Giovanni nods, his eyes observing Sandro. 'Yes, you said he'd be back and here he is.'

Zoran holds up his hands like Jesus. 'There, what'd I tell you.'

'That I'd be back.' Like a dog needing a meal.

'You look like shit, Sandro. You had a bath lately?' asks Giovanni with nothing approaching concern.

'Yes, Giova'. I've been bathing in pity.'

'Giova, for Christ's sakes, you sound like an old queen—go get us some shit. *Dai*! The man is in mourning, for fucksakes.'

The girl finds that moment to appear from the bathroom clothed in a tight dress and make-up hiding her bruises. 'Will I see you later, Zoran?' It sounds more like begging that questioning but her dilated eyes are not going cold. Yet.

Giovanni returns from the kitchen armed with a tray and a plastic coin bag packed with ready-to-be-cut dreams. The girl watches the lines develop on the tray with wide-eyes, magical crystals of beauty, and her tongue slips from her thick lips. Giovanni brings the tray and places it on the floor by Zoran's foot.

'Come here.' Zoran motions with his fat-face at the girl. He sees her hesitate and smiles, holding out his hand. '*Vien' qua, baby.*'

She steps to him holding her stilettos in-hand. Zoran nods at the tray. 'See, baby, Zoran always keeps his word.'

She goes down and just then his hand suddenly slams into her head, grabbing her hair in his fist by the roots and pulling hard so the girl stumbles onto her knees with tears dripping down her screwed-up face. 'But you mustn't *bug* me, baby—okay? If I needed a wife, it wouldn't be some fucking diseased whore like you.' He releases his grip. 'Now fucking hurry up! You can see this bitch is hanging worse than you. You think you're the only coke-whore in town?'

The girl snorts up a couple of lines and stands still rushing to the ceiling.

'It's the new shipment I received from Miami, five days ago,' says Zoran, and watches Sandro snort up lines. 'Came with some horse too. You look sexy doing that,' he says as Sandro cleans his gums with the excess. Then turning to the girl, 'What the fuck are you still doing here?' He slaps her leg, and the sound startles her.

'Fuck off! Go make me some fucking money, go! *Via*! Get the fuck outta here.'

The girl rushes quickly for the door and leaves the apartment barefoot and not at all steady on them.

'What an ass.' Zoran winks at Sandro. 'You should see her give me head, Sandro—Jesus Christ. Sheer art. Nothing better than desperation and head, you know? But of course, you do—that's why Azmi's hanging for you. Giovanni will drive you tonight. Stay here 'til then.'

He hands the mirror back to Giovanni and stands up laboriously. 'And have a bath before you go, buddy. He wants to get away from the fucking desert, not fuck a fucking camel.' He leans forward and suddenly his hand shoots out like a coiled snake. Sandro cringes. The hand grabs his chin, forcing the face up, to stare at Zoran's steady eyes staring straight back at him. 'Your nose is bleeding.' Tenderly, he runs his finger into the glistening rivulet, then wriggles it between Sandro's lips. Watches him eat his blood. 'You must start looking after yourself, buddy.' He releases his grip and Sandro's face bows forward. 'You look like death, man.'

4. Don Harrow: 'Don't Break My Heart'

'You're sure?'

'Yes.'

'Okay. Sure-sure?'

'Yes!' she says and laughs.

Wayne smiles, running his hands gently over Robi's pale face. 'And you have the address in Milano?'

Robi flicks out a notepad from her jacket, opens it to the last page. 'Right here under Z, where it was when you asked me five minutes ago!' she says, wrapping her arms about the powerful man with her eyes staring past his shoulder at the departure lounge at O'Hare. 'Don't worry about me, Wayne.'

He holds her shoulders now at arm's length. 'It's arrivederci then, I guess.'

Robi tilts her head and kisses his veined hand. 'Wait. Here.' She unclips a pendent from her neck and holds it out in her palm, the golden crucifix twinkling below the lights. 'I love you, Wayne.'

'I know, baby.' He lifts the pendent and absently drops it into his pocket, his searching eyes not leaving her face. 'Just come back to me, okay? I'll die without you.'

She watches him walk away, swallowed quickly by the sea of people mulling in the airport as if he'd never even been there.

5. Sabrina: 'Boys'

I

The BMW stretch-limo' speeds up the ramp of an underground parking lot with Pirellis whispering on the tarmac. A blushing moon hangs limply above the lit-up city as the bimmer slips into the trickle of evening traffic. Couple of weeks back and it would have taken half-an-hour to get crosstown. Sandro, slumped on the back seat of the limo' and sipping on a Campari bitter, thinks it's high time he gets out of the city too. It's been a long time. A Marlboro burns in the ashtray beside him, grey smoke snaking to the roof. His gums are numb, his throat sensitive like he's swallowed anaesthetic. The occasional headlight shatters the tainted windows, stinging his dilated pupils. The magnificently carved cathedral drifts past, a silhouetted gothic construction rising in pen-tip-like towers into the muggy night.

Giovanni up front with the wheel in his hands slows for a red light and his eyes glance at the rear-view mirror. 'I'm sorry about Francesca. She was a nice girl,' he says.

'She was a whore, Giova'. What's so nice 'bout that?'

'That's not nice.'

'Why, because she's dead? No one gave a fuck when she was alive. We care for her now? Is that it?'

Giovanni returns his eyes on the road and eases the car gently forward. The limo' sails into the slip-road leading to the Savex Hotel. Giovanni pauses beside the staircase leading to the doors and the rainbowed lobby beyond. He swivels in his seat and extends a fist back, three bills clasped in his fingers. 'Catch a cab home. I have an engagement.'

Sandro downs his Campari. The door swings ajar and he climbs out of the limo', banging his head on the door frame. He stumbles out onto a red carpet and smiles at the kid holding the door open for him with disappointment on his face.

'Coke and tobacco,' Sandro tells him.

The porter slams the door shut and follows Sandro up the staircase to the lobby not expecting and not receiving a tip. Well-heeled folks whisper in hushed voices between the heavy oak furniture as Sandro checks out the crystal displays encased within their glass prisons on his way to the elevator bank. He joins a maid in the elevator, up to the twentieth, and climbs out with the Camera Royale dead ahead of him. There's feint music filtering out from the double doors joining the clouds of hash exuding out onto the hallway. He wraps on the door and waits until a man opens it, one hand slipped beneath a black dinner jacket.

'Azmi is waiting for me.'

The man nods levelly, his hand slipping out from beneath the jacket to wave Sandro in. Pillows have been thrown randomly on the carpet to form a foursome about a silver hubble-bubble. Two naked girls and a man with a white polo-neck sit around the hubbly, each sucking on a rubber pipe extending from the bubbling contraption into their inhaling mouths. The fourth man has a conservative suit, conservative presence, and no hair. He's lining up mountain ranges on a tray, Switzerland, brown bergs with snow-capped peaks. The girls watch Sandro come to stand above them. He squats next to a tube, lifts it, and places his lips on a bronze filter, joining to suck on the tarantula's legs spewing velvet poison through his mind.

'It's good to see you again, Sandro. Zoran told us you would come, and as usual, he has been true to his word,' the man with the polo-neck says.

'It's good to see you again, Azmi,' Sandro says, blowing a long steam of thick smoke and thinking about the damage his majesty had caused on their last tête-à-tête.

'This is Vincenzo,' the man nods at the bald guy creating his mountains. 'You probably recognise him.' The dark, bald man doesn't look up, and Sandro knows better than to pay attention. He glances at the girl beside him instead. Their eyes meet, the girl's got faded, veined eyes, and Sandro looks lower, at the hairless body contracting as she inhales another lung full of dope. The music seems to grow dimmer, the room drifting away in a grey haze.

'Come.' Azmi stands and the three whores follow suit. The dinner-jacket-man is standing before the bedroom chamber, holding the double-doors ajar for the foursome who leave Vincenzo to scale the Eiger. There're scented candles burning in the bedroom, illuminating a tall bed where a sjambok waits on a silk sheet. Beyond the bed, tied together by leather straps, is a DIY crucifix made of snaking branches. Azmi turns to dinner-jacketman with a dismissing hand. 'Leave us. Go keep Vincenzo busy.'

Azmi leaves no room for contradiction and waits for the man to shut the doors in complete silence before turning to his harem of whores on junk. 'You two, lie here,' he says, his eyes glancing down at the two girls who follow his pointing finger to lie naked on the bed, bronzed bodies glistening in the dim, nebulous light. Azmi grabs hold of the sjambok and turns to Sandro. 'They've been bad.'

Sandro accepts the whip. Stares down at the two girls, his nuts tightening as they stare back at him diffidently.

Azmi heads over to an easy chair, stripping off his pants on the way. 'They've been bad. Just like you. But I'll deal with you later.'

II

Amyl nitrate and room deodoriser and coke and Azmi's face and lube for grunting Azmi steam-training away, hands and fingers jabbing and clawing, grabbing and squeezing.

Coughing, Sandro slides open his eyes and glances about him bewildered. Azmi has dried at the back of his throat, and he swallows painfully. The two girls sleep on the pillows with bodies entwined. Nicely striped asses, and Sandro observes his work with something that feels a little like passion. There's a clock ticking in the sultry room. Standing, he staggers about momentarily with an awe-inspiring headrush as his brain spews out toxins and questions. With palms rubbing frantically at his temples, he sets off in search of his clothes. His jeans and shirt have been thrown out from the bedroom. His fingers inspect his tingling body. Blood has clotted, dry and rough on his fingers whose mere touch sends spasms of hot irritation like he's forgotten to clean up after diarrhoea. Dressed, he steals a pack of Phillip Morris from the floor and allows his eyes to take in the girls. He'd been like them once, doing it for the jollies. Not now, now it's survival.

He steps out of the hotel room and shuts the door behind him. The hallway is cool, an air-con purring softly overhead. Beyond the ceiling-high windows at the end of the hallway, a perfectly oval crimson sun hatches a new day and a new beginning.

Summoning the elevator, Sandro gobs up into a succulent growing from an elaborately carved pot. On the trip down he checks out the three bills in his jeans pocket and resolves to buy himself breakfast before returning to the penthouse. In the lobby, Vincenzo with the sparkling bald head is trapped in a conversation with a young woman scribbling in a notebook. The bald guy pauses in his sentence, spotting Sandro approaching. Sandro listens as he passes with a polite, knowing smile.

'The heroin crisis is what our administration is working on day-in and day-out, it's ...'

Dawn is Milan summer-chill when he steps out from the lobby. Streetlamps shine nebulously, casting pools of yellow on the dirty streets. He crosses to a 24-hour faux American diner with a scattering of plastic and vinyl booths and slumps into one near a window, staring at the tall hotel across the avenue from where he'd just come. A plump, yawning waitress walks up and waits while he scans the menu.

'Just give me a pineapple burger and coffee—lots of coffee.'

His hands are shaking when he lights a smoke and allows his mind to drift with the smoke escaping from his lips. Concentration is difficult, the coke and hash and poppers having worn his mind down flat. He tips ash into a tray lethargically and runs a hand through his matted hair. Christ, sticky and matted. On his wrists he can see lacerations, Jesus at 5am. He rips at his hair strands irritably, fingers coming away with a thick lock of black hair. He sets the strands alight in the ashtray and his eyes watch despondently as the flame dies instantly. A polystyrene cup is dumped before him, and he looks up at the girl.

'Thanks.'

'Your burger's on its way.'

'You killing it?'

She understands, she's his age, and they share their common fate with a meaningless joke in meaningless lives. The coffee's warm and soothing to his aching throat. He'd prefer an espresso. It tastes like shit. Perhaps he'll stop over at the Flamingo Club on his way back and have one. *'Flamingo nests are made of mud, Sandro.'* Francesca and her warped fucking ideas.

Jesus, Francesca, why the fuck would you do something like that?

'You say something?'

He blinks up at the waitress, startled, blinks at the steaming food beside his elbow. 'No—no. Nothing.'

The girl shrugs and walks away, but she's wondering about the scars on his wrists for her eyes are too tired to notice incognito. Sandro digs into the seeded bun, forcing down mouthfuls. He's hungry and he chews down the burger with his mind enveloped in a picture of Francesca. Strange, all the memories, all the time condensed in a still-life in his mind, that night he'd met her down in the club in Rimini, outside sharing a joint. Orange light bathes the city in warmth now, and he decides to walk with his boots clapping heavily on the sidewalks, the forlorn city refusing to awaken. Faceless figures sweep past and avoid him on the oily sidewalks. He lights up smoke after smoke. They help him concentrate and focus his scattered thoughts and memories.

And the thought that keeps coming back is that he wants out. Out of this city. Out of this fucking life.

He enters the lobby and nods at the dozing guard waiting to be relieved from his shift. Giovanni allows him access to the penthouse with a scowl, his hands buried deep in his pockets. 'Zoran called.'

Sandro shrugs, showing what he thinks but not daring to articulate his thoughts into words—fuck him—and steps into the sun-drenched apartment. 'When d'he call?' His mind is drifting, skipping realities and he needs his sanity. He needs a nice, long fix.

'—ago,' says tall Giovanni, consulting his Rolex.

'Oh.' Sandro nods appreciatively.

'A friend of his is flying in from the States,' continues Giovanni, following Sandro to a pink-tiled bathroom where the girl had taken shelter the day previous. 'Zoran wants you to look after her—give her a good time.'

'Her?' Sandro clips open the medicine cabinet, staring at Giovanni from the mirror for an instant. He lifts a bank-coin packet from the cabinet and turns to glance vacantly at Giovanni before resting the bag on the pink toilet seat and twisting the bath faucets on.

'That's not yours,' says Giovanni.

'Azmi is happy,' says Sandro. 'And I need a painkiller for my sacrifice. Okay?' He slips off his top and jeans slowly like he's a stripper, smiling at Giovanni before squatting within the rising warm water. 'And you know I don't do girls, Giova'.'

'I'm pretty sure Zoran doesn't want you to fuck her,' shouts Giovanni over the tumbling water. 'Just show her a good time.'

'There's a difference, is there?' Sandro shuts the water and points at a towel on a sliver rack. Giovanni brings it over, his eyes staring down, and watches Sandro dry his hands before inserting a fingernail into the bag and snorting up his brown sugar.

'That shit'll kill you.' Giovanni is consciously looking away from Sandro's body now as he lies back in the warm cocoon with his heroin thoughts.

'It already has.'

Giovanni doesn't argue. 'And it's not yours so put it back where you found it. It belongs to Luca. And she'll be here at two.' He turns and steps out of the bathroom. 'Remember, two, this afternoon. Don't let us down, Sandro, Zoran's losing patience with you.'

Sandro turns on the taps to flood his body and his fading consciousness with cool reviving water before leaning from the bath and taking another snort from the bag. Blood drips from his nostrils onto the tiles. He sinks into the water with his head tilted back. His face is numb. And he's getting queasy. He splashes water on his face, but the nausea won't go, forcing him to climb out to puke the pineapple burger into the toilet. Puking on heroin isn't the same as puking after twenty B52s, it's like gobbing, only he's spewing his insides 'stead of the usual mucus. He gives up the bath and heads naked for the kitchen, still wet and swallowing phlegm and puke, to grab a six-pack of Peroni from the refrigerator. Crosses silently to the bedroom, knocking the tall ashtray over en route.

The ceiling and walls in the bedroom are mirrored, and he watches himself cross to himself naked and dangling invitingly. A king-sized waterbed is behind him, memories of Zoran hazy like the sunlight filtering in from a window and sparkling pink off the mirrors, an outside reflection from within.

Unscrewing a Peroni, he clangs it against its reflection and offers a toast—'cin-cin'—and watches the man swallow. 'Drink up,' says the man, 'we got a whole dozen to get through.' His heart is thumping wildly, perspiration dripping from his brow. Ever present is puke running up his throat. Those girls are haunting him. It isn't the first time he's fucked with adolescent bum-girls but those two—fuck, they'd seemed so young—as old as Francesca, as young as he'd been once, and it makes him wanna puke memories of the first time with Zoran. He gulps down a mouthful of beer and puke, burps fouls smelling air and wonders what's stopping him from getting the fuck out, away from the backyard chemical abortionists of his dreams. He studies his reflection, at a cigarette scar just above his pubic hair. Where the fuck are his cigarettes?

He heads for the shut door. And hears something scuttle outside.

His hearing is sensitive like his flesh. Someone's just shut the front door. There's an intruder and about ten grams on the toilet seat! He stops at the door and listens. Not a sound. Had he imagined it? Is he somehow hallucinating on heroin? Like fuck he's not.

He grabs the doorknob with his breath clutched in his lungs and eases open the door. Peers through the tiny slit, into an empty lounge. No shadows, no noises. If there is an intruder, s/he's taking great pains to stay hidden. A thief? A junky? A rapist? A *sodomiser*? Fucking *think* it through! Obviously, the intruder has slipped unnoticed into one of the rooms in the penthouse.

But which one?

Sandro had not heard another door shut after the first, the front. All the doors are shut now. The kitchen has no door. The intruder is therefore in the kitchen. Let's go, Sherlock, he thinks, and eases himself out into the lounge, carefully treading to the kitchen with his naked feet silent on the thick carpet.

He pauses beside the doorway and slowly, slowly, he twists his head around the doorway and smacks his face on something metallic that hovers at crotch level. Grunting, he falls to one knee with his hands cupped about his nose.

'Fuck!' he grunts as a figure steps quickly past him, into the lounge, and Sandro squints and blinks up at a silhouetted man. The man's short and squat and he's stepping back cautiously. 'Who *are* you,' he snaps, almost tripping up on the marooned ashtray, 'what are you doing here?'

Sandro stands up wearily, fingers stroking his nose and his eyes inspecting for blood. 'Is this like one of those fucking TV shows? Who the fuck are *you*, buddy!'

'I'm looking for Giova'.'

Sandro scratches his pubic hair and realises he's naked at the same time as the guy's eyes slide on down. He steps into the bathroom and slams the door shut. 'He's not here,' he shouts, dumping the bag into the cabinet and dressing quickly.

'Bullshit. I called him no more'n two hours ago and he told me to come right over.'

'And it takes you two hours?' Sandro steps into his boots and walks out into the lounge. Gets a good look now at the shabby man with the metal buckle that had almost sheared his nose off. His head's bald but for a crown of metallic silver spikes, remnants of some messed-up hair-implant. 'No one's here.'

'You're someone,' says the dude.

Sandro brushes past him and heads for the front door, testing the knob. 'How d'you get in, anyway?'

'I've got a key.' The guy dangles it as evidence. 'And you? You one of Zoran's … boys?'

Sandro looks at his clothes. Cheap. 'You can't afford me, buddy.'

'Like shit I can't. But I've come for my package—did Giovanni leave it with you? Have you got it?'

'No. What are you talking about.'

Nodding like he's not buying any of this shit, the man walks to the bathroom and stands in the pink gloom, his eyes craning about. Opens the medicine cabinet and wields triumphantly with his cravat swinging machete-like. 'I'm talking about *this*!' he says, waving the bank-coin package. '*This* is what I'm talking about.' He kicks the door shut and shouts, 'Asshole!'

Closet addict thinks Sandro. But an addict all the same 'cause addicts don't fucking share. Ever. Still, there's hope so he sits on the carpet and stretches to grab a pillow. The clock quivers to twelve-twenty. Something's happening at two. The toilet flushes and the man coughs hollowly beyond the white door. What the fuck's happening at two?

The bathroom door swings open and back he comes, big eyes and big smile, shaky fingers and filmy sweat. 'What's your name?'

Fifty bucks comes to mind.

The man squats beside him before lowering himself onto his broad ass with a long groan. He nods at the pillow in Sandro's hand. 'Can I have that?'

Sandro obliges absently. What the fuck's happening at two?

'I'm Luca,' says the man, shuffling his shoulders on the pillow with his eyes gawking. 'Are you shy? Is there something to drink?'

Sandro looks at the clock. *Think*!

'—name anyway?'

'I don't know.' Sandro stands, running his hands through his damp hair. 'I'm going for a nap. If I don't see you before you go,' he shrugs indifferently and heads for the bedroom and slams the door shut. He lies on the floor with the noonday sun warming his body and dozes off with Giovanni's face before his shut lids telling him something about Zoran and women.

He dreams of planes and Francesca hanging off a building pointing at the sky, *up*, she screams, *up, up is the only way out!* Her hands like tentacles brushing against his groin.

Sandro sits up instinctively from REM confused and fearful. Luca's staring down at him, smacking his lips like he's about to have an appetizer. 'I won't hurt you,' he says and draws out a Gucci wallet as insurance, extracting a thick wad of notes and thumbs 'em out and tosses a few onto the floor. Watches with heavy-hooded, red-as-dead-zombie eyes at the whore who scuttles about trying to collect the drifting money.

Sandro forces the bills into his tight jeans. Looks up at Luca with his pants down to his ankles.

And heads for the ajar door.

'Where *the fuck* are you going?'

'Preparation H,' he says, and Luca can only imagine what's coming next, 'lie down wait for me.' Sandro moves quickly through the lounge to the bathroom with a thundering heart. Where's the old fuck hidden the dope? He throws open the medicine cabinet and an electric-razor tumbles onto the sink, smashing into third-world components. Move! Where the fuck is it? Satisfied, after a crazy search through the bathroom, that the dope has vanished, he turns and steps out to—

'You looking for this?' Luca stands beside the ashtray waving the package before his naked groin. 'Why don't you come here and suck it up.'

Sandro hesitates. Stares at the man, at the door, then back at the grinning man. Fuck this shit. He moves to the door watching Luca standing motionless with the flaps of his nose all swollen and red like his cock.

'Where are you going?'

'Nowhere near you, bud.' Sandro twists the doorknob. Locked. He looks down at the Yale. A hand grabs his shoulder and wields him around. Sandro keep swivelling with a right hook. His fist cracks a path into Luca's mouth. The guy stumbles two steps back with a wide-eyed, staring face, before falling back on his ass like some footballer in Serie A. Sandro throws the Yale and storms out onto the hallway. Freezes. Turns back for the apartment to find Luca on his knees, hands enveloped about his mouth as blood seeps between his fingers.

The package is on the floor beside his feet. He gurgles something incoherent as his eyes settle on Sandro with hate and contempt and not a little fear. Sandro lunges for the package. Luca knows his intention and tries to reach it first. The two men touch hands on the package but Sandro's always too quick, shifting the package one way and slamming an elbow into Luca's throat. The guy roars, hands grabbing his face as Sandro sprints out from the apartment.

He forces the package below his sweatshirt and summons the elevator and smooths the hump at his belly, willing the damn elevator *on*. He's sweating hard when the elevator slides open, allowing him access into the levitating cubicle in the sky. He stares up at the alternately flashing green light, 11,10,9, Jesus, come *on*! What if the asshole has called security? Christ, Zoran will fucking … Sandro feels sick at the thought. He stares as the door splits and before him is the lobby appearing like a different world. He spots the security guy reading his *TV Sorrisi e Canzoni* behind the shimmering front desk.

Sandro eases past and heads for the exit. A woman steps into the lobby, nods at him, tall and pretty with dreadlocks cascading over her shoulders, and her clear eyes stare at him as he brushes past and *out*, scampering into the heat and sensing her eyes on him as he sprints down the wide avenue for a blue Fiat taxi pulling away lethargically.

Sandro waves at it, shouting, 'Yo! *Yo!*' Regardless, the cab must roll slowly to the red traffic lights up the block where it waits for Sandro to run to it with his hands holding the package in place like he's injured.

He reaches the cab as the lights turn to green, lunges onto the rear seats and says, '*La stazione, dai, porca troia, ho fretta!*'

6. Propaganda: 'Dr Mabuse'

Stale cigarettes overpower a tiny office in downtown Milan. A metal desk with files and papers converged haphazardly upon it stands before a blinded window. Metal filing cabinets with dangling drawers line the olive-green walls.

A grey-haired man sits behind the desk scribbling on a pad. A siren gathers momentum beyond the window before being replaced by the monotonous tapping of typewriters outside the frosted-plate door. He lifts a manilla folder, scans the memo briskly and thinks how strange it is that obituaries are always so neatly set out in the department. A tidy end. A convenient state burial at the kin's bequest, teenage suicide in a city turned frantic with indifference. It's so neatly packaged. A problem only arises when the corpse is a Jane or John Doe. Then the police department must fork out money—and God only knows City Hall's running on a shoe-string budget—and time to identify the unclaimed. The unloved. The lonely freaks brooding in the bowels of the city.

The man squeezes the intercom button beside his telephone without straying his eyes from the memo.

'Yes, Chief Inspector Virdis,' cracks a female voice in static air.

'I want Onassio and that Englishman—what's his name—'

'Blake—'

'Yes, him. I want 'em here now.' He flicks off the call without bothering to listen to the inevitable response. Why the hell does the dreaded receptionist feel the urge to have lengthy conversations down the fucking intercom? It's not a fucking telephone! He returns his mind irritably to the page. His eyes jump back and forth, absorbing. Memorising. The intercom buzzes alarmingly. 'Yes,' he snaps punching the button, '*what?*'

'Onassio and Blake are here, sir.'

'Did I ask you to call them?'

'Yes, sir, about two min—'

'So why the fuck are you *telling* me? Get them in here! For chrissakes.' He leans back on his swivel chair as the door is pushed open and two men step in with similar-styled suits. They nod at the chief inspector before sitting on two bareback chairs before his desk.

'I received this half an hour ago,' he begins after the men have swapped pleasantries, 'from our mayor. His honour,' the chief inspector smiles at the grey-haired Onassio, sharing a private joke because he's known the man for almost thirty years, 'says if we don't find a way to curb the recent increase in ODs, he's gonna start reshuffling the department.' He looks at Blake, sitting forward on his seat trying to read the reversed pages on the desk. 'It says,' continues Chief Inspector Virdis, following Blake's stare, 'that there were fifteen overdoses last night, bringing the total for the week to eighty-three.' He lights an MS. 'The city's fucking drowning in dope, gentlemen. Badly cut dope at that. And the press wants blood. So, the mayor, his *honour*, is demanding action. Where does the supply come from? Who is the supplier of this killer batch? How does it get here?' He casts his level eyes on Blake. 'Do you have anything to contribute, signor Blake? What does Scotland Yard have to say?'

Blake exchanges a glance with Onassio. 'Well, we know that a massive cargo of cocaine and heroin was shipped from Miami three weeks ago. Destination Naples. The FBI was tipped off too late.'

'And?' prompts Virdis.

'We lost it,' answers Onassio, 'the ship docked in Napoli on the first, the narc' boys had a search warrant all ready and stormed the ship immediately—'

'—and found nothing but a joint butt,' completes Blake, cleaning his nails absently.

'Who was the vessel registered to?'

Onassio meets the chief inspector's gaze. 'That's where it gets interesting. The Atlas Corporation. The vessel is named Atlas Four—it's one of five owned by a Miami-based conglomerate.' He clears his throat. 'We ran Atlas through Interpol's computers, but—'

'—it's a dummy corporation,' completes Blake, playing with the crease on his silk trousers. 'Layers within layers, the standard drill.'

'A smokescreen,' says Onassio.

'Too sophisticated for the Camorra,' says Blake.

'But not for the Colombians,' says Onassio.

Virdis looks at the pair of them. Christ, he thinks, too early for this comedy show. 'Can you get Scotland Yard onto this, signor Blake?'

Blake nods. 'Already have.'

'Well then let's get to it. Onassio, a word, please.'

Blake stands and seems a little put-out as he shuffles to the door and shuts it loudly in his wake. 'I don't trust that man. God knows why, but I don't trust the fucker.'

'Because you hate anything English, Giuseppe.'

Virdis kills his smoke and runs his fingers over his face. 'I remember it all so different. It wasn't like this when I grew up. I mean, we were as poor as whores, but people were—good, you know what I'm saying? People *cared*.'

'Sure.'

'I grew up near the San Siro.'

'Here we go,' says Onassio and smiles.

'I went past the other day and there's ... druggies and pushers with their goddamn cellular phones peddling shit on the sidewalks to kids, Pierro. These kids, I mean, what have they got to live for? Give 'em some drugs and of course they'll take. Why not?' He slaps the memo. 'I want 'em,' he says and fixes his weary eyes on Detective Onassio, 'I want the pushers. Everyone on our files—bring them all in. I want every available man on this—and I don't give a shit if they're on leave—I want *every*body working on this. You organise the teams. Hit the streets with everything we've got. Bring to me anyone who knows anything about this Miami shipment.' He glances down at the file. 'Jesus,' he spins the folder across the desk, 'the youngest was fourteen. Fourteen. They found a nine-year-old in a subway toilet last week—she'd been … what kind of animals, Pierro, I'm asking you.'

Onassio shrugs.

'You think I'm outta touch, don't you? You think I don't know what's happening out there?'

'I never said that.'

'But that's what you think. You're right. I've been stuck behind this desk for too long. But I know this,' he taps the memo, 'this city's being drowned in the shit right now. And I don't give a *damn* about sociology and psychology and contributing causes to drug addiction—I care only about one thing. We gotta get rid of the shit, Pierro, we gotta get rid of the dope. And then we can sort out the problems. 'cause the dope's killing the kids, they can't think straight on the stuff.'

Onassio stands. He knows the city. Drugs *are* the city. Get rid of one pusher and there's another ten waiting in the wings, smarter and tougher, to take over shipments from Miami and Istanbul and, 'I'll get on it immediately.'

7. Chris Luis: 'The Heart of the City'

Robi finds the front door to the penthouse ajar. She ducks her head in, calls out, 'Hullo,' but there's no reply within the sun-drenched pad with the tumbled over ashtray leaking out its insides over the carpet. She hesitates a moment, checking out the hallway furtively, before entering the apartment. 'Hullo,' she calls again. On the floor, a fresh bloodstain on the rich carpet causes her to shudder involuntarily. Forcing her eyes—her mind—away, to gaze at the empty sitting room. 'Zoran?' she says uncertainty and then shouts, 'Zoran?'

As if in reply, the telephone shrills to life somewhere in the apartment. Plenty of extensions follow, and it sounds like a train-station. Her eyes search for a receiver. She discovers a shrilling one hanging on the kitchen wall and lifts it, listening to a stranger whispering in her ear.

'*Pronto? Pronto?*'

'Hullo,' she replies numbly.

''allo? *Cazzo sei?*'

'Uhm. This—this is Robi?'

'Robi? Ma scusa ... oh—wait,' the voice turns softer, 'wait,' sudden comprehension, '*Wayne's* friend? Robi from America?'

'Yes. Is this Zoran?'

'Yes. Did you meet Sandro? Can I speak to him?'

'No.'

'No? What do you mean "no"?'

'Well, I just walked in—the door was open but—I don't think there's anyone here?' There's a lengthy pause as she listens to Zoran's brain echoing on the line. To break the uneasy silence, she says, 'What does he look like?'

'Doesn't matter because he's gonna look a lot different when I'm done with that sonofabitch. So the door was open, is that right?'

She doesn't want to get whoever this Sandro is into more shit, so she says, 'I bumped into a guy with jeans downstairs, about twenty or so. Pretty face, black hair—'

'That's him,' says Zoran. 'Did he leave?'

'I think so. Maybe he's coming back?'

'Coming back?'

'Like he went to get something or—'

'Like what? Crackers and fucking cheese?'

'I don't—'

'Okay, listen, Robi? I'm gonna be back on Monday. Make yourself at home until then, okay? There's a number above the phone in the kitchen. Are you—'

'I'm here now. Is it this one? 716-1160?'

'Yeah. That's my friend. His name is Giovanni. Give him a call if you're lonely or bored. He'll show you the town, okay?'

'Thank you.'

'Good. And if you need some action, under the bed in the main bedroom, okay? Help yourself. And use whatever bedroom you want. But not mine. The one with the mirrors. That's mine.'

'I don't,' she says but the line's dead because Zoran's spirit has hung up. Robi sits down on the kitchen table, clipping her bag open to extract a pack of Chesterfield. Lit up, she shakes a strand of hair from her eyes and exhales loudly. She'd landed in Rome yesterday, slept the night at the airport hotel before catching the train to Milan. Then the cab and here she is. So much for the great vacation through Italy, she thinks sombrely.

She stands, yawning, and examines the apartment indifferently like an estate-agent making mental figures of worth. Two days in a new country, twenty thousand dollars to her name, and she's bored. Terminally bored. And more than bored—unhappy. What was Zoran's friend's name? She grabs the receiver and dials the number with a hesitant finger. She needs to stop thinking. Simple as that. About her father. About Richard. They're gone. Time to move on. Guilty or not. She thinks about Wayne who she'd tried to call collect last night and who wasn't home. The phone beeps in her ear. And continues 'til she's certain no-one's gonna reply. It's for the better, anyway. She's lousy with people. Can't even recall his name. She replaces the phone on the wall.

'You must be Wayne's friend,' a voice says behind her, and she cries out, side-stepping rapidly and colliding into the kitchen table with waves of pain running up her hip. She stares back at a white-haired man holding a cap in his hand. 'I'm sorry,' he says amused. 'I didn't mean to startle you.'

'Startle me!' She's got a temper this girl, he thinks. 'Startle me?' She rubs her bruising below her skirt. 'You fucking scared the *shit* outta me, you asshole!'

'I'm sorry, *signorina*. Are you okay? I'm Giovanni.'

'Yeah, I'm fine.' She checks him out and then points at the phone number above the receiver. 'You're him?'

'I hope I'm a little more,' he says, 'than just a number.'

She smiles. 'I'm Robi.'

'I know.' The man looks about the apartment. 'Have you met Sandro? Is he here somewhere?'

'No. What's with that dude—everyone wants a piece of him.'

'Everyone?' The guy looks at her. 'Who's everyone?'

'Zoran called. I spoke to him.'

'Ah.' Giovanni smiles, reassured.

'Let's go, Giovanni.'

'Go?'

'Yes, let's go somewhere.'

'Where would you like to go?'

'I don't care. Let's just go.'

It sounds almost as if she's pleading. And maybe she is. He's company speaking English in a strange land. This is what she needs. 'I'm hungry. Let's go eat. Spaghetti.'

8. Round One: 'In Zaire'

The procession rolls beneath a baking sky with a black open-top limousine, surrounded by a dozen police bikes, leading the way. A tri-coloured flag bristles on the enormous vehicle's bonnet, clapping along with the throng that stands six, seven deep on the dusty sidewalks.

The new king. The king is dead. Long live the king. Faces and arms dangle from apartment windows, little flags waved in dirty hands, streamers falling like rain. A fluorescent tape cordons off the sidewalks, khaki uniformed policemen patrolling the perimeters, trying to control the horde. Fists punch the muggy air in unison, words chanted, a song of freedom accompanied by applause and cheering and dancing.

Standing in the half-a-million dollars' worth of German luxury, a big man in a big suit, waving at his people. His people now. Because only forty-eight hours ago the people had belonged to another. To his brother. Dead now. Dead and buried and forgotten.

The blond-haired assassin leans out from his window five storeys above the street, watery eyes gazing down at the passing procession. The limo' slowly rolls directly below him on the pot-holed street and he focuses his eyes on the king with the leopard-skin cap covering his Olympian-sized head. His wife sits beside him with her head twisting nervously about.

The blond assassin stoops over and lifts a rifle from the wooden floor beside his feet and cracks a cartridge into the chamber. He checks his wristwatch and dabs sweat from his brows. The flair will go off in twenty seconds. He crouches onto one knee and sinks the rifle-butt into his shoulder, rests the barrel on the windowsill. He twists his neck until the rifle becomes an extension of his body—a third arm. Blinking away the sweat, he focuses his left eye on the long sights. The crosshairs move until the leopard skin-cap appears in the scope. With two fingers, he adjusts the sights, his arms following the Olympian head along.

Seconds now. Where's the flare? Down below, he spots a man jumping over the cordon tape, waving his hands frantically as he sprints for the limo' that has almost reached the end of the block.

The assassin knows it will turn left and run out of sight: Last chance then. He sees two cops strike the running man with their rifles. The assassin blinks once. Where the fuck's that flare? Where's the fucking diversion? Too late now. He can no longer wait. Typical Third World Revolutionaries, he thinks. Time for his own diversion.

He focuses the sights on the running man. He's being dragged away by two cops. In the scope, his face is bleeding. The assassin takes half-a-breath and squeezes the trigger.

The report's silenced by the festivities. The man springs out of the cops' grip, his head splattered across the tarmac. The cops stare about bewildered. One cop kneels beside the corpse on the dusty earth. He reaches for his weapon. The assassin reloads three more rounds and fires one through the cop's face. The other cop looks at his partner's face vanish and immediately turns to the crowd that's pressing closer now and shouts at them. Silent words from up where the assassin watches. And probably silent to the crowd by the looks of it, because they're marching forward now. A half-dozen cops run onto the scene, waving their arms about and then their rifles. The assassin drops the second cop with a round that enters the back of his skull.

The rest of the cops fall onto their knees and blast warning shots over the heads of the crowd closing in. They don't back away from their forward march, machetes and knives and sjamboks and AKs in hand. The cops open-up for real now, onetime sizzling lead, their firearms ak-ak-ing into the throng. Domino-like, the shouting throng drop to the hot ground in sprays of fiery crimson as those behind run over their slain comrades to race at the clapping automatic rifles.

The assassin flicks the crosshairs back to the limo' and traces the leopard cap. The king is gesticulating at his driver. So close in the crosshairs that the assassin thinks he can observe the words drift in the hot air. Alsatians have been set loose, leaping into quickly evacuating bystanders, jaws snapping through faces and legs, arms and wrists. One of the police bikes pulls up to the limo' and the assassin sees the rider stand and scream at the driver of the limo', pointing him forward.

Smart boy thinks the assassin.

The driver turns in his seat and his mouth is screaming at the royal couple in the rear seats. 'Get down!' The assassin knows the words, has heard 'em shouted so many times, *get down*. But it's all too late. The assassin squeezes the trigger. The queen's head vanishes in a yellow-green explosion. It's the last thing the man who was king for a day will see. Because the next round shatters through his throat.

And now there's just silence. And dust.

The driver stares down at the corpses on the back seat. Should have driven away, thinks the assassin, who takes a final assessment from the scope and then flings the rifle into the room. He ducks his head from the window and straightens his tie. He leaves the room, lighting a smoke and taking a deep drag. And hears a flare bang somewhere outside the room. Fucking idiots, he thinks.

Death always reminds him of those instants after an orgasm, when he suffers the healing nourishment of his soul.

9. Koto: 'Visitors'

Snowcapped mountains stretch before them in the distance, sparkling beneath a clear sky. Giovanni gazes in the rear-view of the limo' at the pretty girl chain-smoking on the rear seat. She stares out of the window transfixed by the villages in shades of red and ochre passing by in the soft light. Between the villages lie green fenced-off cropland with the occasional *contadino* in faded clothing working the land with an unsmiling family. The land is old and difficult to yield.

'You won't see many farms out here,' says Giovanni, 'this is the industrial heart of Italy. Don't believe the geography books— the capital of Italy is Milano.'

'It really is beautiful,' says Robi, having nothing better to say.

'No. The south is beautiful.' He searches for her eyes in the rear-view. 'Up here it's all business. Industry. The mountains have been mined, the seas and rivers polluted. If you want nature, go south. Go to Calabria. Believe me, you'll never come back up,' he says with a trace of a smile, 'except for money, of course.'

Not much need for that. She has a fortune, she thinks. 'Where are we going?'

'There's a restaurant in the mountains. You did say you were hungry—'

'I am. Starving.' She'd eaten her last meal on the flight over and she'd skipped breakfast in her haste for the Rome-Milan train.

Which was stupid. Wayne had been right: trains are always late in Italy. Everything is late in Italy as far as she can tell.

Giovanni drives slowly onto a pebbled road snaking steadily up between tall pine trees with thin limbs huddled together, shutting out the glare. They approach a sharp hairpin and, on negotiating it, Robi holds her breath. Spread out below is a green valley bowled within scraping mountains and a river that meanders across the lush land. Giovanni pulls the car onto the shoulder of the road and lingers with the engine idling. The wind whistling up the valley stings her body when she climbs out. She follows Giovanni silently to the damaged Armco barrier, Robi tightening her leather jacket about her torso.

'Beyond that range,' says Giovanni, pointing, 'is Switzerland. And there is Milano.'

Robi stares. She can barely distinguish the black autostrada slicing through the valley. Richard would have loved it, she thinks. She can almost picture him slinging the trusty Kodak Instamatic Mom had given him so many lifetimes ago to begin clicking away. He'd been too young to understand the futility of photographs; that they can never capture emotions, never capture the wind blowing up into her face or the scurrying of nature before dusk as the dying sun fades beyond the Alps. Or the reason behind a smiling face. Richard. Her brother, he'd ... it was a mistake. A terrible mistake.

'I'm getting cold,' she whispers. Fighting back the tears, she walks back to the limo' with her shoes crunching onto the pebbles.

'You don't like it?' Giovanni steps past her and throws open the rear-door.

'No, it's beautiful.' She climbs into the limo'. 'I'm just cold. Cold and hungry.'

Giovanni smiles, shutting the door and climbing up front behind the wheel. 'You must have Italian heritage. Life is beautiful, but food comes first, no?'

Robi forces a laugh from her throat. The bimmer climbs the pebbled road at a steady pace now, the countryside slowly fading to purple as night falls.

The restaurant's a converted farmhouse in a clearing with silhouetted trees surrounding it. Light oozes out from wooden framed windows to bleed on a deserted gravel carpark. A swaying board above the porch displays 'La Trattoria Della Campagna' in gothic print. Classical music drifts out to them as they enter the warm restaurant. Red and white checkered tablecloths decorate a dozen tables scattered unevenly about the deserted room. A chandelier hangs from a wooden ceiling, delicately illuminating the tables, jittery in the flame of candles. It's always comforting for Robi to see someone has bothered to light candles. There is life here, despite the isolation ... stop, she thinks, *enough*. Just sit back and chill. No guilt. No memories. No pain.

'What does it mean, Tratorea nela Campag-na?'

'Restaurant in the country. *Trattoria Nella Campagna*.'

A short man approaches them with a limp and a belly stretching a stained shirt, a smile cracking his egg-shaped head. He stands before Giovanni, throwing out his hand and shaking his head as the two men shake hands with eyes locked in an embrace.

'*E quasi un anno, porco can',*' says the restauranteur with Giovanni's hand still in his powerful grip. '*Pensavo che eri morto.*' He examines the tall man fondly. '*Ti trovo bene, Giova'.*'

Giovanni goes in for a hug and then turns his attention to Robi. 'Robi, this is Gino.' Then to the man whose hand he's finally abandoned, 'Robi is American—from New York.'

'Chicago.' Robi extends a hand. Gino side-steps it and pecks her quickly on both cheeks with his hands grabbing a bit of ass. '*Bella,*' he says, '*bella.*' He waves at the room. 'You should have called,' he laughs, 'to reserve a table.' The men share a glance and Robi laughs nervously. 'Come,' Gino avoids a chair behind him and leads them to a table near the swing doors leading to the kitchen, 'is this alright?' He pushes back a wooden chair for Robi and drives her closer to the square table as Giovanni sits opposite.

'*E Maria, dov'è?*' asks Giovanni.

'*Sta brontolando nella cucina come sempre. Vado a chiamarla— volete qualcosa da bere?*' He flicks an inquisitive glance at Robi. She avoids his eyes, staring helplessly at Giovanni.

'Gino wants to know if you'd like something to drink.'

'Oh. Damn right I do.'

'Ah—you not understand Italian? Not a word?' asks Gino.

'No, but I think it's a beautiful language,' she tries. Gino nods but his smile has faded, glancing at Giovanni with a tilted brow.

'*Portacci del Lambrusco, Gino.*'

The man limps away and Robi follows him with her eyes through the swing doors and catches a glimpse of a kitchen.

'It's usually very busy—a week's advance booking is normal. But this is August ...'

She smiles at his sweeping hand-gesture, what can be done? She finds a cigarette and lights it as if she's trying to vanish along with the reeking smoke. Gino returns with a green bottle and three glasses dangling from his thick fingers.

'Vincenzo gave this to me,' he says absently to Giovanni while popping the cork to the sparkling wine. It bursts with a powerful clap, grey blue smoke spiralling up from the neck like a pistol ... Jesus, she thinks, stop! He fills two glasses and allows them to taste the strawberry-red liquid. Giovanni gulps it down like Kool-Aid and Robi follows suit, the wine warming her body as it speeds down her throat. She burps silently, hiding her mouth behind a serviette as a woman with thick black hair tumbles out from the kitchen doors. She has fiery black eyes like coal, ablaze as she steps slowly to the table with those eyes fixed on Giovanni and a melancholic smile caressing her wrinkled, tanned face. Giovanni stands and hugs the woman. She sighs, running a hand lovingly over his face. 'Giovanni,' she says.

'Maria.'

'This is my wife, Maria. This is Robi,' says Gino, 'from Chicago.'

'*Che bella,*' she says, extending a podgy hand rife with callouses, the lines of labour. '*Sei qui da tanto?*'

'*Ma cosa dici?*' Gino forms his fingers and thumb in a triangle and shakes it around. '*Non parla una parola d'Italiano.*'

'*Ma no,*' she gives Gino a dirty stare and then turns to Robi and says, 'I have friend, Americano in the war—Johnny, *ti ricordi,*' she looks down at Gino, '*Johnny, da dove veniva?*'

'*Ma che m'interessa a me? E morto da trent'anni, Dio bono.*'

Maria nods whimsically. '*Mah,*' she says as Robi finishes her glass of wine, already tipsy on her empty stomach. Gino grabs the bottle and refills. Maria slaps him on the shoulder. 'What you do— you make her drunk, you dirty old man!'

'*Ma vattene!*' he shouts, waving at the kitchen. 'Go!' He fills the glass to the brim and hands the bottle to Giovanni and then follows his wife into the kitchen with his hand firmly on her broad buttocks.

'Do they have kids?' Robi asks.

'Had. One. Michele. He's dead—overdosed—must be ten years now.'

'They're so close.'

'Forty-five years' worth of marriage.'

36

She kills her Camel and stirring memories. 'Can we order?'

'Of course. May I have the honour of ordering for both of us?'

Robi sips her wine, smiling. 'Please. You've made one good choice already.'

He orders an antipasto of cold meats and cheese, spaghetti with chillies, then a fowl basted in olive oil and a cassata to finish. Robi's overeaten and over-drank and over-talked. She sips at a small espresso and lowers it quickly. Grimacing.

'Don't worry,' says Gino, who has pulled a chair from a table and joins them now for coffee, 'you will get used to the taste. And when you leave, back to,' he points at the ground, 'America, you will always remember.'

Robi lights a smoke and sighs, falling back on her chair. Remembering is what she doesn't want. 'If I keep stuffing myself like this,' she says, 'I won't even fit on the plane back.'

'You have seen our plan. More to drink?'

Giovanni looks at her. 'Robi?'

'What the hell.'

'Maria!' shouts Gino, 'Sambuca!' Then bristling closer to Robi, 'How long will you stay?'

She observes Giovanni watching her with interest.'I—I don't really know,' she says.

'When did—' the swing doors opening interrupts the conversation as Maria walks to them carrying a tray with four small brandy glasses. She deposits the drinks onto the stained tablecloth and drops the tray onto a flanking table. Milky-thick liquid fills the glasses with three coffee beans floating in each. Gino lights the fluid and lifts one in the air, muttering 'Salute' and downs the Sambuca flames and all.

'It roasts the coffee-beans,' explains Giovanni with a smile so she's not quite sure if he's pulling her leg, 'but blow out the flame.'

'Salute cara,' whispers Maria, slowly sipping the Sambuca down. Robi, Dutch-courage besieging her, throws the flaming liquid down her throat. Splutters tears from her eyes and flames from her nostrils. Gasping, she mops away the tears and smiles at the laughing trio with the taste of liquorice deep in her throat.

'I'll—get used to—it, right?' she asks between coughs.

'Brava!' Gino pats her on the back and together with Maria take the plates and glasses into the kitchen.

'Zoran tells me you're staying for a month,' says Giovanni, eyes watching her.

She shrugs. 'I guess that's right.'

'Will you be staying with us?'

'You mean with Zoran? No. No, I don't think so. I've come to get away from a lot of shit.' She meets his eyes across the table. 'I want to see everything here—hitch around a while. I have … things to sort out—and I think,' she adds after a brief pause, 'maybe I've come to the right place.'

'A beautiful woman always has much to worry about, Robi. But also solutions are easier to find *per una ragazza bella*. Do you have family—in Chicago?'

'No. Just Wayne.'

'I see.'

'They're dead.'

'Oh, I'm sorry, I—'

'Don't be.' From her wallet, she finds a faded monochrome photo, crumpled like a small bill from the past. 'That's my brother—Richard.'

'Richard the,' he places the photo over his heart, 'uhm—'

'Lionheart?'

'Yes,' he pays homage to the photo with a respectful glance before handing the face back.

'So what does Zoran do?'

'Zoran? He's—a business executive, yes? Import-export.'

'And this Sandro everyone's looking for?'

Giovanni smiles. 'Don't ask. He's sort of a—sort of a friend.'

'Sort of?'

'An intimate friend, if you understand.'

'Of yours?'

'Of Zoran.'

'I think I bumped into him on my way up to the pad.'

'It's probably for the best he wasn't there. He's a user. In every way, if you follow.'

She clears her throat. 'Well, then I'm glad you came.' Robi glances down at her wristwatch. 'It's getting late.'

'Yes, of course, you must be exhausted.' He stands and pulls back her chair to allow her to wander to the reception table. He walks into the kitchen and Robi can hear voices before the trio walk back out laughing.

Gino steps over and hands her the bill. She looks at it. L123,500.

'Giovanni tells me you will take care of the bill,' he says.

Robi glances at Giovanni hesitantly. 'Sure. But I have no money here. I mean, only dollars. Do you accept dollars? Like, how much is this anyway?'

Maria shakes her head firmly. 'No.'

'Oh,' says Robi, flustered. 'I could—'

'You will have to come back, Robi, and settle' says Gino.

Robi frowns and then understands and smiles. 'Of course. Thank you. This place is—it's magical here.'

Gino leans forward, and she kisses his cheeks this time, then those of rosy Maria.

'Thank you. I will always remember this,' she says.

10. La Bionda: 'One For You, One For Me'

'I think we may have a break,' says Blake, waving a folder at Virdis in the chief inspector's office. 'Arrest report. He was found with twenty grams of coke and heroin paraphernalia, and he wants to bargain. We have him down in the interrogation room. Do you want a look at him?'

Virdis rubs his eyes, glances at this Gucci wristwatch. 'Is he selling the Miami stuff?'

'Possible. I haven't spoken to him. Onassio had the first interview. The guy's claiming he's got Colombian powder direct from the Cartel. Probably talking shit but he's waved his right to an attorney. Says he wants to talk to someone who can give him a deal.'

The interrogation room is at the far end of the dim precinct. Virdis pauses beside a square window and peers into a white-tiled room. A yellow-haired kid sits behind a table, nervously tapping a cigarette in a metal ashtray. The clock above his head shifts to 1.15am.

'You want me to come in?' offers Blake.

Virdis opens the file and briefly scans the stapled sheets. He glances up into the white-tiled room before walking to the door with *PRIVATO* printed on it. 'Watch,' he points at the window, 'when you get my cue, come in fast.'

'Your cue—' but Virdis has nothing more to add because he's already going in. Blake lights up a smoke and watches Virdis appear on the other side of the window. The peroxided kid stands, killing his smoke. Virdis paces to the table silently, grabbing a wooden chair before it and sits, resting the file before him.

'Please, Massimo,' drone the speakers above Blake's head, 'sit down.'

The kid sits down hesitantly, hands dangling at his sides.

'You understand you've waved your right to an attorney?'

The kid nods, strands of yellow hair whipping his face.

Virdis drums his fingers on the table. Where to start? With a sigh, he stands and glances at the mirror.

'Why don't you invite 'em in?' asks the kid.

Virdis turns and checks the kid out warily. Forms a word with his lips, pauses, pulls back the chair one more time and sits with his palms flat on the file. 'What makes you do this? Selling this shit to fucked-up kids who have no-one to tell 'em any better? Fucking up their lives before they even start.'

Massimo avoids the dead-grey eyes, and lights another MS. He inhales heavily, masking his face in a cloud of smoke rising to the strip lights on the ceiling. 'I told the other guy I wanted to talk to someone in charge. Who are you, the fucking priest?'

'Two previous convictions,' says Virdis, tapping the folder with four incessant fingers. 'You're looking at a stretch, you know that, right?' He stares at the yellow hair. The vague, diffident eyes.

'I told the other guy,' says Massimo. 'I know things.' He looks up and meets Virdis' stare momentarily. 'I know things.'

Virdis nods, looking suitable impressed, and makes a production of looking up at the clock. 'It's late, Massimo, and my wife's gonna hit the roof when I get home. So I'm going to get straight to the point. Did the coke you're peddling come from Miami?'

'I already answered that. Besides, what happens if I cooperate?'

'Who's your supplier, Massimo?'

'What happens if I tell you?'

Virdis swings his arm with his hand open and slaps through the kid's face. He returns with his knuckles and Massimo, caught unawares, falls off his chair, his head bouncing off the tiled floor.

Virdis is on his feet fast, climbing over the table and throwing the chair into the wall above the sprawled kid's head. The chair splinters. Virdis grabs the kid's leather jacket, hoists him against the wall and pins him back with one elbow on the throat, faces inches apart. Blood trickles from Massimo's mouth, rolls down over his chin. Virdis slaps him again, then again, and again, first with the palm then returning almost instantaneously with the knuckles. Tears burst from Massimo's face as his head snaps sideways, hair lashing the white tiles behind his head.

The door crashes open, Blake running in and effortlessly hurdling over the table. He throws his hands onto the chief inspector's shoulders, twisting him away.

Massimo falls onto his knees, his hands rubbing a beat-red face. Blood trickles from his nose, joining the stream cascading onto his shirt.

'Jesus, what the fuck are you doing!' yells Blake, a shield now between Virdis and the dope-pusher.

'I was showing Massimo what would happen if he did *not* cooperate,' mutters Virdis like a scolded child. He grabs Massimo's upended chair. 'Sit,' he says, 'we're just getting started here.'

Blake grabs Massimo's shoulder. The kid twists away from him, pushing Blake away with a weak, proud hand. Brushing away his tears, the kid sits sulkily.

'Okay,' says Virdis, 'so now we all know where we stand. Let's begin again.' He grabs his broken chair and inspects it. 'You broke my chair,' he says, and walks back toward Massimo.

Blake looks from him to the pusher and steps ploddingly for the door.

'Hey, where the fuck are you going?' Massimo points a finger at Blake. 'Where's he going? You can't leave me here alone with this ... you saw what he *did!* You can't leave me—'

Virdis makes a production of stretching his back laboriously. 'What, were you expecting a fucking priest? Fine, have it your way. You tell *him* everything he wants to know.' Virdis smiles at the pusher. 'I'm gonna be outside,' he motions to the mirror, 'listening. You give him any shit,' he nods at Blake, 'and I'm gonna come in here and go Old Testament on you. *Capito?*' He turns and steps to Blake and they exchange a brief look before Virdis slams the door violently in his wake. He steps to the window, looking in, and monitors Blake's voice filtering out metallically from the intercom.

'—only about ten grams,' whispers Massimo to Blake. 'I got busted with my whole stash, man.'

'Your supplier—does he channel through to all the pushers?'

'I don't know.'

'When did you buy it?'

'I've already—'

'When!'

'Friday.'

'From who?'

'Arcadia.'

'Arcadia? Like what, fucking Duran Duran Arcadia?'

'What? No, man, he's a dude. From the neighbourhood. Connected, know what I'm saying?'

'Where does he live?'

'I don't know, man. What the fuck, I'm not his buddy.'

A long pause. Finally, 'Cooperate with me, Massimo. This guy,' he jams a thumb at the mirror, 'he doesn't give a shit. He wants you to go down, Massimo, he's from the old school, you understand? You're guilty and you go down. The only way out is if you give him what he wants. Which means you give me what *I* want. Everything you say here is confidential—there's no-one taking notes. I can guarantee your protection. And I guarantee you—'

'I don't know the answers to your questions, man.'

'Okay—okay. So let's try again. How do you buy your stash?'

'What? How do I buy—'

'Yes. Who's your merch'?'

'*Arcadia*, man, I jus' told you.'

The voices fall silent. Virdis exhales grey smoke from his nostrils.

'So you have no idea where this Arcadia scores from.'

'No. I don't ask questions like that. I ask questions like that, and I'll get popped, man.'

'You never followed him?'

'No. What? Why the fuck would I do that?'

'Never asked?'

'No!'

'Okay. Let me get this straight here.' A scrape of a chair. 'You give this dude Arcadia, what, three, four million bucks, and then you sit around and what? Have a wank and wait for him to deliver you the dope? Is that right? I mean, did it ever occur to you he might split?'

'What? Man, I told you, he's connected.'

'And who's his connected to?'

'I don't know, man.'

'So how the fuck do you know he won't skip.'

''cause he just—it's not the way it goes down in the streets, man. We look after each other. We all look after—'

'Save me, mate. Fucking brotherly love, is it? I'm going to weep. How did you meet him? Arcadia?'

'He's always been around.'

'He sells to all the pushers in your neighbourhood?'

'No, not all. I don't think so.'

'A lot?'

'I don't *know! Fuck*!'

'Massimo, mate, if this is all you've got to offer, you'd better get yourself an attorney. 'cause you can forget about any kinda bargain.'

'You fucking promised, man!'

'Yeah, well, you trust too much, Massimo.' Blake's shoes walk away and a moment later he walks into the backroom where Virdis stands watching the yellow-haired kid through the window.

'Now what?' says Blake.

Virdis sits up wearily, brushing gunk from his eyes. 'Now I go home. Get this piece of shit to the lockup. Let him sweat a while with his brothers down there. Let's see if he likes married life. If what he's saying is legit, we may have a pipeline to King Coke himself through this Arcadia prick.'

'King Coke?'

Virdis smiles. 'I heard it on the news this morning. King Coke. Like King Kong, I guess. The king of Milan's drug epidemic.'

'Fucking journalists, Jesus. King Coke?'

Virdis kills his smoke and nods at the window. 'Keep this fuck under your belt, Blake. It could easily backfire if this hits the press. Or the mayor's office. Understand?'

'You got it.'

11. Desireless: 'Voyage Voyage'

Zoran is not what Robi had expected. A powerful aura radiates from his steady eyes that seem never to leave her face as they sit on the floor of the big empty lounge of his penthouse. This is a man that commands respect, she thinks. A man who will not be crossed. A man a lot like Wayne. If Wayne was twenty years older and a hundred pounds heavier.

Giovanni places a tumbler of OJ before her on the floor, and whispers in Zoran's ear before smiling pleasantly at Robi and wandering off into the apartment. Zoran sips on his orange juice. 'I'm sorry there was no one here to welcome you,' he says.

'I had a wonderful time with Giovanni,' she says, sitting cross-legged on the rich carpet.

'Good.' Zoran lights a Camel and tosses her the pack. 'Have you spoken to Wayne?'

She looks up. 'No, I think he's away. On one of his business trips.'

'Business still lucrative?'

'Wayne never talks shop. But I guess so.'

'Mr Go-go,' says Zoran and laughs. 'You're lucky to have him. He's a good guy, Wayne. *Mah*,' he adds after a long sip, 'knowing him, he'll probably appear at the door tomorrow. Wouldn't surprise me. I'd never let someone as beautiful as you run around this country alone.'

'Is it dangerous?'

'Italy? God no. Not really. Not like Chicago, for sure. Full of mobsters! Wayne was very vague about why you're here, Robi.'

She breaks from his glance and stares down at her drink. She sips on it before replying, 'I just—needed some time away.'

Zoran nods. 'Many are the reasons for leaving home. But you made a wise decision to come to Italy. If you don't leave Italy with answers, you certainly will leave—what's the word now? Enrich?'

'Enriched? Yeah, I guess. You're Italian then?'

'Me? No. No-no. I feel Italian sometimes, but it's an exclusive club. I'm from over the border—Yugoslavia. My folks came over when I was seven, refugees, and I've never found a good reason to leave.'

'How—' but she's interrupted by the shrilling telephone.

Zoran stands.   'I'm sorry,' he says, and shuffles his mass surprisingly quickly toward the kitchen. She can hear him reply in short staccato bursts, and as his voice drifts out to her, she realises that Zoran is more than the sum of his presence. His eloquence and elocution have quickly transformed into, 'Yeah, no-shit. Fuck, it's what I—no ... the fuckin'—does he know who he's fucking with? I'm gonna have his balls, man, I'm gonna eat his fucking—*what*? Yeah, yeah, I can't fucking believe—yeah, okay, good, yeah, that's good. Yes-yes, I'll take care of it. You just keep in touch. Yes. *Ciao*.' He returns to the sun-drenched lounge with a pensive frown. 'So where were we?'

'I don't—'

'Never mind,' he says, downing his juice, 'I must be off; something's come up. I'll be back this evening—maybe dinner and an opera? Placido is at La Scala. I'm sure you'll love it.'

'Yes, I'm sure.'

''til tonight then.' He strides for the front door. *'Giova! Andiamo, dai!'*

Giovanni exits the kitchen and has a whispered chat with Zoran by the front door before he glances back at Robi and offers her a smile goodbye before the two men leave together.

Robi stretches and gets up. Mr Go-go? She smiles. The clock shows eleven thirty. She needs a bath. She heads to the pink bathroom and undresses, turning the brass knobs and squatting in the scorching water, bathing her ankles, her legs. When the water's touching her belly, she shuts off the knobs and lies back in the soothing warmth.

Big Brother Mr Go-go constantly peering over her shoulder, her protector against anything—*everything.* 'I hear Wayne's doing well', she mimics. 'Business still lucrative? Perhaps he'll pop on a plane and visit'. Yeah, right.

Wayne has been good to her, there's no denying that. He'd been there when everyone with empty promises had vanished with empty lies. She *is* grateful. Grateful—but not indebted—to him or anyone else. She owes nothing to no one. Not even herself.

And anyway, Wayne had gifted her the cash. And it's high time for her to spend some of it. She soaps herself down before stepping out into the caressing steam and dresses. She collects her money-belt from the guest room and slaps it on before heading down to the lobby where she asks the doorman to call her a cab and leaves a message with him for Zoran or Giovanni on a scrawled sheet of paper. 'Traveling for a while. I'll call. Thank you for everything. Love, Robi.'

It takes twenty minutes for the cab to dump her outside the station. The enormous board just inside signals the imminent departure of the Milano-Napoli express. She figures why not? She's heard of Naples. Elbows her way through the bustling throng in the hall and gets to the ticket-counters. A whistle blows from the far side of the station. Robi slaps money onto the counter. 'Naples,' she says. 'Napoli.'

'Cinquanta milla lira,' says a clerk with diamond-stud earrings dancing on his ears. *'Binario sei.'*

'Where?'

'Six,' says a guy behind her.

Robi retrieves her Three Spears backpack from the lockers, slings it onto one shoulder, and she's barely climbed onto the train before it bounces forward with a metallic clang to leisurely rattle its way out of Milan.

12. Piano Fantasia: 'Song for Denise'

I

Silver-white strobe lights bounce off the mirrored pit, rhythmically silhouetting the snaking, faceless bodies swaying in the confined space of the black-walled club. Figures dangle about in varying degrees of euphoria, Chinese lantern eyes twinkling whimsically.

Sandro slumps over a rectangular bar, oblivious to the erratic lights flickering about him, oblivious to the music. Tilting his head back, he pours the rest of his drink down his throat and splutters as he crashes down the glass onto the scarred bar top. Thousand-Watt speakers scream thoughts into his ear. A woman groans in invalid ecstasy. Sandro glances up into the foggy dimness. The barman, head bowed forward, listens to four gesticulating, screaming women in tattered clothes spraying orders and gob in his face. Two men step beside Sandro with heads too tired to talk, too tired to dance, too tired to live.

Sandro stands from his stool and staggers sideways onto the bar. Pushing himself up with his hands, he turns and widens his eyes, trying to focus on the dancing mass before him. They rise in the pit before his eyes. He blinks, and they return to the floor, then begin to rise once more. God, he thinks, he's pissed outta his mind. He gropes his way toward the dancing mass, muttering 'sorry, pardon, sorry, *scusa*' as he forces a path to the exit and finally throws open the heavy metal door to stumble out into the hot night where he rakes in breath and chokes on the stench of uncollected garbage lining the dank alley. Soft yellow light bleeds into the alley from the road ahead, shadows cast between the dilapidated trashcans buried in a sea of rotten refuse.

He tosses away the butt of his cigarette, shoulders crashing into graffiti-covered walls. Shuffling noises penetrate the silence, red eyes flickering about, surveying him suspiciously until he staggers out onto the road.

Inquiring, invading eyes fall on him as he attempts to follow the groove in the oily sidewalk below his boots. His vision is double. He must stop, staggers into a lamppost, leans heavily on the cold metal and digs out a crumpled pack of Marlboro. Rips the pack open, the world tilting, sorts through a dozen slit cigarettes, determined to find the undamaged article. He does but typically there's no light in his life. Lifting his head, he peers at two men scuttling past him with lowered eyes. Behind them approaches another man with hands dug deep into his pockets and a cigarette dangling from between his lips. A flashing sign on a shop window behind him proclaims **XXX**sadotrans**T**S**X**O.

Sandro pops the smoke into his mouth and unsteadily steps into the man's path. 'You got a light, buddy?' His head sails a stormy ocean as he tries to concentrate on the guy's pale eyes.

'Sure.' The man hands Sandro the butt from his lips for him to fuse cancer together on the third attempt before dragging and absently throwing the man's butt into the gutter.

'Are you going somewhere?' inquires the man. 'I have two tickets to the Sabrina concert.'

A girl in stilettos races past them with stockings torn up beneath a leopard-skin-skirt.

'C'mon,' urges the man, 'my name's Elliot and I'm probably as fucked as you.' He grips Sandro's elbow and pushes him forward. Sandro stumbles and falls with Elliot still holding his elbow. He lifts Sandro effortlessly and slaps him about a bit. 'Jees, you really are fucked.'

Vomit races up Sandro's throat with juices alive and burning and he swallows it down sourly. 'Why are you speaking English?' he asks.

'Because you are.'

Sandro nods. Considers this for a while. 'I don't like Sabrina.'

'You have a better idea?'

'Come.' He leads the man blindly toward a taxi-rank across a well-lit, grey piazza. A junky sits below a lone concrete horseman with a guitar forgotten on his lap. Just sitting and staring. They climb into a Fiat cab. Sandro leans forward to the silent, capped cabby with hands resting on the wheel, Ayrton Senna just before the Monaco GP. *'Trenta-due via delle Pine,'* he says before slumping back on the vinyl seat, exhausted. The Fiat jumps into the trickling traffic, the driver banging his horn at a stationary taxi beside him.

'Your place?' inquires Elliot.

Sandro brushes his hand over Elliot's crotch. Elliot traps his hand and lays the palm over his cock. Sandro rubs it up. Elliot smiles. The cabby drives through the city, heading down for the docks. He pauses the Ritmo at a red light, checks the street numbers and turns left, passing the tall, barbed-wire prison walls. He pulls the car over beneath a squat apartment block and swivels in his seat.

'Venti milla.' He extends a fat hand.

'I'll take care of it,' says Elliot. 'How much does he want?'

'Thirty thousand,' lies Sandro, climbing out from the Fiat. He slams the door and staggers on the deserted street. Identical brown-brick apartment blocks stretch into a purple forever, fenced off tiny gardens facing the prison. Sandro digs in his jeans and slips out a key. The Fiat U-turns and drives off as Elliot joins him on the sidewalk to stare up at the quarter moon winking out a forgotten morse code. Sandro listens to the engine fade away with the red taillights.

'That's the prison,' says Sandro, pointing at graffiti-plastered walls. 'It's the official boundary.'

'Between what and what?'

'What? There're more whores here than anywhere else in Italy. Including the prison, maybe?'

'Where—'

'Except Rome.'

'Yes, do you—'

'And Milano, yeah. Everyone's a whore in Milano. And—'

'Yes, but where—'

'Come,' says Sandro, staggering through a set of rusted thigh-high gates. Elliot follows into a gloomy apartment block, winding up a dark staircase to the first landing. They pause before a brown door with the number nine painted on it in blistered red paint. A naked bulb shines meekly from a cracked ceiling, illuminating the moth-eaten blue carpet stretching down the musty corridor.

'*Fuck*,' says Sandro, 'I've lost my key.'

'Shit.' Elliot watches Sandro lean on the termite-infested door for support and rub down his jeans.

'It must've fallen from my pocket. I haven't even paid the rent yet.'

Elliot laughs, a harsh laugh which makes Sandro take a careful look at the face.

'What's so funny?'

'What's that in your hand?' Elliot juts his square chin forward at Sandro's hand and then he laughs again at Sandro's bemused stare at the key in his hand. Shaking his head, Sandro tries to prod the key into the hole, eventually getting the aim right, and unlocks the Yale before throwing open the door. Elliot's still laughing when he walks into the dank apartment.

Sandro flips the light switch and shuts the door. 'I have a split personality,' he confesses.

A single bed beside a rusted white radiator greets them in the tiny room. An un-curtained window stares out at the apartment block across the way. A red light shines from a window, gleaming out sullenly into the night. A shadow flicks across it briefly. Sandro slumps onto a bed, resting his head on the wall-papered wall, and watches an unsteady Elliot draw out a Dunhill.

'Come sit here,' says Sandro, patting the stained brown blanket with his palm. He leans over to the bed-side table and grabs a Clint Eastwood *Sudden Impact* cigarette case. A neon light flickers monotonously beyond the window. The bed creaks as Elliot slumps down on it, staring quizzically at the cigarette case.

'Sudden Impact,' he reads. Sandro flips it open 'Jesus,' says Elliot. 'Is that?'

'Horsepower,' mutters Sandro.

Elliot slides out his own stash, white and they mix and match and, it looks like ash, ashes to ashes, and it's a terrific rush, the coke picking 'em up and the horse waiting around to let 'em down nice and smooth. But Elliot's party-tricks aren't over just yet. 'I've got some dope,' he says, digging out a packaged newspaper. Sandro stands and headrushes to a sink against the wall with a stain where the water has dribbled out for a century. Two Peroni bottles lie beneath the rusted bowl, and he brings one for Elliot.

'You got a light?' he slurs. Elliot's got a Bic decorated with the Peace on the Planet doves and two crosshairs lined up over their heads. Sandro dangles the flame beneath the bottleneck, rolling it little by little against the compressed fire. A black stain gradually forms about the neck of the bottle. He tosses the lighter onto the bed and grips the bottle in two hands, forcing the palms down. The bottle snaps in a concentric circle and shreds his hand viciously.

'Oh,' he says.

'You okay? What are you doing?'

Sandro hands him the bottleneck flecked with blood. He examines his hand. The cut wells up across his palm and the blood drips down onto the bed in thick globules. 'We're gonna smoke this Joburg style,' he says, and rolls the foiled packet from the Dunhill box into a geometric circle with a gap in the centre. He forces it down the narrow end of the bottle/pipe and blows through. Satisfied, he pours dope into the wide end, packing the dope tight with his finger.

Elliot's dope so he gets first dibs, tilting back his head and resting the bottleneck on his lips. Sandro lights the pipe of peace with the Bic for Elliot to suck and huff and puff and vanish in a thick plume of smoke. He hands it over and Sandro full-moons the fucker with smoke escaping uninvited through his nostrils.

Elliot says, 'What do you do?'

Sandro coughs. 'You want me to say it?'

'Sorry? Say what?'

'Why else are you here?'

Sudden clarity. 'Oh. Jesus. I thought,' Elliot hesitates, looking away at the red light across the way, 'I thought, damn, I don't know—'

'You thought what,' says Sandro with velvet-like smoke erupting from his lungs, 'that I live here 'cause I'm researching a book?'

'No—'

'No? I'm not good enough for that, right? So you think you can pick someone up from a street-corner just like that? Look at you, eh? A fucking gigolo.'

'Well, no—'

'You've got money?' Sandro stands and stumbles into the window 'cause the room's spinning wildly.

'Of course, sure, but—'

'Okay. So why are we freaking? Relax! Chill-out, buddy. Here,' he hands Elliot the pipe, 'light it—you look tense.'

Sandro clumsily strips off his sweatshirt with his back to the bed. He kicks off his boots and wriggles out of his jeans, naked. Elliot watches him strip, eyes drawn to the mosaic of scars on the thin back and ass. White blisters in concentric circles. Elliot extends his hand and touches the flesh. Sandro feels the fingers probing. A lighter flips behind him, and instinctively he tenses. The heat burrows deep into his flesh and he arches his back. Turns to find Elliot pulling a cigarette away, all spent. Burnt flesh smell. He lights it again and stands, the pipe forgotten on the floor.

'You like this?'

Sandro shrugs.

'Go stand against the wall.'

Sandro hesitates, touching this new blister tenderly. It's soft.

'This *is* why I'm here, right? So let's get it on, *buddy*.' Elliot grabs Sandro's wrist and propels him into the window. He forces the naked body wide, palms and toes grazing the wallpaper. Sandro can see a couple on the road below him, lovers walking hand-in-hand-in the night, skipping in the pools of delight cast by the dim streetlamps. He turns his head away from the window. Elliot is unstrapping his belt, running it through his slacks methodically, eyes staring wildly at the naked body two feet before him spread-eagled naked for the world to see.

Sandro turns away. Drugs impair pain but does it impair absolution? Must he be sober to feel the pain of a sinner? The pain of forgiveness? He returns his unsteady glance down at the lovers. They've paused below a streetlamp, the man cupping a flame in his hands. The belt rushes through the smoky air and Sandro cringes, the leather tearing across his ass. At the height of the clawing pain, he relaxes his body and sighs the pain out from his flesh through his gaping mouth. The lovers are moving once more, hands entwined in a sweet display of love. The belt flicks its long tail, snaking about Sandro's back, across his belly. Two red welts follow each other round his body. Elliot gains pace, strapping the belt out with all the power he can muster. The booze and the coke and the dope's numbed Sandro's flesh, his senses, but he can feel the heroin tingling his consciousness. He can see the lovers stepping into an apartment block, kissing lips. Sandro, his body writhing with the snapping belt, finally cries out, 'No more,' with his knees buckling and fingers digging into the wallpaper, 'no more, I can't take no-more, Jesus, no more.' It sounds fake because it is. He has learnt, on the streets, what pain is, understands that he must beg, slow the process down, 'please…'

'This *is* why I'm here, right?'

Sandro slides down the wall, the road replaced by the wooden floor bouncing into his face. He catches a glimpse of something jarring and white jabbing at his head. Elliot's fist smashes into his mouth. His head recoils, banging against wood as he grunts. Another punch sinks into his groin, winding him, 'stop,' he whispers, 'stop, please stop,' but the fist swings into his face regardless. Blood and mucus splatters onto the floor. He covers his head with his elbows, instinct, fends off the blows. He can hear Elliot breathing hard with the energy. A foot boots him in the belly. He shrinks into the foetal position with the kicks spinning him into the wall below the window. And gratefully, he allows the black fog to invade. Welcomes it like he welcomes the sweet caress of heroin.

II

Sudden Impact! Sandro sits up and moans, pain flashing ice-white in his mind. Whimpering, he crawls on all fours to the bed.

It's still there. *Sudden Impact.* He reaches for the case with a purple welted arm. There's twenty bucks on the bed, too. Payment for mercy. A syringe lies beneath the bed, the needle stained with flecked dried blood. A burnt spoon lies beside it, and Sandro reaches for the equipment. He's not strong enough. His mind quits and his body shuts down to collapse on the floor beside the bed.

He's stronger when he wakes, manages to stand, stumbling to the sink with clotted wounds razoring open, pours water into a stained glass and drinks gratefully. Returns to the bed to gather his equipment and begins burning up the juice of life, trembling hands sucking up survival into the syringe. Like a pro-assassin, his own painkiller, piercing into his foot and whimpering as it punctures through a bruise. White is replaced by the cleansing fluid that eases the pain to a blunt stabbing. He realises it's day, consciously, warmth flooding in from the window. He crawls back under the window and squats before it. Cold. He shuts his eyes and rocks on the balls of his feet. The toilet is on the passage. He can't make it that far, numbed, so he allows the stream to ooze out, bathing his feet in warm fluid. The stench is acute in the heat. Tears trickle down to his cut lips. He crouches with arms folded tightly about his chest, sunlight not warming his cold, continuously rocking body. Gravity will always conquer, and he must eventually fall.

It may have been a day. Two? He can't be sure. But he can stand, shielding his bloodshot eyes with his hands to peer out at the white-baked road. A battered car turns at the intersection, driving past the prison. He turns to retrieve his scattered clothes, dresses on the floor by slowly manoeuvring his aching limbs into the material. He collects the *Sudden Impact* cigarette case and helps himself to a line directly from the package inside. On the hallway, two girls try to force their way into an apartment with a credit card. The bathroom's located all the way down the corridor. It's unoccupied and Sandro steps into the reeking room. One wall of has a rusted bathtub attached to it, dripping rust-coloured water. Next to it is a splintered wooden latrine that is missing pieces. He runs the cold water into the tub, placing his head below the cascading water. Dried blood mingles with the water. He rubs his face, testily probing the cuts on his lips and ears. Satisfied, he steps out from his jeans and squats into the tub, directing the spray of water with his hand.

The heat strikes him like a buckle as he steps onto the sidewalk. He has barely taken two steps before a droplet of sweat forms on his brow.

La Luna Bella Pizzeria is a take-away-cum-restaurant-joint at the corner run, rumour has it (and rumour in this part of town is always authoritative), by a former child-prostitute in the fascist regime. Sandro knows the rumours to be true when he steps into the place and first sets eyes on her. She approaches him laboriously, shifting her weight amongst the tables. Wrinkles cut deep in her face, lips aflame beneath a thick smudge of lipstick. But it's the grey-green eyes that betray her, staring out with the aggressive indifference of an old whore who's fucked it all and caught it all—twice.

'We're shut,' she croaks with a throat that's swallowed too much Jack Daniels, 'come back later,' she adds, standing before him in her flowing red floral dress.

'I'm hungry, Rosa.'

'You look like it.' She examines his bruised face, her podgy hand reaching out for his chapped lips. He snaps his head back like her fingers are red-hot pokers and glances away from her invading eyes, back at the street.

'I live over there,' he points at the row of identical apartment blocks, 'that's how I know your name.'

'We're closed.' She juts her head at the scarred wooden tables behind her with chairs balanced upside down above them. 'But 'cause you're so cute?' she smiles with blackened teeth. 'We only have last night's pizza.'

'Thank you, that's great.' He follows the big woman to a table near the kitchen.

'Sit.' She waves at the table and continues through the swing doors into the kitchen. Sandro grabs the two chairs from the table and deposits them on the un-swept floor. It's painful to sit. Watching the kitchen door furtively, he forces the *Sudden Impact* case from his jeans and snorts up noisily. The door swings open, and Rosa strides out towards him, balancing a plate in one hand and a bottle of house-wine in the other. She dumps everything before him, sits on the vacant chair and glares at him with a tight scowl.

'Your nose is bleeding,' she informs him. She slides out a tissue from her cleavage and tosses it at him. 'Wipe yourself clean and never do that here again. No drugs and no fucks at Mama Rosa's, you understand?'

Sandro twirls the tissue in a long strand, snaps it and blocks off his nasal passage. Free now, to break the pizza with his hand, to bring a piece to his mouth and smell two-day-old garlic. Something scuttles just before he slips the pizza into his mouth, and he swallows, gagging. The pizza is cold and tasteless.

'What's your name?'

'Sandro.' God, when had he eaten last?

She unscrews the bottle and takes a long swig of the warm wine. 'Sandro is an Italian name. And yet you speak with an accent.'

Sandro forces another piece of the pizza down. 'I was born in Africa.'

'South Africa?'

'Yes.'

'I had an uncle who went there. Many years ago. What is it like? We see so much on television.'

'It's like anywhere else.'

'Like Italy?'

'Sure,' he mumbles, chewing.

'It seems so bad—what we see.'

'It's bad what I see here.'

Rosa nods at his face. 'You were in a fight?'

He doesn't say anything. Was it a beating? Or redemption?

'I see so much of it—boys, younger than you, walking around,' she waves at her puffy cheeks, 'and pinpricks like crucifixes on their arms.' She shakes her head and fat waves about. 'I raised my boy working the streets—but never once did I beat him, never did he miss a day of school.' She nods at her righteousness. 'Never did he go to bed with an empty tummy.'

Sandro lifts the wine and guzzles down a mouthful. 'Yes,' he says, 'childhood doesn't make the man.'

'I read on the morning 'paper about this twelve-year-old-boy,' she accepts the wine back, drinking to stimulate her mind, 'he was on cocaine and heroin—what do you call it?' Like he should know. 'A highball?'

'Sure?'

'Anyway,' another swig, 'he was stopped by two policemen—this was up in Milano—you want some more?' She hands the bottle over. 'This boy overpowered the cops—I mean, can you imagine, at twelve? Stabbed one cop and then ran into the road and attacked a pregnant woman. When the cops finally got there, he'd stabbed the woman—and all this in broad daylight.'

Sandro gulps down the wine and pretends to care.

'I hear the cops are getting tough on drugs up there. In Milano. Is it the same in Africa?'

'Sure. Worse.'

'And this whole thing with AIDS—'

'It's a rumour,' says Sandro. 'I mean, just the name says it all. Who does it aid? Me? You? Is it a sex-aid? They should call it death—more to the point. Or fuck you.'

'A girl in this neighbourhood got it. So has her father. A good family. It's spreading everywhere. Are you safe? Do you take precautions?'

'It's people like me they wanna kill.'

'They?'

'What?' he blinks. His mind is losing focus.

'Who wants to kill you?'

'Me? Oh,' he nods whimsically. 'We're living a lie, Rosa, it's us against them,' he sips on the wine. 'It's fight or die—die fighting.'

'I've heard it all before.'

He shuts up. Said too much. He staggers onto his feet. '*Grazie*,' he says to the woman. She stands laboriously and accompanies him to the door. 'They've fucked up my world, Rosa, they fucked up my inheritance and I know who they are and there's fuck-all I can do, fuck-all,' he says. 'What do I owe you?'

'Keep your money. I'm always free for the first meal.' She touches his face for a moment, assessing a cut, 'and the last.'

Sandro steps out into the humid day. He crosses the road wondering how many free meals Rosa has given away to departing patrons. In this world, a whore leaves in a state box and no room for a stale pizza at Rosa's.

He finds a pharmacy between two XXX-rated shops, down a flight of concrete stairs in an air-conned windowless cellar. His skin chills as he approaches the counter. 'You got some base? For, like, the face?'

The pharmacist gazes at Sandro's face attentively. 'That looks painful.'

'Feels worse than it looks.'

The pharmacist turns and lifts a jar from the shelf behind him. He struggles with the seal, finally wrenches the lid off and dabs his finger into the white jelly. 'Let me take care of that for you,' he offers, holding up his finger tinged with the cream. Sandro leans forward, resting his hands on the counter. The pharmacist slowly dabs cream on the swollen face and watches him wince.

'Your head okay?'

'I think I'm cut behind the ear.' Sandro catches the man's eyes, looking for something, anything to explain this sudden turn of humanity. Is he mocking him? Is the cream the most expensive in the shop? The eyes stare back at him levelly, the face giving nothing away, the perfect salesman to a point of indifference.

'It looks pretty mean,' he says, applying cream. 'You should get it treated.'

'I am.' Sandro flinches.

The pharmacist cleanses his fingers on his lapel and shuts the jar. 'On the house. And forget the base for your face. You're likely to get an infection.'

Sandro heads up the stairs waiting for the pharmacist to play his hand. When he's back up in the sizzling heat, he gives the kindness some retrospect and explains it off to a lone freak working in the bowels of the ground, lonely and horny and drugged-up to the hilt on uppers.

Passing the squat apartment block, he thinks it looks like a mound of dogshit in the heat with flies massing on the seeping walls, and he thinks fuck it. The docks are within walking distance and beyond them the sea, and he heads down the hill. The closer he gets to the docks, the more kids he sees on the streets, girls with tattered cotton dresses and warm mouths in the hot day chasing uptown ragged boys, cigarettes, and the easy day.

A football match is being played on the street ahead. Sandro watches dirty kids chase an egg-shaped ball, swearing and shoving one another about. Sandro moves on, turning into an alley. A junky's slumped behind a trashcan with shut eyes and sores on his face. He looks dead. Jesus, he never wants to die in some alley from a freak OD. He wants out of this shit. Francesca had found the way out. On her terms. Can he ever do the same? Save himself from this death?

Boys stand on sidewalks behind unstable tables flogging stolen cigarettes from the docks at half price and porno photos of their sisters and mothers and brothers and cousins in varying positions. Distantly, the Tyrrhenian blinks silver in an oozy mess to a blazing horizon, silhouetted vessels drifting along patiently, waiting for permission to dock and off-load their drugs.

Sandro cuts across to a rocky bay beyond a grouping of desolate warehouses. The roaring machines from the docks roll up the hill with the occasional whistle of vessels and foremen. A young boy dashes from the road ahead of him, panting and moaning in near hysteria. Moments later and a group of equally young boys charge after him, screaming obscenities. Sandro catches a glimpse of flashing metal as the boys surge past. They vanish down a side-road with their screams echoing in the sultry afternoon.

Sandro reaches a cordoned off municipal dump with tons of sweating junk abandoned within a gargantuan hole in the ground ready for burial in the polluted sea. The stench is overpowering. He climbs over a four-foot fence with the cigarette case cutting into his groin. Beyond the smoking garbage pit is a rocky hill climbing up into the murky sky. And beyond that, he figures, is the sea. He climbs the hill laboriously. Halfway up, he needs to sit and catch his breath. He can barely see the suburbs beyond the haze of thick grey smog rising from the garbage heap. Flies and mutated insects with dayglo green- and orange-swelled abdomens feed off the beads of salt cascading from his brow. He withdraws the case and snorts up a thick load before shutting his eyes and allowing the violent sounds of the distant docks to filter through his quiet mind. The stench is nauseating, forcing him to stand and, with clawing fingers, continue the arduous climb to the summit. The jagged rocks are covered in broken bottles, bottle necks, empty tablet containers, bloody syringes. But he's reached the peak.

He looks about him. He can see the docks now, a stage for centuries of time-beaten vessels. He slings off his sweatshirt and moves to the opposite ledge with the Tyrrhenian bleeding in-between two brown-white shorelines. The hill terraces down to a pebbled shore where the sea shatters into a small grotto. A body lies on the top terrace, basking half-naked in the sun. Sandro climbs down, his eyes transfixed by the hairless, bronzed body. He walks over to the kid, his boots crunching on loose earth. He kneels beside a shoulder and shakes the warm body. An arm moves, the body twisting on its back and glancing up at Sandro with one hand shielding the eyes from the glare.

'I thought you were dead,' mutters Sandro, standing back. 'You okay?'

The kid gazes back up with dreamy eyes. 'Sure.'

'So long's you okay.' He walks past the kid and stares down at the spraying surf twenty metres below. Down and to the right, he can see a pebbled beach. He begins to climb down.

'Hey!' says the kid.

Sandro glances over his shoulder.

'Where you going?'

'For a swim.'

'Stay. We can talk.'

'About what?'

The kid rubs his eyes wearily. 'Fuck do I know?'

Sandro steps back to him and sits on the warm rocks. 'What's the water like?'

'I'm Andrea,' the guy says. 'And I don't have a fucking clue—I hate swimming.'

'So what are you doing here?'

Andrea smiles.

A gull squawks above them, giant white wings flaying in the thick air. Sandro stares about him, then down to the kid's nipples, down to his underpants. 'What happened to your clothes?'

Andrea stares down at his body, glances about him, shakes his head with a curious frown. 'I don't know,' he cranes his brow and checks out the world one more time, 'I came here this morning ...' he casts his eyes at the sun. 'What day is it, today?'

Sandro gives it a bit of thought. 'Tuesday? Yeah, Tuesday, I think.'

'Oh.' Andrea nods. 'So I came here yesterday morning,' he says. 'There's plenty of dopers here—they probably stole my clothes.'

'And you're clean, of course.'

'And you, a tourist.'

'Of course.' The two share a smile.

'Do you have? *Hai del fumo?*' The kid asks, too eager.

'I have something better.'

Andrea smiles. 'You wanna?'

Sandro draws out the *Sudden Impact* case and shows him.

'Fucking hell,' Andrea says. Behind him, on the hot ground, is a syringe that he lifts with a stretching hand like he knows it's there. 'You have a light?'

Sandro hands over a Bic, peace and doves.

'Better than swimming, see?' says Andrea, doing his bit with a rusted bottle-top and water from a hollow in the rocks. 'Would you like the honour?'

Sandro accepts the syringe with an inspection of the needle. 'You heard of AIDS?'

'Sure. You?'

Sandro does his thing and Andrea does it squatting, shoots in through the groin. Still someone to hide this from, thinks Sandro. Who? Andrea sinks back slowly. Back to looking dead.

Sandro leans forward and retrieves the *Sudden Impact* case, balances it on his lap. The sea is audible now, his brain zoning out the industrial sounds and replacing them with the steady rhythm of the Tyrrhenian clapping on the rocks somewhere below and the sounds of the birds that flap past. 'You got any cigarettes?'

The sun is lower when Andrea says, 'No. I need a cigarette too.'

Sandro stands on unsteady, weakened legs. He has sweet lethargy, but he has another addiction to curb. The case falls onto the rocks. His head feels so heavy, his hair must weigh a ton as he stumbles about lifting cigarette butts from the ground. A boat tugs, a whistle blows for lunch, and the clamour of working people drifts up to him. He says, 'Help me find some butts, Andrea.' There's no reply and Sandro turns quickly. Somehow knowing.

The case is gone ... and Andrea too has vanished into the haze.

He swivels his head about like a radar-kit, eyes wide and ears straining for any sounds. Rocks tumble. Sandro runs, clambering up the rocks with frantically scraping boots. Andrea's head vanishes below the rocky summit five feet above Sandro's furiously climbing body. He reaches the summit, sprints to the other side, and slides to a halt on the edge. To stare down. At Andrea, climbing quickly towards the ground with naked toes grabbing at jutting rocks like a fucking ape.

'Stop! Stop, you fuck!'

Andrea ignores him, jumping six feet down and rolling on the hot earth with rocks scraping against his body. Sandro chases, falling onto his ass and sliding down with pain surging white through his mind and his boots losing grip. He falls with a thud. Stands and watches—gasping breaths and drifting nausea— Andrea sprinting past the rubbish-dump. Sandro limps after him, his ankle twisted, his jeans torn, blood trickling from the cuts on his palms. Tears spring to his eyes as he watches Andrea climb the fence to liberty.

'Stop!' screams Sandro, 'cause now there's nothing he can do. 'Stop!' He comes to a halt beside the rubbish-dump and breathes the noxious air and watches Andrea sprinting away with the *Sudden Impact* case and all Sandro's dreams.

III

The sun has ascended dead-centre in the white-blue sky when Sandro begins the arduous trek back to the apartment.

A stranger, no possibility for dope on credit. And no fucking money even if he could find a merch'. The whores in the district would know—point him in the right direction. He needs cash. Above, thick grey clouds are converging, shutting off the fierce glare of the sun. A cool breeze swings inland, bristling his hair and chilling his flesh. The odd silence before a looming summer storm. The world turns green. And the storm breaks. Thick pelting raindrops the size of tarantulas plunging down from a thick, purple sky. Thunder lashes away, the torrential rain splattering onto the city in a rigid waterfall, gutters immediately unable to cope.

Sandro's soaked through to the skin when he finally enters the dim apartment block. The building smells like a urinal. The elevator stands open towards the back of the shit-brown lobby with red graffiti sprayed onto its wood-panelled interior. LSD & ME & KATIA PUTANELLA.

Ignoring the elevator and the termites chewing at its insides, he climbs the staircase with his hands groping in the dimness, fingers touching the damp walls and flipping off vermin that suck and bite the blood from his hands and wrists. A scream reverberates round the building as he reaches the first landing. Sandro pauses, listening. Silence, now, but for a dripping water pipe above his head. He unlocks his door. A door suddenly bangs on the dim hallway, and he darts his head towards the clamour. He watches a naked girl come storming down the hallway with breasts wobbling into her chin. Her face is gleaming with sweat, her eyes wide sparkling worlds as she jerks her head back over her naked shoulders. *'Serpenti!'* she screams behind her at the hallway, *'Auitami! Auitami!* She sprints past Sandro with her eyes seeing nothing much of anything at all.

The dripping water soon replaces her voice. LSD and Katia, thinks Sandro, walking into the apartment. Sandro's over that shit. Acid makes him feel too good, makes him think too much. Leave it to the college students who can afford the trip. He doesn't like to think too much. Like the girl running naked through Naples on her way to a gang-rape up some alley, thinking isn't for this life.

Sandro flips on the lights in the apartment and carries a wooden chair to the window. Tears roll down the pane to a dripping ledge.

A pigeon has perched itself in a thick crack in the building, shelter from the rain, from the storm that continues unabated. Faded lights gleam in the dark afternoon from the buildings opposite, silhouettes flickering behind the windows in unsteady rituals.

He sits down on the hard chair. Thunderclaps startle him, making him crave a smoke. He glances about the apartment until he finally spots the overflowing ashtray. He reaches for it, deposits it on a scarred cabinet. Rain pelts into the window, the wind gushing up. The single drawer in the cabinet contains nothing but a black bible and Sandro tears out a page at random. Resting the torn page on his lap, his eyes browse the words.

> *Turn away from all the evil you are doing*
> *and don't let your sin destroy you. Give up*
> *all the evil you have been doing and get*
> *yourselves new minds and hearts. Why do*
> *you want to die? I do not want anyone to*
> *die. Turn away from your sins and live.*

Sandro decides whoever wrote the Song of Sorrows knew a thing or two. He mulls what remains of his dope onto the page, cleaning the seeds into the ashtray. It's getting difficult to justify, this whole scene. He cleans out cigarette butts, mixing the tobacco and dope, and sticks it all together. God's word is strong, and he coughs a thick trail of smoke from his raking lungs. He glances through the window at the dark sky. The rain will not let up. The thought of working without a high makes him bilious, the fear causing his bowels to churn. He tugs heavily on the joint. It's weak. The room is so ... present. It exists, and he is aware of its existence, aware of the different shades of shit-brown beneath the hanging, bare bulb. The hole beneath the sink is suddenly, weirdly, threatening. Rats? Snakes? Not snakes. The joint that he kills is not enough to produce euphoria, much less hallucination.

Reality is the nightmare. And he knows there's no choice. Not really. He can't recall now, but maybe he'd sworn never to be like them—never to work the streets, not like that, that's what whores do, and somewhere he figures he's not that, not a whore. It's for the jollies. Isn't it, Francesca. It was for the jollies.

Sandro lies on the bed with his aching body, shuts his eyes and allows the storm to cleanse his mind. It's gonna be a long night. Without a fix. But in truth he just needs to be a good time boy once or twice to find the numb.

IV

The rain has passed, leaving the city weirdly cool in its wake.

A blue Alfa drifts off down toward the docks. A pale man, shadowed by the nebulous glare of the city's lights, drives carefully over the ancient, wet roads. Soft music flows from his car, dimming the purring engine. He holds a cigarette between two fingers, his palms gently resting on a wooden wheel. He brakes for a set of lights, slinging off his necktie that constricts his brain from oxygen, and tosses it onto the backseat. It comes to rest above a black briefcase.

Resting the smoke between his lips, he undoes the top button to his Cardin shirt, his eyes checking out the tall prison walls opposite the intersection. He turns the Alfa left, drives easily towards the Tyrrhenian sparkling with light. The traffic is steady, pedestrians converging on the narrow sidewalks. The man parks his car beside an abandoned warehouse, locks the doors and begins walking towards the docks with a nervous saunter. He glances at his Longines wristwatch below a streetlamp. 10:15pm. As an afterthought, he unstraps the leather band and inserts it firmly in his grey flannel slacks.

It's not difficult for him to distinguish the junky whores from the casual passers-by. Even simpler is identifying the junkies hanging for a fix—which is precisely what he's searching for. He finds them keen and submissive when they're going cold. The man thinks he knows the difference between aggression and passive jonesing. Like the young man who traps his eyes from across the road. He's never seen the face before, fresh meat suit, and he looks away suspiciously. He has familiarised himself with most of the rents on the docks over the years, and he, like the whores, greets strangers with suspicion.

Drawing out a smoke, he pauses mid-stride and lights it with his eyes scuttling about. Something's not right tonight. There're no conspicuous cars on the road. But on the opposite sidewalk stands a man sipping on a can of Coke with a red shirt too rich for a whore and too poor for a respectable citizen searching for merchandise. What's begging for a mugging, aware of it, and doesn't give a shit? Whores move away from their campsites as the man with the Coke approaches, vanishing into buildings and slowly cruising cars. He's a ghost cop without the comfort of invisibility.

The cop's passing the entrance to the Marinaia Club, nodding his head curtly at a lazily smoking girl in Dr Martens. A hand touches the man's shoulder, and he loses sight of the cop when he turns around. A mini-skirted girl stares up at him with a Madonna smile. He looks away. The girl trudges on, whispering, 'Fag.' He watches the girl walking away for a while, before returning his glance toward the club and the cop. He's vanished. Faces have appeared from alleys and buildings and shops and hotels and hostels. Business is back to normal. The ghost has vanished. He turns towards the fresh-face he'd seen standing outside the XXX-movie house, but he's disappointed 'cause a freckled-face girl with three fingers missing from one hand has replaced him. She's winking at him and licking her lips like he's ice-cream. He glances away from her, turns, and comes face to face with brown eyes six inches from him.

'You got a smoke, buddy?' the face asks through cut lips.

The man's heart takes a skip. 'I can get a pack.' He takes a cursory look at the street. 'A pack of twenty?'

'Make it thirties and we're good.'

'Okay. Come,' the man whispers.

The jean-clad whore follows on the sidewalk. Whores jeer, laughing like sirens distantly wailing in the silver-bathed night. The man enters a run-down motel with the whore joining him in the lobby instants later. A girl's kneeling before a man beside the staircase, black hair partly hiding her gulping mouth. The man with the Cardin shirt accepts a key from an indifferent woman behind the front desk, her eyes fixed on a portable monochrome TV. Bill Cosby's having breakfast with his family. Everyone's having a laugh. The woman thumps a palm over her knee and throws out a heavy laugh too while the girl on her knees tries not to swallow.

Cardin shirt walks up the staircase with his whore following at a discreet distance. Music thumps from beyond a shut door where two guys wait outside, randying themselves up with stroking palms. On the second landing, Cardin leads into an unnumbered room, locks the door and tosses a pack of Camels at the whore. He takes his junk out and sits on a double bed. 'You can call me Papa,' he says. 'Now why don't you strip—'

'Papa,' says the whore, 'you owe me a pack of thirties.'

The guy stretches and finds his wallet, strips four bills and rests them up on the vanity. 'Now strip down.'

The whore complies. He kills his smoke in the ashtray on the vanity and inspects himself briefly in the mirror before undressing lethargically. His bruises stress the thin body in the soft, uncertain light. He stands before the man now, naked.

'Go squat over there like an animal,' says the man, pointing at the corner of the room. The whore does. But doesn't move fast enough. 'What do you say!' the man snaps. 'You stupid whore. What do you *say!*'

'Si, Papa?' the whore guesses. He moves to the corner, squats, and glances at the man.

'How many men you had today? How many?'

'None, Papa.'

'You *lie* to me! To *me!*'

'Two, Papa.'

'Why are you beaten?'

'I was bad, Papa.'

'You're shit.'

'Yes, Papa.'

'You're shit. Show me,' he groans with a frantically pumping hand like an ape in a zoo. 'Show me your shit—'

Something thumps against the door. Then again later. The man freezes. The whore freezes. And an instant later, the door explodes off its hinges and crashes down into the room. The whore's running naked for the window as a uniformed cop runs in with a baton-wielding hand. Behind him comes the ghost cop.

The whore's got one leg dangling out of the window into the night, assessing the twelve-foot drop beyond, when he hears a voice shout, 'Stand still! Stand still where you are!'

The whore turns and sees one cop thwack Cardin man on his fat ass. Ghost cop is rushing towards the window and tackles the whore and delivers two powerful close-contact blows. The whore somehow grabs him and together the two fall onto the floor, wrestling about until the cop finds his feet and swings his fist across the whore's bruised back.

'Lie still! Spread yourself, *now!* Do it! You breathe and I'm gonna break your balls, you faggot, you *hear!* Do it!'

The whore whips out a hand, grabs the cop's ankle and thrusts back. The cop loses his balance. Stumbles as the whore regains his feet. The whore hesitates, looking from one cop to the other, busy handcuffing Cardin man. He moves back hesitantly 'til his back presses into the windowsill. He looks behind his shoulder, down at the alley two floors below. The cop before him sees opportunity and springs forward, slapping at the whore's exposed genitals. There's a loud thwack before the whore's face goes tomato red and he collapses onto his knees.

The cop smashes his fist into his face. Blood spurts from the whore's face as his body goes down, his face inches from cop's boots. The cop squats, about to bring the blows, but the whore's working on instinct now, survival, lifting his shoulder and absorbing the first blow with the pain feeding energy to his anger, his adrenaline, as his head butts up into the cop's crotch. Ghost cop roars as the whore stumbles to his feet.

'You fuck!' screams the uniformed cop, pushing the cuffed Cardin man away onto the bed and stepping forward, baton up. The whore's oblivious now, grabs the unsteady cop by the hair and launching his head through the window.

'Jesus,' whispers Cardin man, 'Jesus.'

The cop's body starts to slide through the window, the whore holding him out by the belt, veins protruding from his arms. 'I wanna get outta here!' screams the whore back into the room. He forces the cop further out into the night and now the cop's boots are floating above the floor. 'I wanna get out!'

Ghost cop outside moans as his partner plays it tough and by the book. 'We can't let you go,' he says, but he's not getting closer now, standing and assessing the level of crazy he's dealing with. 'Just chill out, okay? You're under arrest—there's nothing you can do about it.' He glances at ghost cop's ass. 'Let go of him and we'll forget this whole assault shit, okay? We'll take you down to the station, and tomorrow you'll be back here spreading your ass. Okay? Don't make this worse, man.'

He drops his baton and raises empty palms, trying to be calm, but the sweat dripping off his brow is a dead giveaway. He tries two tentative steps towards the whore. His partner's boots lift even further, the whore's body arching out now and gravity's threatening to heave them both out into the abyss.

The whore's eyes shimmer in the erratic light, blood falling from his nose and into his mouth. The cop thinks hard. Blinks away his cover of calmness. He locks eyes with the whore who's sweating hard at keeping the cop up. 'Let him go, buddy. Please.'

The cop with the unsheltered view of destiny's panicking now. His legs kick out and the whore loses his grip. Just for a moment, before grabbing hold of the trousers. But ghost cop's head is heavy and he's steadily worming out toward the other side of the void.

Ghost cop suddenly starts screaming at the black road two storeys below him. 'Sergio! *Sergio!* Help me, Jesus, help me!'

'Let him go!' Sergio the uniformed cop steps forward. 'You got nowhere to go, man, *nowhere.* Don't make this worse on yourself. What the fuck are you doing! *Think about what you're fucking doing!'*

The whore is sweating hard, blood thick on his face as he fights with the squirming weight in his hands. Sergio steps forward again, now just a couple of feet from the window, fighting indecision. The whore blinks. Sergio attempts another step. The whore, wanting to protect himself, loosens his grip on the trousers. Just an instant.

But it's enough. It's too much.

Ghost cop's legs rocket up the wall to follow the body straight out into the night.

There's a scream, sudden and savage. It lasts 'til Sergio dives at the window, hearing the thump that kills the scream before he ducks his head out.

The whore side-steps him as Sergio stares out of the window at his partner spread-eagled on the dim road below. Sergio gazes at his partner sprawled on the dim road below and then shifts his attention to the whore rushing out of the room.

And then Sergio just falls onto his knees, resting his face in his hands. And screams until his larynx dries up while the cuffed Cardin man sits on the bed and sheds tears for his own sins.

13. Spagna: 'Call Me'
I

'All units, in position,' comes Chief Inspector Virdis' voice over the two-way.

'We're all ready for you, chief inspector,' whispers Onassio into his two-way that he now lowers onto the bitumen rooftop. Crouched behind a small brick wall, the city rising in turrets and towers below the setting sun, his fingers caress the rifle balanced on his knees. He scans the rooftops, then the road four storeys below. The Englishman Blake, in a bad suit, sips a tall drink on a sidewalk café partially hidden beneath a Martini umbrella. Across the street, dope-pusher Massimo with the yellow hair is leaning against a lamppost, one hand in his pocket, the other holding a cigarette, body bleeding a dirty long shadow onto the road.

The two-way crackles near Onassio's shoes and he lifts it quickly with eyes never straying from the road.

'Target coming in,' says Virdis over the two-way, 'turning onto the block now.'

A kid appears at the end of the block headed towards the café. Onassio watches him come. Him and, following behind with silver hair gleaming in the twilight, Chief Inspector Virdis. The kid is wearing Dr Martens and an unbuttoned shirt and a denim jacket. He passes the café. Onassio watches Blake nod imperceptibly at Virdis as the chief inspector steps past in the boy's wake. A spectacled man crosses the road, pausing on the sidewalk to glance up at the Hotel Alessandria across from Onassio. Onassio follows his stare.

'It's gonna go down,' drones the two-way, 'I'm pulling back, the kid's getting jittery.' Virdis pauses in his stride, turning to a Benetton-window display to light a smoke.

Onassio watches as denim jacket reaches Massimo, the two slapping knuckles in greeting. Massimo moves back suddenly. Too sudden his movement. Onassio sits up. Watches as denim jacket steps into Massimo. The two touch bodies. Just for an instant. And then Massimo looks up at the night sky. Denim jacket steps back as Massimo falls onto his knees, fingers entwined over his belly. His head's bowed, staring down incredulously at the stream of blood pouring between his fingers onto the sidewalk.

Denim jacket starts to sprint away from Massimo and back towards the café, passing Virdis who stares past his shoulder at Massimo, folded like a lawn chair and bleeding out.

'Blake, he's yours!' Virdis shouts into his lapel. 'Onassio, don't lose him!'

There's a woman with a poodle in her arms standing over Massimo now, her face contorted in a pink, monstrous, screaming hole. Massimo falls onto his face as Virdis reaches him.

Onassio forces his eyes to snap from the chief inspector and onto the running boy—sonofabitch! Grabs his rifle. 'He's yours, Blake!' shouts Onassio into the radio. 'All units, suspect is male wearing a denim jacket and boots and jeans—we want him alive!'

Denim jacket's sprinting hard and doesn't register Blake who comes at him through the café, wrestler-like. The kid sees him too late. Tries to skip away in full stride, tries to alter his momentum. Blake's having none of it. He's onto the twist and change, diving to his right and tapping the kid's ankles as they tear past his face.

Denim jacket keeps running. Only his ankles are lagging behind in Blake's hand. He pitches forward and slams down onto his knees to skid into the tables, rolling with arms protecting his head. Blake grabs a table to stand and falls over clumsily. The kid gets an ankle out of the vice and staggers on, off-balance, arms flaying wildly.

'Heading towards Via Vialli, all units! Suspect about to reach Vialli!' shouts Onassio and watches Blake take up the chase, wondering, not for the first time, why Virdis had stationed him on a rooftop when all the action was inevitably to take place down there on the streets. Why was he not in Blake's position? The kid would never have bolted from Onassio. Down there Blake's not an asset, he's not a beat-cop, the Englishman belongs behind a desk, a forensics man, a computer man. A man of intellect. Not a man of action.

Onassio glances back toward Massimo. Virdis has vanished. His jacket has been thrown over Massimo's face, the body lying limply amongst a group of beady-eyed strangers staring down at destiny on the sidewalk.

Blake's closing in on the kid now. Two blue Giuliettas, *Carabinieri* stencilled on the doors, fish-tail round the bend in front of the kid. They brake hard, one spinning wildly and crashing onto the sidewalk, narrowly avoiding denim jacket who slides to a stop, his eyes darting from the car and back at Blake closing in fast. Nowhere to run, nowhere to hide.

Onassio with the grandstand view shouts, 'Arcadia is trapped. All units close in!'

The kid lifts his head to the darkening sky with arms held up in surrender. His head continues to rise, ripping off from the body in a golden-tinged spray, the headless body crumpling up like a marionette. The carabinieri storm out from their squad-cars waving shotguns at the street, the shops, the rooftops. Blake crouches over the corpse with his Beretta protruding from an outstretched arm.

'We have a shooter!' shouts Blake over the radio. 'We have a shooter!'

Onassio glimpses a silhouette above the Hotel Alessandria across from him, then loses it for an eternity in the land of shadows. Finally, *finally* he tracks it down!

'Gunman on the roof—above the Alessandria!' shouts Onassio, tossing the two-way behind him and shouldering the rifle. It's too dark to get any distinguished impression of the silhouette in his sights as it begins to walk to a hump on the roof, which Onassio figures to be the staircase. Onassio sights in on the target. Exhales. Squeezes off a round. The silhouette pauses, standing motionless. Onassio squeezes off another round. The figure vaults backwards and out of sight. Onassio thinks he's heard a muffled scream. He finds the two-way. 'I've got the fuck!' he shouts, '*the fuck's not getting up! I got the motherfucker!*'

Another silhouette steps out from the hump. There's static on the receiver as Onassio goes for the rifle again, teeing up his shot.

'Don't shoot, Onassio,' whispers Virdis over the two-way, 'you've already blown a woman's face into her washing basket.'

The static dies as Onassio drops the rifle onto the gravel. He had not even thought—he'd just—just reacted, like an animal, and 'What, what did you say?' he whispers over the radio. Nothing comes back but static.

II

Sirens approach violently through the city. The carabinieri have stretched a fluorescent tape from one traffic light to the next, a roadblock already sealing off the road. People scamper out from the surrounding buildings like blood-hungry rats, peering past the shoulders of the policemen, frantically trying to see something—anything—so long's it's all covered in blood and gore.

A voice is shouting from behind Blake, a journo', something about the country having the right to witness the crime on the streets of Milan. 'I demand to see the body!' she shouts. 'Italy demands to see the crime-infested streets!'

Blake moves away, shutting off the voice by concentrating on the wailing sirens homing in on him. A Giulietta sits across the cordoned-off road ahead, blue sirens looping silently on its roof. Virdis sits on the passenger seat with legs slumped out on the road. He's talking into the car's radio. Their eyes meet in the gloom, and Blake steps on over.

Virdis slams down the radio and climbs out, the blinking sirens turning his hair purple. An ambulance has arrived, blaring its horn and siren as it tries to manoeuvre between the jeering spectators.

'How come the ambulance's allowed through? The people have a right to see! Fucking pigs!'

'This shouldn't have happened,' says Blake. He follows Virdis away from the car.

Virdis digs his hands deep into his pockets, shoulders slumped forward and head occasionally rising to check out the proceedings. 'If I'd gone through proper channels,' he says, 'this would not have happened. Agency would not have been granted.'

'It's not your fault, chief inspector. The boy—Arcadia—was obviously marked. They both were—him and Massimo.'

'Massimo knew it was a set-up. I sensed it immediately.' Virdis makes a fist. 'Damnit, I should have bailed us out right there! I could see it happening. Five metres away and I just ... hesitated. I could've stopped Arcadia from stabbing him. But I— held back. We could get him on murder, he'd have squealed like a fucking rat. We'd have squeezed the source outta him.'

They reach an unmarked Giulietta parked opposite the Alessandria.

'Yes, there's no doubt,' says Blake.

Virdis opens the passenger door. Blake notices the motionless figure of Onassio slumped in the backseat. Virdis glances at him briefly through the shadows, holding the door open, before settling his eyes back at Blake. 'We were set up. Someone leaked. There were only a handful who knew about this operation. And one of them leaked.' He climbs into the sedan, slamming the door shut, and the uniformed cop behind the wheel guns the engine for Blake to step aside and watch the car slide forward with barking sirens.

Blake tosses away his smoke distastefully. How much does Virdis know? Probably more than he's letting on. Did he suspect anything? Virdis is a snake and Blake is a foreigner, immediately suspect. Blake's seen the chief inspector at work—it's no wonder the local cops dub him Machiavelli. He has a habit of setting off so many sparks that eventually something must blow. But Virdis' tricks have begun to backfire of late. His entire life's a powder-keg, thinks Blake, from his stormy marriage to the Contessa De Stefanis to his rapidly fading political career.

'There's a man, Detective Blake, sir, says he saw the killer.'

Blake turns in his stride to face a young rookie cop dead in the eye. 'We all know who the killer is. He's the one without the head.'

'No, sir—I mean, the guy who sniped the kid.'

Blake follows the cop towards a squad car parked vertically across the road. A man stands gesticulating at two policemen, his finger pointing towards the flickering green neon sign above the café, ALES AN RIA. The conversation dies as Blake catches the eyes of the spectacled witness.

'I'll take it from here, thank you,' says Blake, waving the cops away. They move off silently like extras in a movie. Blake turns to the frail-looking man. 'What's your name, mate?'

'Gianni Battani.'

'Well then, Gianni Battani, what is it you thought you saw?'

The man hesitates, suspecting there's something insulting in Blake's approach but not quite able to pinpoint it, perhaps it's the accent, so he avoids the Englishman's blue eyes and says, 'Well, I was crossing the road, see, heading towards the café—I saw you sitting there—and I had the impression of something ... flashing, from above the Alessandria—' he pauses while Blake stares back at the café pensively, 'and—'

'How could you see over the canopy if you were at the café?'

'I was halfway across the street—I could easily see the—'

'What kind of—*flash* was it?' interrupts Blake with a vague indulgent smile, 'was it like a photoflash?'

'Light, reflecting off glass.'

'You know this for a fact.'

'Yes.'

'Then what happened?'

Battani digs out a pack of MS, flips one in his mouth and pats down his baggy green jacket for a light, his eyes staring down at the road. Blake springs a flame by his nostrils.

'*Grazie*. I stared up at the roof for a while, but I couldn't really see anything, so I walked into the café. Then I saw the kid with the denim jacket walking—'

'From inside the café, now?'

'Yes.'

'How come you noticed the kid?'

'I don't know,' he smiles, 'how come I noticed you? I just notice things is all.'

'For absolutely no reason?'

'No—well, yes.' He drags heavily on his smoke, flipping off ash with a thumb. 'Look, I saw the kid—I don't know why I turned, I just did, okay?—and then I saw you nodding at a man with grey hair. I was sitting down talking with Arturo—the café owner— when I hear this scream, so I get up and head for the door. As I get to it, the kid runs past, and moments later you jumped and grabbed him. As I got outside, I saw the kid get shot—'

'Did you hear anything?'

'Yes, I heard a shot from above, so I looked up—'

'But there's a canopy above the café, Gianni Battani.'

'I was crossing the street when I looked up,' says Battani impatiently, 'and I saw a man standing with a rifle which had a big silencer—'

'But you heard a shot? Isn't that what you just said?'

'Well, yes, I suppose—I heard a, well, a muffled puff, rather'n an actual gunshot. Like a pop. A spit.'

'So you *didn't* hear a shot?'

'Yes, of course I did, but it was sorta a ... a—'

'Muffled puff, yes, like in the movies. Did you see the shooter? Can you identify him?'

'Yes. Yes, I think so.'

Blake watches him close-up. 'What did he look like?'

'He was tall, thin, black-hair, with a black suit—'

'Was he standing where you think you saw this—this flash?'

'Yes. From a room in the Alessandria. Third story. I could see him clearly because he stood after the shot and—'

'So how come you didn't see him the first time?'

Battani stammers. 'I—I suppose he—'

'*Ma basta!*' Blake lifts his hand and slices the humid night. 'Go home and tell your kids, Gianni. You have the storyteller's gift.' Blake turns from the startled man, stepping away with, 'Don't bullshit us, man, 'cause we got too much shit already.'

The rookie approaches Blake. 'Shall we take him in and get a statement?' he asks, thumping Battani on the back.

'No.' Blake smiles at Battani. 'He knows nothing.'

'But Sergeant Nero said—'

'I don't give a fuck what Nero says. This guy knows nothing. Get me a car,' he smiles evenly at the rookie, 'pronto, pronto!'

The rookie licks his lips like he's tasting blood. 'Yessir. Immediately.'

III

Onassio locks the Alfa's door and tosses away a smoke butt. He perspires freely, the humid night affecting his asthma. He steps sullenly through a metal gate into a delicate rose garden, the flowers like black shadows suspended. The building's squat but spacious, ivy crawling up the bricks to wood-framed windows adorned with hanging flower-pots. He checks the mailbox from instinct before trudging empty-handed up a dim flight of stairs to the first landing. A furry puppy bolts past him, paws sliding wildly on the polished wood. He watches it run with a thoughtful smile before unlocking a thick oak door on the landing.

'What's happened?' A straggly haired woman stands outside the kitchen with an apron declaring SAFE AS MILK. She steps to him with a wooden spoon in a veined hand. 'Giuseppe phoned me. He told me—'

Onassio shakes his head as she reaches for his face with an unsteady hand. He moves away from her silently. His eyes shimmer, as if he's on the verge of tears, and perhaps to protect his ego, his macho, Onassio walks down a dim corridor toward his home office that had once been his son's bedroom before he'd gone off to university and a posting in Montreal.

'I'm sorry,' he hears his wife say behind him. 'There's food in the oven if you're hungry.'

His study has French doors opening out to a tiny metal-framed veranda above the communal rose garden. He sits behind a small desk and pensively lights an MS and a lampshade with the same motion. A cricket shrills and a truck jostles past through the night as he stares at a photo of his wife, monochrome, standing outside La Scala circa '61 ... it's been a long time, and now this.

Suspended. At his age, best-case scenario is early retirement. With a pitiful pension from the state. If he's lucky. How's he meant to pay the bond on the apartment? Or his daughter's varsity fees?

Uomo propone, Dio dispone.

There's nothing left for the trigger-happy Onassio.

He tips ash from his smoke. They will set up the final hearing in a week or so. Virdis will make sure of its haste. But in the meantime, what is Onassio to do? Sit around and stare into space waiting for the verdict? God, will they force him to face criminal charges? *Homicide*? It's happened before.

In his unconscious mind, though, a solution has already been percolating.

Only now, though, safe in his home, does the data trickle into his consciousness, drop by terrifying drop. And it makes sense. All of it makes sense.

But it just—it can't be. Can it?

Is it possible the bastard betrayed everyone?

IV

Blake lifts the mattress from his double-bed and slides an attaché case beneath it. He'll rid himself of it soon, he thinks, sitting down heavily on the bed and lighting a Chesterfield before lying back and giving the ceiling a long stare. He reaches beside him for the telephone and dials.

'We need to meet,' he says when the ringing ceases in his ear. He listens momentarily. 'Tomorrow,' he says, and watches the violet smoke rising from his smoke. 'Yes, I *do* have a fucking problem. Why was I not told—' he pauses, interrupted by a loud voice, listens, dragging on the butt of the smoke as the voice gains a new pitch in his ear. Finally he says, 'Call me at the usual place at six-thirty and lead me in.' He slams down the receiver and kills the half-smoked cigarette in a full ashtray before flicking off the lampshade and undressing in the night.

V

He can't do it!

This evening he'd blown a woman away while she was hanging up her fucking laundry—but he's too selfish, too egotistical, to do it to himself. Disgusted—with himself, with God, with this fucking life—Onassio drops the Beretta onto the desk with a solid clutter. Light reflects off its polished metal from the high-powered lampshade. He mops at the sweat on his brow. He cannot simply blow his brains out over the veranda in downtown Milan. No matter how tempted he is. He can't abandon his Lisa, not after everything they've shared. But Jesus, what's left? With suicide, she can at least claim from his insurance. A fortune-teller had told him once he'd be killed by a gun ... Onassio has never forgotten, and he'd incorporated suicide into his policy just in case the gun was his own.

Hate.

Hate the bastard that set them up. Someone in the department leaked the sting operation. If Onassio can identify the leak, he might be able to salvage his career. There's so much corruption. Who could have done this is not as simple as who would *not* have sold them out for a few extra bucks. And although he will never forget his atrocity—that poor woman—others would in the face of his achievement. Virdis still pushed a lot of buttons around City

Hall. And Onassio knows he can count on Virdis' friendship and allegiance. The unfortunate death of an innocent woman is acceptable when the result is the capture of Milan's biggest drug-baron. And he knows, Onassio, he knows ...

He lifts a pencil from a coffee-mug and stretches forward for a sheet of paper. With a frown, he scribbles a list of names. Start with a fixed variable. Those that were informed about Arcadia before the sting took place.

The list is short ... sixteen names. Five are his colleagues—he's known 'em for over two decades. The sixth sends warning signals through his brain.

He nods, circling a name with a pencil. *Blake.* There really is no other, he knows it. Has always known it.

Even Virdis has mentioned his distrust of the Englishman since Blake's transferal from Naples. The Englishman had first arrived in Italy to aid Commissioner Paulini in the infamous Camora investigation. After Paulini's assassination, Blake had been assigned by Mayor Del'Aquila to assist Chief Inspector Virdis to get to grips with Milan's catastrophic heroin traffic, which had reached epidemic proportions, a second wave far more deadly than anything that had come before.

Onassio taps the pencil on his teeth. No choice, of course. And that realisation sends waves of gratitude to his mind. No choice but to go after Blake and expose him. He finds another sheet of paper and hastily scrawls a message. Standing, then, he deposits the Beretta into his slacks and silently leaves the sleeping apartment.

VI

Blake lies on the wide wood-framed bed with socked feet resting on a woollen rug. He's dressed in a blue suit, the tie hanging loosely as he lazily smokes what made American cigarettes great. The clock on the bedside table flips to 6am. It's time to rock & roll.

Standing, he forces his feet into soft-leather moccasins and checks the pistol on his shoulder-holster. He fingers the cold metal reassuringly before walking to the door. A deserted elevator drops him to the basement, and he finds his Fiat in the underground lot.

Moments and he's joined the thin stream of traffic under the dawning sky. The world's thrown into orange and grey shadows beyond the sloped windshield. He kills the Fiat's headlamps as he joins the autostrada and pushes the needle to 120. He drives to the outskirts of the city, east. Takes a turnoff into an industrial park and parks the car beside a public telephone booth on a quiet intersection. A red Alfa grinds past, struggling for gears, and turns left at the intersection. Blake watches it vanish between the darkened buildings and warehouses.

He climbs from his car, listening to a dog bark in the distance, and walks to the phone booth. His wristwatch, on inspection, shows six-thirty. Birds cherub frantically from tall fir trees, and even though expecting it, the shrill of the telephone startles him. He lifts the receiver. 'Yes?' he says. 'Yeah, okay. Yes. Jesus, how long have we been fucking doing this—yes, fine!' He nods once like a petulant child, slams the receiver down and walks back to his car. He accelerates, turning right at the intersection. Moments later, a red Alfa creeps after him, its exhaust spiralling out smoke into the morning.

Blake swings the Fiat back onto the autostrada and speeds towards the airport. Blotches of crimson highlights the eastern horizon, soft sunlight beginning to engulf the road. He rolls the Fiat onto the first airport off-ramp and stops the car beside an abandoned building just off the motorway. A public phone rings from outside the crumbling construction. Leaving the Fiat to idle, Blake sprints to the screaming phone and lifts the receiver. 'No,' he whispers, glancing up and down the road, 'I'm not being tailed.' He listens at length, before nodding his comprehension. '*Si*, *capisco*, seven-thirty, yes.'

With a glance at the developing day, he climbs into the Fiat and drives off slowly with his eyes stuck on the rear-view. No-one follows. He has an hour to kill. A few miles down the road, he finds a café and parks the Fiat beside the glass-and-brick building. The café's deserted, booths lining the room in three neat rows. He sits near the counter and smiles at a young girl filing her nails behind it. She stands, steps around the counter, and grudgingly dumps a menu before him. Blake orders eggs and coffee. The girl gives him a quizzical look and asks whether he really wants eggs. Fucking Italians, he thinks. Driving at dawn has always made him hungry. A television, yellowed and erratic like a jaundiced junky, is turned on low behind the bar. '—in what mayor Vincenzo Del'Aquila described as an unsanctioned set-up of an alleged drug-dealer, Massimo Brigante. It's alleged that—' the girl deposits food before him.

'There anything else you want? With the eggs?' she asks.

'No.'

'—the mayor in a press-conference late last night said, "although there can be no justification for the accidental killing of this unfortunate woman by the suspended officer concerned, I must reiterate that our mandate with the citizens of Milano was to pull the plug on drugs, and this unfortunate event will not affect our directive...".'

The waitress has begun filing the other hand when Blake washes down his meal with weak coffee. He dumps three notes on the counter and leaves. The day has formed, an infinite blue sky stretching out above him. Leaning against his Fiat, he pulls out a pack of smokes and lights one up with a cupped flame. The occasional car whizzes past. Blake heads for the airport.

His wristwatch shows seven twenty-five when he spots the road-sign. It points to a dirt-road on the left, winding away into a cornfield. ATLAS CORP. Blake slides the car onto the road with the Fiat fishtailing abruptly. He jams down the accelerator and the engine kicks the car straight. A trail of dust rises into the morning as he speeds towards the private airstrip. A Cessna glides above his head, gaining altitude.

There're three hangers before him in the distance. A red and white tower watches over the single airstrip, cutting into the field in a black slashed shadow. He glances into his rear-view, but all he can make out is red dust. It doesn't matter. No one's following. He'd made sure of that.

The BMW limo' is parked within the first hangar, dwarfed by an enormous DC10 with huge wings barely fitting in the metal hangar. Blake parks the Fiat below the dipped nose of the aircraft, kills the engine, and peers into the bimmer's tinted windows. Silence but for the ticking of the engine. Where the hell is everybody? He checks the time. Seven thirty-three. Igniting the engine, he rolls the car backwards, out of the hangar, and realises suddenly where everybody is.

A plume of dust rises from the road behind a red Alfa, storming towards the airstrip.

Blake strikes the wheel. *Fuck, someone was tailing him!*

The Cessna reappears above the Alfa as it approaches the airstrip. It dips, and then rises again in a tight arc above the red Alfa. A jeep roars out from the second hangar, heading for the road. Blake drops the clutch and tails the jeep. The two cars are quickly approaching the dirt road on a collision course with the Alfa that isn't slowing.

The jeep brakes suddenly, tyres locking on the earth. Blake keeps his foot down, running past the jeep and toward the Alfa now directly in his path. The Cessna pulls up, gaining altitude. Blake can see the Alfa's police-plates. Then Onassio's face staring back at him from behind the wheel of the Alfa. Instants before impact, Onassio swerves the Alfa onto the shoulder of the road. The Fiat careens into its rear end. The Alfa slides about in a flash of red, out of control. Blake locks the Fiat's brakes, staring into his rear-view as his car slides on the grain of the road.

The Alfa rotates like a rotor-blade before the rear wheels strike a ditch and the car instantly takes flight, spinning up into the air. To glide in space. Before it crashes down onto its roof with glass and debris splintering out across the field. The Alfa slides onto the tarmac with sparks dancing beneath the crushed metal roof. It finally comes to rest with its wheels still spinning, smoke drifting up into the morning air.

Blake powers the Fiat in a long spin to speed for the wreck. The jeep's already reached the Alfa and Blake can see a silver-haired man squatting beside the crushed door of the Alfa, dragging Onassio out. Blake stands on his brakes, ripping up the handbrake, locking up all four tyres and stops inches from the jeep. He stumbles out and sprints toward the silver-haired man now leaning over the motionless, bleeding Onassio on the tarmac.

'*Giovanni!* Is he still alive?' shouts Blake.

The tall, silver-haired man nods.

Blake kneels beside the body spread on the tarmac. Blood pours from a gash on Onassio's head, the flesh already beginning to swell to a dirty purple.

'Kill him,' says a voice from behind Blake.

Blake looks over his shoulder. Zoran stands beside the jeep with his body eclipsing the sun and his shadow rolling over Onassio's body. Giovanni hoists a Smith & Wesson from his belt, aims it at Onassio's face. Thumbs back the trigger. Blake grabs the wrist, forcing the revolver down as Onassio flicks open vague eyes from the ground.

'Little fuck,' he whispers up at Blake. 'Little fuck.'

Giovanni untangles his wrist. Onassio catches a glimpse of the revolver glistening under the warm sun. He stares up at Giovanni evenly. Blake stares from one to the other before stepping back.

The revolver spits a purple-red flame. Onassio's face disintegrates into the tarmac as the explosion echoes about the hangars.

Blake steps back, his hand rubbing away grey matter that has splattered across his face. He stares at Giovanni. 'You crazy bastard.' He wields suddenly to Zoran. 'How the fuck are we gonna explain *this*!' he demands, waving a hand at the jam-like mess that had been Onassio's head ten seconds ago.

'You fucked up,' says Zoran, turning away.

Blake follows him to the hangar, casting a last glance back at Giovanni sliding his warm revolver under his belt. 'He was a cop, Zoran! A fucking *cop*!'

Zoran slips into the back of the limo' and grabs a tumbler of orange juice. Takes a greedy sip. Then he reaches beside him and slides a briefcase out from the window. 'I've included a substantial bonus,' he tells Blake. 'Your information was not only important but correct. That's a rare commodity nowadays.'

Blake lifts the case. 'You realise,' he says, 'what this means?'

Zoran sips his juice and looks dead ahead.

'Zoran, I've—I thought I should tell you this—I've—'

'—applied for a transfer, back to England. Yes, I know. I hope this bonus will help, old friend. You're an integral part of the team, and it will be a sad day indeed if we had to lose you.'

'It's just getting hot, I mean—'

'But remember,' says Zoran as if Blake had not spoken, 'you are still part of my team.'

'Zoran—'

'And the game, buddy, is not football. It may be highly paid, and indeed great skill is required, but transfers are not allowed. Cancel the transfer. And don't give me cause to worry.'

Blake wants to say something. He has words. But they die in his throat. He lifts the briefcase. Heavy, like his mind. He walks out of the hangar and slings the case into the Fiat, and watches Giovanni drag Onassio's corpse by its ankles to the jeep. The Cessna hovers above the Fiat as Blake drives quickly toward the main road.

VII

The receptionist smiles up at Virdis from behind her Olivetti p/c. He seems tired, she thinks, the eyes and mouth drawn from exertion. 'Good mornin', chief inspector. Your wife been on your back again?'

He nods absently. 'Any messages?'

'Yes. Mrs Onassio called five times. She wants you to call her at home immediately.' She follows him into his office. 'It sounds urgent,' she adds.

'Get her for me,' he says.

Virdis examines the untidy office. He sits behind his desk and rests his hands against the receiver. He hopes Onassio's not done something stupid. The phone buzzes and Virdis snatches it up in an instant. 'Lisa, *cosa c'è*?'

'I think something's happened to Pierro,' whispers the voice.

Virdis can hear the tension, and he swallows, glancing up at his stacked in-tray. 'I'll be right over, okay?'

'Yes, Giuseppe, please. Thank you.'

Virdis leaves police HQ five minutes later. His Volvo's parked at the front entrance, on the busy main road. Life is seeping back into Milan, vacationers having cut their holidays short and returned to the city to enjoy the final, fine days of summer while it lasts. He drives quickly, switching on the radio.

Pierro and Lisa Onassio have been family friends of the Virdis family for over three decades, their kids having grown up together. Virdis and Onassio had joined the force the same year, partnering each other for five years. Virdis can only imagine what the suspension has done to the quiet, unassuming man. He'd been born a cop—and he was a damn good one at that. He'd never shared Virdis' political aspirations, happy enough to help Virdis' career without a thought to his own.

Virdis parks the Volvo beneath a tired but well-kept apartment block in the Borgo Ortalani, green-ivy crawling up the brown-brick. He walks hastily along the path through the rose garden, into the building and up to the first landing. He knocks on the last door on the sunny corridor and waits for the door to be opened, a face peering out at him. Then the door's widened and a woman offers him a shy smile and tear-swept eyes. They embrace warmly, kissing each other's cheeks.

'Lisa,' says Virdis, holding the woman at arm's length. She looks away from him, blushing. 'Tell me what's wrong.'

She shuts the door and bids for him to follow. Together they enter a sun-drenched study and step to the desk before the French windows. Lisa lifts a note from the desk and extends it at Virdis with a shaky hand. Virdis accepts it, reads it aloud. *Lisa, I must leave for a few days. I'll contact you in the morning and explain. Tuo, Pierro.*

'Has he called?' he asks.

'No. That's why I think something's happened. You know how he is.'

Virdis touches her face before walking about the desk. The sun filters in dusty rays from behind the curtains, reflecting off the polished parquet floor. He examines the desk pensively, shifting some papers around. 'Have you touched anything?'

Lisa shakes her head, standing uncertainly beside the big man.

Frowning, Virdis lifts a sheet of paper. Sixteen names. Blake's has been circled. Virdis folds it carefully and deposits it within his jacket. He continues with a cursory search, reading sheets of paper at random, with Lisa peering over his shoulder. Onassio is hunting the leak, he thinks. It's as he had expected. He turns to Lisa now. 'Did he take his pistol?'

She blinks at him horrified, before leaning forward and opening the top drawer. Golden shells roll about the otherwise empty drawer. She nods, drawing her lips onto her teeth as she fights back the tears.

'And his car?'

'Yes.'

Virdis strokes her face, brushing away an astray tear that rolls from her eye. Smiles reassuringly.

'Something's happened to him,' she whispers. 'I feel it.'

'Nothing's happened to him. Come here, Lisa.' They embrace, her arms holding him tight as sobs rake her body. 'Lisa, you mustn't worry. Pierro knows how to take care of himself. He's probably on a stake-out and hasn't been able to contact you, that's all.' He pushes her to an arm's length again, holds her shoulders tight. *'Dai, forza, su con le spalle.* You'll see. Everything's gonna be fine. He's not a rookie, Lisa. Come on.'

She nods, sniffing and attempting a smile.

Virdis offers her his handkerchief as they walk for the door. He turns to her on the threshold. 'I'll keep in touch. Call me the moment Pierro contacts you.'

'Yes, Pino, of course.'

'Trust me, Lisa, he'll be okay.'

Virdis can't avoid a foreboding sense of guilt as he steps down the corridor. After all, it was he that had baited Onassio in the car. He'd baited Blake, too, hoping something would give. And Onassio had bitten. Had Blake though?

He lifts his two-way immediately on climbing into the Volvo. 'Dispatch—this is Chief Inspector Virdis, code triple-one.'

'Yes, sir,' crackles a voice hastily.

Virdis guns the engine, peering at his side-mirror at an on-coming Vespa buzzing like a wasp in the quiet suburb. 'The following is the registration number of a red Alfa Giulietta—MI77924P. I want every available unit scouting the city for it. And send the choppers into the country—I want the car found!'

'Yes, sir!'

He pulls the Volvo out behind the black Vespa, accelerates past quickly, and can't help his eyes from straying on the naked legs of the woman riding the small vehicle. Onassio did all that was left for him to do. Predictably, he has gone after the leak. And Virdis, like Onassio, has his money that leak is going to turn out to be that Limey sonofabitch Blake.

Lifting the telephone beside the handbrake, he dials a city number and balances the receiver between his shoulder and ear.

'Mayor Del Aquila's office.'

'This is Chief Inspector Virdis. Put me through to the mayor.'

'Virdis,' comes the mayor's voice after a moment. 'How are things?'

'Onassio's taken the bait. He's after Blake.'

'As you wished, no?' There's an uneasy edge in the mayor's voice.

'Yes.'

'Can I thus expect a quick and tidy ending to this whole mess?'

'I have every disposable man on it.'

'Very good. I need not remind you what a stink this is gonna cause with the English. So keep it under your hat 'til all the apple-carts are in a row.'

Virdis kills the line, accelerating as the light ahead flips to orange. The city's stretched out before him, concrete pushing up to a blue-white sky. It's so unnatural, thinks Virdis, dialling another number. How can these million-ton concrete mountains expect to endure? They have an air of temporariness. Just looking at the dull brown grey is enough to know it'll all be destroyed in the end—however soon that is.

'Chief Inspector Virdis' office, how—'

'Is Blake there,' interrupts Virdis.

There's a pause before the receptionist says, 'No. And no-one's seen him all morning. Shall I get dispatch to track him for you, sir?'

'No, it's fine. I'll be back at lunchtime.'

He drives to the heart of the city. Onassio has not called, and Blake is missing. Coincidence? His heart misses a beat as an alarming thought crosses his mind. Would Onassio go after Blake with murder—revenge—on his mind? No. No, Onassio is a family man—he's after Blake for his job. Redemption. Onassio is a tough cop, he's learnt his trade well. Learnt his lessons like Virdis had learnt his. He's not the kind of man who would seek vengeance. Virdis speeds through an intersection and reassures himself that Onassio wouldn't destroy the only tangible lead in the investigation.

Blake has a furnished apartment in downtown Milan, in a tall cylindrical building with tinted glass reflecting the morning sun. Virdis drives round the block once, before finding a vacant parking space toward the back of the building.

The lobby's plush with red carpets supporting heavy wooden coffee-tables and chairs. Virdis saunters straight to the elevators, goes up to the tenth floor. He's met with palm trees growing abundantly from over-sized planters on the carpeted hallway. He checks his Beretta—full count of nine—before wrapping on the oak door at the far end of the corridor, 2014 emblazoned on it in velvet red.

He waits a moment, impatiently shifting his weight from one leg to the other. He knocks once more, firmly, before stealthily glancing down the hallway. Opening his wallet, he draws out a metal card and kneels with his eyes level to the Yale lock. Twenty seconds, and the door slips open. He checks the hallway once more before easing himself into the sun-licked apartment.

VIII

Blake strolls to the massive mahogany desk. He lights a smoke while waiting for the front-desk security guy to finish babbling with a blue-haired woman holding a yapping poodle under one thick arm.

'Any messages?' inquires Blake, turning to the porter when the woman hustles away for the front doors, '2014.'

The red uniformed man searches the pigeon-holes behind him momentarily. 'No.'

Blake nods and steps to the elevators.

Virdis, he thinks, knows nothing. If he did, the entire police force would be searching his apartment by now. Onassio had worked on his own—solo—following a hunch. Trying to save his career in the only way available to him.

But how did Onassio connect Blake? That's what's been bugging him since he left the airstrip. If Onassio had discovered his involvement with Zoran, what's stopping Virdis from putting the same pieces together? What's he done to leave a trail? Or was Onassio just following his nose like any good cop?

The elevator rings, doors whispering open and Blake climbs in. That's the only workable explanation—Onassio had taken a wild guess, the joker in the pack. Had Onassio informed Virdis of his suspicions? Because that would be a problem, he thinks. That would be a serious fucking problem. Virdis wasn't a man to be trifled with. And Onassio's death—Jesus, he thinks. That was going to have consequences. No mistake about it. Virdis would take that personally.

The elevator pauses on the seventh floor. A woman in white overalls climbs in and offers him a curt nod. There's a briefcase in his apartment with twenty thousand pounds in it—and another in his car with another ten grand. He needs to get the money to his Swiss account—should have done so this morning. He walks to 2014, inserts his key into the Yale and pushes open the door, kills his smoke in an ashtray on the dining-table and heads for the bedroom.

He notices the drawer hanging out from the bed-side counter immediately. Instinctively, he unholsters his Beretta and slips back the metal foreskin and scans the room, eyes fixing intently on every piece of furniture. Nothing's amiss. Perhaps he'd left the drawer open on leaving that morning? God only knows he's been distracted since that affair with Massimo and Arcadia, who knew far too fucking much about Zoran.

Something, though, is not quite right.

Blake scans the shut bathroom door. He swallows phlegm while slowly stepping to the door. Resting the barrel on his temple, he eases his hand on the doorknob and turns real gently. Before kicking the door open and hurtling into the white-tiled room with his pistol darting about within the confined space.

He forces out a long sigh at the empty room. Paranoid, he thinks.

He replaces the Beretta in its holster. And then he figures it all out in a flash. He steps back into the bedroom and lifts the mattress off the bed. It collapses on the carpet, sucking up air like a vacuum, the lampshade crashing onto the floor.

There's nothing above the springs.

Someone's taken the money.

Blake reaches for the Beretta.

'Are you looking for this, signor Blake?'

Blake swivels. Virdis stands by the bedroom door, dangling the briefcase from one hand while the other holds a Beretta that's pointed at Blake's belly. 'Take your gun with your thumb and forefinger and toss it onto the mattress. *Slowly*! *Piano*! Good … now toss it down. Nice and easy, signor Blake.'

Blake drops the pistol on the matrass and meets the man's eyes with an even stare. 'Chief inspector, if it's not too rude, why are you in my apartment holding a weapon to my face?'

'It's a valid question, signor Blake. So let me ask you something: Where's Onassio?' Virdis takes two steps forward, the Beretta not lowering an inch. 'Tell me what you've done.'

'What I've done? What are you talking about?'

Virdis shakes the briefcase. 'Where is Onassio?'

'How the fuck should I know? Look, mate, this is not what it seems, okay?'

'It's chief inspector, signor Blake. Not mate. And what does *this* seem like?' he asks, waving the briefcase. The pistol wavers as the men stare hard at each other.

'It's *Detective* Blake, chief inspector. And the money you got there in your hand is mine—I withdrew it yesterday morning. I'm putting down a deposit on a house—in Calabria.' He smiles, opening his hands in resignation. 'Come on, chief inspector, put the gun away before it goes off. There have been enough accidents this week.'

Virdis lowers his pistol. 'You know your rights, Detective Blake.'

'I know enough to know you can't arrest me—illegal entry, to begin with. And what the hell are you gonna charge me with? Possession of twenty thousand of my own pounds?' He steps forward confidently. 'Come on, chief inspector, we're all going through it, let's just calm down and look at this rationally, okay? Now what's this about Onassio?' He steps past Virdis and into the sitting room. Sits down on a leather couch, folding his legs and lighting up. Virdis follows him in and sits opposite the Englishman, resting his Beretta on an ivory-legged coffee-table beside him.

'He's vanished. He disappeared last night, without so much as a note, and nobody has heard from him since.'

'So what's the big deal?' Blake shrugs. 'He's got a lot on his mind—what with killing that old woman and his suspension. He probably needed to be alone for a while, get away from his old lady. You know how it is. Sometimes a man needs to be alone, no interference ... what's so strange? He'll be back in a couple of days, you watch.'

Virdis rubs his temples wearily. 'I guess I'm overreacting,' he whispers finally. 'Christ, I'm so fucking tired.'

Blake drags heavily on his cigarette. 'Has anything new come up?'

'No. Where were you this morning anyway?'

'Playing tennis,' comes the immediate reply, 'with an informant. I couldn't call 'cause it was like a ring-and-run situation.'

Virdis nods his understanding. 'We've got nothing to work on, then—we've reached a stone-wall until we can trace this bastard— this leak with the big-mouth.'

Blake kills his smoke. 'Perhaps it's Onassio—and he's bolted?' He blinks as Virdis' face tightens. 'I'm sorry—that was callous. Whoever this leak is, though, we'd better uncover him soon.'

'Yes,' agrees Virdis. 'To think it's someone in the department. One of us.'

IX

They drive to HQ in Virdis' Volvo after Blake has showered and shaved. There's an uncanny silence as the car crawls the five blocks to the commissariat. Virdis parks on the street, and together, the two men enter the squat, imposing building dating to the seventeenth century. A junky's throwing a fit on the olive-tiled floor in the lobby, screaming and wrestling with three cops. A whore stands before a sergeant's desk chewing gum and watches the cops give the junky a beat down, her ripped mini exposing a hard buttock.

'Christ,' mutters Blake as they push the swing doors ajar and enter the Detective's Division. 'Gets crazier by the day, doesn't it?'

Virdis' receptionist, on the far side of the endless row of metal desks, stands and walks to them quickly. 'The chopper spotted the car, sir.' She hands him a note. 'There's a patrol car on the way now.'

Virdis looks at the note, memorises the address. 'Call the car back,' he says and glances at Blake. 'We'll take care of it.'

The two men hurry through the station.

'We're about to discover our leak, Detective Blake,' Virdis says as they climb into the Volvo.

'Whose car have they found?' inquires Blake when the Volvo's on the road again.

'Onassio's. I had an APB put out this morning.'

They drive east, into the sprawling industrial zone out by the airport. Blake settles into his seat. They continue past factories and warehouses with the occasional worker sitting about and staring dazed at the dank day. On toward Segrate where Virdis turns into a dilapidated construction site.

Just behind a shed is where they find a red Alfa baking beneath the noon sun. It's a write-off; all the windows are shattered beneath a caved-in roof. Virdis slides the Volvo beside it, leaving the engine to idle as he climbs out. Knowing. Knowing already what he's about to find.

His shoes grind into the gravel as he strides to the wreck. A bird sings in the distance, the only interruption in the silent day. Virdis crouches beside the Alfa. Wriggles his body through the narrow gap between roof and seats.

Blake steps behind him, observing as the chief inspector searches through the dashboard, the cubbyhole, the footwell. Looking for what?

'How the fuck did he do this?' asks Blake, touching the grazed metal.

'I don't know, but he sure didn't do it here.' Virdis wriggles back out from the Alfa with a note in his hand.

'What's that?' asks Blake. Christ, he thinks, Giovanni had neglected to search the Alfa! The goddamn *idiot*! He steps behind Virdis as he unfolds the note. A list of names, cops.

Blake circled in red.

Virdis feels the metal digging into his spine, senses Blake breathing warmly on his ear, and despite the situation, Virdis can't help but smile.

'Drop your pistol, mate. I don't wanna hurt you.'

Virdis drops his Beretta onto the gravel. Too willing, thinks Blake. He must be careful with the old fuck. Blake steps back with the metal of his pistol scraping away from Virdis' spine. He walks around Virdis with his Beretta levelled easily from the waist like a gunfighter.

'Where's Onassio?' asks Virdis, glancing from the Beretta to Blake's eyes.

Blake says nothing. The silence is overwhelming suddenly.

'Is he dead?' Virdis' hand digs into his hip pocket.

Silence is the affirmative reply.

'For twenty thousand pounds, Blake?'

'No,' Blake shakes his head, 'for much more than that.' He lifts the pistol to aim at Virdis face. 'How do they say it? The gain is worth double the risk?'

Virdis isn't listening.

An explosion destroys the silence of the sultry afternoon.

Blake doubles over with his pistol slipping from his fist as he clasps incredulously at his belly. He falls, losing motor-control, onto his knees. A river of blood streams over his hands, cascading down in a glistening fall. Virdis draws out a smoking .38 Police Special from his holed-out hip-pocket and steps to Blake.

Gore covers his hands and arms as he groans from a tear-filled, pale face.

'It hurts,' he whispers. 'God, it hurts.'

'It's a gut shot,' says Virdis. 'It's going to hurt. And it's going to take a while to stop hurting. You were set up, Detective Blake.' Virdis stands with his shadow falling over Blake's grimacing face. Gooey plasma covers the ground about him. 'Your *mates* set you up.'

Blake drops his head back onto the gravel, gurgling on his own vomit and blood, squinting up at Virdis' black silhouette covering the sun. He's cold, his body shivering involuntarily. It's so fucking cold. 'It's so cold,' whispers Blake to the silhouette that reminds him of a plague doctor.

'You're dying. But hell, they tell me, is warm this time of year.'

Blake swallows. His saliva's choking him. He tries to move his head up, but there's no strength left in his numbed body.

'Where is Onassio?'

'I don't know.'

'He's dead?'

'Yes. Fucking help me.'

'You killed him? You killed one of us? Is that what you're taking with you to hell?'

'Help me.'

'Give me a name first.'

'Jesus.'

'Give me another one.'

'Zoran. Zoran fucking Santana,' whispers Blake, spitting blood onto the ground. He can't keep his eyes open, heavy. The darkness seeps through his body. He's never felt this weak, this tired. Footsteps crunch on the gravel, moving away from him. Blake extends his hand with clawing fingers. 'Help me,' he whispers. A car door is shut, an engine gunning to life. 'Don't leave me.' Tyres scrape on gravel and an engine fades into the twilight. 'I don't deserve to die alone.'

Cold. The bird has begun its call one more time.

14. Answering Service: 'Call Me Mr. Telephone'

'So now what, Virdis?' asks the mayor, sitting behind his tidy oak desk high up in City Hall.

'I wanna put a tap on this Zoran Santana's phone.' Virdis paces the mayor's enormous office with a sightline across the city stretched out below the windows. 'We've lost a lotta good people on this case, sir. It's time this fuck goes down.'

The mayor nods. 'Do what you must, chief inspector.' He replaces the spectacles he'd taken off twenty minutes previous and returns his glance at a file spread open on his desk. 'But I remind you, illegal wiretaps are, uhm, yeah, illegal. I deny all knowledge.'

Virdis walks for the door. The mayor's voice stops him.

'Remember, I assume no responsibility. I won't take any flack if this backfires in your face. And I hope you've got a good explanation for Onassio's death. For the press. Like guilt. Shame. Suicide.'

Virdis nods, knowing the mayor will get all the credit when Zoran Santana's put away. Not that he gives a shit, he thinks, leaving City Hall. He has a job to do, and it's personal now. Lisa's still not aware of her husband's death at Virdis' request. The news can only come from him. Zoran Santana is going to pay for that. Of this, Virdis has no doubt.

The evening's turning to shit. The city prepares itself for rain as orange-red dust clouds approach from the south, from the Sahara. It's begun drizzling crimson when Virdis finds a parking space outside the quaint building with the crawling ivy and yellow lights bleeding out into the murk.

Virdis climbs the stairs with the weight of destiny following him up and knocks on the last door on the landing. It's flung open within moments. Lisa looks up at him. And recognises death.

'*Sei un stronzo!*' she screams, lashing at him with her hands and scraping at his eyes. Virdis moves back, blood trickling from three cuts on his cheek ala Bruce Lee and the entering dragon.

'Mamma!' shouts a voice from behind Lisa. A teenager runs into the room, flicking a hasty, confused glance at Virdis. Onassio's daughter. Lela. Virdis had been there for her birth.

'Get this cunt outta my home!' spits Lisa, staring up at Virdis. 'You said he was okay,' she says at his lowered head. 'You said he was okay!'

'Lisa, I—'

'Go! Leave. *Fuori*!'

The young girl hugs her mom. Virdis swallows hard. 'I'm sorry,' he whispers, 'if there's anything I can—'

'You've done enough. *Vattene! Disgraziato!*'

He brushes away an astray tear when she slams the door shut. He stares down the hallway. End it all, he thinks on his way down the staircase to the rain, end it all and let's start afresh without cops and robbers and wars and drugs and *shit* ...

15. P. Lion: 'Happy Children'

A golden sunset with Vesuvius silhouetted across the bay and twenty-thousand dollars in a money-belt strapped around her thin waist. What more could she want? A flood of replies swamp Robi's mind and she smiles wryly, sipping on her Manhattan, eyes straying from the window beside her table to the packed restaurant.

Starting over, she thinks, is everybody's dream—at least, everyone she's ever known. Except, possibly, Wayne. With his ten-roomed mansion in the Chicago suburbs and Maserati in the parking bay, he probably wouldn't gain much more from any redo.

Forcefully detaching herself from her thoughts, Robi returns her gaze to the window. A yacht has entered the bay with sunset following, an oozing golden slosh on the Tyrrhenian, and she can imagine lovers on board swapping sundowners and whispers and—

'*Qualcos' altro?*'

She turns to the waiter hovering beside her. 'Another,' she says, pointing at her glass. The guy nods, walks away, and Robi follows his tight buttocks. He catches her staring and Robi snaps her attention away. Feeling his stare continue, she glances at her wristwatch before flipping a Camel between her lips. The waiter's back fast and holds a flame for her. She inhales and blows out the match between his fingers. He's nice and young with a strong face and huge hands. He glances about the mellow restaurant before wielding a pencil from his red blazer and scrawling something on a matchbox for the Pompeii Restaurant. Then, acknowledging a wave from a table across the spacious room, he drops the matchbox and hastens off.

Frowning, Robi lifts the pad and tries to read it.

Aspetami fuori alle undici. Antonio.

She glances up, confused. The waiter is weaving amongst the occupied tables, making a conscious effort not to look at her. At the kitchen door, he steals a glance, and Robi shakes her head. He frowns and vanishes through the doors. Christ, she thinks, what the hell's he written here? She reads the Italian again, figures the guy's name to be Antonio and what comes before is probably a dirty line from a toilet-wall. Antonio. It has a nice ring.

He's out of the kitchen again, walking to a couple sitting by the windows. She lifts her arm to him. He ignores her. Moments later another waiter steps beside her.

'*Si, signora*?'

'Uhm,' she smiles at him, she's learnt a smile can go a long way on the lips of a pretty young woman in Italy, 'may I have some bread?'

He offers her a bemused glance before walking off. Robi forces back her blush as she spots the basket of bread on her table. She looks up and sees Antonio smiling at her and again she shakes her head. He creases his brows and makes his way over to her with a determined face. '*Scusa*,' he says, '*scusa, ma pensavo che—*'

'I don't speak Italian,' she interrupts, 'no capish.'

Antonio blinks, trying to understand her Italian-mob-boss-accent. Comprehension suddenly dawns on his face as the other waiter deposits another basket of bread on the table, flipping his eyes from the girl to Antonio and back again.

'*C'e qualcosa che non va?*' the waiter asks Robi.

'*Parla solo l'Inglese*,' Antonio says.

'*Allora*?'

'Sorry,' says Robi suddenly, 'I was just asking Antonio—'

'*Si-si*,' says the other waiter, hastening away. Robi smiles up at cute Antonio with the dimples and innocent big-puppy-dog willing-to-please eyes.

'I'm sorry. I just couldn't read your message.' She lifts the matchbox, and Antonio accepts it with a disappointed grimace.

'*Si*,' he says, '*va be*.' Depositing the matchbox into his jacket, he turns looking put-out and walks away.

Night has fallen when Robi settles the bill and leaves the restaurant. She has dined lightly and drank heavily, her mood brewing like the front that moves in over the sea. She wonders why she's here—what insane impulse had led her here, to a foreign land ... what the hell is she supposed to be doing anyway? Visiting museums? Tasting the food? The *wine*?

How would Wayne react to her walking alone from the restaurant, down this hill silhouetted in pale nebulous light? He'd freak out, she thinks. He'd tell her to get a cab from the restaurant to the hotel. She could be walking into the projects without even knowing about it. Though Robi is not naive. She knows the streets like any girl brought up in a '70s American city, can smell trouble before it happens. Usually. Robi knows that pain, here on the city streets, can be as simple as someone taking a liking to her shoes.

It's not as she recalls, back when she and Richard had been kids growing up in suburbia. So much has changed, so much violence, so much—injustice.

Like the girl Robi sees sitting on the sidewalk. They share a look in the gloom, a beautiful girl with black hair tinged with fiery red and eyes like a bull. Robi thinks they have something in common—nice Doc Martens, she thinks. Robi slows, smiling uncertainly.

'Are you okay?' she asks.

The girl frowns. 'Okay?'

'Yes, you're okay?'

'*Non capisco.*'

'Sorry?'

Two space beings unable to communicate and yet linked in time because Robi feels the urge to step to her under a rumbling sky. 'My name's Robi.' The girl frowns. Robi taps her chest. 'Robi. Roberta. Robi. Me.'

'*Ah. Sono Lidia.*'

They shake hands, the girl squeezing with an anaemic strength, nails painted black. Robi checks out the street. Narrow and badly lit with shut stores lining the sidewalks sealed behind metal, graffiti-filled shutters. Dazed light bleeds out from apartments carved into stone relics oozing centuries of accumulated gunk. Wayne would certainly not approve of this neighbourhood, thinks Robi.

She offers a Camel. Lidia accepts. She has a light that she fishes out from black Levis, cupping her hands about a flame that bathes her gaunt face in sulphur. 'English?'

'American.'

The girl shifts up on the sidewalk, glancing next to her. Robi follows the eyes with her ass, sits on the hard, cold concrete, and stares out from Lidia's perspective. There's a pharmacy across the road, '24-ore' neon sign saddled between two porno shops. As she watches, a kid steps out of the pharmacy and onto the street with a package under his arm.

Lidia stands to welcome the approaching kid. Robi does the same. The guy's wearing a leatherjacket, strong of build and his face, Robi thinks, is pretty enough, framed by thick hair. But the eyes that scowl out at her as he walks on over are guarded in the dirty light.

'Lidia,' he says, standing before the two women, *'chi è?'*

'Cazzo ne so io? Si chiama Robi. Americana. Non parla l'Italiano.'

'No?' The guy measures Robi up suspiciously. *'Neanche una parola?'*

'Perche non la chiedi, Andrea?'

He smiles blackened teeth at Robi. 'Tu-rist?'

'What? Oh. Yeah. Sure. *Si.*'

Andrea waves the packet at Lidia. *'Andiamo. Portala con te.'*

'Perche?'

'Perche te l'ho detto!' he snaps and Lidia flinches.

'Look, hey, *arriva-dersi*,' says Robi, not liking the vibes suddenly and tossing her cigarette on the sidewalk.

'No.' Lidia touches Robi's shoulder with hands that squeeze in deep. *'Vieni con noi. Dai.'*

'Sorry?' Robi watches the girl play charades on the quiet street, pointing at Andrea, then at herself, then at Robi, then her fingers do the walking in the cool drizzle-swept air. *'Ballare,'* she says, gyrating her hips provocatively and boogying '70s style while Andrea watches darkly. *'Ballare.'*

'Dance?'

Lidia nods. 'Night-clue-b.'

'Nightclub?'

Lidia smiles, thumbs up, an arm about Robi's shoulders to lead her along now, back to Andrea and the mysterious package he hides below his sweatshirt.

'Nightclub,' he says, leading the way on the cobbled streets.

Through the city in a labyrinth of identical avenues and streets he leads, and if Robi were aware, she would notice the narrowing lanes, the fading lights. She does get a sense of danger though when they turn into a narrow alley, as dark as the pestilence that had once run through Naples. Robi slows, glances at Lidia, seeking reaffirmation, assurance. The girl, caught in mid-thought, forgets to smile. Because she's fumbling in her black jeans and suddenly unfolds a steel blade with a flick of her wrist.

'What the—' Robi doesn't get a lot more out 'cause from behind her, Andrea places a jagged blade that's now stretching the flesh on Robi's throat.

'Money,' says Lidia, 'money.'

Andrea slits the skin of her throat to draw a globule of blood. 'Money,' he whispers in her ear, and she can smell his foul soul.

'Okay. Okay! Just—' she undoes her blouse to expose her vinyl money-belt.

Lidia motions for Robi to unclip it, to hand it over. She does. Lidia grabs it.

'It's just traveller's cheques. American Express. I've gotta sign for them,' says Robi

'American Espress?' Andrea leans over Robi's shoulder to gawk at Lidia's hands that unzip the contents.

Suddenly, from behind them, a shout. *'Eh! Eh!'*

Andrea spins Robi about without releasing the knife at her throat. There's a man coming at them from the road. *'Che cazzo sta succedendo!'* he shouts.

Lidia moves quick, instinctively, losing no time. Andrea hesitates. Pulls the knife deeper into Robi's throat as the man storms at them. Andrea panics. The man looms ever closer with a jacket like a cape behind him, some weird, masked adventurer. Andrea shoves Robi into the silhouette's path, the knife sliding over her flesh. She careens toward the man. He's seen her coming, side-steps easily, and keeps the chase alive. Closing in fast to the sprinting Andrea, the two men swerving into an alley and out of sight as Robi falls to the ground.

Swallows deep. Fear. Panic. *Her money*! She looks for Lidia, but the girl's long gone. Faintly, if she listens hard, she can hear the girl's galloping feet—no ... she's mistaken ... the sound ... the sound is violence. Of knuckle pounding flesh. Pain. She knows this sound. It originates from the alley.

Robi stands and runs toward the sounds. She figures she owes that stranger who just saved her life. And if he's in trouble ...

There's no need. The stranger has everything under control. He's got Andrea pinned to the dirty ground in the alley as Robi turns the corner. The rain is pounding now as Robi watches the stranger deliver two hard punches to Andrea's face.

'No,' gasps Andrea, 'no!'

The man stands and boots Andrea in the head. Fiercely, without betraying an inkling of emotion. Before realising he's being watched. He turns his head and glances at Robi. And blinks.

'*Ma lei,*' he doesn't continue, stands and steps out from the shadows to unveil his face. '*Sono* Antonio.' He touches his chest with a finger. '*Antonio dal ristorante.*'

It all comes flooding back now. 'Antonio,' she says, thinking of the matchbox with his message. He's not listening, though, because Andrea is trying to crawl away, and Andrea boots him in the ribs. '*Dov'è la ragazza! Dov'è!*'

Andrea tries to speak another boot in his face shuts him up.

'*Dov'è!*' shouts Antonio.

The threat of another boot has Andrea crumpling up in the foetal position, elbows covering his head. '*La trovi da Rosa. Da Rosa!*'

'Rosa?'

'*Sì.*'

Antonio wipes blood off his knuckles on his jeans. '*Vieni,*' he holds Robi by the elbow, '*dai,*' he says, dragging her away from Andrea who's crawling along down the alley moaning and dripping blood from his skull.

Antonio seems to have a destination in mind, his striding legs purposeful as he leads her through a labyrinth of cobbled streets, closing in on a piazza and a sudden smattering of people.

He leads her on, through red-lit streets in the raining night. Neon palpitates out, shuddering in the cold, and in the rain, girls in sloppy clothes show legs and asses and mounds of wet flesh. Antonio cuts through an alley. And suddenly pauses mid-stride.

Robi walks straight into him.

'*Sta calma,*' he tells her. '*È lei?*' He nods his head imperceptibly behind his shoulder at the street beyond the alley. A girl strides through the rain with black hair plastered on her head.

Lidia!

'That's her!'

Antonio nods. *'Andiamo.'* In single file, they exit the alley behind the girl on the street. She's but yards ahead. Antonio, though, curiously, does not make his move. Content merely to follow.

Lidia turns left ahead, into another alley with concrete barriers prohibiting motorised access. Now, *now* Antonio moves, breaking into a sudden, violent sprint. The girl's aware, doesn't hesitate, doesn't even look back, just angles her body forward and picks up speed down the alley.

She's too late. Robi watches from the mouth of the alley as Antonio trips the girl up with an angled slide. She loses her feet in a big way, no hope of regaining her balance as she flies face-first into trashcans and a dumpster.

Antonio's not scared to dirty his hands, digs his fists into the trash and scuttling vermin to drag the girl, covered in gunk and gore, out by the hair. She screams, clawing at his fingers like a big fish on a hook. Antonio twists her head back, hair gripped by its roots, and punches her face hard and square. Her head bounces on the trashcans and she grunts as Antonio stares stupefied at the clump of hair in his fingers. For an instant. 'til he recalls what he's after. The girl tries to crawl away. Antonio goes after her.

'No, Antonio, stop, please *stop* it!' shouts Robi.

The guy's not listening. He waits for Lidia to rise onto all fours before booting her cleanly in the kidneys. She keels over. Groaning like an injured horse. Robi runs at them now, at Antonio, 'Stop, just *stop!'*

He does. For under Lidia's raised shirt, Antonio can see the money-belt tied to the tight belly. He flips out a blade. Bends down to the squirming girl.

'No!' cries Lidia, *'no, no! Dio no!'*

Robi's too late. The blade shivers, glinting. He grabs Lidia by the hair with legs straddled about her torso. Lifts her face like he's reigning in a horse. With the knife between his teeth, he rips up her shirt and gets to the money-belt.

'Lasciami!' hisses Lidia with tear-filled eyes. *'Lasciami!'*

'Let her go!'

Antonio's not listening. He knees the girl viciously in the belly. Her body tries to follow the momentum away from his striking knee. Fails 'cause she's held tight by her mane.

'Stop it, Antonio,' with her voice frightening even her, so calm. 'Let her go.' She steps to him. Stands over him. He gets up and meets her eyes. With a look that freezes her blood. And misses his back-handed fist whipping across her face. Pain as Robi stumbles back and suddenly she's staring at tears, water—rain and a pink shivering sky above.

Robi is on her back on the damp ground. Sits up dazed. Antonio is standing over Lidia. Shouting at her. She squirms from his anger. Begging. Sobbing. Bleeding. Antonio waves the money-belt around, hits her over the head with it and shouts, what? What is he saying? And then Robi, squatting now with a numb pain spreading over her face, watches impotent as Antonio slips the belt below his shirt.

'Hey, that's mine!' she shouts.

And the suddenly a voice comes from the dark. *'Sta fermo!'*

The voice belongs to a woman. She's standing outside an ajar door deep in the alley. Music flows out from behind her giant frame. The woman steps forward through the rain. A massive woman in a summer dress. Antonio watches her draw near.

'Non è quello che pensa,' he tells the woman. Robi can hear the stress in his voice.

From the ground, beaten Lidia crawls at the woman to negate Antonio's innocence. *'Rosa. Mi ha menato,'* she whispers.

The fat woman bends over to touch Lidia's face. Like she's inspecting merchandise, damaged goods. Antonio swivels, knowing the girl's blood-smeared face is his incrimination. He looks to this right. To his left. Realises his only way out is behind Robi, and he runs, now, back down the alley through which he had misled Robi.

'I soldi,' whispers Lidia, *'sono di lei.'* Lidia points at Robi who shifts out of the way from running Antonio. Because he's not going far. Two figures have appeared at the head of the alley. To stand in the waterfalling rain. Waiting for him. Antonio slows. And watches the men step forward toward him. Menacingly. He doesn't even fight. Just stands there as the two men set to work. One holding his head to attention while the other uses his knee to whip Antonio's groin. Once. Twice. Again.

'Basta!' the fat woman bellows at the men with a voice that cracks the sky in a silver slash. *'Portalo qui!'*

The men, brawn with shaven heads and veined skulls, drag Antonio to Rosa, standing there waiting like an impatient mother, legs spread and pudgy hands at her hips. Lidia is sitting in the lotus position at her feet, tenderly touching her swollen face. Rosa's bull-like eyes fix themselves on Antonio getting dragged by his elbows down the alley by the two men on either side of him. He's out on his feet, and they dump him onto the ground at Rosa's feet. Lidia stands unsteadily. And then boots him full in the face. Blood beads over her Docs, nicely broken in now.

Rosa holds out her hand. One of the bald goons hands the money-belt over. Then he searches Antonio's clothes, fast, frisks the body to unveil a wallet, a blade, and a *Sudden Impact* cigarette case.

'*L'hai rubata?*' Rosa asks Lidia, holding the money-belt.

The girl pouts. Sullen. 'Andrea,' she says.

Rosa glances up at Robi and the two meet eyes. Robi swallows. She feels little for Lidia. Only regret at the situation.

Rosa beckons Robi over with the waving money-belt and the *Sudden Impact* case. '*Voglio chiederla scusa—*'

'*Non parla l'Italiano,*' whispers Lidia. '*Americana.*'

Rosa glances at Lidia, then back at Robi. 'I am sorry. For you. You must be careful. Is dangerous here.' She hands Robi the *Sudden Impact* cigarette case and the money-belt.

'Yes, but this—' she doesn't complete her sentence 'cause Rosa wields around with a fat hand. Walloping across Lidia's face. To come back again moments later. Lidia sprouts tears over her bruised, blood-coated face. But doesn't try to ward off the blows. Just bows her head compliantly.

'*Vattene!*' Rosa fakes another slap at Lidia's crying face. '*Chiama un taxi per la signora e vattene! Domani ti agiustero. Vattene, Lidia, prima che ti prendo a schiaffi!*'

Lidia limps for the ajar doorway.

'I am sorry,' says Rosa, turning back to Robi. 'She will call you taxi. Are you okay?'

Shaken, shivering, but, 'Yeah, thank you. I'm fine.' She holds the money-belt and cigarette case. 'I'm fine, thank you. *Grazie.*'

Rosa nods. Points at Antonio at her feet. '*Portalo via,*' she tells the goons. 'Come,' she draws Robi close and escorts her down the alley toward the street.

'Wait.' Robi breaks the grip of the woman's fat hand to turn and shout, 'Lidia!'

The girl pauses at the door.

'Lidia, this is your friend's.' She holds the *Sudden Impact* case. Lidia looks away like it's a dirty thought, down at her boots, a guilty child before the thrashing she knows is now coming.

'Give it to me.' Rosa holds out her thick hand with her hard eyes drilling through Lidia's mind. 'If this is what I think this is,' she says, and slips the case from Robi's hand to unfold the lid and expose brown powder stirring within like the shifting sands of the Sahara. 'Lidia!' Rosa is quick, belying her whale-like constitution. Even so, Lidia has plenty of time to quiver at the pain drawing near. Before an obese hand grips a handful of her hair from her scalp. *'Puttana!'* she screams at the girl. Then, in English, obviously for Robi's benefit, 'You think I am stupid!' before tipping the contents of the case over the girl's head. Mixing heroin with her hair and her tears and the rain.

'Stop it!' screams Robi.

Rosa kicks Lidia up the ass. Slaps her around a bit, but the girl won't even block the blows and it's this, Robi realises, it's this indifference to pain and humiliation that makes her shout, 'Please, stop!'

Rosa turns to her. 'I have a rule here, Mrs America. You know what the rule is?'

'No.'

'No? The rule is, *no drugs*. You can stay with Rosa but no drugs. But this *puttana*,' turning to Lidia with brown heroin tears running down her cheeks, 'this whore *will not* learn!'

Lidia hides her face behind a mask of straggly hair. And licks and licks the falling heroin tears.

'Go get the taxi!' shouts Rosa, regaining her composure. Hits the girl viciously over her head. *'Adesso!'*

'Why?' Robi turns away from Lidia as the girl smiles bloody teeth at her under the rain. 'Why do you treat her like that? Don't you think she's suffered enough? She's not a fucking animal!'

'Why?' Rosa barks out a laugh, sarcastic, insulting. 'Because she doesn't *need* you, Mrs America. These two, Andrea and this *puttana*, they have been through hell together. They have lived through things you—you want to come and give—give what! *What*! A job? You want friend, America?' Rosa's eyes note the cab pulling up on the street behind Robi, 'you go to church on Sunday you want friend. You just want to go! Go! *Vattene!* There is your taxi, *madam.'*

'Fuck you,' Robi whispers. She turns and hastens to the cab, climbs into the backseat. 'The station. *Stazione.'*

The cabby pulls onto the main drag heading back through the red-light district. The road's congested with early-evening traffic and lights flashing in the rain. Robi catches the cabby's eyes staring at her from the rear-view and shudders involuntarily. The traffic has stopped ahead, a series of red brake lights exploding. He swivels in his seat with hands holding the wheel blindly. '*Sei turista, si?*'

She looks at him like she's heard all this before. 'Sure.'

'You look to get high?'

'Sorry?'

'Hash, cocaine, xtc—you want? Heroin from Afghanistan.' The car behind flashes its lights. The cabby swings about and eases the car forward with the traffic. His eyes inspect the rear-view, meeting her eyes darkly. 'You want,' he repeats, 'you want?'

'I don't—'

'Good hash,' he interrupts, knowing what to sell her now 'cause no self-respecting tourist would say no to drugs, only the squares, and they aren't trawling the streets of San Giovanni a Teduccio. Ggood hash, from Morocco, fresh, fresh. Two thousand for one.'

'One what?'

The cabby thinks fuck, won't sell her the rough-stuff, she'd probably smoke the little pebble as is, so he clicks open the glove compartment and withdraws a white gum-papered joint. Waves it at her. 'You can smoke in here,' he points at the A/C knob with the joint, 'clean air will get away smell.'

Robi shrugs. She hasn't had a joint since—'Yes, okay, sure,' she interrupts her memories. Strange, she thinks, how every tragedy can be captured in one frame—like tonight and that girl, Lidia, one full-colour frame of the girl's face when she had smiled humiliation and bloody teeth, the pain from her soul, like that night with poppa and Richard, eternities ago, a small boy—*no!*

'Here,' she peels two thousand lira notes from her money-belt. The cab driver stretches back, the joint in his palm. Robi accepts it, dumps the bills in the hand, and lights up. He flicks on the air-con, shutting up the car tight with auto-window-rollers. The stench is overpowering, dusty dreams as Robi sucks hard on the hash. Exhaling, she shuts her eyes, rolls with the headrush, and gives herself another toke.

'Good?'

Robi smiles. 'Yes,' she says, 'You want?'

'I say no to drugs.'

Robi laughs with the cabby. Laughs and keeps on laughing with the night a dark mass of impenetrable space beyond the cabby and the wet streets refracted beyond the dirty windows. She's floating nice and comfortable in the Citroen's cocoon when it pulls up to the San Gennaro station. The contentment of life after a brush with death on the city streets.

'Can I have another?'

The cabby nods and hands her his last joint with her change. She thanks him and climbs out into the night that smells of damp and sickly sweet, fresh urine. The station is abuzz with frantic motion. Three barefoot boys come running at her as she steps through the glass doors. Their hands are begging and filthy, eyes pleading and bruises calling out for empathy. She flips 'em some notes and immediately she's surrounded by more toddlers with hands grasping at her dress. She pushes hands away and runs. A shouting man kneels before a café ahead, passengers walking well wide of him. He looks like Jesus. The preacher from San Gennaro. Voices reach a crescendo about her. Loud and constant. Open-mouthed faces brush past, her ears catching snippets of conversation in foreign tongues and Robi thinks she needs to get the fuck outta here. She hurries to the lockers, forcing herself to be calm, rational. It's just paranoia, wild and desperate, just paranoia dancing behind her eyes.

She recalls her locker number and hustles to the fourth row. Robi finds the key in her jacket and opens the locker. She withdraws her backpack, balances it on her back, and makes her way through the station. Exiting into the warm night, Robi exhales and trudges to a Volvo cab. She dumps the bag onto the front seat and climbs in at the back.

'Take me to the motorway,' she says.

'*Scusa*?'

'Just,' she says, shaking her head in desperation, 'just *drive!*' She throws money over the seat. The cabby looks at the notes, then at Robi in the rear seat waving him forward and engages gear.

Naples is like Milan—like any other big city anywhere in the world. Robi craves for a deserted beach somewhere where she can just sit and think. And get away from *this*.

16. Black Box: 'Ride On Time'

The pale rays of light bathe a figure on the edge of the autostrada. The truck slows, hydraulic brakes screeching and hissing. Gears crunch down on the massive vehicle hauling a Coca-Cola trailer as it gradually creeps to a halt. The cabin vibrates, a car passing blaring its horn. The figure runs to the truck and hoists himself up into the cabin.

'You looked desperate,' says the trucker. Blonde hair falls over her shadowed eyes that watch the figure slam the big door shut and sits back on the seat beside her.

'I am. Thanks for stopping.'

She revs the engine, big and plodding diesel rupturing the night. 'What's your name, handsome?'

'Sandro.'

'Sabrina.' The woman pumps his hand with her callouses before grinding in first gear on the massive lever. The truck rattles and rolls, gaining momentum slowly, Sabrina veering the snake back onto the autostrada.

'How far you going?' asks Sandro, watching a pack of Dunhill slide across the dashboard.

'Cosenza. Have one,' she offers, nodding at the smokes. 'Light me one up too.'

Sandro lights 'em simultaneously, the smoke invisible in the dark cabin. He surrenders one, twisting his head toward the window.

'Where are you headed, Sandro?'

He peels away from his reflection in the window and turns to the trucker. 'Cosenza, I guess.' He tugs on the Dunhill. 'I don't s'pose you got any coke?'

Holding the massive wheel in one hand, she twists in her seat and lifts a can from the bed-compartment behind them. Sandro nods his thanks. He gulps down and burps silently, resting his head back against the red vinyl seat. He lifts his feet onto the dashboard, reclining his head, comforta—

'Don't do that!' shouts Sabrina. She strikes his boot firmly with an open hand. 'It'll bring bad luck.'

Sandro drops his feet onto the metal deck and sits up. Christ, he thinks, how much worse can it get? Sandro sips at the caffeine. With a last tug of the Dunhill, he rolls down the window beside him and flicks the butt out. He sticks his head out into the warm air that rustles his hair before his eyes. The butt explodes beneath the trailer, and he watches it vanish in a flicker of red.

'Shall we?' Sabrina nods at a silhouette cast within the rays of the Oshkosh truck, waving on the shoulder of the road ahead. Sandro dips his head back into the cabin, his eyes squinting on the figure approaching in the yellow-tubes of light, hitching outside a gas-station.

'We could rape her,' he suggests. Sabrina laughs like it's an alternative, squeezing the brakes. Her right hand kicks down the gears, the huge truck bucking and rearing. Sweat thick on her brow, Sabrina withdraws the clutch to bounce the truck to an abrupt halt.

The figure runs around the cabin with dreadlocks caught in the light. Sandro throws open his door and jumps down to the road. He squints at the dimly lit autostrada, then at the woman's ass climbing up into the cabin. She's hoisting herself up with the aid of one long side-mirror. Her sneakers, clutched on one tyre, suddenly slip, her backpack sliding off her shoulder and pulling her down. Sandro pushes her instinctively, grabbing a piece of solid ass. She slides further down before grasping Sabrina's hand and vanishing into the cabin. Sandro tosses the Coke onto the road and follows her up, in, and bangs shut the door.

'I'm tired of big cities,' the girl is saying with a vague smile. 'I come from Chicago, so you can understand. I'm so glad you speak English.' She turns to Sandro beside her now, bodies touching in the cramped cabin. 'My name's Robi.'

'I'm happy for you,' he says. She glares at him until his eyes meet hers, irate. 'That's Sabrina,' he says.

'We met. I think we've also met,' says Robi, glancing at Sandro. 'Have we?'

'I think maybe not,' he says, lighting another Dunhill.

'So where you go?' inquires Sabrina.

'Somewhere not here,' says Robi. 'I just need to get away. Somewhere safe.'

Sabrina whistles a lonely tune and gets the truck moving.

Robi lights up a Camel. 'Just, people are strange out here, you know? It's so different—I'm not quite sure,' she looks at her travelling companions, 'if I trust anyone no more.'

'So why you hitching?' asks Sandro.

She smiles. 'You wouldn't believe me. Wait, I have some hash,' she says. 'Anyone want?' She turns to Sabrina.

'Sure.'

'I'd love some, Robi,' says Sandro, all attention now as Robi digs out the joint from her purse and hands it over.

'From Afghanistan,' she says. 'Or was it Morocco?'

Sandro nods like he doesn't give a shit and flips his Dunhill out. He leans forward to light the joint, cupping his hand about it like it's a pipe, making sure no smoke escapes, and tugs heavily through his fisted fingers. A half-dozen raking drags later, he hands the half-smoked-away gum-paper to Robi. Coughing up phlegm, he sticks his head out of the window and spits away into the night. 'Did you not like Napoli?' he asks after a while, smelling the dope about him, lifting his spirits.

Robi passes the joint over to Sabrina. She smokes it one-handed, the other steady on the fat wheel. 'I hated it,' says Robi. 'There's so many—so much poverty. And I honestly don't understand the culture.'

'How did you know she just came from Napoli?' inquires Sabrina. Then, to Robi, 'Did you?'

Robi nods.

'This is Napoli street-hash. It gives you a seriously fucked buzz. Like pesticide.'

Robi laughs. 'Tell me about it! I freaked out at the station. Everything was like, *crowding* in on me. I just run away. And I had this—so strange ... I just wanted to drive, you know?'

Sandro looks out at the night. 'Try their microdots sometime. You won't run though,' he says like he's tapping from personal experience, 'you'll float through.' He laughs at the silence. Robi eyes out the kid momentarily. The lights zip past, drawing thick black shadows below his deeply sunken eyes. Where the hell does she know that face from?

'If you look for somewhere quiet, come all the way to Cosenza,' says Sabrina. 'Is a dead town.'

'I think Villammare is where you should go,' says Sandro. 'There's all these little coves where you can be alone. And if you want to shoot up, I could give you an address—'

'I don't do drugs,' interrupts Robi, 'but it sounds wonderful.'

'We're there in under one hour,' says Sabrina.

Robi looks at him. Assessing. Thinks what the hell. 'You know,' she says and turns to Sabrina, 'will you drop me off there?'

'No. We'll drop you off at the Hotel Policastro,' replies Sandro with glistening eyes staring straight ahead, 'it's about five minutes from the village—but it's a cool place.'

'It will be full,' ventures Sabrina, tossing the 'roach from the window, 'full of Germans.'

'Will it?'

'No.' Sandro taps his chest. 'Tell 'em you're a friend of mine.'

'A friend of Sandro?'

'Yes.'

'And that's it?'

'Sure.'

'You're serious?'

Silence as the Oshkosh rushes the night, the headlamps catching a sign up ahead—Salerno 10. They speed past the town in the night, headed for Sapri. The Tyrrhenian is visible now, below the twisting road, spewing into the Gulf of Policastro. Sandro has fallen asleep, his head jerking to the Osh's bouncing suspension.

'That's the hotel,' says Sabrina, pointing ahead. Robi checks it out. Nothing much, but it's down near the sea. She grabs hold of her backpack from the rear bed-compartment. The strap licks Sandro's face, and he awakens dozily.

'Sorry,' mutters Robi, dubious about the whole trip here. Sandro sits up on the seat as Sabrina slows the truck.

'This is it,' says Sandro, reestablishing some credibility. Sabrina pulls the truck off the road before a softly lit tunnel and Sandro jumps out, listening to the soft call of the sea.

'Thank you,' says Robi, climbing down and out into the warm night. She nods at Sandro and points at a hacienda-style construction on the rocky beach down a short incline. 'Is that it?'

Sandro nods. 'The one and only Hotel Policastro,' he says before climbing back into the cabin. Robi watches the Oshkosh with its long trailer pull away and enter the tunnel before she follows a path to the hotel's entrance. She glances at her wristwatch. 3:47am.

The night man is dozing behind the reception desk. The lobby's otherwise deserted, cushioned bamboo-chairs framing the white walls in soft shadows. The man peeks up at her sleepily when she dumps her backpack on the tiled floor with a sheltered thump.

'I'm looking for a room,' she announces with a smile. Christ, she's gonna sleep until next month.

The guy frowns like he's trying to see her hidden motives. 'You have *reservazione*?'

'No.'

'Mi *dispiace*. We are full.'

'Yeah, that's okay. Sandro sent me—he said you'd be able to sort me out.'

'Who?'

'Sandro.'

The guy shrugs his shoulders. 'I am sorry, *signorina*. Maybe next month?' He watches Robi sling her backpack over one shoulder and walk angrily away.

She crosses through the parking lot. Takes a moment to observe her surroundings. And then ambles to the pebbled beach. The Tyrrhenian is black beneath the moonless night. She finds a small cove—at least that much is true, she thinks—and sets up her sleeping-bag on the hard earth.

Christ, what a fucking country full of assholes!

PART TWO

17. Righeira: 'No Tengo Dinero'

Sandro gazes up at the dark sky. He judges it to be about nine—nine-thirty. He's hanging … badly. Cosenza is a viceless little town. Colours trickle into his mind and with them events—not single events in succession, but in unity. Francesca is not a midnight walk under a raining Milanese sky with her bare feet sending sprays of water from gleaming pools into the dense fog. She's not a groaning beast on all fours in the mayonnaise light of a squalid apartment in downtown Parma. She's not the lifeless, staring corpse lying in a pool of plasma and blood in her rathole apartment.

No. Francesca is all these things now. And his guilt—his guilt … what more is there? *He* had killed her. As sure as if he'd cut her veins himself. Christ … just like he'd thrown—*thrown* that cop from a window. He'd crashed into the apartment like an animal, grunting with more energy that he'd ever experienced, so completely raging on a small dose of PCP. Carrying tunes and screams. Francesca had begged, on her knees she'd begged and someone—he, fuck it, *he* was slapping … her face, Francesca's face—bleeding and swollen …

He needs to get fucked.

He needs a fuck.

And maybe not in that order.

He walks the dead streets of Cosenza, drawing out a Marlboro and lighting up. He knows this: gas stations offer rides-for-smiles, and railway stations have bucks-for-fucks.

And the station is where Sandro walks with an itch running over his body like wildfire, insatiable even to his scratching, bloody nails that have ripped chunks from his flesh. His clothes stink, unwashed like his body, diseased like his mind. A putrid stench of urine traces across the town and over the old, quaint buildings.

Sandro makes a turn round the block and enters the station through the rear entrance. It's a provincial town and there's not much thoroughfare, even at this time of year. The bathroom, though, is spacious and clean with a dozen or so booths lining the right wall. A flickering light illuminates two showers stretched out on the far side. Sandro climbs into the shower and strips before igniting the cool water over his face. The stream of H_2O stings his lacerated back, and he allows the water to cascade over his face. Shutting off the dial, he stands naked in the cubicle, shivering as he drip-dries his body, caressing his penis, numb and superfluous and growing in his trusted hand as the water drips into the croaking drain pink and black. He dresses quickly before running a hand through his long, damp hair. A young man walks into the bathroom with a backpack slung over his broad shoulders. He smiles at Sandro briefly before labouring the heavy bag from his back.

'You got a smoke?' Sandro asks and helps with the pack, eyes searching for an undone zip where he can slip his hands through. Nothing.

'Yeah, sure, buddy.' He finds his Camels in his jeans and offers one. 'Glad to find someone speaking English. You live around here?'

'Why do you ask?'

'You have a funny accent.'

Sandro accepts the light and winks at the guy. 'I was about to say the same about yours,' he says, before lighting the smoke and stepping out into the station with his hair forming teardrops at the ends like beads on his thick black hair.

A train's arrived on *Binario 2* with a crowd converging onto the platform from the coaches. Sandro moves quickly to the exit, leaning back on the wall outside with one leg up like a flamingo and the smoke dangling from his full, blow-job lips.

He blows smoke from his nostrils while studying the faces approaching him. Not much on offer. Until he catches the eyes of a man at the tail of the crowd. Their eyes meet. Slowly, the body comes to view. Two pony-tailed girls hold on to his hands at his sides. Sandro watches them pass and follows the trio down the stairs toward the small park with the fountain and fir trees where he'd slept that morning.

He tosses the butt away and watches the trio climb into a cab. He runs his hands through his hair, feeling the sweat on his palms. His body shivers. Looking about, he realises there's no-one around, no chances, no familiarity. He looks at his hands that tremble uncontrollably. Sweat covers his body again, cold and bitter in the cool wind blowing down the hills. Craving junk, wondering what the fuck he's doing in this shithole town in the middle of fucking nowhere.

He could wait a few days and meet up with Sabrina. Get back to Milan. Home turf. She's going back up in three days. Or so she said. It's where the money is—where the dope is. And where Zoran is. It'll mean a beating, no doubt—but how pissed is Zoran gonna be, really, over a stolen ten grams of horse or whatever the fuck it was?

Somehow, though, he will have to survive for two more nights. In this shithole. Another day sleeping in the gardens. Not the worst thing in the world, he thinks, if he can avoid the fucking cops. And if he can find a fuck, just one, he'll be back in business, score a bit of dope for the trip back to Milan with Sabrina. Somewhere in this godforsaken town there must be a fag lonely for a piece of ass.

Why the fuck had he run? Yes, he thinks, why? Aside from a fistful of Zoran's Afghan heroin. And that prick in the apartment. Luca … the fucking prick.

IL BARON flashes neon above a beaded doorway ahead on the street, light splashing out of the front door and onto the cobbles. Sandro pauses under a streetlamp and watches the action.

The sidewalk overflows with a dozen cars and enough Vespas for Italy. He figures the bar must be packed. He's found a local hot spot. Two men stagger through the beads with arms clasped about each other and instinctively Sandro figures he's hit pay-dirt.

He watches for a few more minutes, then steps forward and parts the beads to enter a small room with a desk standing beside a heavy oak door that's vibrating to the thud beyond. A man stands behind the desk smoking a brown filter cigarette. A tattoo of something like a mushroom decorates his muscular forearm that's rubbing sweat from above his pebbled eyes. They stare back at Sandro levelly.

The oak door behind the desk opens and a man staggers out of a black room with the thump of music following. Sandro recognises the tune. *No Tengo Dinero*. He hates that tune. Head slumped, the man walks through the beads and shuffles outside. Sandro heads for the oak door and opens it to glance beyond. A strobe-light cuts the blackness for an instant, illuminating a dense mass of humanity swaying on the dancefloor.

'You can go in,' says the dude behind the desk in broken English. Sandro nods his thanks and enters the reverberating club, wondering why the bouncer had spoken in English. Crashing into a man in the mirrored mazed dimness, the thought slips from his mind, numbed and tired without its vitamins and unable to take a thought through to its conclusion. He forces his way to the rectangular bar and sits on an abandoned stool. He glances about the narrow club—not like those mega arenas in Milan and Verona and Rimini—and at the pale bodies snaking about in the unsteady, jabbing light.

The barman signals him with an inquiring gaze. Sandro shakes his head. A hand taps his shoulder. Sandro swivels with a smile all ready and genuine and finds two cops standing an inch behind him.

The cops lift him from his stool and drag him roughly toward the door. Heads turn as the trio barge their way through the club, hands slapping and pushing the ravers out of the way. Vicious stares fire at the *pula* dragging Sandro out, Sandro who can no longer control his emotions, lowering his head as salty tears roll down his face.

Reaching the oak door, Sandro jerks his arms up to break the cops' grip. Two punches sink into his kidneys almost simultaneously and push him forward, through the oak doors and into the antechamber where the bouncer with the mushroom arms steps keenly around his desk.

'*È lui?*' he asks, pointing at Sandro, 'is that the son of a bitch?

One cop nods. 'It's him. Thank you for your cooperation.'

The bouncer steps up and inspects the whore. 'It's only a pleasure, officer. You know our policy here at Il Baron. I recognised this piece of shit immediately from the picture you dropped off this morning. Saw him standing outside, exactly as you described him. Son of a bitch foreigner.'

The policemen shove Sandro onto the street. A patrol-car's double-parked at the entrance with blue-lights silently flashing. They spread-eagle Sandro onto the bonnet. Hands frisk his body, squeezing his balls real hard. They pin his arms back. He hears the handcuffs clang, and he knows this is the moment, the last chance to swivel and break away. The cops are way too quick, smashing him in the face with a tight-fisted upper cut. His head bounces up, teeth chattering. The cuffs snap tightly over his wrists, and he's lifted by the collar and thrown into the car's backseats. One cop hustles in beside him, shutting the door while the other gets up front and guns the engine. The car lurches forward. Sandro glances through the rear windscreen and the vanishing Il Baron.

It's a quick drive to the carabinieri station. The building's a renovated two-storey block across from the station. Sandro's escorted into the quiet station, down into the basement, where he's locked into a private, dank cell.

On the bare-wooden bed, Sandro begins to sob, his body crumpled into the foetal position. Nothing moves about him. Nothing scuttles in the dim silence.

He had killed a cop and what? Expected to get away? He'd been so fucking *naive!* So fucking stupid. He stands and paces to the grey rusted bars. An astray tear rolls into his mouth, allowing him to taste his fear as his hands grip the bars with tight white knuckles.

'I want my fucking phone-call,' he screams at the darkness, 'I know my rights, you *fucks!*'

He turns from the bars, kicks the bed loudly and digs his hands in his pockets. Paces the room irritably, his mind unable to concentrate, sending warning messages to his psyche, error reading Drive B.

Keys rattle somewhere. Footsteps, growing louder. A cop in a uniform inserts a key to Sandro's cell. Back-peddling, Sandro watches as the uniformed cop pushes open the barred-door to allow a jean-clad man into the cell.

The man nods courteously at the prisoner, dishevelled and unshaven, as the metal bars behind him snap shut with a tight click. The uniformed cop goes and stands a few paces away.

'I'm Inspector Lupini,' says the man in jeans.

'I want my phone-call.'

'Who would you like to call?'

'Your mother.'

Lupini pulls out a pack of MS pensively, like he's about to have a good crap. 'You want one?'

Sandro nods and the two men light up.

Lupini says, 'You know, of course, why you're here.'

'Because some fucking cops arrested me for nothing.'

Lupini sighs out a long trail of grey smoke through his nostrils and examines the tip of the smoke. 'Let's not fuck around here,' he says. 'It's late and I've had a shitty day.' He steps to within inches of Sandro's face with hard eyes boring. 'I've been sitting around here since this fucking morning waiting for you to emerge somewhere. A truck driver named Sabrina identified you from a poster yesterday. Recognised you immediately. Told us she dropped you off in town. What did you think? Did you think you could get *away*? Get away after you killed one of *us*? You did, didn't you—kill that cop in Napoli. He had a family. Two kids and a wife, you *scum!*' The guy blows phlegm down his throat. 'Listen, you're lucky you're here and not down in Napoli. Believe me. So all you need to do is tell me what happened and I'll talk to the prosecutor in the morning.'

'About what?'

'About drug addiction, desperation, mistakes, accidents. Whoring.'

'Manslaughter?'

The cop frowns. 'What are you, a fucking lawyer?'

Sandro turns from the cop and goes to stand in the corner of the windowless cell, dragging heavily on the smoke. 'How long we talkin' 'bout?'

Lupini shrugs. 'Do I look like a fucking judge?'

'I want to use the phone.'

'You have no one to call Alessandro Lago. Yes,' says the cop when Sandro glances back at him, 'I know everything about you. I could put you away with what I know. So,' the cop tosses the smoke on the floor and grinds it dead under his sole, 'let's get down to the ass fucking 'cause I hate foreplay. You tell me what happened, give me a confession, or—'

'Or what?'

'Or else you go down, *Ale*ssandro, you go down for a long stretch.'

'What do I give a fuck.'

Lupini stands wearily and stretches his back. 'Way I hear it, giving a fuck is all you give.'

'Sure.'

The cop clangs on the bars with his ring. 'Well, you got years of getting fucked waiting for you. Always look at the positive. That's what my mom always says.'

The uniformed cop unlocks the door for Lupini to step outside, where he waits for the clang of metal shutting Sandro in before he says, 'You think about what I said.'

Sandro watches him walk away down the long corridor to freedom. 'Fuck you!' shouts Sandro. He sits down on the cold floor and finishes the smoke. 'Fuck you,' he says again to the empty world. 'You and your momma.'

18. Matia Bazar: 'Ti Sento'

The cell flares as the first lavender rays of sunshine enter through the bars and stretch across the ceiling. Birds chirrup at the rising sun, peaceful and melodic within the cell that stinks of wild nightmares and spilling loads of fear-shit. Sleeping on the coarse bed has left him with an aching body. His mind is continuously flashing white, and the sweat will not cease trickling from his body. His bowels cramping, the bucket in the far corner of the square cell waiting like shame.

His breath escapes in frantic gasps as his body fights the chemical imbalance. It's only the—is it the third day that he's been clean?—and even if his addiction is not 100% physical, he can feel the froth form in his mouth, the aching limbs in a tube of bright hot pain. The shaking limbs on his body will not slacken. He needs.

He needs his horsepower.

Melancholia—deep and hurtful to his cramping belly—faces passing in the glaze of time, lovers and friends and random fucks, smiling and laughing with never-altering glazed eyes, always so beautiful, never to be seen again.

Francesca.

What's the point?

'Mr Lago,' announces a voice from beyond the bars.

He looks up.

The voice belongs to an attractive woman in her late forties with an attaché case dangling from one limp hand. 'I'm your attorney, Jessica DeLario.' The uniformed cop unlocks the cell and the woman steps in. The cop wants to stay, but she glances at him and out he goes, locking her in with the whore.

She digs out a hand at Sandro, but he ignores it, his pupils the size of UFOs. She can smell his addiction, can smell *him*, like he's a wet dog with foam at the corners of his mouth.

'How have they been treating you?' she asks.

'Like the shit that I am.'

'That's good. The self-hate angle always plays well.'

'They didn't even give me my fucking phone call. I want out of here.' He grabs the woman's shoulders. She meets his eyes close-up, evenly and calmly, and Sandro jerks his hands away to turn his back on her. 'Look, Jennifer—'

'Jessica.'

'Yeah, look, I don't need any hot-shot lawyer fucking with my life, okay? I'm up shit-creek here—it's nothing unusual—'

'It certainly isn't,' she interrupts, 'arrested three times in Milano for soliciting. Once in Parma for possession of a schedule one narcotic—'

'Oh, *so* give me a fucking break.'

Jessica nods. 'That's exactly what I want to do. How you managed to avoid prosecution for any of those crimes is not something I probably want to know but I can guarantee you, that isn't going to happen this time. A cop was killed, you understand? So your best defence right now is to put yourself at the mercy of the court and—'

Sandro spits white phlegm at the ground. 'I don't need mercy,' he whispers. 'I need a fucking break.'

'You got yourself into this and now suddenly you want the world to feel sorry for you? There's only one victim—'

'I don't need a fucking lecture. I know what I do—you don't.'

'You mean there's more to you than some rent spreading his ass for anyone with ten bucks and a hard-on?'

He stares at her levelly. Before clapping his hands with three distinct bursts. 'Thank you for that.'

'You know what I hate most in life?'

'I don't know. Sex? Your fucking mother?'

'Defending assholes like you, too stoned to realise the shit you're actually in.'

'That's your job then, is it? To educate me on the shit?'

'No, I'm here to save you from—'

'I don't need your fucking *help!*' says Sandro.

She measures him up for a moment with her big eyes and then bangs her briefcase on the bars for the cop to let her out from the cage. The cop gives Sandro a menacing snarl. Typical fucking hetero' looking to make an impression on the sexy attorney, and Sandro's in no mood for this shit. 'You wanna help me, you cunt, get me a fix! And my phone call!'

The footsteps have vanished.

Lazily, the world turns blue. Later, who knows how long, the guard, standing beyond the cage, rattles keys in his hand. 'You still want that phone call?'

Sandro nods. The keys are inserted, the cage opened for him to follow the guard out into the passage. Empty cells pass like a film background for a '50's Hollywood production. A telephone hangs beside the exit door and the guard points at it with the keys. 'You got one minute. One.'

'Is that sixty seconds?' Sandro lifts the receiver. '*Gettone*?'

The guard flips a coin and Sandro dials an out-of-town number. '*Pronto,*' comes the reply down the receiver, '*chi parla?*'

'Giovanni?' Sandro says, hearing his own desperation. '*Mi senti?*'

'*Ti sento, chi*—'

'This is Sandro.'

'Jesus Christ. Are you crazy?'

The line dies in Sandro's hand. He looks at the guard. 'You got another coin?'

'You're entitled to only one call.'

'Yeah, but I dialled a wrong number.'

The guard hesitates. Then digs into his uniform to find another. 'You're lucky you have that Jessica bitch as your attorney. This is it,' he says, handing the coin over, 'better make sure you get it right. And you got fifty-three seconds left.'

Sandro redials. 'Giova',' he says after the call connects, 'I'm in prison, Giova'. I wanna get out, man. And I'll bargain with everything I got if Zoran don't get me the fuck outta here.'

Silence.

'*Giova*'?'

'No, this is Zoran, Sandro.' A chill runs through Sandro's body. 'What the fuck are you playing at, buddy?'

'Zoran, man, I need your help—'

The guard touches his shoulder. 'Twenty seconds.'

'Zoran, I'm in Cosenza. I'm up against a murder rap.' Silence. 'Zoran?' Silence. 'Zoran, *fuck*, if this is the way you want it, just don't forget, man, don't forget what I *know*—'

The guard's hand slices the air and cuts the connection.

19. Klein MBO: 'Dirty Talk'

'So what do we have on this Lago character?' asks Virdis in his tobacco-stained office with the grey smoke of his cigarette licking cautiously at a lamp-shade.

A shadowed figure steps forward into the light that cuts across his dark, tanned face. 'He's got a rap-sheet. Three arrests for soliciting, and one for possession of heroin—'

'Nothing else?' interrupts Virdis.

'Not that we can trace. But we haven't had much time—we only got his name this morning. The tap on Santana's line was a good idea, chief inspector.'

'What tap? That would be illegal, Franco. What else you got for me?'

'Only some background. Alessandro Lago, born in South Africa of Italian parentage,' the man sits down and spreads a file open on the metal desk opposite Virdis, 'but his childhood's sketchy. Seems as if he avoided the draft back in South Africa, but other than that, he's got no rap-sheet back there. He left in,' the young detective checks the file, '1985.'

He flips a photo across the desk. 'And that's our most recent photo of him—in Milano—he was staying in an apartment with a Francesca,' again the detective checks the file, 'Francesca Segreto. She was an h-addict and prostitute who sliced her wrists a few weeks back. And these are Lago's mugshots. As I said, he was arrested four times, but somehow never spent a night in prison.'

'What are you saying? He has connections?'

'Look at the arrests. Detective Blake claimed he was an informant. That's how he got out with no charges.'

Virdis lifts a photo and stares at the face. 'Blake, eh.' He drops the photo onto the desk and stands laboriously, sighing out a long stream of smoke. 'I have a hard day tomorrow, Franco. Come,' he says as he shuts the light, plunging the office into darkness, 'walk me out.' On the hallway, Virdis turns to the tall detective and says, 'You get hold of Cosenza and you tell 'em to look after that piece of shit. Tell them I'll be coming down personally after tomorrow to chat with him.'

'He's appearing in court tomorrow.'

'Good.' Virdis steps out into the Milanese night and Franco watches him cross the road to his Volvo with his shoulders slouched and head slumped. Franco thinks it will indeed be a hard day to come for Virdis.

20. Baltimora: 'Tarzan Boy'

I

Day turns to night, lunch to dinner. And the shivering is worse. His body shakes as if some demon is possessing him, twisting his insides with demented hands. He wheezes desperately for the dank air with a bitter gaping mouth, biting at the oxygen in foul bursts. He's weak, barely able to stand. The food makes him wretch all over himself, white puke flecked with blood and madness. Thoughts appear and vanish with no logic, erratic explosions of violence and sex and frustration replaced by lethargy. Curl up and die.

He can barely recall the last three years. Years faded in a haze of frenzy. On the bunk with his eyes shimmering pools in the light burning in from the lamps beyond the cell and beyond the inferno of heated desire. Cleansing blood pumps through craving veins. Sleep is not possible, his mind hyper-aware, images, nightmares so solid he can touch them—so far from the liquid fog his life had become. His body aches with fever, his torn and raked-raw flesh from savage, scratching fingernails demanding more, deeper mutilation.

Almost as if his is mind is suddenly taking advantage of this newfound lucidity, like the dying man confessing his sins, channelled incidents ripple into his psyche, forcing him to relive, experience, that which had always been dreams that were sucked away into a needle. There's no coherence. Guilt, disgust—nostalgia for what was and could so easily have been. He'd left so as not to kill in a wrong war. Now he has murdered in his own war—their war—his war for survival fought in the battlefield of a liquid-energised-mind. Where the grey and yellow mucus spits out nausea. Nausea as black as eyes from a corpse that glare out at him accusing. Jesus ... twisting, he pukes on the floor, gasping for breath. Foam like a dog as Francesca smiles from the floor, drowning in his filth.

Jesus he's about to die ... in a deserted cell in Cosenza.

Francesca. *Ti Amo.*

The night wears on, his thoughts more coherent with every passing hour. If it wasn't for the cramps, the fucking cramps that take his muscles and rip them apart for him to scream and gyrate on the floor in fits of singing pain ... if only ... incidents anchored in his psyche come to life, fully realised. Visions of a life. His life. Without a thread of time.

With the dawn, Sandro finds rest. Sleep. Heavy slumber.

The guard wakes him at seven sharp, informing him that his court appearance will be heard at two while depositing a tray of bread and cheese and coffee, the sight of which forces blazing acid up Sandro's throat to be puked out in the bucket, nothing but air and pain, searing pain running up his oesophagus as the guard assures him the attorney will, of course, 'Consult with you later this morning. After you've washed up.'

He leaves Sandro puking up acid in the corner with his piss and shit and puke staring up at him crawling with maggots.

They wash him down that morning alright, into the cell the cops extend a water-hose and hose him down like he's diseased livestock, stinging his naked, lacerated body as the spray hits his genitals and they laugh and leave him naked and cowering in the corner for Jessica to arrive as the heat in the cell becomes unbearable.

She's dressed in a black suit, hair tied in a tight bun. Ready for court, steady and confident. She deposits her attaché case on the concrete floor and stares at Sandro lying on his bunk clad only in jeans and scars jaggedly cutting his body in a perversely beautiful mosaic of different shades of purple pain. She smiles at him, but there's no reaction, his eyes sunk deep in his pale face. He's thin, ribs visible on the hairless torso, nipples hard under the heat.

'You want a smoke?'

It tastes good, poison for his toxic body. She has withdrawn a manilla folder from her briefcase when Sandro looks at her standing in the middle of the damp cell. He sits up with an aching, attentive body.

'So how do we plead?' she asks, dragging on her smoke and sitting warily beside him on the bunk.

'You're the attorney.'

'How about rehab?'

'Where's that coming from?'

'Is it an option for you?'

'No,' he says.

'Why?'

'Because I don't trust you.'

Jessica nods and opens the folder. 'The evidence, I must tell you, Sandro, is pretty damning.' She scans the pages.

'So what's new.'

'One witness—a cop—has given a positive identification. And the attendant at the, uhm, the hotel where they tried to arrest you. And, of course, let's not forget Piercarlo Battista—'

'Who the fuck is that?'

The woman flips ash onto the poured-concrete floor, eyeing the scarred, handsome kid with level eyes. 'Your client.'

'You mean the fuck that was in the room?'

'Exactly. His evidence is most damaging.'

'What does he say?'

'You tried to kill him—made him sit in his own excrement—'

'That's crap!'

'Precisely.'

'He wanted—he made *me* do that!'

Jessica shrugs. 'It doesn't really matter. He's obviously copped a deal. The problem here is this; you're a cop-killer and what you did or didn't do to Battista won't change that. My advice is this: we plead guilty and leave it to the mercy of the court. Deranged heroin addict—'

'Deranged?'

'Beaten, homeless, a prostitute—it happens, frustration and aggression from—your experiences—lead to a violent attack on a cop. As I said, it happens, I've seen it a hundred times. You didn't mean to kill the cop right?'

'Sure.'

'But I must tell you, Sandro—'

'Let me guess—'

'— that rehab's your best option. It's either that or prison. And you won't enjoy that.'

Sandro stands, flipping the cigarette butt against the wall. He shuts his nostrils with index and thumb, snorts up phlegm before whispering, 'I'm scared.'

Jessica stands, drops the folder into the attaché case, and gazes at him briefly. 'You should be,' she mutters and steps to the cell-door. 'You sure about rehab?'

'It's not an option.'

'Why not?'

'I told you already.'

'Tell me again. Because it's a simple matter,' she says, turning to him. 'There are things you may know. And people who are keen to find out.'

'I figured. And I'd be dead in a week if I spoke to them. Who are they?'

She shrugs and taps on the cell. Finds a pack of Camels in her jacket and tosses 'em on the floor. 'I'll see you later.'

'Do I have a choice?'

II

He's smoked the entire pack before Jessica returns. She has a suit with her, dark and conservative, and she waits for Sandro to dress before her.

'You'll be driven to the court, and I'll meet you there. You're sure about not accepting rehab?'

Sandro shrugs. 'You mean kill myself?'

'Well, between us, at some point, those fellas in Milan are going to come down here. I've seen it before. Plead not guilty and then wait and see what happens. Okay? Maybe they're desperate enough to give you a better option. Between us, they seem keen.'

'Sure,' he says.

III

He's escorted to a blue van by two armed carabinieri with his wrists cuffed tightly behind his back. The bench inside the van's made of hard metal, and he must fidget to collapse the muscles of his ass. One guard sits opposite him, shutting the doors to the van as it pulls off. It's difficult to maintain balance with his arms tied and Sandro's head crashes into the wire-mesh windows behind him with every bend. He thinks maybe they'll have an accident and he'll be dead before he's sent to life in prison.

Sunlight, warm and tranquil, pours into the van, his brows sweating. The van careens into a bend and the guard grabs hold of the metal-bench. Moments before the impact.

Sandro is thrown clear across the van, his head smashing against the bench with a crunch. Exploding pain as the van flips, his body suspended in mid-air for an instant that lasts a lifetime before the van returns to earth on its roof, sliding with a scraping scream, and Sandro hits the floor hard with his face.

He can hear voices. Shouting. The van's doors are being pried opened. Sandro forces his eyes ajar. His vision's doubled by blood. He crawls to the guard, lying still on the floor-roof. He's bleeding over his face from a deep ravine in his skull. Keys are fastened to his thick belt and Sandro grabs at them and flips the locks to the cuffs. Something's banging on the door. Through the chicken-mesh, people's faces peer into the van, their eyes and mouths lusting for the sweet aroma of death. They crouch and stare. Suddenly the doors have been slung open and Sandro throws himself out into the sunlight, his shoulders crashing into bodies. He falls heavily, crawling between shoes and sandals and toes. Hands grasp at him, at his jacket, tearing it apart as he fights with all the fury he can muster, kicking and scratching and punching blindly and wildly. Wrists snap away as he screams, sledgehammering his arms and elbows about with cartilage and bone giving way beyond the reach of his knuckles. He lunges on blindly, staggering onto his feet and with flaying fists breaks a path through the crowd.

Sirens closing in.

Sandro keeps running, turning left, forcing his legs on, concentrating on his boots. Step after step, his lungs about to burst. But he keeps moving. *Must* move! Run! Fucking run!

IV

His legs can no longer hold him. He realises it too late, stumbling forward and down, scraping his hands and knees on the muddy ground as he tries to soften the impact on the waiting, absorbent earth. Writhing, gasping, blood trickling down his face as he stares up at the sun. Low on the horizon. Fuck, where *is* he?

Pain as he pushes himself to a sitting position, surveying his surroundings. Instantly, he realises he's out of Cosenza. He's sitting in a tomato field, the earth damp beneath his pants. A road stretches out beyond a fence he doesn't recall climbing. Above, the sky is darkening, promising rain, shadows vague and long. Almost night. The cut on his forehead's deep but not serious. He's fit and free.

What else is there?

Now he needs to get to—keep moving—get to Naples and ferry away somewhere—or find his way up north—sanctuary, Berlin, Hamburg, fucking Geneva … who cares! Whatever!

Keep moving. *Keep moving!*

21. Advance: 'Take Me To The Top'

It doesn't rain. The graveyard is aghast with piercing sunshine, blinding and hot. Only the widow had survived the entire ceremony without shaking off a layer of clothing. Two kids pinch each other without moving, tight smiles and choked giggles as beside them a man struggles to light a smoke with a faulty lighter.

The priest in purple and black calls for silence.

And there was a light for a cigarette.

Virdis turns and whispers to the widow. *Lisa, it'll be okay.* No, he can't stay. She understands, of course, apologises for her behaviour. She has always been understanding, Onassio arriving at all hours of the night—Lisa is a strong woman, she has endured much, and this, presumably, is her reward.

Virdis allows the tears to roll unabated down his cheek as he walks away from the funeral alone, following the brick-paved trail through the plush, green lawn there between the silent poplar trees. It's like the earth will suck out the marrow of the dead to restore the balance of what the dead had stolen from the earth.

He drives the Volvo back to HQ, forcing the engine into the bends with his hands raking at the gearbox, keeping the tachometer at red line in low gears. He arrives sooner than he intended, parks the Volvo in a plume of burnt tyre smoke before the commissariat, and walks across the road to Il Gatto Silvestro.

Silver is polishing glasses behind the varnished, dark-wood bar, his bald head shimmering and armpits wet beneath his Venice Beach, California t-shirt. The humidity is thick within the bar and Virdis cannot recall when it had been so hot in Milan.

'Back in '67,' replies Silver. 'So how was it?'

'Why didn't you come?'

Silver shrugs his wide shoulders. He'd been a wide receiver once, back in the States, before ducking the draft in Europe and ending up in Milan. He returns his attention silently on his glass, thrusting a soiled cloth into the nozzle and rubbing angrily. 'I've been to so many, Pino,' and nothing more is necessary. Virdis has never felt so completed—so defeated. He has achieved nothing.

'Give me a scotch, Silver. Triple.'

The big man lifts a bottle of J&B from the rack behind his head and deposits it before Virdis. He grabs two glasses and allows Virdis to pour two heavy doses for the men to down together in silence. The liquor tears a path through Virdis' throat and guilt. Immediately he feels more relaxed, pours another, and again the men drink a silent toast to those who have been lost, those each had known and loved and mourn. Those who had died in the pursuit of justice.

'When are you retiring, Pino? I'll sell this dump and you and me, we can buy a café in Portofino. Leave this city to the barbarians. The fucking savages.'

Virdis stands from the barstool, slightly off-balance. 'It's not possible to dream anymore, Silver. We are the savages, old friend.'

Silver nods with a smile playing on his lips. The bar's reflected off the wooden floor where the sunlight splashes.

If it was raining, Silver would cry.

Virdis uses the side-entrance into the station and avoids everyone but his secretary, sitting anxiously in his office, waiting for him. She stands up immediately when he walks in, her eyes following him silently around the desk. 'Was it okay?'

Virdis lights up a smoke. 'It was a great funeral, yeah. Everyone had a smashing time.'

She blinks and Virdis can see tears form in her eyes. 'Franco's been up here five times this morning, sir,' she says. 'He even sent a car to the funeral, but you'd already left.'

'Franco is too young,' he says, 'still thinks enthusiasm can make a difference. What are you waiting for?'

The secretary frowns, then understands, and heads for the door.

'Dani,' says Virdis.

She turns to him.

'I'm sorry.'

She smiles. 'It's not needed,' she says.

Virdis tugs on his smoke, watches the blue toxin form intricate patterns, blows circles from between his lips like signals of a misspent youth. There's a hasty rap on the frosted-plate door, a silhouette beyond stumbling in frantically, the figure of Franco sweating hard in the heat.

'Cosenza,' he stammers, 'they lost him. They fucking *lost* him.'

'Lost him? Lost him where, exactly? Like, under the couch?'

He approaches the desk uncertainly, like the fault is his. 'They fucking lost Lago.'

'Who's in charge down there?'

'Inspector Lupini. I've been trying to get hold of him all morning, but he won't take my calls—'

Virdis snaps up his receiver and barks, 'Get me Cosenza, *now*!' He waves at a chair before his desk and Franco's hardly sat when, 'This is Chief Inspector Virdis ... yes, from Milano, I want Inspector Lupini—I don't care—I don't give the smallest fucking shit if he's blowing the pope in the gents ... who is this? Sargeant Luigi Spuglia? Spuglia? Really? Listen to me, Spuglia, how do you fancy a five-year stint in Bolzano?' Virdis flips ash into a 'tray and then, with a quick glance at Franco, 'Lupini, what the hell's happened, I—' he listens with creased brows, and his eyes lift again to fix themselves onto Franco, 'yes,' nodding his head twice, 'yes, I understand, yes, a sour business indeed. No sign of the killer? Yes, of course ... yes ... I appreciate that—no, thank *you*, inspector. Yes. I'm waiting anxiously. Thank you. Yes, I'll be sending one of my detectives down. Arrivederci.' Virdis replaces the receiver, sighs, and drags heavily on his smoke before killing it in the ashtray.

'Well?'

'Lago was being driven to court. A sniper blew off the driver's head and another cop died in the ensuing accident. Apparently, Lago fought his way through the crowd and vanished. They've got their entire force combing the area but it's summer and everyone's out on leave so they're shorthanded.' Virdis lights another smoke, swallowing disgust down his throat.

'Incompetent southerners, as always.'

'One thing's for sure,' says Virdis through a plume of smoke, 'Lago must have some dirt on Zoran Santana to warrant an assassin.'

'You think—'

'No, Franco,' interrupts Virdis, 'I don't think. I know. Santana wants him dead. And I want to know why. You heard that call Lago made. He knows something. And that means we've got to get to him before Santana. Or we'll find our little Mr Lago in three pieces with his cock down his throat.'

'Can we trust Lupini?'

'No. I want you to go down to Cosenza. Use the chopper. You'll lead the search. I'll authorise it from this end.' He watches Franco head for the door. 'And Franco. Be careful. Please.'

22. Romano Bais: 'Dial My Number'

Reflecting silver in the midday heat, the BMW limousine snakes across the autostrada. The air-con's radiating about the leather cocoon. The limo' swings off onto the off-ramp with a blue Fiat following. Zoran's sipping Campari on ice on the backseat, scanning income statements as Giovanni drives the bimmer deep into the northern exurbias, past the tenement apartment blocks and deserted warehouses with graffiti sprayed about and a giant H that extends up three floors of a condemned building.

The bimmer slows beside the wall and Giovanni turns in his seat. He watches the blue Fiat roll past as Zoran finishes his glistening red drink, crushing ice with his teeth.

'He's been following us since we left the penthouse.'

Zoran rubs sleep from his one eye. 'Lose him.'

The 3.5 litre modified engine screams to a frenzy as Giovanni drops the clutch at 6500rpm and swerves the enormous vehicle into a wide-arched turn with tyres kicking up a fuss. He gets lost in a series of roads that run through the industrial estate.

After ten minutes, he slides back onto the autostrada. There's no sign of the Fiat in the rear-view. Zoran twists in his seat and studies the empty road behind. 'We're good,' he says. 'Now let's move. We're late.'

The limo' re-joins the stream of traffic on the autostrada and heads out of the city. Heading for the airport before taking the off-ramp and Zoran watches as they turn into a dirt road with a sign pointing left: ATLAS CORP.

'Giova',' he says, 'we pulled in 300 kilos of horse this year. *Porca troia.*'

'How much coke?' Giovanni asks, eyes monitoring the rear view and seeing nothing.

Zoran laughs. 'Half of that went into the entertainment account, impossible to tell.'

Giovanni parks the bimmer within a huge hanger below the wings of a DC10 stationary within it, its gigantic wheels dwarfing a waiting, blue Alfa GTV. A silhouette is visible behind the tinted windscreen of the GTV, motionless as the limo' approaches.

Zoran and Giovanni get out into the vast silence of the hangar. The Alfa's passenger-seat door swings open. Zoran motions for Giovanni to wait, and steps toward the Alfa. He peers inside before climbing in and snapping the door shut behind him.

Giovanni steps cautiously to the BMW and leans on the hood with ever-watchful eyes, his one hand inside his jacket like Napoleon. Holding what Zoran knows is his Beretta.

Zoran turns to his companion in the GTV. 'How was Africa?'

'Hot. But not as hot as this fucking place.'

'We're having a heatwave. It's good to see you. It's always good to see people you can count on. People you can come to with a problem.'

'Is that what's happening here?'

'I have this whore. He's become a problem.'

'He?'

'Don't judge. The cops are after him. He was stupid enough to kill one of them.'

'How is that your problem?'

'He can cause my operation some—harm.' From his jacket, Zoran slides out a thick envelope. 'One of my guys screwed up. The whore was in prison, about to spill his guts. Or so I heard. What could I do? I got my guy to take him out. The guy fucked up. A simple job and the asshole—'

'Everyone's got a guy. That's the problem with having a guy.'

'Right.'

'So what happened? The police still have him?' asks the blond assassin.

'No—he got away. So at least that. My guy assures me he's hot on the trail. But I find that difficult to believe. Because he's a moron. And I'm getting some heat from the locals. Nothing I can't handle, but this shit's all happening at the same time. That's why I called you. I need to know this shit's going to get cleaned up.' Zoran lifts the envelope on the dashboard. 'The usual fifty K. Will it do?'

'Unless there's something you're not telling me.'

'Nothing. My guy will meet you in Cosenza. You'll find everything you need in the envelope. There shouldn't be any problems.' Zoran clips the door open and slides out from the GTV.

'How—'

'I don't know,' interrupts Zoran, shutting the door.

The Alfa bursts to life with a thick growl and idles its way out of the hangar. Zoran runs his hand through his hair, watching it speed away. Spits onto the tarmac and walks to Giovanni.

'So he's doing it?' asks Giovanni, hand slipping off his Beretta.

'He took the money.'

Giovanni opens the rear-door of the bimmer for the fat man. 'You told him about—'

'No. It's his problem. Like Sandro running around is my problem. That fucking whore ...'

'Yeah,' Giovanni watches the streamlined GTV driving out into the blistering heat and dust, 'but you said it yourself,' he juts his chin at the vanishing Alfa, 'he's the best money can buy.'

23. Mike Mareen: 'Double Trouble'

I

He can't risk hitching because he knows that all roads will be patrolled. Cop-killer on the run. Cops arrest you the first time, thinks Sandro, the second time they just blow you away. He has no money so even if he was stupid enough to find a train, every station will surely be staked out.

But, Christ, he can't sit in this fucking tomato field forever! The circle is tightening. He can feel it. He needs to move—walk— north. The night will shadow him.

The insanity of his escape continues to baffle him. Why had the van spun and crashed? If it was luck, it certainly wasn't meant to help him, the king of swerve. He finds railway tracks barely visible in the acid-gilded moonlit-night, follows them below his boots. Concentrating on every step forward, forward with a mechanical rhythm, eyes fixed on the tracks and his marching feet. He collapses at dawn, finds a small grotto with the early grey light and passes out.

He awakens with a start. The grotto is awash in golden light piercing his bloodshot eyes. He crawls out disorientated. The heat is like a rush of water over his head, his body oozing out salt-water below the noonday sun.

Sandro slips off his jacket, wraps it about his waist and peers about. The train lines extend past a copse, heading towards a village dwarfed within a lush valley with a river that meanders past. Sandro wonders how far he'd travelled during the night. Regardless, he will pass through the village and find food.

It's over an hour's walk to the village, following the tracks down the hill. His whole body is damp with perspiration when he passes the first of the lonely stone houses, and he can swear he sees the ghosts of the *contadini* who worked the unforgiving land under the merciless *mezzogiorno* sun.

He's passing the village's central square before he sees anyone. A child runs towards him with her bare feet clip-clapping on the cobbles and black hair tumbling over a dirt-smeared face. She spots him and slides to a halt, her eyes quickly darting behind her at the deserted road leading into an ugly piazza.

'Where is everybody?' asks Sandro, approaching her with the sun behind his back and his shadow falling over the girl.

'In church,' she replies in a heavy dialect that's closer to Arabic than Italian.

Sandro squats before her and gazes into the girl's black eyes. 'What's your name?'

'Antonia.'

'Antonia—' he touches her hair softly, 'do you know where I can get some food, Antonia?'

The girl treads back from him, sensing danger, shaking her head with eyes now fixed on her feet.

'There are no restaurants here, cafés?'

'Today is Sunday, *signore*—nothing's open 'cept for the church.'

Sandro stands up sighing. Not much to be found there. The body of Christ does little to feed his churning belly.

'But there's a restaurant,' she says, pointing up into the green hills. 'The rich people come on Sundays.'

Sandro follows her finger. When he looks back at her, the girl is creeping past him and he scratches her head before she sprints in the direction she had come, back towards the village.

The hills surrounding the small-town bake in the humid afternoon. There are houses—villas dotting the hills. Big villas.

Sandro walks through the village, mostly two-storey houses with windows hiding behind wooden shutters, the ancient stone constructions casting shadows over the archaic cobbles below his boots. The main road leads on to a square with a fountain that no longer spurts precious water, and the stone houses have names on their walls here: La Trattoria di Garibaldi, Parruchiere, Il Bar Partigiano. And each with a tag hanging within the clear-glass doors: CHIUSO.

The church is unmistakable, a huge white construction built on the edge of the village with a belltower reaching up into the spotless sky. A choir can be heard drifting up the hill. Ave Maria. It's pointless staying. Sandro makes his way onward, up the hill, towards the villas. Perhaps he can find one with a stock of food.

The climb takes longer than expected. The valley is already cooling with the approaching night, and a cool breeze chills his sweaty flesh. Clouds approach from the west. A storm's coming.

There's a road cutting jaggedly up into the hills and snaking within a covering of richly textured trees and blood-red rock. The remnant of the day is sheltered by the tall acacia trees with the road pitch-black even at dusk as he follows it on, eyes adjusting to the dimness.

A gate appears to his right, hanging unsteadily off a hinge with a name printed in yellow. Sandro jumps over a short brick wall and follows an unkept path deep into trees and shrub. He can distinguish a clearing ahead. Carefully, in the purple shadows, he breaks the covering of trees.

A long, manicured lawn surrounds a stucco villa, handsome and squat and dark. Sandro runs across the lawn with his boots silent on the thick natural carpet. Two mahogany doors on a thick porch serve as the main entrance. He tries the doors, but they're bolted shut. The windows at the front of the villa, too, are secure. But at the rear, on the second and top floor, a tiny window lies open and inviting. And it's an easy enough climb up a drainpipe.

Grunting, he forces himself within the narrow gap in the window and falls heavily onto dark tiles inside. He quickly regains his feet and blinks spasmodically, acclimating to the gloom. A bathroom, big, and with the door shut before him. He grabs the handle and turns, pushing into the door with his weight. And smashes his face into the locked door.

Who the fuck locks a bathroom door from the outside?

His hand instinctively searches for the key, but there's none to be found. He locates the light switch. Flips it but nothing happens. Cursing his luck, he sits back on the toilet seat and, as an afterthought, pulls down the soiled pants to relieve himself.

He must get into the house. It's too late now to continue his search, his body too worn. Tired. He needs sleep. More than food, he needs to rest, and the enormous bathtub will serve as his bed. In the morning, he'll figure out how to plunder the house.

II

He *did* hear it. The door handle twisting, snapping. It's reality! Terror. *Move!* Someone's outside the bathroom door. *Inside the house.* Trying to enter Sandro's sanctuary. Silently, Sandro creeps out from the tub, listening. Cold sweat drips down his spine.

Listens to the silence of the night.

But he *had* heard it!

He knows his instincts—trusts them like only a junky can, knowing his unconscious will always protect him. There's someone on the other side of that fucking door. But why the silence? The dark is impenetrable. Is someone working the lock? Turning the—

Sandro wants to cry out, shout, 'Who is it?' His fear prevents him, churning through his belly, making him bilious. Christ, he's gonna puke! Why can't it just *stop!*

The door suddenly trembles in its frame, a deafening bang echoing through the villa. Sandro feels his bowels loosen. Whoever is beyond the door, they know Sandro is inside. And the thought forces him to back-peddle from the door instinctively. The door trembles again as *something* strikes the wood forcibly. It's going to give. Any moment and the door will crash down to expose *what* nightmare? It does, suddenly crashing inward with a tremendous thump. Sandro screams, lurching himself at the doorway and the darkness beyond.

A fist slams into his solar-plexus from the void, and he doubles-over. Catches sight of a knee heading for his face, and he tries—does—twist his body so the impact crunches into his shoulder. Off-balance, he rolls away, pivoting on the floor. Instinct, groping up onto his feet, stunned and reeling from the blows. Sees a black-suited man charging at him. Swings a fist in desperation, a punch that's blocked before an open hand connects into Sandro's forehead. Explosions rack his brain as he falls back, fingers scraping the wall for balance.

'Who the fuck are you!' he screams at the faceless man.

There's silence, then, before two blows slice the air with a frightening pace, whipping Sandro off his feet. Blood pours from his mouth as he falls and crawls away desperately through the darkness. He senses what's about to happen, rolls away to his left instinctively. There's a grunt as the assailant crashes onto the wooden floor with his knees where Sandro's head had been but moments before. Sandro lunges at the kneeling man, his fist connecting squarely with the face. A grunt. Something cracks. Sandro finds his feet, goes for a second blow. It's blocked, and his legs are swept away from under him. Sandro manages to somehow keep his feet by crashing his back against the wall behind him. Only there is no wall. No ground. Just the void.

And now, screaming, he's tumbling down a flight of stairs backwards with windmilling arms, down, rolling, out of control, grunting down into the abyss.

He hits the floor hard.

Rolls onto his belly. Nothing broken. *Move!* He stumbles to his feet. There's nothing but the dark. But he's running anyway, running through the unfamiliar darkness with his legs crashing into furniture and fittings and arms reaching out like a blind man. Distantly, he can hear the assailant thudding down the stairs behind him. The doors are ahead. He glimpses them in the silver-slither of moonlight oozing through the porch windows. He reaches the doors, fights with the locks—fucking *open*! Get out! God, *open!*

It won't! Fucking. *Budge!* He can hear the man's gasping breath closing in behind him, instants now ... and turns to watch a man enter the hallway. Sandro crouches, fists at his sides, his body swivelling sideways. Coiled like a trapped stray cat. The man lifts his arms and simultaneously there's a spit and a flash and the window behind Sandro's head shatters.

Sandro turns and dives in one fluent motion, headfirst through the shattered window. Splinters cut into his face, shredding his belly, his body relaxing instinctively as he drops out onto the porch. He's up fast, sprinting now for the trees. For survival! He hears screaming. Realises it's him. Shuts up. And keeps sprinting. The clearing is larger than the universe. Explosions follow him, divots of grass ahead of his feet disintegrating.

But it's too late! He's made it! He's within the trees now, sprinting through the heavy undergrowth, tripping, stumbling, moaning hysterically from a bleeding mouth into the night, *running*.

He won't allow his body to stop, sucking nutrition from his blood down his throat, his arms machete-like as he fights a path through the trees, destination not important. *Run!*

III

The black-suited-man on the porch lights up a smoke. His face glows in the night. A beacon. To be homed in on. On the frequency of the blond-haired assassin bleeding out from the shadows at the rear of the villa. Silent. The black-suited-killer does not hear the approach. Is not aware of the assassin feet away from him now on the porch. Assessing. And then asking, 'What happened?'

The black-suited man's cigarette flips out of his fingers as he sucks in air, one hand drawing for his pistol. He spins and recognises the blond-haired assassin. Swallows hard. His body slackening. 'Jesus *Christ!* I could've *killed* you!'

'You found him? I heard shots.'

The suit stoops to retrieve his smoke from the porch. 'Yeah. Sonofabitch has God on his side.'

'Where?'

The man points out at the silhouetted trees in the night. Looks back at the assassin. 'Can't get far. We'll head him off with the dawn.'

The assassin looks up at the dark sky. 'Now he knows we're after him. He will be more careful. More resilient. More inclined to help the cops. More difficult. He will run and I will have to chase. It will take more time. And that gives the cops time to close in. 'cause if we found him, it ain't long before the cops find him.'

The black-suited man shrugs. 'We'll get him. I know his type. He'll crack on his own.'

'You fucked up, buddy.'

An instant drawn out like guns from holsters. Both know, understand, are aware of death fluttering like their souls on the porch, can smell death in the air. The black-suited killer draws faster, first to trigger lead. Whizzing a bullet that thuds beside the blond-haired assassin's head. And in the shattering interval before the suit can squeeze off another round, two slugs have ripped through his chest to send him spinning off the porch. He slumps on the lawn with his gun flipping through the air like a rotor-blade.

The assassin holsters his smoking pistol. Brushes his fingers through his hair with his killing-hand. Everyone has a guy. And that's the problem with having a guy.

24. Brian Ice: 'Talking To The Night'

Franco stands above the corpse on the lawn stretched out in the morning sun. The ponytailed forensic man from Cosenza Station's squatting by the body, inspecting bullet holes with a tweezer deep in the lead-sprayed chest. The photographer's having a chat with a carabiniere, the two pointing down at the black-suited body like they're checking out an engine. This one's a write-off for sure—no overhaul possible.

'How long's he been dead?'

The forensic man looks up at Franco. 'No more'n six hours. Shot twice at close range with a .45. Clean hits to the heart.' The young guy in the ponytail motions with his head at the body. 'He knew it was coming. He died standing there,' pointing to the porch, 'died before he even hit the ground. Shot one bullet at his killer that hit just under that window, the broken one.' The guy stands up laboriously. 'He had a .38.' He juts his chin out at the lawn. 'We found it with five slugs missing. But there's no way he shot 'em on the porch. And he had a cigarette lodged in his throat. Swallowed it after he was hit. You wanna know what I think?'

Franco nods encouragement.

'I think there were two of these guys,' he waves at the morgue guys coming closer with a black bag, 'him,' tapping the corpse indifferently with his shoe, 'and an accomplice. And the two of *them* were after someone else. Who ran into the woods,' pointing, 'over there. Come.'

Franco follows the man over the lawn. Sweating in the heat. On the soil, patches of grass have been wedged up. 'Divots,' explains the pony-tailed forensics man. 'We scraped up the bullets. Belong to dead guy over there. The guy they were after ran into the trees. Over there.'

Franco follows the pointing finger. 'Any ID?'

The forensic guy adjusts his spectacles. 'Nothing. Clean. My guess, some sort of hitman.'

The forensics guy escorts Franco into the villa, jabs a thumb toward the broken window beside the door. 'The guy they were after jumped through this window,' he says. Furniture lies scattered about the floor and Franco side-steps his way to the staircase, stepping up behind the forensics guy with alert eyes. The door to the bathroom's shattered and lying on the floor. Fresh pools of blood stain the wooden floor on the passage. Franco touches the blood with his index-finger. Still warm. Fresh to his lips.

'Inspector Rinaldi!'

Franco turns his attention to a cop climbing the stairs with a girl trailing behind him. 'This is Antonia, sir,' says the cop once he gets up on the first landing, 'she lives down in the village. I think she saw the fugitive. Lago.'

Franco Rinaldi is a young man with not much patience for unreliability and watches the girl trip over the last stair in a new pair of shiny shoes with distaste. He kneels and smiles at the girl anyway, withdrawing a photo from his breast pocket. *'È questo l'uomo che hai visto?'* he asks, holding the monochrome photo of Alessandro Lago before her black eyes. The girl nods. 'When?'

'Yesterday. At lunchtime. He wanted food—'

'Do you know where he went?'

She shrugs. Franco touches her face tenderly. 'Don't worry,' he assures her, 'you're not in any trouble.'

Antonia nods.

'Do you know where he went?' repeats Franco. 'Did he come here?'

'He went into the hills,' she says, 'but I don't know where.'

Franco scratches his scalp and then it clicks. 'You must have been good,' he says to her shoes, 'to get those.'

'A man gave—' she begins, only to hesitate with widening eyes. A shiver sweeps through her body as she avoids the eyes of the cop.

'This man?' asks Franco, pointing at the photo.

'No,' Antonia looks around nervously, 'another man. He gave me thirty thousand lire—he too was looking for him,' she points at the photo, 'I didn't know—' she blurts out, glancing at the bathroom door on the floor behind Franco, 'I wasn't sure, so I told him he went up into the hills, and the man went up too.'

'What did he look like?'

Antonia shrugs.

'Was he as tall as this one?' Franco taps the photo.

She studies the photo levelly with creased brows in exertion. 'No. He was bigger, and he had black hair.'

It's a start. 'Is there anything else you remember?'

'No,' she pauses, 'except—'

'Except?'

'No, nothing.'

The cop slips out a few notes and hands the bills over to the girl. 'Nothing?'

'There was—another man with him. I saw them talking—'

'Another man with him?' Franco points at her shoes.

'Yes. They spoke for a long time in a car. I think it was an Alfa. A blue Alfa.'

'What did this other man look like, Antonia?'

She shrugs, frowning to recall. 'I think he was blond.'

'Good. And where did he go, this other man, this blond man?'

'He drove off.'

'Where?'

'He just left.'

'Alone?'

'Alone.'

'And this man?' asks Franco, nodding at her shoes.

'He went up into the hills. Like the man in the photo.'

'Walking?'

'Yes.'

'Come,' Franco holds the girl by the hand to accompany her out onto the lawn. The corpse has been rolled into a body-bag, but it hasn't been zipped up yet. 'This is going to be scary,' Franco squeezes the girl's hand reassuringly, 'but you must be brave.' They stand above the filled body-bag. To look down at the face basking under the late-summer sun. 'Is it him? Is this the man?'

The girl stares. No horror in her eyes, thinks Franco. Just a cold, curious detachment. Farm stock, he figures; death is nothing new. 'He gave me the money,' she says.

'Thank you, Antonia.'

'Can I—'

'Yes, you can go.'

The girl bolts away to a waiting squad car with the notes crumpled in one puny fist. Franco watches her go. And frowns, trying to work out what the fuck had happened here.

25. Paul Paul: 'Good Times'

'This looks nice.' Robi points at the villa on the desk within the frame of a 4x8 print. 'Is it close?'

The woman smiles the estate-agent way. 'Just up here in the hills. And it's cheap—five hundred thousand a month. I've had four inquiries already,' she adds, the fear of loss as a close, the deal is a dead cinch now. 'But you must lease it for two months.'

Robi flicks an astray strand of black hair from her eyes. 'That's fine. Can I take it immediately?'

'*Certo, signorina.*' The woman crosses the sun-drenched office and extracts a file from a metal-cabinet. 'If you'll just fill in this form and give me your passport—'

'No.' Robi meets her eyes and doesn't blink. 'I will pay you in cash plus two million as deposit.' She stares at the woman evenly. 'Please, I'm—I just need to be left alone. My husband, he—I just want to be left alone for a while. Do you understand?'

The woman replaces the file. 'It's not such a strange request,' she muses to no-one in particular.

Robi digs out a thick wad of notes, separates 'em on the desk. The woman doesn't bother counting. 'The keys are inside,' she says and hands over a manilla envelope, 'and directions, of course, on how to find it.'

The heat outside the small office is oppressive. Villammare is alive with tourists and bicycles and bathers—the youth of Europe tumbling down onto a sleepy seaside village with cars parked in every conceivable turn, the roads so narrow Robi thinks she's gonna scratch her rented VW as she drives up into the hills.

The directions are simple and precise, and it takes less than ten minutes to climb up the cliff overlooking the village and the seaweed green Tyrrhenian. Melting tarmac scrapes upon the VW's Pirellis as she swings the Golf through the curves with a smile and U2 blaring from her speakers.

The chalet is set-back from the road in a lush garden, tall poplar trees steady in the morning breeze. She parks the silver VW on the sunbaked road and walks toward the chalet. It's small, with a veranda on the second floor gaping out at the Tyrrhenian far below. Green shutters are shut, and a gecko climbs up the stucco wall, fleeing as she inserts the key in the lock and opens the front door.

It's musty inside, but spacious enough. The refrigerator holds a six-pack of ice-cold Peroni and Robi cracks one open before heading up for the bedroom and the veranda where she rubs the iced bottle over her forehead. A yacht creeps across the Gulf of Policastro directly in line with a restored Norman castle on the cliffs above the beach.

The beer tastes good, cooling her body. She sits down on a beach-chair to light a Camel. Stares out. This is what she needs: time to herself, to think, to understand—time to accept. Time to heal. Time perhaps to forgive.

Maybe even ... but Robi knows she will never forget. Or forgive. Herself, or her father. Wherever the fuck he's rotting. Hell. If there was any justice. Bastard. There was, in the end, only one way to exorcize him.

What are you gonna do now, Robi? How are you gonna look after your brother, Robi, he's only ten. And you're only fifteen—only fifteen. Old enough, right, old enough ...

Bastard!

She kills her smoke on the floor, crushing it beneath her bare foot. So what choice did she have? Composing herself, she brushes away an astray tear and stands, draining the remnants of her sixth Peroni. She has so much to come to terms with—so much to accept. Two months here, she thinks. Will it somehow help her replace the lost bits? The broken pieces?

26. Righeira: 'Vamos a la Playa'

If he doesn't find a way out soon, they will find him. They'll expect him to head north. Freedom, Europe, is north. So instead, he'll head back to Villammare. He knows people down there. He needs time for things to quieten down, then maybe a ferry, to Greece, or Sicily or fucking ... Morocco ...

He crouches on the verge of the narrow mountain road, watching. Waiting. Opposite him is a scenic lookout with a bench constructed on the side of the road in the shade of orange trees. The Tyrrhenian coast spreads out in the distance in a postcard vista of Italian summer dreams, jagged, rocky cliffs following the windswept coast south toward Tropea. It's only a matter of time before some tourist following the coastal road stops to take photos of this scene.

Sandro is exhausted—his body not functioning, not wanting to move, his mind wanting only to sleep, to shut his eyes and allow destiny to run its inevitable course. But he's not Francesca. He doesn't quite know how to quit.

It happens just gone noon. A car comes to a stop across from where Sandro waits, hidden in the bushes on the side of the road. He watches a man step out from the parked Alfa GTV and Sandro waits. Body tensed like a sprinter on blocks. Smelling his own fear. And fearing his own madness. The man stands with his back to the Alfa, blond hair blowing about as he stares out at the vista while pissing a golden trickle on the thirsty soil. He's left the driver's side door open to the day …

Sandro sucks up the warm, stifling air. He was hoping to find a lonely tourist who'd give him a ride, but this … Jesus, this is his chance. He bolts across the road. Gets to the GTV unseen. The man is twenty metres away, back turned. Sandro checks out the ignition, real casual, like he's a tourist, like he's admiring the leather interior. The keys dangle in the ignition. His eyes target in on the Alfa's logo on the keyring, a man being sucked up by a serpent like a drab of spaghetti. Sandro gazes at the man. He hasn't turned around. Now or never.

Sandro slides into the bucket seat, fingers trembling, fumbling at the ignition. Christ! He turns the key. The two litre engine spins into an aggressive growl. The man turns with a liquid spray circling about his feet, eyes staring wide at Sandro with something more than surprise. Sandro guns the engine and screeches onto the road with revs somewhere at 7000 before he slams in second with a squeal of tyres. He watches the man vanish in his rear-view as the Alfa banks into a curve. Sayonara, fuck-face, he thinks. Sayofuckingnara!

It's a fast drive down to Villammare—only 45 minutes on the SS18 that meanders up the coast. He keeps going, takes the road to Vibonati, heading up into the hills, and it's 1:15pm on the Magneti Marelli clock in the Alfa when he abandons the car behind an abandoned factory. He figures it's about an hour's walk down to Villammare. Before leaving, he searches the Alfa. Nothing in the cabin warrants closer scrutiny, but under the hatch-back, *paydirt*, a thick attaché case resting in the trunk. It's a numbered lock. He flips the catches anyway. And the clips flap open. To reveal a fresh set of clothes—a cotton shirt and slacks—and beneath that, an envelope. Sandro lays the clothes to one side in the trunk and lifts the envelope out to finger it as if it were a gift. Thick. Money? He rips open the seal and takes a peek. At papers. Nothing but fucking papers! He reverses out the contents, sheets of paper falling into the trunk. *Fuck!* A photograph falls face down. He's about to turn it when his attention is drawn to tyres, an engine, *approaching!*

He slams down the hatch, and crouches to watch a car speed past on the road beyond the building. Expecting to see the blond-haired man with the cops. But it's a VW Combi with tourists hanging out of doors and windows, waving and shouting in an alien tongue blown away by the sultry August air.

Move!

It's only adrenaline that keeps him moving, and the sun is already drifting away when he finds his way into Villammare and the anonymity amidst the tanning bodies of youth littering the little streets of the seaside village.

He makes his way to the *Farmacia* on a cobbled alleyway off the main drag, sunglasses displayed on a rack at the entrance, reflecting the glare in ultra-violet-free-rays. There's a kid working the counter with hands waving at two packages on the glass-counter as he explains something to an overweight girl in a bikini with flesh burnt to a crisp. The pharmacy is tight and small, as suffocating as Sandro recalls it to be. He waves a hand at the guy behind the counter but he's too busy and Sandro's forced to move forward toward the counter, barging before an American couple half-naked and lobster-red.

'Excuse me,' says the James Dean lookalike, 'we *were* first.'

Sandro stares at him. '*Che vuoi?*' he asks with fingers of one hand joined in a triangle. '*Cazzo vuoi?*'

The Yank's confused, not his language, frowns while his girlfriend looks down at her feet. Sandro turns his attention to the pharmacist. 'Ciao, bello!'

The guy looks up. An unblemished, sincere face. Sandy hair. 'Sandro,' he says, looking at the bruised face and tattered clothes, 'what the —you okay, man? What the fuck happened to you?'

Sandro leans over the counter and places his mouth on the guy's earlobe. With a quick bite, he giggles and whispers, 'Can you get the afternoon off, Stevie?'

Stevie rubs his ear with his fingers. 'Does it look like it? Some of us have to work you know.'

'It's summer, Stevie. Come on, live it up a little.'

'Excuse me,' comes the foreign English of the Yank, 'but we *are* in a hurry.'

Stevie turns to the guy and nods his head. 'One moment, sir.' He returns his glassy stare on Sandro. 'I'll see you tonight on the beach, okay? After I close up. Same spot—you know where.'

'Yeah. Great. Listen, Stevie, can you lend me some bucks, man—I lost my wallet—'

Stevie places his forefinger on his lips before digging out two bills and dropping 'em on the counter. 'You're always talking shit, Sandro,' he mutters, turning his attention to the Yank pushing past Sandro now, at the end of his tether. Sandro bangs the girl on the shoulder on his way out.

There's a restaurant-cum-café on the boardwalk, tables under Martini umbrellas scattered about at random, waiters in varying colours and styles of swim-shorts running about in the heat. Sandro finds a table near the rear, under the reed roof that leaks sunshine and dreams, and orders a tequila sunrise and a lemon *granatella* from a waiter who speaks in broken Italian, his Nordic features scorched beneath the Mediterranean heat.

The sunrise tastes good, refreshing and warming simultaneously. He steals a newspaper from the table vacated behind him, lifts it and there he is, staring out at himself on fucking page three. For a moment he thinks it can't be, no way—and yet the headline's accurate enough—COP KILLER ESCAPES CUSTODY. Heart thundering, he scans the restaurant quickly, like a celeb' in search of the paparazzi. Only this kind of fame will buy him nothing but a lifetime as the wife of some primate in a state pen'. *Porca troia.*

He scans the article, mercifully short and sketchy, allegations rather than fact. The police van that was driving him to court had lost control for unknown reasons. And then there's the second-last paragraph that alleges the policeman driving the van had been shot by a mafia hitman because Lago was not only being sought for the murder of a rookie cop in Naples but because of his underworld connections.

Jesus, he thinks.

'Hi, you remember me?'

Someone has recognised him! He folds the paper real slow to unearth his face. Gazes up at faded blue eyes. The face is familiar, black dreadlocked hair. Who—and then he places her. The American—*the girl in the truck.*

'You have the wrong person,' he says dismissively.

'Robi,' says the pretty girl, pulling back a chair opposite him, 'you mind if I sit?'

Sandro would rather she fucked off. But he says nothing.

'What a coincidence,' she says and sits. 'It's sandy, right?'

'What?'

'Your name. Sandy.'

'Sure,' he says.

'Right. No, it's Sandro, right?'

'Whatever.'

'You're a wanted man, Sandro, you know that?'

Sandro goes cold. Meets her eyes. They're playful. 'What?'

'Milan,' she says. 'I knew I recognized you from somewhere. Zoran Santana?'

Sandro blinks. 'Who the fuck are you?'

'I'm Robi. And you,' she reaches over the table and reaches for his bruised face with her fingers, 'don't look too hot.'

Sandro snaps his head back.

'I'm sorry,' she says, and checks out the restaurant in search of a waiter. 'I know how it feels.'

'What?'

'Never mind. What a weird coincidence, right? We almost meet in Milan, and then in a fucking truck—'

'Two o'clock,' says Sandro suddenly.

'What?'

'I was meant to meet you. At two.'

She frowns. 'I don't get it.'

'Never mind.'

Robi smiles, pulls out her Camels from her purse and lights up. As an afterthought, she spins the box at him as an invitation and he accepts the light from her hand. They smoke silently for a while, watching the Tyrrhenian swooping gently on the pebbled beach opposite.

'I never did find a room in that hotel,' she says eventually, disturbing Sandro from overhearing a conversation between an elderly couple and a young girl sitting behind his chair. He takes a scoop of his melting *granatella* as a waiter arrives with two menus and a smile, his English better'n his Italian.

'Just a beer, please,' she says. 'Any will do so long's it's cold.'

The waiter turns to Sandro, who waves at his drink as dismissal.

'Did you tell them I sent you?' he asks once the waiter's out of earshot.

'At the hotel? Sure. No-one knew you from a bar of shit.'

'And here I was thinking I was a wanted man.' Sandro smiles as she glances at him. 'So where did you go?'

'Sorry?'

'After the hotel—'

'Oh,' she nods at the waiter depositing her beer before her, 'I slept on the beach. And I realised I actually like it down here, it's really pretty—'

'Isn't it.'

'Yeah, really swell. Anyway, I decided to stay, so I rented a house up on the hill. A *villa*. Fancy. You should come over. Are you staying?'

'No idea.'

'I'll make dinner.'

He studies her face, the high cheekbones shadowing the flattering light. 'I have things to do.'

'Here?' She waves her arms about. 'What could you possibly do in this medieval village besides fuck and tan?'

'Swim,' he mutters.

She waits for him to say more. He doesn't. 'You don't say much.'

'What do you need me to say?'

'It's not a sin to be shy.'

Sandro runs a hand through his hair. 'Your fancy villa have an address?'

It has, and she writes it down on the tab which she insists on settling, folds it and hands it over. 'Do you have any shit on you?'

'Shit?' He reads the address before sliding it into his shirt pocket.

'Hash, yeah, you know ... blow.'

He stares at her. 'No. Do I *look* like a dealer?'

She stares at him openly and in a way that he finds disconcerting. 'Kinda, I guess. I was just asking, since you knew the hotel staff so you must be, like, connected and shit.'

'I can get. If you want. Twenty thousand should cover it.'

She slips out a wad of notes and slits one off. 'Will I see you tonight then?'

'Yeah, I'll, see if I can make it happen.'

27. Firefly: 'Love Is Gonna Be At Your Side'
I

The main beach is deserted at dusk but for a man jogging on the pebbles with his poodle pacing itself alongside him. They fade into golden-hued silhouettes running before a crimson sun. It's the twilight hours, the void between late afternoon and when the tourists will come back to hit the restaurants and bars, the time for napping and showers to prepare for the night. Sandro watches the Tyrrhenian turn shades of dark, smoking cigarette after cigarette. He has stripped off his shirt. Occasionally he glances back behind his shoulders, looking out for Stevie.

He lights another Phillip Morris, shielding the flame with cupped hands. The trail of rainbowed lights along the boardwalk floods onto the beach. He's sitting beside a boulder with his body swamped in imperceptible shadows, only the red glow of the cigarette-tip signalling his presence. Bryan Ferry drifts lazily through the night, the sea crashing and drowning the music out in sudden bursts of potency. Distantly, the roaring, clanging trucks pass, bouncing on the jagged road headed for Naples.

Footsteps crunch on the rocks beside him. He gazes over to watch the unmistakable frame of Stevie stumbling over the boulder.

Stevie sits down beside him in the gloom and lights up a smoke. 'Sorry I'm late,' he says, and flicks his head about, checking out the familiar scene.

'What's wrong?'

Stevie shrugs. Avoids Sandro's eyes.

'Tell me?'

'I saw your photo in the paper,' he says, returning Sandro's stare suddenly. 'What the fuck, man? What the fuck are you even *doing* here?'

Sandro swallows uncertainly. 'It's a set-up. The cops want me to testify, so I told the cops to get screwed, fucking pigs, and now they've pinned this dummy rap on me—'

'You talk a lotta shit,' interrupts Stevie, 'you lie so much you've forgotten the fucking truth.'

'I'm not lying, Stevie. Christ! I wouldn't lie about something like this. Come on ... we've known each other for three years, man. I would never—do I *look* like a killer?' He holds his hands out like Pontius Pilate. 'Seriously, man. Do I look like a fucking killer?'

Stevie considers this. 'Nobody knows you, Sandro.' He stands wearily, brushing off the seat of his jeans. 'You're a different person with everyone you know. You're *false*.'

Sandro grabs hold of Stevie's jeans, raising himself onto his knees. 'Don't go,' he says, staring up at the pretty, shaded face staring out at sea. 'Stay with me.'

'What do you want from me? Fucking killer on the run, what do you want from me?' He rips his leg away angrily, steps back. 'You're not here 'cause you got nothin' better to do but *vacation*. So what do you want? Tell me. Tell me what you want.'

'Stevie, *hey*, buddy—we're friends—we've been—'

'Just fuck off, Sandro. We fuck when we see each other, and that's it. Every time you're here, you want money from me. Man, it's like you're a fucking a whore. You *are* a fucking whore!'

'Stevie—'

'D'you want money, man? Is that what you want? How much you want, huh? How much *are* you?'

'Stevie, you're—'

'How *much*!' yells Stevie. 'I read on the paper you're *connected*. To a wire up your fucking ass! Fifty-thousand, is that good? Huh? Is that good? Is that what you *go* for?'

'Stevie, you're wrong. I care—'

'Fifty thousand. Take it or leave it, whore. And this?' He tosses two tinfoil squares on the ground. 'You gonna do me for that, huh?'

Sandro shifts his eyes away from Stevie's threatening face. 'Sure.'

'Yeah? Yeah? I'll give you your fifty thousand bucks, man.'

A front of clouds tumbles in above the restless sea. Surf sprays from a rocky outcrop, glinting salt-water tears caught like pearls in the silver ray of light. The wind is up, the moon slipping away unnoticed, yielding to the void. Except for the sea that pushes higher now, splitting the land in jagged outbursts of rock. Groaning to protest the inevitability.

Stevie zips up his jeans. Looks up at the blackness, the thunder now registering in his weary mind. Sandro turns onto his back. Stevie digs out a few bills from his wallet and chucks 'em down at Sandro, lying there with his pants around his ankles and naked ass cold on the pebbles.

'Stevie—' Sandro watches the notes scatter like a ticker-tape parade in the wind. He crawls after them. Traps a couple of notes under a hand. Before, 'Stevie ...'

But Stevie's gone, leaving Sandro to shepherd in the rest of the numbered herd. When he stands, he can see Stevie bucked over near the boardwalk, puking out his guts.

Rain splatters itself on Sandro's face, the drops running down his face cold. He pulls up his jeans and rushes in the opposite direction to Stevie. The rain is falling hard now, his body already drenched. Only when he gets to the path jutting up a small embankment does he realise he's left his shirt on the beach.

He thinks fuck it and follows the path up. The pizza he'd eaten at the café has done him good, but his body still aches. And Stevie hadn't helped much. He emerges onto a palely lit road, the rain hitting hard. He shivers, aware suddenly of the chilled wind sliding up the hill from the turbulent sea. Crossing the road, he finds a footpath heading into the darkness and follows it up with an itch invading his shoulder that will not abate even beneath his clawing fingernails. It's humid, his breathing difficult as the rain pelts down between the succulents.

Via Delle Rose is a gravel road perched up high above the hills with only three chalets sharing an uncompromising view of the world beyond, of the lights across the bay that are barely visible tonight with the heavy storm clouding out the Tyrrhenian.

Robi watches from her sitting room. There's something about a storm, she thinks, something primal and human and ... suddenly there's a distant knock on the door downstairs. Robi stands, figuring Sandro has braved the weather. He has, sopping wet, naked chest and tight jeans—cool look, she thinks—his face gleaming as he steps into the lounge dripping.

'You're soaked,' she says, and leads him up into the house and waves him into the bathroom. Sandro strips, towelling himself down furiously. He retrieves three packages from his soiled jeans, snort a healthy dose from one, and the others he carries back with him to the lounge where the American girl is sitting on a couch, her legs crossed in the lotus position, bare feet below her knees. Watching him. She says, 'I'm glad you came.'

Sandro points at a copy of *Vogue* on the table. 'Can I use that?'

'Sure.'

'I got your stuff,' he sits beside her on the couch, 'pure Malawi gold,' he says, taking out a wrapped banana leaf from one of the packages and starts mulling the rat-shit-like dope on the magazine. 'The real McCoy from a guy that works at the post-office. He's also an ex-South African.'

'You're South African then?'

He shrugs, glancing about him. 'I'm a citizen of the world. This is cool.'

'Cheap, too.'

'Yeah?'

'Half-a-million a month.'

'Christ.' He watches her light two Camels simultaneously. 'Give me another,' he says and rolls out the tobacco and replaces it with dope and a sprinkling of tobacco. 'Don't mind seeds, do you?'

'I don't really care.'

'You should,' he fixes the joint between his thick lips and sucks up the smooth dope into his throat. 'Seeds,' he tells her after a while, with smoke fleeing from his mouth, 'can make you sterile.' He passes her the furiously smoking joint with a grey haze filling the chalet.

'I wish my father had been.' She drags on the joint as an impressive clap of thunder echoes down the hill, the rain clattering on the roof, a million insects trying to swim in the heavy wind as distantly a window-shutter bangs. She hands him back the joint with, 'so how long were you there?'

'South Africa?'

She smiles at him, holding in her breath.

'Fifteen years. How long you been in the States?'

'All my life. But that's boring—'

'So is South Africa.'

Then silence as he sucks the joint dry.

'Where are you staying?' she asks.

'Here and there.' He kills the roach in the ashtray.

'Is it really impossible to create conversation with you?'

He turns and fixes his eyes on her enquiring stare. 'No, I just like listening.' He glances about the room once more. 'This *is* nice. Not worth half a million, but nice. Listen—' he twists his head in an obvious gesture, ear strained at the raining night beyond their den. Motions for her to be still. A gutter drips somewhere outside, clip-clapping heavily. 'Don't you love that?'

'Yeah.'

'Drains always bring back memories,' he says whimsically.

'For you too?'

'Oh, yeah. Gutters play an important role in my life.'

Robi laughs, not able to stray her eyes from the beautiful, bruised man beside her with the scarred body. She hadn't been attracted to him earlier—well, not overly attracted—she'd just been lonely. Wanted to talk—to communicate. But his aquiline features grow on her, his voice deep, expressionless. Facts are facts and everything else is bullshit. Her father had been like this. Playing kind games, forcing her to admit her guilt with subtle threats, then beating her for lying with that thong. And justifying the beating with, 'If you're innocent, Roberta, never admit your guilt.' He—oh, *stop*! What has Sandro just said? He's staring at her with a quizzical expression, thick brows creased, purple rings surrounding his eyes as though he's been wearing shades in the desert from birth. 'Sorry?'

'I said, it's good stuff?'

She smiles at him.

'Yeah,' he lights up a smoke and starts to mull more dope, 'my fondest memories are raging about Joburg stoned outta my mind on this shit. Actually,' he continues after a pause, 'I was mostly fucked on mandrax and jut.'

'Sounds like fun.'

'Not really. I was a draft-dodger in a fascist shithole. And eventually—'

'—you came here to get away from all the shit.'

'Not my greatest idea,' he says but watching the way he destroys the smoke in the ashtray, she figures it's best not to ask why. 'I was an idealist. Thought South Africa was so evil, so bad, then I came here, to Europe, and realised it's all the same shit. It's all the same system, see,' like he's an intellectual, 'in order for us to survive, we must sell our souls to evil—'

She's not interested. 'You want some Scotch?'

'Yeah, straight.'

'That's the only way it comes here,' she informs him while heading off into the kitchen and returning with a bottle of J&B and two wineglasses. She dumps it all before him as he lights up the joint. She heads for a c/d player against the wall. She's got three c/ds she'd bought from the record shop. She goes for Tears for Fears.

Sandro swallows his drink with a huge gulp and returns it to the table to pour himself more. Struggling to imitate him, she splutters as the warm liquid burns her throat. She composes herself, rubs away some tears, and grabs the bottle. Lifts it onto her lips and swallows a thick gulp.

'Many of my memories,' she tells him, 'are of stumbling through Chicago fucked on this stuff.'

He lifts the bottle and raises it for a toast to life and the thunder answers him. 'Bottoms up,' he says, gushing down the whisky with his Adam's apple rising and falling rapidly.

'So tell me about your scars.'

He laughs throatily. 'Why?'

'Looks like you took a beating,' she says.

'So what more d'you wanna know?'

'How?'

'How? I'll tell you the truth if you keep prying.'

'I'm not frightened of reality.'

'You should be,' he says. 'How about I tell you I'm a whore.'

She studies him levelly, nodding her head as if her assumptions have turned out to be correct. 'You enjoy it?'

They break down laughing, the tension fading like the smoke drifting away and leaving behind a clarity stained with the sweet odour of dope.

'Not many people joke about it,' he says with their eyes locked.

'Not you, for sure.'

'It's hard to laugh with a cock in your mouth.'

'I've never felt the urge to laugh with a cock in my mouth. Except once,' but he's giggling, and she joins in, drinking the night away. Until the bottle, in a drunken exchange, slips and crashes to the floor, splintering for them to laugh at its inevitability. Her hand falls on his crotch. Instinctively, his hand pushes her face to his lips. Their tongues meet, heat, their eyes open and staring at each other from a hot breath away. His hand creeps below her t-shirt. She slides it up and off, her small breasts falling between his fingers. He squeezes hard, and Robi tilts her head back. She bucks forward now, her hand fondling his zip. 'You feel so good,' she whispers, flipping him out. He watches her lower her face onto him, her mouth exploring, tongue playing. His hands caress her naked, strong back, touching, and he must open his eyes to see what it is his fingers are tracing—three pink scars that run up her back—and she moans with his cock in her mouth. She lifts her head, stumbles off the couch and draws down her skirt. Naked, she paddles to the wall and spread-eagles herself with palms and toes touching the wallpaper and face staring up at the ceiling. Sandro walks to her, stripping. Noticing her scars, those three pink serpents curling alluringly from a bygone age. He touches her ass, firm, kneels with his lips and tongue slipping in the crack of her ass. She gyrates into his face, and he stands, stepping back and finding a way inside of her. She is searing hot. Her hands slip down the wall, arms swinging behind him to squeeze his ass, forcing him in deeper 'til her muscles inside grip him and crush out his climax.

II

Robi rubs away the sweat from her face, realises then that the storm has passed, the only remnants a drain dripping lazily into an otherwise silent night, the dawn creeping in over their entwined limbs soft and pink. He stiffens as his body becomes aware of her flesh, of her presence, and barely awake, they make love, blindly exploring, probing, their mouths and lips meeting, parting, meeting. But their eyes remain shut because vision would destroy this splendid dream, vision would cause the nightmare's return.

It's past two when Sandro awakens again. He lifts himself onto his elbows. Glances about until sighting the Camels on the coffee-table. Looks at Robi with her one arm extended over his chest. He slides away from her and places her arm gently on the floor.

Ripping open the pack, he searches for a cigarette. None left. Then he recalls the pack he brought, in his jeans, in the bathroom. Naked, he paddles from the lounge, touching himself gingerly. This is the third woman he's ever had. He looks down at her while climbing the stairs, his mind processing thoughts that plunge him into a weird sense of despair. Who had tried to murder him in the house? He takes consolation from two thick lines, clearing out his stash, sweet sugar warming his senses, cocooning his mind within a nest of calm as he steps down the staircase and sees the doorknob to the front door *swivel*.

They've found him! He moves fast, crossing to the lounge, noticing that Robi has vanished—*where*? She's set him up! The door swings ajar. Sunlight washes in. He runs into the kitchen … back door, he thinks, the bitch betrayed him! He's running, looking back behind his shoulder at the shadow that steps in through the front door. And crashes into Robi, the two falling amidst a shattering of eggs. He doesn't slow, naked feet slipping in the runny fluid as he stumbles for the rear-door, eggshells fragmenting below his soles.

'What the fuck are you doing? *Sandro*, what the fuck's happening?'

The door is locked! He wields to her. 'Where the fuck's the key!' He can hear footsteps approaching. 'Give me the fucking key, Robi!' He has seconds, no more!

'Don't fucking *yell* at me!'

It's too late. He watches as the figure enters the kitchen, realises it's the body of a woman wearing a worn cotton dress. She gawps at him for an instant before blinking her enquiry at Robi, standing in a puddle of yellow slime. 'Have I,' says the woman with a lobbed smile, 'come at a wrong time?'

'What the fuck ...' stutters Sandro.

'—is going on, Sandro?' asks Robi. And then she looks at the woman. 'And who the fuck are you?'

'I'm your housekeeper,' announces the woman, glancing from Robi to Sandro. 'If I've come at a wrong time—'

'No, not at all,' interrupts Sandro, stepping past her now and the two women listen to his feet paddling up the stairs.

'The agency didn't tell me about a housekeeper.'

The woman nods. 'Yes, well, signora Fieri thought a signorina like you could do other things here besides cleaning this old place.' She laughs. 'Seems she was right. So she thought maybe I could help, since I can speak English.'

'That's great.' Robi extends a hand, smiling. 'I'm Robi.'

'I'm Mary. Actually, it's Maria, but I don't mind Mary.'

'Okay, Maria, fantastic. We'll come to some arrangement—'

Maria dismisses her with a waving hand, attention now on the eggs slimed across the terracotta floor. Robi brushes past her to the stairs. She can hear the shower dripping and she runs up to the steaming bathroom. She can see his thin body silhouetted behind the frosted-plate glass shower, and she slides open the door. He stares at her like he's been waiting, all hard as she strips to join him below the warm water.

'Are you going to stay?' she asks.

'I don't know.' And he doesn't—there are so many questions that need answering. All he wants is for it all to stop. To wake up from his nightmare, so he can—what? Keep whoring and doping? Christ, if he can only get outta this mess, he'll stop with the drugs, the whoring, derail himself from the express train to pain.

Her hands touch his face. He allows her access to his mouth with her fingers, his hands cutting across the jutting water and playing with her hard nipples. Their eyes meet and lock. His hands fall from her breasts as he moves forward with the waterfall directly over his head and the spray shielding his face. He holds her, her arms about his back, and they cling onto each other with their bellies sticking with the smashing water.

'I haven't felt like this for a long time,' she whispers. He holds on tighter, as his tears mingle with the spray. Sobs rake his body as he slides to the wet tiled floor, cowering naked in the corner. Robi squats before him with the water falling off her back. She touches his face, but he pushes her away, moves from her reaching fingers and cries his invisible tears.

'What's wrong?' she asks.

He looks at her with bloodshot eyes. He wants to explain, let her in, so badly does he want to share his anguish. The night had been beautiful. Surely, she won't betray him. Her tenderness has finally broken the wall he has created between his mind and his emotions, the survival wall, impenetrable and fortified by pain, betrayal and the insanity of those that have tried to climb it—

'What's wrong?'

'I'm dying,' he whispers. 'I'm dying.'

III

Maria has prepared them a light lunch of cold meats and boiled eggs with fresh bread. Robi brings two plates out with her from the kitchen to the veranda where Sandro sits staring down at the bay with nothing on but his jeans. She sits down beside him, depositing one plate on his lap.

'Does anyone want wine?' calls Maria from the kitchen.

Robi glances at him. 'Yes!' she calls.

They've eaten by the time Maria brings up the bottle of local table-wine with two glasses. 'I'm leaving,' she says. 'I will see you tomorrow.' Her eyes take him them in. 'At ten,' she adds, and they can hear her laughing on her way down the stairs. Robi waves at her as she walks out below in the garden.

'What did you mean?' she asks after having sipped the wine. 'Are you sick?' She thinks of HIV.

'You didn't read the papers yesterday?' He swirls the wine in his glass before downing it in one gulp.

'Which paper? I don't read Italian.'

Sandro stands pensively, lights a smoke and leans on the metal veranda. The Tyrrhenian glistens beneath the afternoon sky. Taking a sip of the chilled wine, he lets out a sigh, his face covered in shadows from the sunlight pouring over his shoulders. He has no choice here. Not really. 'I'm wanted, Robi—by the police.'

'Seriously?' He doesn't look away from her gaze. 'For what?'

'Murder.'

Robi stretches for her smokes.

'I just lit the last one,' he says, and takes a deep drag on it.

'Did you do it?'

'What do you think?'

'Why don't you tell me?'

He turns from her. 'No. Of course not.'

'So then why don't you tell 'em you're innocent?'

His eyes focus on the distant bay below. 'Because they know.'

Robi frowns. 'What does that mean?'

'They framed me for the murder of a cop in Napoli—they want me to testify against—someone I know. Someone dangerous. They think I know enough to bury him.' It's the only thing that makes sense. But how can they know of his connection to Zoran—and why would they *care*? Why would Zoran fucking care? Had the killer in the house been one of his boys? Who the fuck else, he thinks.

'Do you?' she asks.

'Do I what?'

'Know enough?'

'I don't know shit, Robi. And if I did, I wouldn't say shit.'

'Who is it?'

'You don't wanna know.'

'It's Zoran, right?'

'You don't wanna know, Robi. Believe me. You really don't wanna know.'

Robi stands and walks back into the bedroom to return moments later with a new pack of smokes. She balances one between her lips, flips a light and drags thoughtfully. 'Why didn't you tell me—last night?'

'Would it have made a difference?'

'No.'

'So then what's it matter?'

'It makes a difference now.'

Sandro steps past her silently, tosses his smoke into the garden below. 'I knew nothing 'bout you either. I came here looking for shelter, okay—not to con—'

'So you fucked me for a place to stay. Like a whore.'

It hurts him. Robi can feel the tension suddenly as his eyes darken. 'I'm sorry. That was below the belt.' She smiles at her words. 'Sorry. Jesus, I'm just confused.' She turns from him, heading indoors.

'So'm I, Robi.'

She pauses mid-stride. Turns. He steps to her, and she holds him close. 'God,' she whispers, 'you must be. You really must be so freaked out.' Their lips lock hungrily, hands grasping, and for a brief moment they're transported into a world in which they long to live.

IV

Dusk has fallen, the lounge invaded by pools of crimson and pink straining in through the windows. Sandro lies on his back, watching the patterns form and spoil on the ceiling. Robi rests her head on his chest, her fingers drawing imaginary patterns on his groin, listening to his heart.

'Sandro, I know cops—my dad—they're a tribe. You hurt one of them and you go to war with all of them, you know?'

'Of course, I fucking know.'

'So what are you gonna do now?'

'Run. As far and fast as I can.'

'Where to?'

'Greece. Morocco. Joburg. I don't fucking know.'

'Do you have money?'

'Not a cent.'

'When are you leaving?'

He inhales heavily, caressing her scalp with his fingers, the dreadlocks thick in his hands like serpents. 'It must have taken you a long time to curl your hair like this.'

'Can I come?'

'Where?'

'Wherever you're going. I'll pay my own way—'

'People wanna kill me, Robi. I'm the last person you want to be around.'

'So we'll be fugitives together. Bonny and Clyde—'

'No.'

'I have twenty-thousand dollars. Well, eighteen, I guess.'

Sandro pushes her head off him. 'I'm not someone you want to be around.'

'I know. You're a whore—'

'You say that—just like—'

'Please,' she interrupts, 'take me with you. If it gets dangerous, I'll leave, okay?'

'It's dangerous already.'

'You know what I mean.'

'Robi—'

'I don't wanna lose you, Sandro.' She swallows down emotion. 'I don't wanna wake up tomorrow morning without you. I don't wanna say goodbye—'

'You promise to leave when I say it's too dangerous?'

'I promise.'

Sandro lights a smoke. Turns to the naked girl standing beside him. 'I'm leaving tomorrow.'

'So soon?'

'God, don't start bitching already!'

She laughs throatily. 'Come here and I'll show you how hard I can bitch.'

28. Giorgio Moroder: 'Chase'

I

Inspector Franco Rinaldi walks into the packed pharmacy, a uniformed police officer following closely on his heels, shaded eyes checking out the bikini babes. The shop clears out magically before them. The chemist, a young man with beach-blond hair, smiles at the cops and walks around the counter. He shakes hands with the inspector, nods curtly at the uniformed cop, and waves them toward the rear of the shop.

'I'll be back now,' he calls to a young girl smoking a cigarette at the entrance to the shop, out there in the quickly fading light of evening. She nods her head indifferently.

The chemist leads the cops into a storeroom. He flips a naked bulb to bathe the room in a dim yellow light. 'Can I get you guys anything?'

'We're good,' says Franco Rinaldi. 'But we are in a rush. This could be a matter of life and death.'

Stevie nods. 'Of course, I under—'

"You've seen this man?' interrupts Franco. The policeman slips out a photo. He raps on it with a blunt pencil. 'You're sure, yes?'

'Oh yeah, sure I'm sure,' says Stevie, taking a quick look. 'I called you as soon as I could.'

'When was this?'

'When was what?'

'When did you *see* him?' says Franco.

'Oh. Right. Last night,' replies Stevie, watching the silent cop scribbling on a pad with his blunt pencil. 'It must have been about nine.'

'Nine?'

'Around.'

'Last night?'

'Yeah.'

'And that's as soon as you could?'

'Sorry?'

'You said you called as soon as you could. It's,' Franco checks his wristwatch, 'ten to eight. Almost fucking twenty-four hours since you saw him.'

Stevie shrugs. 'Yeah, right. Well—'

Franco says, '*Where* did you see him? Here?'

'No. On the beach. Well here first, then on the beach—'

'Did he say anything? Where he was going?'

'He said you guys had put a bum-rap on him—to force him to testify or some such shit. I didn't believe it, of course,' he adds quickly. 'Sandro's always been full of shit—I only see the prick when he needs money or dope or whatever—'

'Did you give him any?'

'What, money?' Stevie nods. 'Yeah, I did. I mean, he seemed desperate, so I gave him cash and told him to get lost. Can you believe it—after knowing a guy for three years—'

'Where did he go?'

'Well, I told you when I called, I don't know. I don't. I left him on the beach last night. Maybe he's still there—I don't know.'

Franco digs his hands deep in his pockets. 'Show us where you left him.' The cop shuts the pad and together the trio walk back through the shop. An elderly couple with red and blistered flesh argue over the merits of cream and UV protection and Stevie tells them he'll be right back.

Voices drift to them from the boardwalk café. Tourists stroll on the piazza sweating in the humidity and licking hastily melting ice-cream. Chatting, laughing lovers hold hands on their way through paradise. Light from the boardwalk floods the pebbled beach, causing the Tyrrhenian to reflect yellow as the translucent surf washes up. Stevie leads the cops onto the beach, then a set of old slimy concrete steps that runs over a seeping pipe. He points at a cluster of rocks and a massive boulder jutting up on the beach.

'Over there,' he says.

The cops follow him on, slipping on the pebbles. Stevie takes them to the boulder, around it, over it, and into in a small cove.

'Here?' asks Franco, inspecting his surroundings.

Stevie nods in the dimness. 'Listen, I need to get back—if you need anything else—'

Franco ignores him. Watches him climb back over the boulder. Turns to the cop. 'More than friends,' he says.

The cop raises his brows. 'Sword fighters,' he says and laughs.

Franco ignores him. Looks around. 'You got a flashlight?'

The cop does. Franco grabs it and together they comb the darkness for something—anything. Franco finds a still-damp shirt on the rocks near a grotto in the cove. It's flecked with blood. He lifts it carefully, like it's a booby-trap about to go off.

'Think it's his?'

'Possibly.' He hands the dripping shirt to the cop. 'Let's go, there's nothing here.' They climb back over the rocks, into the light, and hastily step to the boardwalk. They cross the cobbled road, climbing into an unmarked Giulietta, and drive away.

The blond-haired assassin watches them drive off. From the boardwalk café sipping on a cappuccino. He targets-in on Stevie crossing the piazza. He considers following the Alfa briefly but thinks better of it. If the cops had got anything, they wouldn't have been on the beach. Which doesn't mean the pharmacist doesn't know shit. It just means he didn't tell the cops. So first, find out what the pharmacist knows. He lifts his head up at the purple sky with watery blue eyes focusing on the half-moon.

He's close, now. He can sense it.

II

In a silver-slashed carpet does the moon reflect from the horizon on the Tyrrhenian, serenity seeping through Stevie's lips to raise his soul with peace and serenity. Stevie has always loved the sea, a sense of nostalgia for his childhood in Cornwall. He wonders if he'd done the right thing, informing the cops of Sandro's whereabouts. Not that he told 'em anything damning. Nevertheless, he has betrayed an old—well, not friend, lover, he supposes, and thick with thoughts and maybe tinged with regret and a little guilt, he finds himself strolling through the warm water washing up on his ankles. On impulse, he strips naked and dives into the warm cocoon, plunging under the water. Exhilarated. He stares up at the infinite black universe, treads water with his legs, begins swimming out with agile strokes of his powerful arms.

He swims out a long way, careless and confident in his strength against that of the tide that pulls him out with the lights of Villammare and the villas on the hill distant like the stars above. Distant like the world. It's all different out here where Stevie treads, splashing his hands in the suffocating silence. He dribbles the moonlit water between his fingers, body awash with the dark waters of the Tyrrhenian, alone but vital within the eternal space surrounding him.

Something scrapes against his ankle. The hairs on Stevie's body rise erect. He twists his body, staring into the water, looking for shadows beneath the clarity of the moonlight. Nothing stirs down in the black water. It must have been a fish, he thinks. What else! Shaken, though, he realises how very alone—vulnerable—he is out here. Crazy to have swum so far out—alone. He should make his way back to shore.

Whatever it is, it strikes again, harder now, across his buttocks. And suddenly pain shoots through his body as the silver-carpet alters to crimson about his shoulders. Something has fucking attacked him! He sinks his head beneath the water, kicking frantically with his legs. He touches the gash on his ass. It's warm and deep. The night gets dark awful quick, the water chilled. What the fuck is it? He glances around. Panicked.

It's time to *move*!

Get the fuck outta here!

Too late.

The water breaks before him, a silver-cut man rising from the blood and the water. Diabolical pain rushes through Stevie's belly to his throat. He gurgles, watching the blade in the man's hand curl into his throat.

The face is inches from his, *talking*. 'I'm gonna gut you like a pig.'

The blade digs deep across Stevie's neck, cutting off the boy's shout mid-throat. His eyes are wide, pools that shimmer out at the assassin. He wants to shake his head, to plead, *no*, but he realises the smallest twitch and the huge Bowie knife held in the powerful fist will slice through his larynx. Blood is thickening about them, warm as the assassin speaks, so close to Stevie's ear he can feel the words.

'Where is he?' The assassin's power is incredible, legs pushing his thick torso out from the water almost to his belly, his arms free to dig the knife in further. Stevie's sinking further, the blade slicing through flesh. The assassin grabs the kid's hair and twists the head back to release pressure on the thick blade.

'Who,' gasps Stevie, 'who? Who!'

He is nearing hysteria. The assassin has too much experience to allow the boy to freeze. He slaps the kid across the face viciously with the butt of the knife, bone snapping.

'Sandro Lago. What did you tell the police? Where is he? *Tell me!*' The blade's back on Stevie's lacerated throat, the steel beginning to vanish and the blood that drips from the throat thick upon the tranquil Tyrrhenian. *'Tell me now!'*

Stevie gurgles something unintelligible, lips quaking, eyes shut-tight. The blade lifts, allows him an instant to speak—'I don't—know, I don't—' he begs with his face a mask of pure fear, 'please—I don't want to—*die*'—and then he tries to scream but the blade slices the sound away. Terracing the flesh under the blade for the assassin to tear it out with peeling sinew clinging on like Stevie's soul.

'Why did you call the police? If you knew nothing, why did you call the police? You're *lying* to me!'

'No!' Stevie gurgles out blood from his trembling throat, opening his eyes to meet those of the assassin's. 'No!'

The Bowie knife bayonets into his throat. The blade sinks in, slicing through flesh and nerves. Stevie's head bloats, blood streaming from his severed throat. The blade penetrates in further, Stevie's face just a massive black-gaping mouth with a hollowed-out throat vomiting blood and bubbling air. With a vicious jab, the assassin rips the blade out and the boy's insides with it. The head collapses onto its shoulder marionette-like, tendons and muscles gaping like a smashed machine. A pink cloud drifts over the moon as the assassin cuts through the water heading for land with the knife a fin for the powerful arms and striking legs.

III

The car whistles past with its headlights outlining two figures in the Giulietta heading towards Cosenza at 180km/h. Franco searches the blood-stained shirt methodically, excess water dripping onto his crotch. The pockets are empty. He tosses the shirt onto the back seat. Thinking. Frowns suddenly at a matted scratch of paper on his crotch. He lifts it to observe from the light of an approaching car. The police officer at the wheel glances at it swiftly, at the paper in Franco's hand, before returning his stare at the road. 'What is that?'

Franco shrugs. Gingerly, he tries to unfold it, but it's so wet it sluices apart between his fingers. The writing—if there'd ever been any—has faded. 'I don't know, Luigi,' he answers finally, storing the paper within a tiny plastic-bag, 'perhaps the lab will come up with something.' Franco's exhausted. Can't face the hundred-kilometre drive back to Cosenza. 'There's a hotel, there,' he points at an antiquated construction with a neon light flickering at its entrance, Hotel Policastro. 'I'll get a room here. You get this to the lab, okay? As soon as you hear anything, call me. I'll leave a message with reception.' He hands the forensics bag to Luigi, who slows the car at the hotel entrance.

Franco climbs out wearily. He gets a room fast—'If you don't co-operate with me,' he points out to the night manager who'd just informed him there were no rooms available, 'I'll have to inspect every employee's passport starting with yours'—with a splendid view of the Gulf of Policastro. Franco smokes a last cigarette on his balcony and stares out at the dark water before snuggling up in the comfortable bed.

Alessandro Lago is about to get himself killed. He's running from the police straight into the bullet of an assassin. But right now, Franco doesn't give a shit. He just needs to sleep.

To be awakened by the shrilling phone on the bedside table. With shut eyes, Franco searches for the screaming contraption, lifts the receiver with sleep thick in his voice. 'Yes, what is it?'

'Inspector, good morning. The lab's come up with an address, sir—off the paper. It's a chalet in Villammare. It's a rented villa. There was also a name scrawled on the paper.'

'Name?' Franco slides open his eyes and is surprised to see a bright new day out there beyond the shut-tight curtains.

'Robi.'

'Robi?' He throws off the sheets, the sunlight already warm on his naked flesh. 'Pick me up, Luigi. Now!' he orders before slamming down the receiver. Only to lift it again as an afterthought to order breakfast from room-service. He grabs a shower before the food is delivered and washes it all down with four shots of espresso.

His wristwatch shows 9:30am when Luigi finally screams into the parking lot below a morning sky that's turning sombre. A thick grey mass covers an equally grey Tyrrhenian, rushing distant and brooding.

With Franco riding shotgun, Luigi pushes the Alfa to its limits, throwing the car into a series of tight bends and heads up into the hills. Franco wonders if they're not too late, as Luigi manhandles the sluggish engine up the tight road. He slows to turn left onto Via Delle Rose and drives half-way up a gravel road.

'There it is.' Luigi points to a small chalet nestled behind a cluster of tall pine and poplar trees. He parks the car, and they watch a woman walk through the entry gate. She strides to the front door and vanishes inside.

'Stay here,' says Franco to Luigi. 'I'm gonna check this out. If anything happens, call in reinforcements. Understand?'

The cop nods. Disappointed.

'And remember, if you see Lago, do *not* do anything to harm him. We want him alive. Do you understand me?'

'Yes, sir.'

Franco draws out a Beretta from his shoulder holster and checks out his magazine before climbing out from the Alfa. There are no cars in the driveway, the chalet dim beneath the thickening clouds. He creeps to the side of the house, peering in through the kitchen window as a scuttling lizard half-frightens him to death. He observes the woman walking about, shouting. What is it she's saying? Franco studies her lips. Roberta? Is that what the woman's calling? Roberta? Robi ... of course ... Is *she* not Robi? Quickly, Franco paces to the front door and slams his knuckles against the wood. He's about to force the handle when the woman opens it with words already formed on her lips before realising it's not who she was expecting. '*Buongiorno*,' she says, blinking. '*La posso auitare*?'

Franco flashes his badge and brushes past her into the chalet. 'Where are they?'

'Where is who?' she asks, following him as he as he begins to search the house.

Franco slips out a photo from his breast pocket and waves it irritably before the stocky woman's face. 'Him. Have you seen this man?'

Maria shrugs. She's from the south and anything north of Florence is not to be trusted. 'I don't quite—'

'Don't bullshit me, signora. He's a killer—and he's dangerous.' He sees something in her eyes. 'Who is renting this place? Where is Robi?'

Maria shrugs. 'She's gone.'

'Gone? Where?' demands Franco, replacing the photo in his pocket and glancing at the stairs. 'What do you mean—*gone*?'

'All her clothes are gone. Everything.' She pauses, staring into his eyes as a thought traces her mind like constipation. 'D'you think he,' she nods at his breast, 'you think he—'

'Killed her?' Franco helps out. 'He *was* here, then.'

Maria nods.

'Last night?'

'I saw him yesterday afternoon.'

'Did she—Robi—did she have a car?'

'Yes. A grey one.'

'Was it rented?'

'I don't know.'

'What was the registration?'

The woman shrugs.

'And she's taken everything? Clothes, toothbrush—'

'Yes. I went upstairs when I came in thinking they were still, uh, asleep, but—'

'Who leases this place out?'

'Signora Fieri, she's got an agency in town.'

Franco runs to the Giulietta, jumps into the cabin with, 'Turn around and get to Villammare!'

Luigi drops the clutch and slides the car into a noisy 180-degree turn. A red Fiat Ritmo crawls down the hill ahead of them, Franco banging the dashboard with frustration. Christ, he's so fucking *close!* Hours and the fucker would've been his!

'There's an agency in town that rents out villas—'

'Yes, signora Fieri.'

'That's it!'

IV

'No, I've never seen this man,' replies Fieri, studying the monochrome photo on her desk. She looks up at Franco standing above her. Nice eyes, she thinks. Green. 'Should I?'

'You rented a chalet to a woman named Robi—up on the hill. Via Delle Rose twenty-seven.'

'Yes, and so?'

'Where are the papers?'

'The papers—'

'The lease agreement,' snaps Franco. Christ, every fucking second is critical. 'The fucking rental papers, signora. Now!'

'Look, there's no need—'

'I'll get a warrant in five minutes if you force me—'

'There are no papers. You see, she didn't want to sign any documents. She said she valued her privacy.' The woman shrugs. 'I assumed she was trying to get away from something—someone. A bad marriage. Some man—'

'And you allow this type of thing?'

'She paid the lease in advance, inspector. Plus two million for any problems—'

'What you did,' interrupts Franco, 'is highly unethical. Not to mention the circumspect legality.' He leans forward over the desk and eyeballs the woman. 'I'll be sending a colleague here this afternoon. I want you to cooperate fully. Is that under*stood*?'

Signora Fieri nods her head, lighting a Dumont and watching the inspector leave. Nice ass, she thinks.

Drizzle is falling lazily onto the cobbles now when Franco lowers his head and hurries to the Alfa across the piazza. 'Where can we rent a car around here?' he asks, climbing in.

'Inspector, if you wish for a car, out motor-pool will be quite willing to supply—'

'Answer my *question*, fuck it!'

'The closest is Sapri.'

Franco leans forward and punches the dashboard. Luigi flicks on the wipers, the rubber screeching away tiny spittles of rain. 'Hurry,' says Franco, 'to Sapri. We have little time.'

The gulf has vanished behind a thick mass of fog rolling in from the west. Small fishing barges are abandoned along the coast filling with rain and the grey sea crashing mercilessly over the pebbles. Luigi twists on the headlights, the fog and rain diminishing visibility on the tight road.

The rental agency is a private enterprise near the Sapri train station, its dirty showroom crammed with VWs and Fiats. Franco establishes from a floor rep' that the M.D. has not yet arrived, but there is a senior sales-manager, a small man sitting with his legs on a metal desk at the back of the showroom, a receiver completing the gap between raised shoulder and tilted head.

'Thank you, darling,' he mutters into the phone, twisting his body and glancing up at Franco. He motions for him to sit, cupping the receiver. 'I'll be with you in a moment,' he whispers, then nods firmly, 'yes, yes, of course, dear. I'm still here. Look, I have to, yes, I love you too, darling, but I must—no, but ... I—yes, yes, I must go,' he smiles up indulgently at Franco, 'yes, I'll—I'll call you later. Ciao.' He drops the receiver and accepts Franco's badge with a steady hand. 'How may I be of assistance, Inspector,' he checks out the name, 'Rinaldi. I have an aunt named Rinaldi, from Parma—'

'You rented a car to a woman—'

'About ten, fifteen a day, yes,' interrupts the manager, returning the ID. 'That's our business, inspector, hiring cars.'

'I need to see your files for the last two weeks, starting August tenth.'

'Do you have a name?'

'A first name. But it may not be correct. She rented a VW.'

'If you return this afternoon—'

'Signor, uhm—'

'Leonardo. I'm not a Rinaldi, that was my—'

'Signor Leonardo, I need this information now.' Down south, if information is wanted, there's only two methods to get it, thinks Franco: one is to bully these jerks with state power. The other—more efficient and timelier—is to hand the manager a couple of bills and, 'Will this help speed things along?'

Leonardo smiles, standing from behind his desk and makes a show of picking up the bills and counting them. 'You northerners think everything can be bought with a few lire,' he says, holding the cash out at Franco, 'but bribery is unnecessary, Inspector Rinaldi from Milano.' He leads Franco to the filing room. Metal cabinets line the walls, each drawer printed with a month. He opens AGOSTO and slowly skips through the files with his thumb. '*Ecco*,' he says, drawing out a manilla file. 'All our files for this month. Would you like to take a seat, inspector?'

On a plastic chair with the file spread on a metal desk, Franco flips through names, names beginning with a R ... like this one in his hand, this silver Volkswagen GTI I series registered to a Roberta Johnson, on the sixteenth of August, American passport, twenty ... two years of age. Franco nods. Instinct. This is her. Roberta Johnson—*Robi*. Who the fuck is she?

'May I keep this?' Franco inquires, back in the manager's office.

'I'll make you a copy.'

They return to the showroom. A red Fiat pulls up onto the sidewalk outside, headlights dim under the sweltering rain. Leonardo inserts the file into a photocopier, waits for the exposure to slide out, and hands the paper to Franco. 'Five hundred for the copy, inspector.' He waits for the money before turning and walking back to the filing room. 'And best of luck.'

Franco folds the page and deposits it into his pocket. It's only time now before the VW is located. He's found Lago. The only problem is the woman. Where the hell had she come from? Why is she assisting him, this dirty, drug-addicted whore? Where does she fit in?

There's a payphone further down the block. Franco lifts the collar to his jacket and runs out into the wind and rain. The Fiat has its headlights on, the driver silhouetted behind a misted-over windscreen, a constant plume of smoke drifting up from the exhaust.

Franco shuts himself within the cubicle with the phone and the ghastly scent of urine. Lifting the receiver, he places a collect call with the operator to Milan. 'Chief Inspector Virdis, please.' He waits a while, before, 'I've got it,' he says, 'I'm going to set-up a roadblock, all points heading north. He's with a girl by the name of Roberta Johnson, American passport number,' his eyes stray toward a tobacconist shop with the local paper in the window, the headline screaming into his mind, the photo staring out accusingly from behind a tear-filled window. 'Listen, chief inspector, I'll call you later. I gotta move.' He hangs up the receiver abruptly, eyes unable to stray from the photo. The stench is suddenly nauseating, like the smell of death, and he's grateful for the cleansing rain as he steps out of the booth and walks toward the tobacconist in a daze. He lifts the local paper and flips a coin at the tobacconist. Rushes back to the Alfa where Luigi waits with a smoke dangling from his lips.

'Look at this,' says Franco, and throws the paper at Luigi.

Luigi scans the photo and first paragraph briefly before lifting his head. Franco stares out from the misted-over window, at a pool of water rippling under the fierce downpour on the pools on the sidewalk.

'Do you think Lago did this?'

'Who else?' replies Franco, staring at the photo and the headline. MAN FOUND DECAPITATED ON VILLAMMARE

BEACH. 'Come, Luigi, let's get some espresso somewhere. I'm tired, and I have a story to tell.' He grabs the police radio.

Luigi starts the engine and rolls down his window. He tosses the paper out onto the wet sidewalk and rolls over it. It catches a gust of wind, the front page separating and rising, Stevie's face sweeping into the windscreen of a red Fiat Ritmo accelerating away from the rental agency.

Fishermen stumble about town in drunken stupors, slipping in from one bar to the next knowing their barges, rotten and hardly seaworthy, will not be launched today and there's nothing for it but to wait the storm out. Eventually, the clouds will break, and they will again fish and the children will again be fed, and the wives will again spread their legs in the heat of a Tyrrhenian summer-night.

29. Doctors Cat: 'Feel the Drive'

I

'That handle there, I think,' offers Sandro, pointing at a thin stick exiting from behind the VW's steering-wheel. She tries it and the wipers scrape off the water from the rear windscreen. Only it's a car in front that slams on brakes suddenly with red taillights fluid in the rain. Robi hits the brake pedal too hard, the GTI fishtailing for an instant. Instinctively, she counter-locks the slide. The VW contemplates spinning out of control before swinging its ass back on course.

Robi swallows. 'Jesus.'

'That was great.'

'Cars are dangerous.'

'That's the idea. Only shit drivers get scared.'

'My mom died in a car accident,' she informs him with a hot glance. 'Was she a shit driver too?'

'I never met her,' he replies, lighting a Camel. The smoke is heavy in the car, fogging the already misted windows.

'Will you *kill* that!'

Sandro slips open the ashtray and crumples the cigarette. 'Is something bugging you?'

'No.'

'Look,' he persists, turning to her, 'if you're having second doubts or—'

'Thoughts. And I'm not.' She flashes him a re-assuring smile. 'I'm just a bit on edge.'

'Didn't notice.' He touches her naked leg and squeezes. 'Let's stop at the next hotel.'

'Yeah, okay, I think that's a good idea. This weather's really shitting me off.'

Red lights explode ahead, a stream of them, each applied within a fraction of the next. The car ahead brakes and Robi slows the VW and takes a long right hander. And then they see it. Blue lights flashing in the nebulous light of the rain and wind.

'Cops,' she whispers, glancing at Sandro. 'It's a fucking roadblock!'

'*Porca troia.*' He should have expected a roadblock. He's being so stupid! What's wrong with his fucking *mind!* Okay,' he says, 'this is what we're gonna do. I'm gonna jump out and cross the block on foot. You drive through it, and I'll meet you on the other side. Now slow down, but don't stop.'

'Sandro—'

'*Do it!*' His eyes stare ahead at the road littered with three blue Giuliettas silhouetted purple in the twilight. 'If you get stopped, deny everything. I'll meet you in Milano. Do you know—'

'I know nowhere in Milan!'

He brushes his hands through his hair irritably. 'Let's hope you don't get stopped then. If you do,' he touches her cheek, 'then destiny's destiny and you don't deserve me.' He swings open his door, forcing her to touch her anchors instinctively when his body vanishes out into the gloomy day. The door dangles open. Robi curses, leans over and slams it shut. She checks out her rear-view, but he's vanished. She thinks he's lucky. The car ahead stops, Robi following suite, peering again at her rear-view. There's a car behind now, its headlights bright and wet in the gloom, but it isn't making itself conspicuous. Sandro has made it!

The car ahead pulls off with a cop in a fluorescent yellow uniform waving it on. The cop waves her to a halt and she watches him step to her with a flashlight lighting the cascading water in gold. He gestures for her to roll down her window. Robi complies, her heart thundering. The cop shines the flashlight into her eyes, then directs the beam onto the passenger seat. A pack of Camels lie on the seat. The cop redirects the beam into her eyes.

'*Sono le tue*?' he asks, pointing to the cigarettes with his flashlight.

She shrugs. 'No capish Italian,' she says. Then, with hesitant hands, she takes out a Camel and offers it to the cop.

'No,' he says, '*aspetta qui.*' He shines the beam about the car one last time, then flips it off and walks back to one of the patrol cars blocking off the road. The afternoon light is dying now. He speaks into a two-way, body caught in the VW's headlights with water falling heavily on his yellow raincoat. His head is turned to her. Christ, why is he taking so long! She lights the Camel and takes a heavy drag, watching through a haze of smoke at the cop returning slowly towards her. He pauses at the head of the car, leans over and shields his eyes from the glare of the headlights to check the registration. Then he steps around the car to appear at her window once more.

'*Passaporto.*'

She leans over to her money-belt. Zips it open. Extracts a roadmap, then a passport that falls to the floor. She unbuckles her seatbelt, smiling apologetically at the carabiniere before leaning over the gearshift to retrieve the passport. Gives him a good look at her tits. Hands over the passport with a big smile. He flips through it, checking something out on his clipboard.

'Mrs Roberta Johnson,' he announces, snapping the passport shut.

'Miss,' corrects Robi. Big smile.

He nods his head, hands back the passport, and waves her on. Robi shifts the gear into first, her palms sweating on the lever. 'And drive careful.' She forces the clutch out and rolls away, passing the flashing blue lights before accelerating away, remembering suddenly to breathe!

Now where the hell is Sandro? Night has set in fast.

A silhouette suddenly appears on the road ahead of her, arms waving frantically. Robi slams on the brakes, the VW gripping tar and sliding to rest two feet from the figure that runs through her headlights. The door on the passenger side cracks open and Sandro climbs into the cabin. He's wet, face shimmering. He slams the door, the cabin lights extinguish, and he waves them on. She slips out the clutch, front tyres slipping momentarily. She glances in her rear-view. Two headlights follow distantly.

'You took so long. What the fuck happened?' he asks, running his hands through damp hair.

'They just checked out my passport.'

'Did they say anything?'

'Yes. They told me to be careful.' She turns to him. 'I'm here, ain't I?'

Sandro shrugs. 'It's destiny I guess.'

The car behind has caught the VW, headlights on bright, casting crazy shadows within the cabin. It pulls out from behind the VW, and they watch as a Giulietta speeds up beside them, slowing to their pace. The driver flips on a flashlight in the Alfa, waving it up and down in the darkness.

'Who the fuck are they?' she asks.

'Cops.' Sandro lowers his body in the seat. 'They tricked you, Robi. They fucking tricked you! Pull over. This is where it gets dangerous. Pull the car over. There.'

'No.'

'Do it *now*!' he snaps with his voice overriding the two engines and the noise entering as the two cars speed side-by-side.

'I said no!'

The flashlight focuses onto her eyes, blinding her. Then sirens whoop from the car. She twists her head away, eyes straying from the road. She slams down two gears, the VW kicking forward on its powerband. The Alfa's headlights swing in behind them as Robi changes up to fourth without lifting her foot from the accelerator, the revs reaching the limiter and forcing the car to stumble off-stride. Ahead, in the darkness, blue lights and headlights appear from above the crest of a rise. The wipers whip furiously at the storm striking the windscreen at over 180km/h, focusing and un-focusing the approaching lights in Robi's windscreen.

'Jesus, we're going straight at them!' Sandro says.

Robi turns to him, her eyes searching his purple profile for aid. Please, Sandro, this is all for you, can't you understand?

'There!' Sandro points through the rain. There's a slip-road ahead, closing in rapidly along with the approaching flashing blue lights. The Giulietta following finally forces its way beside the VW once more, its horn screaming now.

Robi slams her feet onto the clutch and brake pedals simultaneously, the car lurching sideways on the wet road. She flips down to second, lets out the clutch, and loses the VW completely. It fishtails on two-lane road, heading for the tall pine trees flashing before the spinning car. She jams on the brakes and handbrake, the car skimming on, tyres scraping off speed 'til it smashes into a tree. Sandro's door bends inwards, but the impact's easy, the engine still turning and Robi slams in first gear and kicks the car forward. Front tyres spinning, the VW struggles for grip. The Giulietta's stopped a hundred metres up ahead, lying broadside across the slip-road. Behind them, police cars close in fast.

'You haven't got space!' shouts Sandro as they approach the Giulietta. Two silhouettes are visible within the blue Alfa as Robi doesn't lift, foot flat, wheel gripped white-knuckled, and charges right at the Giulietta.

'Jesus!' screams Sandro.

Robi tries and fails to fit the VW between the stationery Alfa and the pine trees for access to the slip-road just beyond it.

'What the fuck are you doing!' shouts Sandro as headlights shatter and the Alfa is barged sideways by the VW tearing through with a biting stab of shattering glass and shearing metal.

Robi keeps her foot down. Takes the narrow slip-road that heads uphill now, trees whipping past, the VW's tyres scratching for grip on the wet earth. Sandro turns in his seat, staring back at the headlights chasing. 'They're gaining,' he says.

'What now?'

'I don't know! Fuck. I thought you were a careful driver!'

'I am. What now!'

'I don't *know*!' He falls back on the seat, slamming his palms onto the windscreen. 'Fuck this rain!' The road narrows even further as they enter a small village, their headlights silhouetting figures and obstacles whizzing past in a galactic whirl. Stone buildings hang over the road claustrophobically as Robi weaves this way and that, inches from collecting cars parked on the diminutive sidewalks.

Sandro turns in his seat, thumping the headrest. 'We're losing 'em.' The police can't compete. Sandro realises this suddenly. Where they have survival, the cops have only procedure. Innocent bystanders must be protected at all costs. They won't shoot through a village at 160km/h. It dawns on him suddenly that escape is feasible, the VW lifting in the air, falling hard. Hits the bump-stops. But Robi's got it covered, her mind working at faster than the 175km/h registering on the speedometer. The road ahead forks and Sandro says, 'Take a left!' as he suddenly recognises the road from some party back-when with Stevie.

She does, swinging the car left and onto a gravel road. The road's unlit, headlights flashing bends with instants to spare as Robi forces the VW hard into a deepening forest. The road rises steeply now, the bends sweeping incessantly as the sliding tyres throw up gravel and mud. She catches a momentary glimpse of headlights glimmering erratically through the trees. 'Where does this road go?' she asks, shifting down for a sharp right.

'Into the mountains. There's a four-way intersection ahead, you keep going straight.' They lose speed as the VW struggles up a long incline. Robi slings the car into second and they go airborne over the ridge. The intersection lies ahead, four tiny roads splitting off into the trees, four rotten signs on a pale post proclaiming God-forgotten places, one horse towns where the horses died as foetuses. She keeps accelerating straight on the road that climbs once more. Sandro watches the horizon brighten behind the VW as a car approaches the crest of the hill behind them. It fades, the back windscreen wipers swinging away the thick water for the lights to be replaced immediately. Now!

'Kill your lights!'

Robi hesitates.

'Fuck it!' he screams, swinging his hand past her shoulder and onto the light-switch. The world flips to black in an instant. Instinctively, Robi floors the brake pedal. The headlights behind are almost over the crest. Moments and they'll be over and know which road they've taken! Sandro punches her hard, on the leg, forcing her foot to wield off the pedal. The car lurches, momentum shifting convulsively. And suddenly they're spinning away into the night, the windscreen shattering and trees and stumps smashing through into the cabin. Sandro's body gets thrown about as the car starts to roll and tumble away.

It rolls onto its roof in slow motion, smoke rising in the rain. Robi unbuckles her seatbelt and collapses onto the roof and slithers through the shattered windshield. She crawls to the edge of the car and glances into it. Sandro's not in the wreck. She blinks, smelling gasoline, and watches headlights vanish as a car on the road high above the thick barrier of trees about her speeds past. She listens. Expecting to hear it slow, voices, but the engine's fading, *leaving*! She realises she's unhurt. Though her legs will not cease shaking.

'Sandro!' she calls. 'Where are you! *Sandro*!'

'I'm okay,' he says, walking up beside her with his footsteps muted by the thumping rain on the soft soil. He runs his arms about her shoulders, holding her close and smelling her fear. 'You were fucking awesome!'

She cracks his face with an open hand. A fearsome slap that knocks him back a pace. 'Why did you hit me?' she says, waves at the wreck. 'You could have fucking *killed* us.'

Sandro rubs water from his face. 'We're still alive, aren't we? They woulda seen your brake lights—they would have found us, worked out which road we took. I just wanted to pull to the side of the road,' he adds. He looks at the wreck and laughs. 'Hey, you sure have a story to tell now.'

'Yes, and no one to tell it too.'

'Get your stuff and let's get the fuck outta here. Leave your backpack.'

'Are you crazy—'

'Trust me, Robi.'

The rain's subsiding a bit, the night damp and cold on their wet bodies as they begin to trek. Sandro trails first, taking the lead and heading deeper into the forest. He rips at the branches and twigs with his free arm. 'Shield your eyes!' he warns and Robi gasps when a twig slices across her face, her legs still stumbling with delayed shock and drying adrenaline. 'Keep moving. Keep walking!'

The ground is muddy, their shoes sliding as they keep climbing. Her breath comes in gasps as she forces her legs onward, his arm half-dragging her along. She can't keep up with his pace, twisting her perspiring hand from his. He slows for her, waiting between thick brush with his shirt dirty and shoes brown with clotted mud. 'C'mon, Robi, we can do this. Just focus your mind! Pain is ecstasy.'

'Fuck you,' she says, but grabs his moist hand anyway as he forces her forward. Loses his footing and stumbles in the mud. Maintaining pace becomes impossible, the trees too compact, the underbrush jagged and treacherous. But he still won't cease, creating a path for her in the void, stumbling, falling. The ground gives way beneath her feet. She falls chin first.

'C'mon, Robi!'

'Fuck you,' she hisses, but she gets up and pushes on, anyway.

Her legs tremble with exhaustion. Cramping. A peculiar greyness falls about them. The wind is fresh, cutting the mist. The rain, somewhere in the night, had ceased without her noticing and she crashes onto her knees for Sandro to drag her on for a while before realising that she's not getting up. Releasing her hand from his vice-grip, Robi grabs for her leg, nauseated at the tearing pain on her calf. He slaps her calf hard, rubbing the flesh as she bites her fists. Then the spasm lets go and she lays back, wasted. Sandro falls beside her. And sleep comes instantly with the first rays of dawn.

II

He's awakened by the sound of chopping. Not trees. *Choppers!* He brushes open his eyes, blinking at the harsh light that stings his consciousness. The chopper's somewhere above, but he can't spot it, the canopy of trees about him blocking out the pursuers. Robi sits up beside him, listening.

'Are they—'

He holds up his hand, demanding silence. Robi finds her overnight and lights up two smokes. Hands him one.

'They looking for us?' she asks as the rotors fade into the day and the forest explodes into a buzz of a thousand sounds.

'Yeah, for sure.' He stands wearily, dragging on the smoke. 'You have something to eat?'

Robi shakes her head. She surveys the thick cluster of trees about her, shadows falling on the dark, muddy ground. 'Any idea where we are?'

'I'm no Cousteau.'

She smiles at him. 'Nature's calling.'

Sandro watches her squat behind an immense oak tree. Food is now everything.

'What time is it?' he asks as Robi steps behind him, drip-drying.

'Two. Just past.'

'We must move.'

'Did you have something else in mind?' she asks.

He smiles ruefully. 'There should be a village around here somewhere. It's fucking Italy. We'll find something eventually.'

'I hope so, Sandro. I'm starving.'

Sandro leads her on, up-slope, his arms and legs grabbing at trees and roots for the slope rises precipitously for about two hundred metres. The grass is thick here, helping them grip the ground, the trees stable under their grasping hands. Finally reaching the crest, Sandro climbs up and finds a dirt road. He kneels and studies the tyre prints. They're clear and fresh. Robi clambers up onto the road, sweating and swearing. The day is thick with humidity, the air stagnant and dense. There's no sign of yesterday's storm.

'What are you, Tonto?' she asks.

'Who?'

'The—oh, never mind. What are you doing?'

'Car tracks,' he says, and shows her. 'Means someone's used this road during the night. Means somewhere here there's something worth driving to.'

They follow the road north. Conversation is too much effort as their bodies ache at the sustained pace. The light fades, plunging the road and the forest into eclipse-like-shadow. The sun has descended completely when the road twists into a village of red-stone houses in the gloom of dusk.

A donkey-cart passes them, the animals' hooves clapping on ancient cobbles. Children run about dreamily, lights already on in the stone buildings. The village rests at the foot of a tall mountain peak that rises above the village for hundreds of feet, grasping the darkening sky like an accusing, jagged finger.

'You have money?' inquires Sandro as they pass the oak-doors to the Albergo delle Orchidee. Robi nods. Sandro swings open the door and enters a small lobby with a chandelier illuminating the yellow-pool wood. A man stands behind a small reception desk, scarred like the walls, and tosses two letters into pigeon-holes behind him.

'Buonasera,' calls Sandro, standing before the desk. *'Abbiamo bisogno di una stanza,'* he says in halting Italian when the man turns to cast thick malevolent eyes onto them. 'We—Americani. Turisti. Only dollars, is okay?'

The man looks from him to Robi. *'Sono cinquanta mille lira al giorno. Ciascuno. Per quanti giorni?'*

'How long we gonna stay?' asks Sandro. 'Two days?'

'Yeah, sounds good.'

'Due giorni. Cinquanta dollari al giorno?'

The man nods. *'Bene. Firma il libro, per piacere.'* He reverses the reception book at Sandro, who scrawls illegibly. The header on the book reads 1879—1929. The man rings a bell and a porter saunters down a flight of stairs.

'Stanza cinque, Beppe,' the old man hands the key over to the porter before turning to Sandro. *'Avete valigie?'*

'No, stiamo faccendo un hike. Prima che ci sposiamo'

The man smiles and watches the couple follow the porter up the stairs. *'Buona fortuna col matrimonio,'* he mumbles to their backs.

In the room, Robi says, 'What did he say?'

'He wanted to know where our bags were.'

'What did you tell him?'

He looks at her. 'I told him we were on a hike. Before our wedding. It's just our thing.'

She frowns. Looks at him. 'You look like you've been married for a century,' she says, pinching his swollen, dirty cheeks. 'Do you think the cops have put out our photos?'

He shrugs. 'Down here in the south, it won't matter,' he says and hopes it's true.

30. Italian Boys: 'Midnight Girl'
I

Franco sips the espresso from a tiny cup, a cigarette burning idly in an ashtray by his hand. He glances at his wristwatch for the dozenth time. Eight am. Virdis will have arrived at the office. He dials the number on the hotel-room phone.

'Chief Inspector Virdis' office.'

'Hi, Dani, it's Franco.'

'Franco, he just walked in.'

There's a click and Virdis' voice echoes down the receiver. 'Franco. What's happening?'

Franco takes a deep drag of his smoke before replying. 'They ran through a roadblock, about fifty kilometres north of Sapri.'

'I don't quite follow, Franco.' Oh, he understands, thinks Franco. What's there not to fucking follow? Only Virdis has a strange way of dealing with disappointment and mounting anger.

'I organised five roadblocks on all the major routes out of the Villammare region. Orders were to stop the Volkswagen only if Lago was in the car. If he wasn't, they were to allow this Roberta Johnson girl to pass through and to follow until she contacted Lago.

'At about seven last night, the VW was seen heading north on the SP16 towards Tortorella. Lago was not in the vehicle, so they let the girl pass. She picked him up less than a kilometre past the block. They—we pursued—but Lago gave us the slip by running through a goddamn village at two hundred kilometres an hour. This kid is outta control, chief inspector.

'We discovered the car this morning at five, completely written off down a goddamn ravine. But there was no trace of them. We called in the dogs—however, it's proving difficult to track them 'cause the area's so hilly and unpredictable. And, of course, they had a ten-hour head start. A chopper's been scanning the area since dawn, but again, chief inspector, they came out empty. I'm afraid there's been nothing positive. They're somewhere in the Parco Nazionale del Cilento, that I'm sure of. But—it's pretty wild in there, a whole lot of nothing and nothing else but. And we can't count on the locals, you know what they're like down here, they'd sooner help a serial killer than have anything to do with the cops.'

Silence for a while before Virdis says, 'If you could apprehend criminals, Inspector Rinaldi, like you file reports over the phone, we'd live in a crimeless world.'

Franco kills his smoke. 'Inspector Rinaldi', he thinks. Not a good sign when Virdis uses your official title. He sips on the cold coffee, listening to Virdis breathe.

'Okay,' says Virdis eventually. 'While you've been away, we've dug up some interesting things on this Roberta Johnson girl. I'll fax you the stuff via Cosenza. There's nothing in it to help you, though. Nothing to explain why she's involved with Lago.'

'She has no connections?' Franco lights another MS, watching the flame of his matchstick momentarily.

'No, not as far as I can see. But I have some contacts in Chicago, I'll see what more I can dig up. There's got to be something of course, some link between those two.'

'She's a damn gutsy driver,' mutters Franco, regretting it instantly.

There's a heavy silence before Virdis speaks. 'We're running a story on all the major newspapers—and on radio during the day and the main news bulletin on RAI tonight. There's a suspicion that Lago murdered that guy in Villammare—uhm—'

'Stevie Friers.'

'That should at least tighten the net over our Bonny and Clyde—'

'That could be dangerous, sir. Lago's an addict and probably suicidal. And this girl doesn't take any credit when it comes to caution.'

Virdis sighs down the receiver. 'It's a risk we've have to take. The word on the street is Zoran's hired a big-time assassin for the kill. He's serious about wasting Lago. And that tells me this Lago knows something we want to know. We just need you to bring him in, Franco, bring him in breathing and able to talk.'

'Has surveillance on Zoran Santana picked anything up?'

'No. The assassin is here. That's all we know. But that's not your concern. I will cover that end. You lead the search on that end.

This assassin comes with impeccable credentials, Franco, so find me Lago before he finds this killer's bullet.'

'You have zip on the assassin?'

'Nothing. 'cept this: the corpse you found at the villa. His name was Luca Bergamo,' Virdis says, 'a rap-sheet the size of his intestines. Four convictions, assault and bodily harm. And that's it. Except for that Stevie guy.'

'What about him?'

'I figure the assassin killed him because he knew that Friers spoke to you, Franco.'

Franco blinks. 'What do you mean?

'I'm figuring the assassin followed you to Villammare. Saw you interviewing that Stevie guy.'

'Jesus,' whispers Franco, trying and finding no other conclusion. 'Jesus.'

'Which means he could be near you right now, you following me, Franco? I need you to be careful,' says Virdis. 'And whatever you do, don't lead the killer to Lago. You understand? Because then it'll be both Lago and your fucking funeral we'll be attending.'

Franco crunches the MS into the overflowing ashtray and drops the receiver pensively.

II

It's dusk when Sandro climbs off the vast bed with its solid oak pillars and paddles to the veranda with his feet sinking into the plush carpet. The valley is awash with shadow below a golden-streaked sky. A chilly breeze blows up at him from the hills, causing him to shiver and rub his arms with his palms. A hand cups his scarred buttocks, fondling him quickly, and he turns to Robi with a cautious smile.

'You look real sexy standing there.' She slips beside him, flesh on cold flesh, her hair messy and tangled. She stares about her, folding her arms about her breasts and fingers massaging her shoulders. 'It's getting cold.'

'*L'Estate sta finendo*,' he says.

'What?'

'Summer's coming to an end. It's a song.'

Sandro follows her into the room, shutting the veranda doors behind him. She collapses on the tiny couch and lights up a smoke.

Sandro jumps onto the bed, finding a smoke and catching the light she tosses at him.

'You did good the other night, Robi.'

'It feels like a dream.' But when her eyes gaze at him, Robi recalls the fear with too much clarity, even for a nightmare. 'We broke through a police roadblock, escaped from God-knows how many pigs, and we hardly even know each other. That's strange, Sandro. This is *really* strange.'

'We know each other.'

'Yeah, I guess we do, don't we. Even if we know nothing about each other.'

'The past is irrelevant, Robi. What we've done alone, we've done alone, and it means nothing now—now that we ... have each other. Who gives a shit how many fucks you've had in your life, or, or, what results you scored at school—'

'Do you wanna know?' Robi stares at him through a cloud of smoke.

'Know what?'

'How many times I've been fucked?' She smiles as his cock stiffens. 'The past helps us understand the present,' she tells him. 'Helps us understand each other better.' She stands and paddles before him, naked. As she kneels up on the bed to lay her head on his crotch, he watches the purple-brown bruise on her leg. She drags on the smoke. The breeze grows louder beyond the room, a car audible somewhere below. Music filters from one of the adjoining rooms—Duran Duran? A clock ticks beside the bed, long hand vibrating with a mechanical heartbeat. To be that beat, thinks Sandro. Constant and experiencing nothing.

'Why are you doing this?' He sucks up nicotine down a phlegm-raked throat. 'Why you fucking up your life to help me? I just don't understand, Robi.'

'Tell me something first.'

'What?'

'Why did you—that night, you remember, in the truck, why did you tell me you knew people at the hotel?'

'I do.'

'Don't lie to me, Sandro.'

He cleans out an ear-hole. 'Truth?'

'No more lies.'

'You said something, that night, something about,' trying to recall in the mist of his mind, 'about trust, or—' and it comes back, 'not trusting anyone anymore. So I thought I may as well give you a reason. Does that make sense?'

'No.'

'Well, that's the best I got. So why are you doing this?'

'Does it sound corny if I said I want to do something—' she hesitates. Why? She recalls asking herself that question before falling asleep last night after dinner, after having made love to him—why *is* she helping him? To do something that matters—something—'Right.'

'I'm not a good cause.'

'You're innocent, aren't you?' She glances at his silent face gazing back at her.

'That still doesn't answer my question.'

'If you understood where I came from, my past, you'd understand.'

He smiles, lowering his gaze on his smoke. 'You told me your mom died in a car accident.'

'Yes, when I was fifteen. Are your folks still alive?'

Sandro shrugs. 'I don't know. We drifted apart. Last time I spoke to my mom was about two years ago, I think. Were you close to your family?'

She smiles with obvious warmth in her recollections. 'Mom was my only friend when I was growing up. My dad ran out on us when I was young. I didn't even remember him. I raised my brother in the afternoons after school, you know? In the evenings, we'd sit around and, you know, just hang out and help with my brother—Richard—with his homework and crap.' She blinks away a tear and nods. 'Yeah, we were close.'

'It must have been a bummer—her death?' Sandro plays with her hair in his fingers, the room gloomy with the setting sun beyond the veranda.

She lights up with his Camel. 'My dad came back after mom's—after mom died. To—*take care* of us. I was far too young to support myself and my brother. He was only ten. What was I going to do? Run away with him and work the streets?' She glances at him quickly, glassy eyes shimmering in the gloom. 'Instead,' she says, 'I became ... For months after he came back, he told me if I didn't give him, if I didn't give him a good time, he'd ... That's how it all started—him beating Richard so often with this fucking *thong* and Richard trying to be a big man about it all. Jesus. I'd sworn on Mom's grave to look after Richard, no matter what—it's what she would have expected, you know? And he kept beating Richard, and never me. Until the day it all made sense. If I was prepared to—if I … he would stop with the beatings.' She swallows hard, the tears now unable to resist the form of her face to roll into her mouth. He holds her tight, not knowing what to say. Holds her, pain escaping from her warm body. Knowing, understanding—and completely incapable of casting away her agony. She composes herself, brushing away the tears. She clears her throat and whispers croakily, 'It went on for almost a year.'

His hands play with the hot tears on her face.

'And then—this—I was coming back, from a club, not exactly sober, you know, and I—outside Richard's room and I heard someone—moaning, and so I walked in—and—and there he was, my fucking father,' Robi stares into the room like it's all happening before her, 'his body smashing into, just—'

Robi stands and drifts away from him. 'So I ran into his room, I knew where he kept his gun, you know, and—' she spreads the thin curtains from the veranda doors to stare out at her pale reflection. 'When I got back to Richard's room again, he—he was pretending, you know, that nothing happened, you're drunk, Robi, and Richard, he was, he was just sitting there staring at me, like he expected something, just staring at me, willing me—so I—' she turns to him with her mouth twisted in disgust, 'I shot my dad,' she says, her eyes shut and body numb, 'I shot the sonofabitch. I aimed that gun at his chest and I pulled the trigger and I shot him. And the bullet, the bullet—the bullet somehow went through his neck and—and—I shot 'em all,' she whispers and doubles over, 'I killed them all,' she says, 'I fucking unloaded the entire—I killed them both,' she says and bends over and wretches on the carpet.

Sandro steps from the bed and helps her up. He carries her to the bed like she's deadweight, laying her down gently. He touches her fever-hot flesh. Wipes the vomit from her lips with the back of his hands. He strides to the bathroom, finds a towel, wets it with warm water. She hasn't stirred when he comes back and begins mopping up the still-warm, oozing fluid on the floor.

'I'll do it,' she whispers wearily. 'I'm sorry, Sandro. I don't know what happened. I thought …'

He twists the towel into a bundle and steps past her. Dumps the towel into the bathtub, holding back his own nausea, and washes his hands while staring at his face in the dark mirror. What the fuck is he doing? he asks his reflection and answers, surviving,

Sandro, you're surviving as always. And you've done worse than clean up puke.

Sitting beside her on the bed now, he touches her warm forehead with his lips. 'You're beautiful,' he whispers.

Is it only survival?

Robi holds him close. He can smell the vomit in her breath, and it does not disgust him. *'You're* beautiful, Sandro.'

He understands, slowly penetrating her now, drawing her up gently, rhythmically, as the last rays of day vanish beyond the valley and the mountain is a giant silhouette over the black land.

III

They're back. In violent waves of a million polluting heaps of processed metal clogging the roads in gaseous clouds of bestial desire, butchering one another in sublime, ghoulish ignorance. The sidewalks are bursting, spewing forth filth—girl-whores and boy-whores, woman-whores and men-whores, rats and pigeons and beggars, winos, druggies, muggers, clerks—*vermin*. And staring down at them all—the infector of the vermin. Welcome to the new century, thinks Zoran, looking down at Milan from twenty floors above in the golden-hued Torre Velasca.

Assholes.

Zoran leans over the veranda of his penthouse, hands clasped about the metal railings, and hurls a chunky piece of gob down at the vermin. Milan extends far into the hazy night. Lights never ending as a three-quarter moon ascends anaemically.

'Phone call from your buddy,' rasps Giovanni from within the penthouse. 'He sounds irritated.'

Zoran takes a last glimpse at the city, then up at the blackness. He sighs, turns, and follows Giovanni into the penthouse. He grabs a Peroni from the refrigerator and the phone off the wall.

'Hey, what's happening?'

'We need to meet,' says the voice in his ear.

Zoran sips on the Peroni. 'Is it done?' He shrugs at Giovanni, listening in the doorway.

'At midnight. The station. Bring cash. Fifty grand.'

'What—' but the line snaps and sizzles and then dies. 'Hullo?' There's no reply and Zoran slams down the receiver. 'Christ, fuck it!' he explodes, brushing past Giovanni. 'He wants to meet—tonight. He wants more fucking money.'

Giovanni says, 'That's unusual.'

Silently, Zoran marches to the veranda and vanishes outside. 'Fuck you all!' he screams down at the vermin, 'you fucking peasants!' And hurls the Peroni down into the night.

IV

It's happened! The assassin's made contact! Virdis storms into his office, grabbing the phone and barks, 'I want all available detectives here in my office in an hour! *One* hour!' He hangs up, grabs his chair, and thinks, Christ, he's *this* close, as close as the phone shrilling by his elbow. He grabs the receiver fast. '*What*!'

'Giuseppe, ciao.'

'Gina? Gina, what's wrong?' His wife hasn't phoned him at work in—must be three years, he thinks, since their daughter Rina had left for college. 'All okay with Rina?'

'Nothing's wrong, *bello*. You coming home soon?'

'Why? I mean—'

'Just come. I've got dinner in the oven, candles, champagne. It'll be like the old days.'

'Darling, I wish I could—'

'So make all your wishes come true, *amore*,' she interrupts promisingly.

'I can't. Something's about to break—'

'Our marriage, Giuseppe. That's what's about to *break*. Please, *amore*, I can't stand this any longer.'

'Gina, look, after tonight it'll be different. I promise. I love you, *carissima*. I do. But tonight is important—'

'*To me*!' shouts his wife. 'It's our fucking anniversary!' The line dies abruptly. Virdis stares at the phone in his hand, curses, and stoops to re-dial as a man steps into the office.

'Inspector Dabia, reporting for duty, sir,' announces the tall, bearded man.

'Are you alone?'

'I passed Pascale on the corridor.'

Virdis replaces the receiver and crosses to the detective.

'I'm going to the boardroom. I want you to assemble everyone and get them there. ASAP.'

V

Zoran steps through the massive swing doors and into Milan's central station. The house Mussolini built. Fat and grandiose, Zoran thinks. Just like every other man of substance. The huge all-night cafeteria is practically empty but for a Japanese trio conversing over espressos. A young girl stands just outside, browsing through a copy of *Vogue*. The girl spots Zoran over her *Vogue* and looks him over with a heavily tarted-up face and rouged mouth forming a concentric O. Zoran swings his stride in her direction with eyes alert and erratic.

'Do you have a message for me?' he asks the girl. She stands taller than he in six-inch stilettos.

'Depends on who you are, *amore*,' she whispers, touching his face.

He grabs her wrist and bends it without exertion. 'Don't fuck with me, *puttana*.'

'You haven't paid, baby,' she says, not in the least intimidated by the pain etched on her face.

Zoran draws out his Gucci wallet and peels off a few notes to slip into her blouse with his finger touching her nipple. 'Where?'

'In the subway.'

Zoran spins away from her, hurrying back towards the exit. He steps out, down to the road and further, into the sharp-lit subway. A shuttle wheezes off into the cylindrical shaft. Squatting before a vast underground map, a hiker cross-references with a pocket-map in his hand. A kid rests in a heap beside a pillar covered in graffiti. Two suited men are discussing something in harsh tones, hands waving about. Zoran stands and looks around. And then, finally, he spots the assassin. He has been there the whole time, a man dressed in a grey suit and charcoal shoes, standing to Zoran's right near the public lavatories, blond hair indistinguishable beneath a baseball cap. Their eyes meet. Or Zoran now meets the eyes of the assassin that have been staring at him for how long? Zoran waits. For the assassin to step to him.

'Meet me at the cathedral in an hour,' he whispers, passing by like a stranger in a train station, 'and you're being tailed, you fucking clown. Lose them.'

Zoran blinks at the assassin, watches the man run up the stairs. Zoran turns and looks about casually. Catches the eyes of two men in suits. They avoid his stare abruptly, and Zoran makes them immediately.

He strolls for the stairs. Half-way up, he breaks into a sprint and comes up onto street-level and runs for Giovanni waiting in the gleaming limo' outside a burger-joint where kids sit about on the curb chewing on a million hectares worth of jungle, polystyrene boxes laid open on their crotches.

Two figures appear from the station, following Zoran as he jumps into the limo' and shouts, 'Drive, Giova'!' He stares out through the back windscreen as Giovanni drops the clutch and accelerates his way out towards Brera. 'Just keep going,' says Zoran. 'We're being tailed, just keep going, keep going!'

It takes almost an hour until Zoran is satisfied there's no-one tailing him. 'Okay, Giova', find a dark corner near the Duomo and drop me off and go home. If someone's on your tail, take your time getting there. I'll meet up with you later.'

The bimmer pauses up from the grand old cathedral, and Zoran climbs out with a briefcase. The limo' slips away with its red taillights joining the stream of traffic.

VI

Virdis sighs, parking his Volvo before the villa in Brera. They lost Zoran Santana and with him any chance of identifying the assassin. Although two cops down in the subway had seen Zoran swap brief words with a blond man in a grey suit—could *he* be the assassin? An identikit had been formulated and sent by fax to all EC police forces and Interpol and the FBI. Perhaps one of those databases, which Virdis doesn't understand at all, will be able to make a connection with a face, an identity. The identity of Zoran's assassin.

Lost because of incompetence, thinks Virdis. And that's best-case scenario.

In his day, back when he was on the beat, cops were *cops*—they weren't on the take, they didn't have unions and a cop would risk his life for the people he was sworn to protect. Now ... He swallows down bile. Now they're all tainted, the cops are either green with kickbacks or yellow with fucking fear.

Virdis unlocks the door to his apartment, thoughts of Zoran expelled as the conversation with Gina his wife invades his mind. He checks his wristwatch, 3:15am. Christ she's gonna be pissed, he thinks, and it's the last thing he needs. But her anger is right, he thinks. This fucking job. He moves quietly through the silent house, up the carpeted staircase and down the corridor. The door to the spare bedroom is ajar, as is, he suddenly realises, the main bedroom. Odd, because Gina always sleeps with the doors firmly shut. Virdis slips out his Beretta and eases to the main bedroom. Enters the dimness with his pistol, an extension of his darting arm.

'Gina?' It's too dark to see whether there's someone below the duvet. Virdis flips on the lights, thinking that if she's asleep and he wakes her up waving a gun at her head, she's going to seriously give him a slapping.

The room's in disarray, empty drawers hanging out from the cupboards, clothing—his possessions—scattered on the thick carpet. He thinks for a second that they've been mugged. And then he sees it.

There's a pink envelope on the bed-side table, propped up by an empty glass, GIUSEPPE printed upon it. Giuseppe. Not Pino. Not good, when his wife refers to him by his full name. He shuts off the light and turns and wanders off to the spare bedroom. He can guess the contents of the letter. If he reads it, he will not sleep. And right now, Virdis needs to sleep with his pistol lying limply on the floor beside him.

VII

On the back pew of the cathedral with fifty thousand dollars cash in a black attaché case, Zoran waits with an impatiently tapping leg. His eyes are aware, watching the doors, the altar, the confessional, waiting.

A boy suddenly steps into the cathedral. He stands just within the doors, inspecting the twilight. Before he sees Zoran in the shimmering house of God. The boy genuflects, in the name of the father, the son, and the holy ghost, and then steps toward Zoran. And walks right past him, to kneel before the altar. When he gets up and walks away, Zoran notices that the boy's left a note on the marble floor where he'd knelt. Zoran walks over and stretches for it. Crumpled for him to unwrap like a gift.

Café across the road. 3 minutes or I leave.

Zoran leaves immediately. Watching the time on his wristwatch. One minute, no more, and he's seated inside the cosy coffee-bar. Orders two espressos. Looks down at his Longines.

Three minutes. The chair opposite him scrapes back. Zoran looks up mystified at the blond man in jeans sitting down opposite him, tense and tight blue eyes staring at him.

'I've paid you already and unless you've completed the assignment, I don't see why I'm here,' says Zoran. 'And what the fuck's with the spy routine? You're not in the fucking CIA anymore.'

The assassin lets this all sink in while a waitress deposits two espressos on their table. He keeps his face in the shadow of his baseball cap and waits for her to leave.

'So?' prompts Zoran, 'what the fuck's happening?'

'You never told me there was gonna be two.'

'Two? Two what? You mean Luca? Buddy, that was *your* call. I don't pay if you have a personality clash with one of my guys and shoot the fucker. Not that I'm not grateful though. Prick had it coming.'

The man sips down espresso. 'He was your guy indeed,' he says after scanning the tables about them, 'but that's not the problem here—Luca is on the house. Call it a favour.' The assassin leans forward. 'No, the second person here is a girl that's teamed up with your whore. To get to him, I will need to get to her. And to get to her, I need more cash. Because this ain't a two-for-one special week, you following?'

Zoran blinks. 'A girl? He's a fucking faggot, for chrissakes. Who the fuck is she?'

'I don't know who she is.' The blond licks his espresso-stained lips. 'A young cop named Franco Rinaldi. He's heading the search. So I've been tailing him. Why don't you work your sources at the cop shops and find me a name? That would be useful.'

'So where the fuck's the whore?'

'He's vanished.' The assassin shakes his head at the waitress about to pause at the table. 'The cops don't have a clue where he's holed up.'

'And you do?'

'A clue? No. Whoever he's with got him out of the cop's sack. With some inspired driving.'

Zoran sits back in his seat. 'So what the fuck is it you're saying here? *Spell* it out for me.'

The assassin sips down the espresso and leans back in his chair indulgently. 'The cops are figuring he's gonna turn up, eventually. Because they have certainties. Like, one, all borders leaving Italy are shut tight, so he ain't fucking leaving. Which means, two, he's going to run out of money and options eventually. So they're holding station and waiting. And that brings us to three, which is, when he does run out of options and money, he's gonna have no choice but to—'

'He has money now?'

'Seems like it. I think that's why he's tied up to this girl. He'll know the cops are closing in—knows it's just a matter of time before they nail him. Knows too, thanks to your guy Luca, that you have your own interests regarding his—health. So he's only got one option available, really. That's three. You following? And I will be waiting.'

'What the fuck are you saying? Waiting? I don't get it. Where? *What* option?'

'You'll figure it out,' says the assassin. 'But in the meantime, you got some more pressing issues.'

'Like what?'

'Like spreading the word on the street.'

'The word?'

'About your concern over Lago's well-being. About how much you're prepared to pay if anyone knows his whereabouts. The cops have got the media. You got the streets. The streets always win.'

'Done. This town belongs to me.'

The assassin places his coffee cup down and meets Zoran's eyes. 'You think so, buddy? So tell me then, why d'you have a wire on your phone?'

'What the fuck are you talking about?'

The assassin slides out from his chair, about to stand. Dabs his lips clean with the disposable hanky. 'You're slacking, Zoran. You should get off the powder.'

'How the fuck do you know—*what* wire?'

'You didn't tell anyone about our station rendezvous. Am I correct in assuming this?'

'Yes.'

'And yet there were cops for Africa waiting at the station. What does this tell you?'

Zoran stares.

The assassin stands holding the attaché case. 'I'll be in touch.'

'Just don't call,' Zoran says and burps foul smelling air. 'Send me a fucking postcard.'

31. Macho Gang: 'Naughty Boy'

I

The soft embrace of a bitter dawn basks the plush valley as they tangle together over the muddy trail, the footpath slopes up into the mountains barely distinguishable. The heat is already rising, Robi's vest drenched with sweat. She follows Sandro at a healthy distance, the swollen air trapped about her, her hands protecting her face from the whipping branches as he fights his way through the dense growth.

Robi's feet ache. She'd found a cobbler's shop in the village and purchased a pair of leather boots the day before, but they're taking their sweet time to break-in. Her back foot slides, and she crashes down onto her ass with a yelp.

'You okay?' Sandro walks back to her and extends his hand. She grabs it and lifts herself up, their bodies embracing and her breasts squeezing on his chest delightfully. He can smell her, gasping breath hot on his face. Quickly, her hand slips onto his crotch, fumbling over his hard-on.

There's a tiny gap between fighting and fucking.

II

Cigarette smoke drifts up into the dense air, reeking in the vinyl morning. 'This is one thing I didn't expect to find in sunny Italy.' She waves about her with her naked breasts gleaming. She snatches a dribble with her finger and feeds it to his waiting mouth beside her. 'You fuck like a whore,' she tells him.

He kills his smoke. Dresses. She watches him pensively as his clothes mask his scars. 'What's wrong?' she asks.

'This whole thing's such a fucking mess.'

'You're frightened.'

'I'm sober.'

Robi stands and finds her vest, flicking it clean and sliding it on. 'What does that mean?'

'We need to keep moving.'

Conversation is too taxing now as they steadily climb up-land into the mountains. She holds forward her hand for him to drag her along, slackening her body and allowing her legs to follow in-step with his momentum.

With the darkening of the sky, they find a small clearing amongst the trees and Sandro says, 'Help me gather some wood.'

Fire crackles in the night, red ash flickering away into the darkness about them as they sit beside each other hungrily eating from cans of beans.

He gulps down a last spoonful of beans and throws the can into the brush. 'When your cause goes sour and you're about to die, then the man counts more than his cause,' he says.

'You're full of shit,' she laughs, her hands touching his face tenderly. 'How the fuck did you get yourself into this?'

'Behind every whore there's a hard-luck story.'

'Do you see yourself as just that ... a whore?'

'No, more hard-luck story.'

She looks at him. Sees him. 'You're so much more than you even realise.'

He lights a cigarette, using the excuse to pull away from her.

'Why do you hate yourself so much?' she asks.

He smiles. 'Do I?'

'Yes.'

He meets her eyes in the chiaroscuro. 'I'm not sure,' he says, and comes closer to her, 'you're in a position to be judging anyone, you know. I hate myself? It's better than you feeling sorry for yourself 'cause your old-man wanted a bit of a fun with your ass— I've fucked—' she slaps him, hard, and Sandro stumbles onto his ass.

'Fuck you,' she whispers.

'Fuck me then.'

She crawls to him, unfastening his belt and jeans and squats over him. She trembles as he slides in. She stares down at his shadowed face in the erratic light. 'What can I do to make you love?'

His hands find her breasts beneath the vest. 'Hurt me,' he whispers, grasping her breasts cruelly. She winces, wielding from his clawing fingers.

She moves on him, sighing. 'I would never.'

Their eyes lock, and she sees his thick lips form words in the darkness. 'Hurt me.'

'I can't.'

'You want to.' He begins to unleash the belt from his jeans. 'Hurt me,' he whispers with his tongue touching her lips. He twists and she rolls onto her back, and he places the belt over her heart like temptation. His hips grind rhythmically into her. Robi holds the belt uncertainly, eyes searching his, staring down at her with a ferocity of indifference that makes her heart stutter. *Do it*, he mimes silently. Hurt me.

Robi shuts her eyes and swings the belt through the darkness. She's no stranger to pain, not about to hold back her strength now that she's committed to it. The buckle strikes her on the leg, and she cries out. Sandro's hand grabs the welt and squeezes it until tears trickle from her wide eyes. Her breath catches in her lungs, mouth agape and wet. Wanting.

'Double it,' he says. She does, using her mouth. Swings the belt again. It cracks across his back, and he sinks deeper into her with the pain. 'Again,' he whispers, 'you know my pain.' She does, 'again, again, again.' The further he draws her in, the harder the belt flays until, grunting, she stops wielding the belt to grab onto his beaten ass and fucks him with her teeth drawing blood from his lips.

III

'I'm sorry,' she says, tracing the welts with her fingers as he lies beside her, the grass itchy to his perspiring flesh. 'Does it hurt?'

'Can you see the welts?'

She traces them with a finger. 'I'm sorry.'

'No,' he rests his index-finger on her lips, 'you're not. And neither am I.'

The sulphur catches the night unaware as a cigarette crackles to light. Sandro tosses the box at her. She lights one up and tosses the match into the embers of the dying fire. Her eyes stare at his body lying naked on the blanket, arms folded below his head as he watches the black sky. 'You bring things out of me,' she says.

'So do you,' he replies, smiling.

'Shut up, I'm being serious. What are you thinking about?'

Sandro shrugs.

Robi crawls to him and rests her head on his shoulder. He flips a strand of hair from his mouth and allows his heavy lids to shut.

'I love you,' she whispers. She slings her arm about his chest and kisses his lips. 'I love you, Sandro.'

IV

It's dawn when they waken and once again continue the trek on the tapering path. At noon, they break from the dense trees and stare down at green hills and a valley stretching endlessly below them. They stand at the top of the world with their bodies bathed in a soft breeze. An ancient village lies in a white haze on a ridge in the shimmering distance. Villas sit glazed under the cloudless sky in the hills above it.

They follow a footpath towards the village of San Matteo, the name scrawled on a wooden pole on the outskirts of the small community. The roads, cobbled and red like dried blood, slope down crookedly between white stone dwellings with welcoming open shutters.

L'Albergo Pozzi stands just off the piazza on via Regimentale. It's an old, white-washed building with a date above the entrance. 1702. The lobby is small, stone and pine, dark and cozy. A woman sits behind the small reception desk sorting through mail below a pale light. Sandro steps to her.

'*Solo quelle?*' she asks, pointing to the two small bags on the wooden floor.

'*Si*,' Sandro says. '*Siamo Americani. Sposati. Appena.*'

The woman smiles at Robi and slides a key across the desk. 'You good stay.'

'*Grazie*,' says Robi, following Sandro up a staircase with anti-fascist propaganda and pro-Yank bullshit from a long-forgotten war lining the wooden walls on either side of the richly carpeted staircase.

Room 23 is at the end of the corridor on the second landing. The room is sunny, light gushing over the ancient wooden chairs and the massive four-poster bed. Heat floats in from the French windows that open out onto a small metal-grilled veranda and, beyond it, the valley that undulates thick and verdant.

The bed is soft beneath her body, so cool and comforting, lulling Robi to sleep. Sandro slumps on a two-seater couch, unable to sleep with the bleeding thoughts, the twirling blue smoke thick about him in the early afternoon.

He figures he hasn't been this sober since—Jesus. Lucidity is beautiful and frightening because there are no hidden chasms of the mind to bury fear.

There are places in these mountains, he thinks, where a man can hide out forever without ever being questioned—or even found. All he needs is a place to rest for a few months. Wait for everything to blow over. And after that—a job. A life. He still has a lot of doors open. And for the first time in years, he falls asleep knowing there are to be no nightmares. His mind is clear, his body clean. If only his life can now fall into step with his consciousness.

V

It's as if … as if she can *feel* again, thinks Robi. Passion—lust … love? She'd taken what Wayne had offered and she had given him her body. Now she gives Sandro her body and her soul as a union of pain—with its scars and its imperfections, both accepted.

She touches his hair as he lies sleeping on the couch, eyes shut and trembling. Silver moonlight falls into the room, his face thrown into deep shadows. Lightly, Robi blows on his ear, and he awakens with his eyes searching her face blankly.

'Is something wrong?' he asks, sitting up and glancing around into the shadows. 'Something happened?'

'No.'

He blinks wearily, standing. Switches on a lampshade, tracking down his smokes and lights up. 'You hungry?'

Robi smiles at him. 'For you.' Their eyes lock, the room closing in as their bodies search for strength within their souls. 'I love you, Sandro.'

Sandro breaks from her and wanders over to the veranda. The night is bitter, the piazza lit and bustling with dozens of locals, dancing and shouting below an opal moon. Some feast or another. He turns to Robi. 'You're crazy.'

She touches his hand now, standing beside him. 'Why?'

He shrugs.

'Have you ever been in love?' she asks.

Sandro hesitates. Yes, he thinks. And she comes to him. Francesca. Beautiful, kind—dead Francesca. 'Yes.'

'Who was—' she hesitates.

'She. Her name was Francesca. She was—we were close 'cause we were both fucked in the head.' He drags on his smoke and exhales audibly as a teenage girl below kisses a policeman with hands grabbing his ass.

'So what happened?'

Sandro moves away from her, lies on the bed. He stares up at the ceiling with shadow fingers pointing in obscene angles. 'She died.' Died in a pool of her own blood, stupid bitch. 'How about you,' he says, forcing his mind on, 'you ever been, *in luuuuv*?'

Robi sits beside him, not sure if he's mocking her, so she grabs a smoke and watches him for a while. 'Before you, you mean? I s'pose. He's much older than me. His name's Wayne.'

'It sounds present tense.' He stares at her carefully. 'Does he know where you are?'

'Yeah. Well, not *here*, but sure, he like—sponsored me on this trip.'

'And he'll be okay with you blowing his dough on hookers?'

She slaps at him playfully. 'Wayne's a good man, as kind as they come. But it's over between us. What we had was good, special, but not meant to be forever.' She glances at him. Sandro has become her future now. 'Why do you do this?' she asks.

'This?'

'This,' she brushes his cock with her finger.

'What else am I gonna do? Work as an accountant?'

'Why not?'

''cause it's all whoring.'

'That's not, no,' she says.

'I don't like the world, Robi, I don't fit into it.'

'Tell me about where you came from.'

He shrugs. 'Not much to tell. I just turned out bad.'

She understands, spanking his leg playfully. 'Bad boys get punished.'

'Yes,' he whispers.

Her eyes grown dark with guilt and unexplained desire. 'Let's just fuck,' she says.

VI

A stream of sunlight sweeps over Robi's thigh as she sits on the veranda. She fixes her eyes on something only she can see, somewhere in the afternoon sky. 'So where do we go from here?' she asks eventually, turning her attention to Sandro lying on the bed with shut eyes. 'We have to leave. I'm getting a bad vibe.'

'Me too. But I got nothing. No plans. Do you?' he asks, as if her revelation will be intrinsic to his future.

'No.'

'No? You sure? Because if you have any ideas, I'll be happy to hear 'em. Otherwise,' he lifts his hands and flops them back on the matrass, 'shut up.'

Robi tosses her smoke over the veranda and joins him on the bed. 'Don't be angry. I'm on your side.'

Sandro locks eyes with hers. 'Yeah.'

'We've got money. We can leave here—leave Europe and—I don't know. Get lost. In Jamaica.'

'We'd get arrested within a kilometre of any border post or airport. It's impossible.'

'False papers.' Robi shrugs. 'You're the one with the contacts.'

Sandro sits up, studying her face pensively. He blinks now, working it out. 'It means we gotta get back to Milano. And it'll cost a packet.' She sees nothing to contradict. 'But it's possible.'

'We could fly away, far, far away, and no one could ever find us again.'

She feels good. She grabs his cock. Power. She looks down at the bruises across his naked ass. Her bruises. She takes him roughly, sitting on his cock whispering, 'Give me your face,' and when he lifts his face to her outstretched hand, she slaps him lightly and when he doesn't flinch, she slaps him harder and his continuously ajar eyes stare into her soul until she comes with an actual shudder of her body.

VII

They'd settled the account with the innkeeper at sunrise with an iced wind whistling up the valley. The nearest train station is on a secondary route jutting deep into the mountains, a thirty-minute hike away, and Sandro has figured it will be safe, now, days from the hunt and deep in the ancient country where the partisans had hidden during the second war, and the bandits before them. There's a train to Isernia leaving at 5:45am, a two-hundred-kilometre trek north of San Matteo. Sandro has decided this is the most promising destination.

The train is late, but the compartment is big enough to allow them both to lie on the bunks as the desolate train rattles up through the mountains and miles of dark tunnels.

Isernia is a small village in the shelter of olive and orange groves, cobbled streets and old, squat buildings leaning up one on the other like old brothers.

The autostrada runs past on the outskirts and Sandro has decided it's a safe spot to hitch a ride on the highway bound north, heavy with traffic as the last of the holiday-makers storm back home. He leaves Robi to stick her thumb out and it's a matter of minutes before an olive-green Alfa slows for them on the shoulder of the autostrada.

'Carlo,' says the driver, digging a podgy hand at Robi riding shotgun, Sandro left to the rear seats, *'dove andate*?'

Sandro shakes his head stupidly. 'We don't speak Italian.'

'English?'

'American,' says Robi, glancing quickly at Sandro sitting hunched in the back seat.

'*Turisti*, yes?' The driver watches Robi nod, casually surveying her tight vest and the mounds of her breasts. 'Hot,' he says, waving a hand at his face and laughing, 'really hot.'

He slides onto the left lane and brings the V6 to 210 km/h on the clock with his face passively scanning his rear-view at a Maserati closing in. Fast. With headlights flashing irritably. Carlo slides the car right to slow behind a Fiat, allowing the Maserati to sweep past with brights still flashing, and then throws the Alfa inches behind the Maserati. The driver up-front panicks at the sight of the Alfa scraping his rear bumper at over two hundred. Taillights shine red for an instant, Robi inhaling loudly as the Alfa almost touches the rear of the Maserati Bi-turbo. Carlo drops down a gear to fourth, slip-streaming the Maserati until the silver car ahead inches away from the Alfa, Carlo willing the Alfa faster by bouncing on his seat and glancing at Robi with a huge grin.

'Where you go?' he asks over the reverberations of the tight engine.

'Milan,' answers Robi, watching the road ahead for him, 'if you don't kill us before then.'

'Me, Parma.'

'That's close enough,' mutters Sandro, checking out the rev counter from the back seat. 'Your engine, it's a beast,' he tells Carlo, and Carlo smiles proudly, Robi forgotten on the seat beside him.

They're in Parma in under four hours, Carlo driving them to the Hotel Cosmopolitan on the outskirts. Sandro knows it well; a business hotel where he'd spent a few evenings with Francesca and easy marks back when. They're shown to a room on the first floor by a bearded kid chewing American-gum and quoting precedents for an upcoming exam for his law degree. The room is comfortable, and sleep is easy after room-service and love.

32. Ryan Paris: 'Dolce Vita'

Sandro is awake before dawn with tearing bowels, cramps, nausea—*fear*—and lies naked in bed chain-smoking and waiting for the day to begin. Everything will start again in Milan. Francesca—the image of that—*her*—body lying on the bloody floor. Heroin had wiped away the memory. But he recalls her now, *Francesca, ti ricordo*, black hair tinged with red like strands of blood and thin body almost sexless, androgenous in its skeletal beauty, the face sagging, yellowed with recurring thrombosis, the arms thin, anorexic and scarred with bubbled blisters and clots, the eyes black in death, staring up like she was stoned, like she was alive, and her laugh, God how he'd loved that goofy laugh. He can never return to Francesca, but he senses here, in this place, and the things she did here.

Francesca, what the fuck is still left?

Just a forgotten child in a world that has a billion worse, begging and fucking and stealing for a living fix until the inevitable—the welcomed—death. *La morte, Francesca. Com'è?* Living for death. That had been Francesca's addiction. She'd accepted the evil, happy to fuck you with all she had, and she was not destroyed because she rejected the evil, she had embraced that longing for the brown happiness the colour of shit that had caressed her when first she'd found her true lover that cocooned her in a warm paradise like that NATO-surplus coat that kept her warm from the eternal cold of addiction.

Francesca.

Sandro wonders if he'd been better off before, was he not happier a few weeks back? Before sobriety—sanity—had taken over. Before he'd met Robi. He can't stand his mind any longer as the first rays of grey dawn spill through the yellow curtains. He shakes Robi awake, whispers, 'We gotta move,' in her ear, and ambles to the bathroom. Now he recalls—now everything comes back so clearly. And never has his craving for horse been so strong.

The ash of purity that was her life.

Ti amo, Francesca.

They're on the autostrada at seven, in Milan by ten-thirty. Sandro leads her through the city, into the bowels of Boviso where raggy kids with hungry eyes see too much and pretend to see nothing at all. He knows the old neighbourhood, and Robi follows him into a maze of tight cobbled alleyways and tiny walkways, syringes and filth, dirty underpasses and threadbare parks.

They pass a church that attracts Robi's attention, the façade ornate and weirdly unkept, the windows dipped in technicolour from the noonday sun. She follows him down a dank alley behind the church and then through a small opening at the base of the wall that leads to a flight of concrete stairs leading down into what he says is an underground bomb shelter dating back to the second war.

Below, in the vague, soft shadows of candlelight barely lighting the brick vaulted ceiling, they find two girls sleeping on a bug-infected mattress. A tunnel leads on behind them, the grey, dripping walls vanishing in deep shadow, leading deep below the metropolis and into the maze of forgotten passageways.

One girl has a syringe in her throat. Robi turns away, gagging on the smell of dried blood and warm filth and spewed fluids and decades of grimy dreams. The other girl rustles and casts two heavy, confused eyes on Sandro when he nudges her awake with his boot. A flash of recognition sweeps through the mud-brown eyes, and she sits up slowly, weary.

'Sandro? *Pensavo che eri morto*.'

Sandro squats beside her. She sits up and the two embrace. 'Only the good die young,' he says. 'How's it going, Katia.'

'Is she okay?' asks Robi, pointing at the pale girl with the syringe sticking out of her neck.

Katia glances up at Robi, then down at the girl. '*Dio che cagacazzo*,' she says, wrenching the needle out, the hole suddenly visible like a burst blister. Blood trickles out, fresh, running down onto a stained pillow. 'Always the same with this one,' Katia tells Sandro and the two share a laugh and some private insight while Robi tries to control her nausea, the stench in the basement overpowering.

'I'm going outside for some air,' she says to no one, walking back up the stone staircase where a condom, still flecked in shit and come, makes her gag some more.

Katia watches her walk away into the dark. 'Who's the princess?' she asks. And then, 'You're crazy to have come here.' Katia meets his eyes and smiles. She's missing a tooth. 'But I'm happy you're here. Gianni's dead, did you hear? He OD'd last week. And Paola's in prison, she freaked out and stabbed her dad. And Francesca's gone, and you—' she shakes her head, 'everyone's left, Sandro. I feel so fucking old.'

You're nineteen for fuck sakes,' he says. 'You're ancient.'

'Twenty. Last week.'

'Happy birthday.'

'*Fanculo*,' she says. 'Where've you been?'

'You don't know?'

She looks at his eyes. 'What happened?'

'I made a mistake,' he says.

'And now?'

'Now I need to get out, Katia, I need papers.'

'Papers?'

'Passports.'

'For what?'

'To leave.'

'You wouldn't leave me alone. We're the last of the tribe.'

'Do you still have that contact? The Russian? At the Soviet Consulate?'

'Sure.'

'Could he do it?'

'Probably. But it'd cost. A lot. It's not our world, Sandro.'

'I've got the money.'

She looks up at the stone stairs. 'You found a rich princess? Nice, Sandro. I always knew you'd whore your way to a better life. You got something?' Katia stares at his eyes, trying to read something, like he's given her kinetic powers, her hands touching his arms, then his face. She frowns. 'You're fucking clean, aren't you?'

'Yes.'

'Fuck!' she throws her hands about him like she's genuinely pleased. 'I knew it. Francesca always said—she always told me you were always gonna get outta this shit.' She laughs, but it sounds empty. 'I'm happy for you.'

And suddenly Sandro sees the pathetic loneliness that had attracted him to Francesca. To this life. A sorority of isolation.

Katia stands unsteadily and wavers to the shadows of the tunnel, naked but for her t-shirt, drug-thin, firm assed, nothing has changed, and does her business in a bucket. 'You have a smoke?' He lights two and tosses one at her, watching as the smoke spins in the sultry air to fall and roll to her naked, dirty feet with purple, gangrenous looking wounds stretched upon her soles.

'Fuck,' she says, dragging with relief while running a hand through her hair before a shattered mirror on the wall beside a poster of the Sex Pistols, 'my legs are so fucking stiff. This stuff we're getting is laced with, fuck, I don't know what the fuck—'

'Strychnine.'

'Yeah.'

'Katia, you still using Massimo?'

'Fuck no. You don't know? Massimo got popped.'

'So where's you merch'? Is he close?'

'Yeah. Can we get?' she asks, turning to him with big eyes.

'That and more. Let's go.'

Robi's playing football with a group of kids on the street, smiling and sweating beneath the oppressive sun. Sandro steps to her, crossing in the ball's path. He controls it, dribbles two kids before the exertion forces a headrush, and he squats at Robi's feet, dizzy.

'I need to score some shit for Katia. She's not doing too well.'

Robi stares past him, at Katia leaning against the wall before the entrance to the underground shelter with matted blonde hair falling in thick strands over her face, cotton dress tight on her thin body and feet covered in scarred, broken-in Dr Martens.

'Must I come?'

Sandro shrugs. 'No—if you don't want to. I just need some bucks. Fifty thousand should be enough.'

Robi digs into her money-belt and hands him some bills.

'I won't be long,' he says, stepping back to Katia without a backward glance at Robi, who watches the two walk up the block.

'I'll wait here,' she says.

Katia leads him into a condemned apartment block down from the Parco di Villa Litta, the corridors stinking of shit and age. The dim, nebulous walls are covered in graffiti, and 'roaches scuttle for cover on the wooden staircase as Sandro follows Katia up, gripping a rickety banister for support.

Katia's dealer is a tall man dressed in flowery jeans and a paint-splashed Nike sweatshirt. His apartment is barren of furniture but for a worktable covered in a techno-rainbow of oils, a mattress in the corner, and an easel with a massive, frantic blood-red canvas of a stencilled orgy scene in the foreground. The walls are covered in leftist propaganda, Marxist and neo-Marxist words and some Red Brigades and Red Faction posters from back-when, the days of the *lotta continua*.

GIVE BACK THE WORLD TO THE WORLD

FIGHT WAR NOT WARS
SIATE REALISTI: DOMANDATE L'IMPOSSIBILE!
ORA E SEMPRE RESISTENZA!

'This is Sandro,' introduces Katia. 'Gianfranco.'

The two men shake hands in the turpentine smelling space before Gianfranco vanishes into the only other room of the pad. He comes back moments later with a foiled-package in a red-stained hand. 'Let's do it now, okay?' he says.

Katia examines the large canvass. 'It's nice.'

'It's not meant to be,' says Gianfranco, cooking up another dream. 'It's about the deprivation of man, about man's alienation from humanity, it's about man's alienation from himself.'

'It's very red,' says Sandro.

Katia sits opposite the artist and winks at Sandro. 'Sit,' she says, patting the wooden floor beside her.

'I don't—'

'He's kicked the habit,' she explains to Gianfranco, who holds a Zippo with an American flag on it below a cooking spoon. 'C'mon, Sandro. Just once. With me, for old times' sake. You remember how it was? How it is.'

Sandro remembers too well and sits down to complete a circle on the dirty wooden floor. He glances about at the sketches balanced in rows up on the wall, twisted, masked reports in seeping, loud colours. He watches Gianfranco offer the syringe to Katia. Ladies first, just in case the cut's lethal. She accepts it, goes for the jugular, lower, does her bit and hands the syringe over for Gianfranco to share the blood of life. He offers the remnants to Sandro. Not worth the push, he thinks, as Katia smiles wearily at him. He hands the syringe back to Katia and says, 'Do it for me.'

'Always the same, the tourist,' says Katia, leaning forward with a searching needle before going in for the kill. Sandro pulls back. Gazes at Katia, then Gianfranco with their small, weary eyelids. He digs out the money from his jeans. Tosses the notes at Katia, who doesn't think to catch them. They float onto her lap.

'Money, money, money,' observes the neo-Marxist artist.

'I'm going back to Robi, Katia. I'll come tomorrow morning with our photographs, and you can tell me how much you want.'

'Who says I'm gonna do it for you?'

'Because we're friends. Katia, please.'

'Unity is strength,' offers Gianfranco, glancing from one to the other. ''Tis the final conflict, let us unite and tomorrow, The International will be the human race,' he sings.

'Come early,' says Katia.

Sandro holds up a left fist and smiles at the pusher. Then he stands and leaves, the taste of heroin like regret on his lips.

33. Joe Yellow: 'Lover To Lover (For Sale)'

I

Sandro awakens them early. Katia's got a pimple growing on her nose that looks infected, and she asks for a smoke while idly squeezing the puss out. Rina struggles to find anything but chaotic confusion in her mind, attempting to sit up on the mattress before giving up, casting dark eyes on Sandro. She flashes her ear-ringed nipples and breasts that are a lot whiter than her teeth.

'Sandro?' she says, blinking. 'Why are you here?'

Sandro looks down at her. Can recall when they'd been close, really close, when first Rina had spiked. It was Sandro who'd popped the virgin vein. She'd been smart and drop-dead gorgeous then, the daughter of someone or another high-up in government, he can't remember now, she was studying art at Parma University, heavy into politics, but these are not thoughts to live with. 'You don't look too good, Rina.'

'Thanks. You look like the prick you've always been. I've been having a hard time, that's all. I think I'm sick.'

Katia gazes at the entrance above the stone staircase, but there's no-one there. 'Your friend's nose too sensitive?'

'No,' Sandro says, 'her eyes are too sensitive.' He passes an envelope to Katia. 'The photos. I want two EC passport under any names you care to come up with.'

Katia un-flaps the envelope and digs out the two photos. 'The happy couple. Yeah, this'll do. How about Francesca and Alex Segreto?'

'That's not funny—'

Katia laughs. 'I can have 'em in about a week.'

'I'm sorry about Francesca,' says Rina, shut eyed. 'Really sorry. She was the best.'

'Two days is all I got, Katia.' He looks back at Rina and shakes his head. 'Strangely, she meant a lot less to me that I imagined,' he says for no reason at all.

'You should have told her when she was alive,' says Katia.

'He's right, though.' Rina finds a rare moment of lucidity, and her words are just short of a mumble. 'What's a whore like Francesca worth compared to his new sugar-mommy?'

Sandro wields to Rina angrily.

'Forget it,' says Katia.

Sandro looks away, back at Katia.

'I can't possibly get it done in two days,' she says.

'I must be out in two days, Katia. I don't think I even have that long. We haven't slept for two nights; we've been wandering about the streets like ... We took the photos at five this morning 'cause any hotel here's too hot for us.'

'Next time don't steal from Zoran,' says Rina.

'Fuck do you know about it?' asks Sandro.

'Everyone knows, Sandro,' says Katia. 'You're a wanted man.' She laughs. 'Like a fucking—fucking—*Diabolik!* But then everyone's always wanted your ass.'

'Especially Francesca,' says Rina. 'But she meant nothing to you, right?' Rina swallows some phlegm. Decides she can't swallow it all and spits the rest on the floor. Black.

Katia says, 'There's nothing I can do before then, Sandro.'

'Fuck. Why?'

'Because that's the way it is.'

'When next week?'

She thinks about it. 'Tuesday.'

He nods, digging crumpled notes from his jeans. 'Here's a million to see you guts through. Is that enough?'

'Sure. That's enough.' Katia accepts the bills and Rina finds motivation to sit up. She shares an unpleasant glance with him, snatching the money from Katia's hand and begins counting slowly, mumbling the figures to herself. By the third note, she's forgotten her count, and must begin again in earnest with saliva dribbling from her thin, purple lips.

'It's gonna cost you another ten million on Tuesday,' says Katia with her body gold in the stream of morning sunlight peering through the entrance.

Rina's eyes grow wide at the sum.

'Come,' says Katia, 'I'll walk you out.'

She wiggles into a tight pair of soiled jeans with stains on the crotch and a sweater from a pile of clothes in the corner below the mirror. She senses something, and reaching below the

Benetton green, she seizes a 'roach crawling on her flesh and squeezes the fucker to death between her fingers, staring at it until it dies.

The first day of autumn is hot out on the street. Silently, Katia walks with him into an alley around the corner. Turns to him now. 'I want to stop all this.' She waves about her at the mounds of garbage spread about the alley. 'I've had enough, Sandro.' She searches his silent face, traces his lips with her dirty fingernails. 'You know when you feel like you're going to—and you realise you're already dead but, somehow—'

'You want to keep on going.'

'Yes. That.' She hugs him, and his hands come to rest above her buttocks, squeezing her to him. 'We're friends, right,' she breaks contact and looks up at him, 'we're all that's left, Sandro. Me and you and Rina. We're it now. We had such good times together. You remember?' She smiles at him. 'You remember the old days, Sandro? You and Francesca, Gianni and Rina? Hanging out in Rimini, raving and watching the sunrise on the beach? Do you remember? And Francesca swimming naked? With Paola? We were so close then. *Ti ricordi, Sandro? Ti ricordi*?'

Sandro says nothing.

'So where do I go now?' Katia looks about her. 'I mean, as you say, Francesca means nothing now—she's just some dead *puttana*—and Gianni, you remember Gianni, when he climbed the cathedral and that cop—you remember—*ti ricordi*, Sandro?' She grabs his shirt and holds on for a moment. 'Now Rina's trying to off herself with every fix. And you—you're getting out.' She scrapes away what looks like a tear but is probably just dirt in her eye. 'And I'm the only one left.' She taps his shirt back in place. 'I'm scared, Sandro. I'm scared to be alone.'

Sandro has no reply. He senses her future—slumped somewhere, probably in that fucking bomb shelter with a syringe up her arm and a bad cut exploded in her heart. He hopes it will happen soon. What else is there? Francesca had understood it all. She'd always been too good for this life. Gianni too ... and Rina, 'though she was too far to even understand now.

And he had found Robi.

'I don't want to go like this, Sandro.'

'I gotta go, Katia. I left Robi at a café across town.'

She grabs his arm. 'You'll be back?'

'Yes. On Tuesday. With ten million cash.'

'Then we talk. Like we all used to. Remember? You going on about racists and South America and Francesca and her devils. You remember, Sandro. *Ti ricordi*?' she says forcefully, as if his remembering mattered.

He nods. He does. But the memories to which she clings so deeply make him bilious.

'Those were the best days of my life, Sandro. The best. Remember the way we were? Hanging out at Club LeRoc? You—'

'Yeah, Katia, they were great days. I gotta go. I'll see you Tuesday,' he says, turning and walking away with hunched shoulders and bowed head and shoes kicking a Coke can with the clamour following him until he exits the alley.

II

Robi's on her third Chinotto when she finally sees him. The piazza across from the café is quiet. A couple of tourists with backpacks slumped beside them sit on the sidewalk terrace studying a menu. Sandro pulls back a seat and plunks down across from her.

'A week,' he says. 'It'll take that long.'

'So now?'

'So now we gotta get out of the city. We're not safe here.'

She studies his face for a while. Her hand holds his across the table. 'You're going through hell.'

The waiter appears beside them, a straggly haired youth smothered in a tight red jacket.

'*Un caffe*,' orders Sandro with a vacant stare, watching the man vanish into the tinted windowed café. 'You don't look too good yourself.'

'I'm just tired.'

'Yeah.' He squeezes her hand. 'We'll go into the mountains. I know the perfect place—we'll be okay for a week.'

'I love you, you know.'

'Yes.'

III

They sleep in a park that evening, in a clearing Francesca and he had come to snort and shoot in the good ol' days, her park, the one she'd brought Sandro to one night, to be closer, she'd said, chemical cocktails and yellow-jacketed pill picnics while they touched and made love. Nothing has changed and Sandro must swallow his memories, lying on the cool grass to stare up at the cloud formations. So little of it matters, a spike and a high, two kids fucked in a fucked world loving each other the best they could. But in the end, it was each for themselves. Sandro could not help Francesca, could not give her an excuse for life. And it was her decision to quit, to leave him alone, to leave him here with his memories, his recollection of bygone days when Francesca had slept, like Robi does now, slept with her sweet chemical dreams ...

That night they get a taxi to the autostrada and hitch through the dawn—the safest way to travel, he tells Robi when she suggests they hire a car, no trace—and in the eat of the next morning they've reached a hostel in Schio, a sleepy town a hundred kilometres or so north of Venice with the small Dolomites jutting up as backdrop beyond.

They roam up into the mountains, swimming in the pebbly, icy streams, conversations of severed childhoods while staring out at the green hills and valleys and cool lakes reflecting the bursting sunshine. Hands touching, whispered voices and long vacant stares. Minds drawing closer, exploring, understanding, loving; acceptance. Living moment for moment, loving expression for expression, making plans, and knowing it's the moment that counts because there are no certainties. Except that this will not last forever and all things must end.

Somehow the world seems to fit on those long, first days of autumn, life about them waiting, sombre but brave still, for the dragging winter to come, rejoicing in the last hot sprays of sunlight before the dark, dreary months. Time slows to a crawl and all they have is each other, their bodies and their minds, sharing fantasies and dreams, sharing fears and screams ... their pasts, their thoughts, their joy. The past and the present, and sometimes, a glimpse of what could so easily be.

The future, the real tomorrow, Milan, is taboo. An unspoken wish for two kids to find what they never believed existed.

A bond created as she sheds tears of frustration for his self-imposed seedy past in the Milan ghettos, and he listening to the silent pain of her fond recollections of a lost childhood that was anything but self-imposed. Who they are and what was is irrelevant—they have each other now, only themselves and the gaping world below the climbing feet. Their love will conquer all.

That's what she says. They have found a tunnel through which they can process their deepest thoughts and fears, to analyse what had—can—never have been examined before. What could never have happened before.

'Scream!' he shouts, and she does, *'Ti amo!'* she shouts at the valley stretched below her and the golden-hued Dolomites that rise about them and *ti amo* comes the reply from the great earth, *ti amo, amo, am ...*

They eat too much soft cheese and drink too much hard grappa and speak of love and make dirty sex with the scent of mucus filtering in the drizzle. Nothing else matters 'til that Monday night, packing their overnight bags in the soft room neither wish to leave and neither will ever—can ever—forget, when Robi says, 'I feel like I'm leaving home.'

He nods, shutting his sack and walking to her. 'I love you.'

'I think everything's gonna be okay now. We have each other. They can't hurt us now.'

'Yes,' he says, 'no one can ever hurt us again.'

34. Paul Lekakis: 'Boom Boom'

Mayor Vincenzo Del'Aquila straightens out his tie, jostles into his jacket, and heads across his office. Opens the door with an ingratiating smile to shake the hand for, 'Minister Bandiera. It's an honour, sir, to welcome you to City Hall. To what do I owe this unexpected visit?'

The minister is an imposing man, what with his silver-flecked, immaculately trimmed beard and attentive eyes magnified behind tortoise-shell spectacles. He peers about the mayor's office, at a loud, blood-red oil painting on the wall of a seascape at sunset. 'Portofino,' he says in a thick drawl with its origin in the south, *deep* in the south. 'Please,' he points to the mayor's swivel chair, 'sit. I'm not here officially.'

The mayor sits. 'A social call, then, sir?'

'You can say that. Do you mind?' He lifts a trophy from the desk, reads the inscription. 'Tessa. Your daughter?'

'Yes.'

'Beautiful. Will she be representing us in the Olympics, Vincenzo?'

Mayor Del'Aquila lights a smoke. 'What can I do for you, sir?'

'Enrico, please, none of this "sir" ceremony.'

'Enrico. I've held this office for two years, and never the pleasure of your—'

'Well then,' the minister grabs a seat on a bare-backed chair before the desk, 'this visit is long overdue.'

'Thank you, sir, but—'

'Enrico, please!' The minister crosses his legs like a virgin. 'I don't want to take too much of your time, Vincenzo. You're a busy man. What with rising crime, spiralling drug-abuse, inflation, murder—you must have your hands full, isn't that right? Milan is Europe's epicentre of the heroin epidemic. I read that in the *New York Times* today. Tragic. Tragic.' His eyes focus on the mayor now, insectoid eyes not blinking, green gems sparkling under the light on the ceiling. 'Vincenzo, is that okay? May I?'

'Of course, Enrico.'

'Vincenzo. Good. Let me speak openly. I think you're the best thing to hit this town since,' he searches for an historical analogy, eyes blinking just once to hide any trace of uncertainty, 'the House of Sforza.'

'Thank you, sir, but I assure you I'm just one player on a team committed to this city's future.'

The bearded man nods distantly. 'Excellently put. I have, in fact,' he leans back on the creaking chair, 'been following this Alessandro Lago affair—in the papers, I mean. I believe Chief Inspector Virdis is dealing with the case?'

'Yes. He's very close to an arrest.'

'An arrest?'

'Yes, sir—'

'Enrico, please.'

'Enrico. We think,' the mayor leans forward over his desk to whisper conspiratorially, 'we may be days away from nabbing Milano's biggest supplier.'

The minister leans forward himself now, to reach for the mayor's pack of smokes on his desk. 'Do you mind?'

'Oh, I'm sorry. I didn't realise you smoked.'

'I don't,' laughs the minister, lighting up. 'So if you ever see me again, don't offer me a cigarette in front of my wife!' The minister watches Del'Aquila laugh forcibly. 'This young man—this Lago— how much does he know?'

'I'm sorry? Know about what?'

The minister's face looks away, down, at the cigarette between his fingers. 'Is he your star witness?'

'Against whom? Minister—Enrico—you're aware that I'm not permitted to discuss an open investigation, even with the Minister of the Interior—'

'Yes, I'm quite aware of this, mayor. That's why I'm here not in any official capacity, you understand?'

'Vincenzo, please.'

'Vincenzo. Look,' he kills the smoke distastefully in a filled ashtray on the desk, 'as I said, *I* think you're doing a terrific job here with limited resources and budget—'

'Yes ...'

'But some of my—colleagues ... Look, there's no easy way to say this. There's pressure, Vincenzo, from,' he nods up at the ceiling, 'to force your resignation.'

The mayor pales visibly.

'They feel this Lago situation has been—badly mishandled. A shambles. There's concern that Lago has been able to avoid capture because of,' he searches for words, 'well, let's not pussyfoot around—corruption within the police department. They find the actions of the police department, of Chief Inspector Virdis in particular, rather suspect—'

'Minister, I can assure you—'

'Enrico.'

'Enrico, Chief Inspector—'

'The accident with that Englishman—'

'Blake.'

'Yes, Inspector Blake from Scotland Yard caused us,' he smiles sadly, 'immense embarrassment with the English at the Farnesina—'

'Yes, I can well imagine, but he was a dirty cop, Enrico—'

'Over and above that, Vincenzo, the drug pandemic here is— alarming. To say the least. Quite alarming. And this open drug policy you're championing: I don't need to tell you how deeply unpopular that is in Rome, right?'

'Which is why we have focused all our resources of capturing the biggest distributor of—'

'King Dope,' says the mayor like it's a punchline to a cheap gag, 'indeed.'

'King Coke,' corrects the mayor.

'Dope, Coke, whatever. I read about him in the papers. Ridiculous name. Let me ask you, Vincenzo. Just between you and me. This Lago character—how much has he told you?'

The mayor slumps back in his swivel chair. 'What you're asking of me is difficult, sir. This is an ongoing investigation—'

'Enrico, cut it out with the sir already, Jesus. And yes, I get what you're saying. And me coming here to warn you of an imminent investigation of your office is equally difficult for me. Believe me. However, you give me a favourable report,' he shrugs at the inevitability of his power, 'and I'm sure I can dissuade my colleagues from continuing what I believe would be a worthless witch-hunt.'

'What do you want to know?' The mayor tips ash pensively. 'We don't—we haven't, as yet—had a chance to—' he pauses, emulating the minister, 'interview Lago.'

'So how do you—'

'We just know. You're going to have to take my word for it.'

The minister nods. 'You think Lago knows enough to bring, uhm, this King Dope—'

'King Coke. And yes, we believe he knows enough to put the bastard away for a thousand years.'

The minister takes time out, glances at the trophy again. 'My daughter,' he says, 'she was also a swimmer.'

'Is she—'

'Let me throw you a curveball, Vincenzo.'

'A curveball?'

'What if I,' he pauses, meets the mayor's eyes, 'if I had to supply you with evidence that your—King Dope—is not who you think it is?'

The mayor frowns. 'I don't think I follow. And to be frank, Enrico, I would reject your evidence out of hand, anyway. It's incorrect.'

'Ah. You are that convinced, then?'

'Yes. But I don't understand how you—'

'Well then,' the minister leans forward, 'I suppose all that's left is to come clean.'

'Sir?'

'Enrico, please, Vincenzo.'

'What do you mean, Enrico?'

'You're not a fool, mayor. There's no need to act like one in my presence. This is not bureaucratic bullshit we're discussing here. Vincenzo, this is your career. And mine. Let me be straight with you,' he waits for the mayor to sit forward attentively himself before, 'Zoran Santana is not your man.'

'Santana?'

'King Dope.'

'Coke. Where did you get that name from?'

'King Dope?'

'Zoran Santana.'

'I'm the Minister of the Interior, Vincenzo. How do you think? Now listen to me. Zoran Santana is not, and never has been, involved in any kind of illegal activity, much less illicit drug-dealing. He runs a legal, and might I add, highly profitable, corporation that brings millions to this country in foreign revenue and taxes. This man is a pillar of his community. Contributes lavishly to charities. He donated half a million dollars to upgrade this very building. Did you know that? Do you understand what I'm saying to you, Vincenzo?'

'With funds he's extorted from helpless children addicted to this shit that he sells—'

'Vincenzo—'

'I lost a *child* in this war, minister.' Mayor Del'Aquila lifts the trophy on his desk like he's just won it and shows it to the minister. 'I lost my girl to this *shit*—'

The minister blinks. 'I'm sorry for your loss, Vincenzo. But please, calm yourself. *Calma*. Now listen to me. First, your evidence, your entire case against Zoran Santana, rests on the testimony of a—a goddamn queer, a fairy selling his asshole for twenty bucks a shot. *Un sfigato*, Vincenzo. *Un culattone*. Not to mention a drug-addict and a whore.'

'None of that invalidates—'

'And a goddamn *cop-killer*.'

Vincenzo blinks at the tone of the minister's voice echoing in the office for a moment. He says, slowly, 'That doesn't negate—'

'And two—'

'Sorry, no, just one—'

'*And two*. Zoran Santana has already confessed to knowledge of a drug-smuggling operation running through his corporation and over which he has no control—'

'*Knowledge!* He's making a million bucks a day!'

'*Knowledge*, Vincenzo. Not collusion. *Knowledge*. In fact, when he was appraised of the situation by my office, he was more than happy to cooperate with our investigation.'

'Appraised?'

'Appraised.'

'By your office?'

'That is what I said.'

'*Your* investigation?'

'Yes, Vincenzo.'

Mayor Del'Aquila sits forward in his chair. 'What the fuck are you telling me here?'

'I'm telling you,' says the minister, 'that we've uncovered who your King Dope is.'

'Yes, we do too. Zoran fucking Santana is King Coke—'

'A man by the name of Giovanni Belladonna.'

'What?'

'That's your King Coke.'

'Who the fuck—' the mayor interrupts, before—'wait. Wait a second. Giovanni Belladonna? Santana's *butler*?'

'Belladonna is Santana's right-hand man, Vincenzo. Has been for twenty years. He knows everything about Santana's operation. He's your man, Vincenzo. Giovanni Belladonna is King Coke.'

Del'Aquila sits back in his chair. 'Are you fucking mad?'

'I suggest you watch your tone with me, Vincenzo. This is a delicate moment for you. And your administration. And I *seriously* suggest you forget about Zoran Santana. You have no evidence against him. A case that hangs on the highly dubious word of a rent-boy and a *cop*-killer is not one you want to hang your career around unless you want to end up hanging along with him.'

Mayor Del'Aquila blinks. Works it out slowly. Then, finally, he says, 'May I be direct with you, minister, as you have been with me?'

'Enrico.'

'What if I tell you my office has full-proof, one hundred percent evidence of Santana's guilt? What would you say then?'

'Impossible.'

'Do you honestly think I'd want to arrest a man with Santana's connections on the testimony of a drug-addicted *frocio*?'

'What more do you have?'

'Plenty.' Like the phone-tap, thinks Del'Aquila, that was fucking illegal. 'But I need you to answer this question for me— Enrico. Why are you protecting him?'

The minister sighs. 'I'm not protecting anyone, Vincenzo.'

'So why are you here?'

'Don't get cocky.'

'Tell me, Enrico. Why are you here?'

'Zoran Santana, Vincenzo, is a useful man. And I suggest you leave it at that, okay? Going to war with Santana will not win you any friends over at the Palazzo del Viminale, Vincenzo. Do you understand?'

'Is that a threat?'

'Don't be a fucking drama queen.'

The mayor gives it a moment. Finds a cigarette and lights it. 'Enrico,' he says, 'let me explain something to you. I have a mandate from the people of this city. To stamp out crime. To stamp out the illegal trade in hardcore drugs. And I will *not* bow to any form of intimidation. I understand very well how much power a man like Zoran Santana can wield. But he is *not* above our laws.'

'That was admirably put.' The minister claps twice. 'And not unexpected. I was warned about your hard-nosed attitude—'

'So my reply, *sir*,' Del'Aquila pauses as the minister's hand vanishes below his jacket to reappear holding an envelope, 'is to tell you to take your fucking—'

'Before you say anything regrettable, Vincenzo,' the minister hands the envelope over, 'I'd like you to consider this.'

'What is this? A fucking bribe?'

The minister pouts desolately. 'There is no corruption in our republic, Vincenzo, dear Gid, man. Are you mad?'

The mayor slits open the envelope. Slips out a monochrome photograph. His face whitens. He slides out the rest of the photos slowly. Photos of him smoking a hash-pipe in a hotel-room, here snorting lines, here lying naked on a bed of pillows joined in the next photo by a girl, oh my God, two girls—

'How old were they, Vincenzo? They look hardly pubescent. You may keep them,' the minister says.

Del'Aquila looks up from the photos. 'What is this?'

'Clearly not a bribe, Vincenzo. Giovanni Belladonna. He's your man. And your—constituents—will be grateful when they read of your great work bringing King Coke to book. Now I will send you the incriminating information that we've uncovered in our investigation. Highly incriminating, Vincenzo. Open and shut case, really.' The minister stands and offers his hand. Vincenzo just gapes at it, tears in his eyes. 'I'm sorry, Vincenzo. Santana is too important to us. And to our American friends. You follow? We're at war with the communists, Vincenzo, and Santana is ideally placed to hurt those terrorists on the extreme left. Now I'll call you next time I'm in town. My wife has been dying to meet you. Perhaps dinner? Next week?'

35. Clio Faces: 'Feel The Fear'

Below his NY baseball cap, he has his long hair folded up. He's grown a stubble. He observes the world from behind square shades. A boy slumped on the sidewalk. Two girls chatting to a soldier smoking American cigarettes up the block. The detached face hanging out from a window in the apartment building above him. Up the block, Robi gives him a thumbs-up. He takes one last look about him, and then walks on and meets her at the small opening that leads down the stone stairs into the bomb shelter.

'You wanna wait here?' He surveys the narrow alley. 'I'll be quick.'

She checks out the alley nervously. 'I don't like this.'

'So wait here.'

'No. I'm coming with you.'

Down the stairs with the light darkening and the stench worsening with every step. In the gloom, they spot Katia on the mattress in the corner staring up at the rounded, rotten-wood-ribbed ceiling, a smoke between her fingers trailing blue in the shivering light of a candle-flame.

'Sandro,' she says, seeing him and sitting up.

'It's Tuesday.'

'*Si, sono due ore che ti aspetto.*' She smiles at Robi. Sits up. 'How are you?' she says in English, and giggles at the sound on her lips.

'We're good,' says Robi and folds her arms.

Katia crouches and lifts the mattress. A bug crawls out, scuttling up over her foot, and scurries at Sandro, who stamps it dead under his boot. 'I could only get these,' she holds two EC passports at Sandro as Robi tries to understand what she's saying in Italian, 'Belgian. You speak German?'

He knows better than to contradict Katia. She still has her ideas buried in the past far away from this shelter, back in the days when she was first in her class, back when she was still a child. 'These are great,' he says, paging through his new passport. 'Where's Rina?' he asks, glancing within the gloomy tunnel, there where the lights fade to black. He feels something—a presence—and ignores his instinct.

'Don't know, she's been missing for two days.'

'She's not looking too hot.'

'None of us are. But look at you.' She looks at Robi instead. '*Amici*,' she touches Sandro's face with filthy nails, '*siamo amici vecchi.*'

'We're old friends,' Sandro translates and steps back from Katia. Eyes focused on the tunnel.

'*Ci volevamo così bene, ti ricordi, Sandro?*'

He says, 'We loved each other once,' with eyes firmly set on the tunnel. Itching to move. 'We gotta go. Now. Give her the cash, Robi. Give her—' but it's too late.

Sandro watches as a silhouette bleeds out the darkness into the nebulous light of the bomb shelter. Katia follows his stare. And sees Rina, a knife in her hand, stepping out from the tunnel.

'I want you to come with me, Sandro,' says Rina with white gob dribbling over her lips. 'Now. Zoran wants to see you.'

Sandro glances away, from Rina to Katia. 'What the fuck's happening?'

'What the fuck are you doing, Rina?' Katia says.

'Sit down, you stupid love-sick bitch!'

Katia falls back onto the mattress. Watches Rina close toward Sandro now, the blade shaking in her grasp. 'Zoran wants you,' says Rina.

'Rina—'

'*Shut up!*' Her eyes are fluttering, breath escaping in gasps. '*Tu,*' she waves the knife at Robi, '*dove sono i soldi?*'

Robi glances at Sandro.

'She wants the money,' he tells her.

Robi lifts her shirt to unreel the money-belt.

Sandro reaches over, grabbing the belt from her hand. 'Here. There's ten thousand dollars in here, Rina. Take it all. We just want to go.'

Rina extends her hand. Sandro lashes the belt out into her face. It slips from his grip on impact, flying deep into the tunnel. Rina stumbles back with a fat welt forming on her cheek as she slams back against the wall with the mirror crashing and shattering at her feet.

Sandro flings himself at her, his body crashing into her and they both fall onto the floor, the knife scuttling away from her fingers. Katia's on to it, as Sandro punches Rina heavily in the face.

'Stop it!' screams Robi, paralysed. She watches Katia lifting the knife. To run at Sandro, holding it up. And jabs the blade down through Rina's wildly flaying leg. Blood spurts out. Rina holds her leg screaming, her body twisting.

'Go!' shouts Katia. 'Take this!' she hands the blood-flecked knife at Sandro. 'Now go! *Go!*'

'Too late!' screams Rina with her eyes staring up at them menacingly. 'Too late!'

There's a sound from the tunnel. Sandro swivels. Sees a silhouette moving through the shadows. Indistinct. But a man. He grabs Robi's hands, pulls her with him for the stairs in one fluid motion. Leads her up for the day, freedom—

'Sandro, the money—' says Robi.

An explosion behind them, reverberating through the bomb shelter. They turn. Katia spins into the wall, her throat gushing blood. A flame flickers from the tunnel. Another explosion. The wall beside Sandro's head fragments.

'Get out! Move!' He forces Robi up the stairs, following her out into the sunlight. Grabbing hold of her arm, he propels her forward, into a labyrinth of narrow alleys. Gasping, their shoes snapping on the ground, they keep sprinting with wielding arms, lungs tightening and hearts about to explode.

There's a church ahead, turrets and towers and a magnificent façade of stone angels staring down at them as they tumble through the doors. The house of another's God appears deserted, with the wooden floor reflecting the light that dances through the immaculately stained-glass windows. They stumble to the front pew and sit down heavily. Breathless.

'Oh God,' Robi wheezes, 'oh God! What's happening? What's *happening!*'

Sandro deposits his head into his palms. The altar is awash with sunlight, a crucifix hanging from the tall ceiling from chains.

'What do we do now?' she asks. 'What do we now!'

'I don't fucking know!' he says. 'Ask God!' he adds, pointing to the altar, to Jesus with his head bowed, staring down at his persecutors. The doors suddenly crash open behind them, a silhouette running in with his face masked by the bright light. Sandro stands, moving to his left, to the aisle. The silhouette lifts its arm.

'No!' screams Robi.

The arm bucks with thunder.

Sandro lifts off his feet. Spinning over the pew and crashing onto the marble stairs leading up to the altar. Splattering blood across the floor as he slides backwards.

'No!' screams Robi, staring at the silhouette stepping cautiously forward, a pistol held in two hands.

Their eyes meet.

Robi blinks tight, focuses once more on the blond-haired assassin walking toward her, the pistol aimed at her face. The assassin stands ten yards from her now.

And then comes his voice.

'Robi?'

'Wayne?'

'Robi,' he whispers, stepping forward, 'what the fuck are you doing here?'

'Wayne,' she says, because she has nothing else. 'Wayne?'

Sandro's crawling toward the raised altar with a carpet of crimson blood following him up the marble. Wayne brings the pistol up. Aims. Robi flings her body at Sandro. Falling over him. Sheltering him now with her flesh, her eyes staring back at the assassin. 'What are you doing, Wayne! He's just a *friend*. What the fuck are you *doing!*'

'I don't wanna hurt you, Robi.'

She shakes her head at him, confused. 'Please, Wayne, I don't understand ...' Robi watches the assassin approach. Shielding Sandro with her body, she reaches her hands out at Wayne, beseeching. 'What are you doing?' She swallows hot fear. 'Who *are* you?'

Wayne strikes her across the face with the pistol's barrel. She stumbles sideways. He lifts the pistol and takes quick aim at Sandro, who crawls up the stairs, groaning and whimpering.

'Wayne, no!' Robi flings her body at the pistol. It fires as she hits his arm, and a hole appears between the eyes of the man hanging on the swinging crucifix. Then comes the explosion. She fights to grab the pistol, but Wayne is too powerful. Sweeps her legs away and she falls heavily with a shudder that rattles her spine.

Sandro has staggered onto his feet, the knife held limply in his left hand as blood cascades from his shoulder. Robi bites into Wayne's calf. He takes a moment to glance down at her. Sandro reacts. Diving over the stairs in a desperate lunge to embed the blade through the assassin's chest with his momentum forcing them both down. Robi's scream echoes in the church. Wayne's pistol scuttles from his grip. She dives and grabs for it as the two men lie together, not moving on the floor in a union of blood and pain.

Sandro's moving. She helps him up and off the motionless assassin. Wayne. Jesus, Wayne, she thinks, seeing the knife rooted in his chest, only the butt visible, blood streaming and pooling about him on the floor.

Sandro leans into her, she can smell his blood as she holds him and staggers forward. Towards the doors, the day—

'Robi! *Stop!*'

She wields around. Sees Wayne as in a dream, a fierce dream molten in pain, with a gun pointed at her. The knife is still buried deep in his chest. He's pale and sweating hard. Shivering, a snub-nosed .38 aimed at her. Struggling to even stand.

'No, Wayne.' She lifts both arms, joins them about the butt of the Beretta, and extends it out.

Wayne, slow with adrenaline and bodily morphine, squeezes the trigger to his police special. The bullet thuds into the stone basin of holy water beside her.

And now Wayne can hear, so clearly can he hear the click of the Beretta in Robi's hand, as the bullet swivels down the barrel. And then the pain. As the slug hits him in the face. He spins away. As a second slug hits him in the throat. And again, in the chest, as he goes down hard, smashing his head on the marble steps, his face shattering as if he's made of clay.

36. Savage: 'Don't Cry Tonight'

Silence. Except for the rocking Jesus on the cross. And the holy water spilling on the ground from the basin besides Robi where Wayne's bullet had ended its life. She looks down. At Sandro. Lying on the ground.

'Sandro!' She squats beside him. He's not conscious. Breathing ... breathing and bleeding, thick and odorous. She grabs his arm and wraps it about her shoulder, drags him up, on, *out*, 'Come fucking on!'

She can hear sirens. Closing! *Move*! Faces peer at them out on the street. She drags him on, into an alley. On. Pain is ecstasy. 'Hold on, Sandro,' she says, dragging him on into a series of ancient alleyways. She must find shelter—safety! For Sandro, who she places gently within a narrow alleyway that runs to a brick cul-de-sac. Dark. Quiet. Behind a dumpster that shields them from the street and prying eyes.

Sandro!

Now, with the sanctuary of the dim alley and shielding garbage dumpsters, her thoughts come flooding out like blood from her lover's body.

Wayne. She'd fucking *shot* him. *Killed* him! Jesus, she's fucking killed him ... As she had killed her father. Her—Richard. And Sandro lying below her. She turns to him, the blood caking through his shirt. 'Christ, where must I go!' she screams at his passive, pale face. '*Where!*' Wayne. What has she done? She looks at her hands, those killer hands that have caused so much pain, so much pleasure—she realises the automatic is still clenched between her fingers, an extension of her flesh. Of her soul.

She throws it into the wall, and it skitters away under the dumpster, and she buries her face into her hands that smell of death and cordite. Sobbing. Tasting her foul guilt like salt to her tongue from the tears that well down. Sirens. Close. Loud. Coming from seemingly everywhere. Sandro stirs, his eyes drifting apart and staring up at her vaguely. Her hands touch his face, her fingers gentle on his lips as he tries to speak.

'You've lost a lot of blood. What must I do?' she whispers. 'You need help.' His eyes shut as a siren screams past. '*Sandro*,' she whispers. 'Stay with me. I'm not losing you too.'

'You must—doctor, Rob ... 'cause I feel—bad—doctor.'

'I'll take you to the hospital.'

'Cops ...'

'You're—we gotta get you to a hospital, Sandro, nothing else matters, you just gotta hold on, you just gotta hold on, please—'

'There's a—Via Gialli—doctor. Money.'

'We left the money, at Katia's,' she swallows back her puke. 'We have no money. Sandro, you're *hurt*.'

He's silent for a moment, wheezing up breath into his weakened, bleeding body. 'I'm so thirsty. Robi.'

'God, what must I do!' she screams 'What must I fucking do!'

His hand finds her and squeezes it limply. 'Don't freak—you said—everything will be okay.'

She brings her face to him, shuffling back his hair from his perspiring face. 'How much money? I can get the money—I can get money. How much money!'

He can no longer keep his eyes open. Slowly, his heavy lids fall shut.

'The address, Sandro. The doctor—'

'Thirty-two—via—Gialli. Abortion—clinic but—money first. Money first or no go ...' His breath is strained, his blood flowing so dark. She walks about the alley, searching through the dumpsters, collecting reasonably clean boxes and newspapers and whispering to herself. As she had done while the sounds of her brother—she'd shot him too—lifting and examining garbage to ascertain its cleanliness. Finally, she returns to Sandro and dumps the boxes over the bleeding body. 'City camouflage,' she whispers. 'You'll be okay. I'll get the money and you'll be okay. Stay here. Stay here, I'll be back with the money.' She runs out from the alley. Only to pause at the mouth. To look back. But she can no longer see him. No longer see him. Her lover. Sandro. No longer hear him whisper in his junk-bed.

He raises his eyelids to the concrete sky. Shivering. Ice cold sweat and so hot. Watching through a soft focus. At the Vaseline sky flecked by scuttling worms. The pain is no longer pleasurable.

'Francesca,' he tries to find her with his heavy eyes. But his head weighs too much to lift. '*Francesca, ti amo.*'

The bomb shelter, when she gets near, is crawling with uniformed carabinieri, ambulances and squad cars parked haphazardly outside. Robi ducks into a side-street, running and crying hot tears that roll into her gasping mouth. Who the fuck does she know? Who—

Giovanni!

She stops mid-stride, examining her surroundings. On the corner, she spots an antique shop. She runs to it, entering with a clanging of bells like the call to Sunday Mass. The shop's musky and brown and an Indian man at the counter is reading an Umberto Eco paperback. He looks up as she approaches the glass-counter.

'Your phone, where is it?' she says.

'*Scusa?*'

'Your phone!'

'Fon?'

'Telephone!'

'*Tele—ahhh—telefono! Non—*'

'What? *What*!' She leans forward with her hands gripping the counter. He looks down. Stares at the blood-soaked fingers and white knuckles. Then up at the blinking, sweating face.

'*Li*,' he points at the corner of the shop, to a stand and a brass telephone above it. She rushes to it. Her hands shiver, like her mind as she dials.

She doesn't have the fucking number!

'Information,' she shouts back at the Indian man, 'information!'

'*Informazione? Tre tre tre.*'

'What!'

He jumps up, startled. Intimidated. Holds up three fingers, three times. *'Tre.'*

She dials it, 333, a message, words, what the fuck does it mean? She holds on, sweating, rubbing the dampness from her brow, smearing blood over her face.

'Informazione, buongiorno.'

'English. Do you speak English!'

'Uhm, yes, little bit.'

'An apartment, wait!' But her money-belt's gone. Along with her money and the fucking address book. Jesus, Sandro, just hold on for me.

'Pronto?'

'It's a big apartment block, here in Milano.'

'Street? What is the, *indirizzo*?'

Fuck! 'Santana! Zoran Santana!'

'Is name?'

'Yes! This is an *emergency*, operator!'

'No Zoran Santana in Milano.'

'But he's here!'

'No Zoran Santana.'

Giovanni, she can't recall the number on the kitchen wall. She's so fucking stupid! Call an ambulance! Now. And she's about to—the restaurant! In the country. The restaurant in the country! 'The restaurant Nella Campagna!' she shouts. 'Near Milano!'

The operator takes a while. 'We have a Trattoria Nella Campagna, in—'

'That's it!'

The operator's got the number. Robi dials it. It rings. And rings. And rings. Until finally a man answers. *'Pronto.'*

Can it be? 'Hullo?'

'Pronto. Trattoria Nella Campagna.'

'Gino?'

'Si. Chi parla?'

'Gino, this is Robi.'

'Chi?'

'I came with Giovanni, the American girl, you remember, *Robi!*'

'Ma si! Robi! Yes. How are you?'

'I need your help, Gino.'

'What's the matter? You sound scared.'

He has the number, Giovanni's, persuaded by Robi's tone, and now there's just blinding frustration as the phone just rings in her ear again, just keeps fucking ringing, *on and on*, until, *'Pronto.'*

'Giovanni!'

'Si.'

'Giovanni, this is Robi.'

'Robi? Where are you? Wayne was looking for you—he's in town—'

'He tried to kill me, Giovanni.'

'What? Who?'

'Giovanni, he shot Sandro. A friend of mine, Sandro. He's hurt—'

'Sandro? I don't—'

'He's hurt bad, Giovanni. We need your help—'

'Tell me where you are.'

She looks around at the antique shop, seeing for the first time, stares helplessly at the Indian guy. 'The address, *here*!'

'Scusa?'

'L'indirizzo,' shouts Giovanni.

'Come here!' Robi holds the phone up at the guy. *'Come here*!' Pointing at her shoe. The guy gets the message and walks to her. Shaking his head innocently. None too sure. She grabs his wrist and screws the receiver between his fingers. For him to speak uncertainly at the talking contraption. He rattles off something, via this and that, before he hands the phone back.

'I'll be there in five minutes, Robi. Just stay there,' says Giovanni.

'Hurry, Giovanni, *hurry*.'

The Indian guy cleans the blood on his hands across his jeans. Stares at Robi with creased brows. Watches her walk out into the day. To stand outside on the curb. Waiting.

Jesus, how *long!* Minutes, five minutes, come *on!* Giovanni will help. Sandro'll be okay. Just fucking wait, Sandro. I'm coming! The cavalry's coming! Whatever shit went down between Sandro and Zoran doesn't matter; they can sort that shit out—all that matters is getting him to a doctor.

The street runs one-way. Robi stares up at the far corner. Willing that fucking big BMW on. Where the fuck is it? A BMW limo' spins around the corner with squealing tyres. Heads for her quickly. She strains to see in the smoggy afternoon, closer, closer, and finally, with the BMW locking up tyres before her, she recognises Giovanni behind the wheel.

Robi takes a step towards the BMW that's stopped just ahead of her. She sees Giovanni climb out, silver-hair ruffling in the breeze.

And then she hears it.

A siren bellowing behind her.

She swivels. Sees a squad car spurting blue, flashing lights, speeding at them. She turns back to Giovanni. His hand is below his jacket, like Napoleon. He blinks. At her. Then at the approaching squad car.

And then runs back for the car.

'Giovanni, no, what are you doing!' she shouts as he jumps behind the wheel.

The squad car doesn't slow—rams into the BMW, knocking it sideways in a sickening explosion of sound. Two cops vault out, revolvers flashing in the afternoon. They sprint at the bimmer that suddenly leaps away, blue smoke from one punctured tyre as it violently charges up the street. The cops get into firing position and empty their magazines at the fleeing car. The rear windscreen shatters into tears. But Giovanni keeps raging on regardless.

And so does Robi. Sprinting away from the BMW, the cops, the bullets.

The cops shout something. Before splitting, one chasing Robi on foot, the other hopping into the Alfa and powering after the BMW with the engine hitting the rev limiter down the block like gunshots.

Robi crosses over the road, up the block, left onto a main drag and rushes the traffic, jumping onto the hood of a tiny Fiat 500 that misses her by an inch. She forces herself on, sliding right and into a tiled shopping mall. Glazed people walk beneath white lights, silent in the recesses of the massive construction. She sprints down an escalator, shoving shoppers aside, then back out into the dying day on a different level. There's an alley to her left and wheezing, she presses herself on through the alley and on to the next block. Moaning, she slows her cramping legs to a trot, her hands squeezing her sides, cramping hard, her back hunched. She casts a furtive look behind her shoulders.

No-one chases.

She's lost the cop.

Dusk is heavy as she retraces her steps towards the church. It's night when she passes the bomb shelter. A fluorescent tape shields off the entrance, *Polizia* printed upon it. *VIETATO L'INGRESSO.* The neighbourhood is alive, transformed within the blanket of the night. Whores line the sidewalks in an endless procession of flesh as curb-crawlers slowly pass, checking out the merchandise with hungry eyes flashing neon and sex. Sandro's world. Christ, Sandro, I'm coming. Music filters out into the streets, dimming voices, noise, anxiety. A car pauses beside her, the hooter blaring once. Robi looks at it, at a young man leaning out from the window. Two cars brake behind him, waiting patiently, understanding.

'*Andiamo,*' says the man.

'I don't speak Italian,' she tells him. Her knees are shaking.

'That sure helps, babe. Jump in.'

'You're American?' she says.

'I'm anything you want me to be. How much?'

'Two—three hundred thousand.'

Means nothing to him. 'Jump in.' He veers off the road onto the sidewalk, fondling out his wallet. She gets into the passenger seat. 'So where you from, honey?'

'Let's just do this,' she says. 'I'm in a hurry.'

'Damn, not like the girls back home,' he says and laughs. He pulls into a parking lot, rolling up cylindrical levels, snaking up for the roof. He settles for a murky corner where the lights flicker erratically. Hands her crisp notes.

'What's with the blood?' he asks, seeing her now for the first time.

'What blood?'

He smiles. 'The blood on your face. Is that your schtick?'

Robi knows what's required. Daddy will always be back to scar her soul. It takes nothing. For life. She goes down on him, slides down his zip. He leans back. She bangs away, sucking and licking and willing it on. Come *on*! He wants more. On the backseat, he wants to screw her like the babes back home with a condom, like college, the good ol' days, kissing her face, forcing himself on with Robi's legs split high on the roof.

'Say my name, baby, say my name.' It turns him on, the mere thought making him enlarge within her, 'say it!'

'I don't—'

'Elliot!' He slaps her face. Hard. 'Say it.'

'Elliot,' she whispers, grabbing his hair and sticking her tongue up his mouth. Grinding her hips into him, willing him on. 'Come on, Elliot!'

He slips out. 'Fuck!' The condom's off. He tries to manoeuvre in the constricted space. Can't.

'Just stick it in, Elliot. Fuck me!'

He does. Can't help it, so close to paradise. She grunts him in. Fucks him, smelling her own filth in the car, thick and overpowering as he orgasms, pulling out. Kneels on her chest, holding her hair now, wriggling—

'Get *off!*'

He does. Awkwardly.

She slides out of the car with her pants wrapped about one ankle. Bounces around to pull them up.

'Your asshole's bigger'n your cunt,' he tells her.

She runs to the ramp. Beside it, in the dark, a girl is on all fours while two men wait their turn sharing a bottle of wine.

She counts the money in her hand, Robi, three hundred thousand. She has enough. Runs, now, down the ramp and onto the street.

She's out of breath when she finally reaches the church. Now she must find the alley. Sandro! Searching the alleys like a starving child, the dumpsters, the garbage. Where the fuck—

Sandro! *Hold on! I'm coming.*

Sanity stumbling in the identical little alleys, knowing that somewhere—*somewhere* here Sandro lies waiting—waiting for her, waiting for the money in her fists.

And finally, finally she finds him.

'I've got the fucking money!' she says, brushing off the garbage from his body. Tossing the boxes aside frantically. 'Sandro! I have the money! It's okay, Sandro. I told you—everything's gonna be okay!' She lifts his pale face and kisses his still lips. 'It's okay.' She allows his heavy head to drop, to bounce on the ground. She stares down at him in the nebulous light. 'Sandro?' she whispers. Bows her head to his lips. Something leaps up at her face. A maggot crawling down her arm. She jumps back swiftly. But her eyes don't waver from his beautiful face, knowing, somehow, that if she looks away ... 'Sandro—'

She nudges him with her foot. Crouches to hold his limp wrist. Staring at his face, so pale, so—

She wants scream at the unforgiving sky but all she can muster from her numbed body is a deep moan that bleeds from her belly as she lowers her head on his blood-caked chest. Then she looks up at his face and she swears he's smiling.

'There's no more pain,' she tells him. She stands over him. Exhales tremulously. 'There's no more pain,' she whispers, and walks away.

36. MoonRay: 'Comanchero'

'Fuck it, I don't *know*.' Giovanni slams a fist onto the kitchen table. 'I was *this* fucking close, Zoran.' He shows an inch between thumb and forefinger. '*This* fucking close.'

Zoran blows nasal mucus down his throat and swallows. 'How did this happen?' he asks, sitting on a stool with orange juice at his elbow. 'I don't understand.'

'Zoran, look, she called, I told her to stay put—'

'—and when you got to the shop, the cops were waiting?'

'*This* fucking close.' Giovanni's eyes peer back behind Zoran's shoulder to the telephone. 'How did they know I would be there?'

'You tell me.'

'Unless the fucking phone's tapped.'

Zoran takes a sip of the juice. 'No. I got 'em checked out after my meeting at the cathedral with Wayne. They're clean, Giova'.'

'So then how? How did the cops know where she was? Where we were meeting?'

'Quite a few ways.' Zoran sips his orange juice. 'One, Robi called them. Two, the guy in the shop called them. Three, anyone on the *fucking block phoned them*!'

Giovanni blinks at Zoran's tone.

'Are you fucking stupid?' Zoran stands from the stool and draws near the silver-haired man. 'What the fuck are you doing going into a situation like that without back-up? You don't know any better? *She* called the cops, *imbecile!* She fucking made a deal with them— trade you in for a plane ticket back to fucking New York!'

Giovanni swallows at the face inches from his. 'Chicago,' he says, stepping back cautiously. 'Zoran. I thought—' he knows better than to continue. Waits for Zoran, but the man's gone back to his orange juice. Giovanni allows him a sip before he asks, 'So Robi's been arrested?'

'No, she's fucking vanished. But we ain't heard the last of that slut.'

'So who called the cops then?'

'It doesn't fucking matter! Who gives a shit who called the cops! It was *your* mistake. The phones are *clean*, Giovanni! And she spoke only to you. I didn't even know about this.' He considers the juice. 'Just chill out. We got other problems to deal with.'

'Like what?'

'Like what? Like this girl—this *Robi*,' like it's a synonym for shit, 'she knows now. Because of you, Giovanni, she knows about Wayne, about you, about *me!*'

'Wayne's incompetence was not—'

'Bullshit! He walked into a trap, you *idiot*! Sandro told her and those two, they figured this all out.' He waves his hands about the kitchen. 'And now Wayne is dead and you're trying to shoot the fucking whore like, like fucking—*imbecile!*' He slams a flat palm on the table. The glass jumps in fright. *'Dio Porco!* I'm surrounded by fucking idiots! And you, you imbecile! You are the most—you are a fucking cunt!' Zoran calms himself. Blows deep throated air into the kitchen.

'—Zoran, this is not my fault.'

The fat man raises his hands, palms up. 'I,' he says, 'I have created an *empire*, Giovanni. In ten years ...'

Giovanni knows better than to interrupt the lengthy pause.

'In ten years, Giovanni, I have learnt the secrets. And no girl from, from *Chicago*, no whore from the fucking *streets* is gonna fuck-up my paradise. Question is, Giovanni, are you bored with paradise? Do you want to go down,' jutting his triple-chin at the window, 'down to those people?'

'You know where my loyalties lie, Zoran.' He says it dead pan. 'I was there when you created paradise.'

Zoran slaps the glass. It flips in an orange spray to disintegrate into the wall. Shattering glass like snowflakes upon the floor. 'So was God,' he says. 'And now you are gonna resolve this fucking mess for me.'

37. Righeira: 'L'Estate sta Finendo'

She finds a hostel with bed and board for thirty thousand lire a day. The bed is comfortable, but she does not sleep. Sleep. She's not even alive. She has nowhere to go. No family, no money—no Sandro. She bites her lips before the mirror as the scissors cut away her dreadlocks to expose her pink scalp. She's in a country of foreigners and from where she can't escape. And even if she finds a way to leave—where does she go? Back to Chicago and the projects? God, if she'd never met that whore! If she'd never met him, if ...

Robi tugs on her smoke and steps to the curtained window. Un-parts the brown curtains and looks out into the night. Raining, autumn has set in fast. Turning, she half expects to find Sandro staring at her from the bed. Tears fill her eyes as she stares around the empty room. Whispers his name through a gob-filled mouth.

She tried to end it all. In the room with a razor blade, she tried to swap life for something else. But the razor would not slash her veins that pumped hate.

Survival's all that's left then. Sandro is gone. So is Wayne. But not Robi—she's back where she'd been at sixteen. When Wayne had found her working at a diner in Roseland. Alone.

Except now there is Zoran. And Sandro ... Sandro. She sees him now in her mind, she sees him stepping through the sun-drenched revolving doors of an apartment building in Milan and suddenly it all clicks.

There's a phone out on the landing and she tip-toes to it from her room, creeping down the long, silent corridor. How can she forget? She lives with sorrow clutching her throat, just a face, an emotion, a whisper, irrelevant and yet wrenching the breath from her body in a vice. When she shuts her eyes, she can *feel* him, feel him holding her from behind.

'*Pronto?*'

'Giovanni?'

'*Si. Chi è?*'

'Robi.'

'Robi? Jesus, *finally*! How are you? *Where* are you? What happened—'

'I want to speak to Zoran.'

'Zoran? Why? Listen, Robi—'

'No, *you* listen, you old fuck. Put me onto Zoran or the next call I make is to the cops.'

There's a hesitant pause. 'Okay. Hold on. I'll see if he's here.'

A moment passes as Robi listens to the ticking of a clock somewhere within the hostel.

'Yes, Robi, hi, it's Zoran.'

'You son of a bitch!'

'Yes,' agrees the voice. 'Where are you?'

'With Sandro. I know Wayne was working for you. Sandro wants a million dollars, Zoran. For his silence.'

'A million,' she hears a laugh. 'You've gotta be outta your fucking mind.'

'I am, Zoran,' says the bald girl with the rash on her scalp. 'I'll call you tomorrow with instructions.'

'Wait—'

She replaces the receiver. Perhaps this is where her life's been heading all along.

38. Kano: 'Another Life'

Virdis slugs a whiskey down his gullet. Burps out at the bald Silver with a frown and a calculator, busy balancing his cashbook that's spread over the bar counter.

'You know what the problem is, Silver?'

The bald guy doesn't look up. 'Not enough cash, too many debtors?'

Virdis adds a few fingers to his ice-ridden tumbler. 'It's these idiots who think we can make the world a better place by giving the kids what they want.'

'Is that so bad?'

Virdis thinks about it with the burn of the firewater. 'Yeah. Because our job's to protect them. Not help them fucking die. That's our jobs. That's what being a cop is about.'

'Like being a priest?' The old guy laughs and Virdis smiles at the sound. A shadow falls over the bar. Silver glances up, behind Virdis' shoulder. Virdis follows Silver's glance, swivelling to face Franco Rinaldi standing behind him with a smile.

'We got him, chief inspector.'

'Sorry?'

'She called.'

'Who called?'

'Roberta.'

Virdis frowns. 'The American?'

'Yes. She says Lago is still alive.'

'He's in the fucking morgue.' Waiting for a state burial.

'Yeah, but your instinct not to tell the press was genius, sir. Santana doesn't know. But get this—she's blackmailing him, she's blackmailing the son of a bitch for a million bucks!'

'A million lire? Not much considering—'

'A million fucking dollars.'

Virdis takes a moment. 'How do you know this? They got rid of the tap—'

'You'll never believe this.' Franco smiles. Big and wide.

'Try me.'

'Our mayor.'

'What about him?'

'He got the info from the ministry.'

'What ministry.'

'Interior. Seems they've been running an investigation on Zoran as well. And they got a wire into the apartment.'

'Santana's?'

'Yes.'

Virdis takes a moment to process. 'The mayor told you this?'

'Off the record. I just spoke to him. Fucking cloak and dagger— he met me at a café, like a fucking spy.'

'And she's blackmailing him—'

'For a million dollars.'

Virdis laughs. No humour. Just a flat, cold laugh. 'Are you kidding me?' And then, 'Go fucking figure,' he says to Silver, and watches him punch keys on his calculator with a tongue sticking out of his mouth, 'that girl's got balls this size,' he holds the bottle and pours another stiff shot. 'I'm gonna supervise this one personally, Franco. I don't want the girl hurt. I want this Santana. So bad I can taste him.'

'I'm not quite sure I understand—'

'No, Franco,' Virdis pats the stool beside him, 'I don't think you do. Let me tell you a story. You too, Silver, have a drink. It's a story about a girl and her brother growing up in Chicago ...'

39. Easy Going: 'Fear'

A stream of dusty sunlight beams over her eyes. She blinks. Sits up slowly. She knows what must be done. Thoughts of Sandro, probably rotting in that fucking alley, feeding the rats with his flesh ... now she thinks of Wayne, her sole source of survival. Why? What the fuck was it all about? She dresses quickly, walks out of the room, downstairs. The woman behind the desk flashes a gold-capped smile at her.

'I hear you walking all night. Thump, thump, thump. You miss breakfast, but I do not wake you. You need sleep.'

Robi smiles. 'Thank you,' she says. Steps away, to the phone. Zoran answers on the third ring. 'You got the money?' she says.

'Yes. Listen, Robi, this thing with Wayne—'

'Fuck Wayne. Fuck you and fuck Wayne.' Where does she meet him? Where does she *know*? 'The bomb shelter—where Wayne killed that girl. You know it?'

'Tell me what you want.'

'I'll pick the cash up. Tonight. Make sure it's there. All if it. In a—in a white sports bag.'

'A white sports bag?'

'What did I fucking say? A million dollars.'

'How do I know he won't talk?' His voice sounds strained, the breathing heavy and erratic.

'We just want to walk away.'

'I want to see him.'

'No,' she lights a smoke and exhales slowly. 'Impossible.'

'No whore, no million.'

'No.'

'That's the only way. Otherwise, we end this now and fuck the consequences.'

What choice? 'Okay. Tonight, at ten, at the bomb shelter. He won't speak to you, though.'

'So then—'

'But you'll see him, if that's what you want.'

'Fine. Robi—'

Robi lowers the receiver. Kills the smoke on the desktop ashtray and wonders out into the cool morning. She crosses the road to a café, her mind only working on the present—on the man serving her, still showing his summer tan, on the Martini umbrellas lining the sidewalk, dripping cold rain, at the cappuccino steaming at her elbow, on the man walking past that looks so much like Sandro.

After breakfast, she decides to sleep. Returns to the hostel. Sleep does not come. Eludes her with feral visions of maggots, chewing on her corpse. She sits up on the bed. Sweating. Staring out at the street nakedly.

Dinner. She's dead-on time. Her fellow residents gather in the mess room, clanging spoons on soup plates in a noisy game that makes them giggle. She eats slowly, alone on a corner table, without appetite, drinks a litre of orange juice, and leaves for the night.

She reaches the church as the belltower strikes nine. This time, though, she finds the alley immediately. Enters. And finds Sandro gone. They have found him. Moved him. But it's too late now for anyone to care. A bloodstain commemorates his deathbed. Maggots chew at the dried fluid. Behind the dumpster is where she finds the Beretta. And kneels in the bloodstain to save a prayer for Sandro's soul. Just in case. Lord, he was a good man. Spare his soul,

Lord. And then she's out. Her emotions buried too deep now to surface. To intervene. Even Sandro is a hazy dream. Maybe he got up and walked away.

The tape has been lifted from outside the bomb shelter. She inquires the time from a passing man in a coat, standing where she had that day when she'd played football, wondering if Sandro would return sober or stoned. So insignificant.

It's five minutes before ten.

The streetlamp casts a pool of nebulous light on the street. Ahead, she can see the whores going about their death. An unoccupied Volvo is parked just beyond the shelter. She glances about her, touching the Beretta slung into the back of her jeans. No-one.

She crosses the road and halts outside the shelter's entrance. Peers down the street. And then vanishes down the stairs. It's pitch black now, and Robi gropes for her lighter. Flips it. The flame casts an erratic shadow within the endless space. She steps down. Listening. Moving one step at a time. One step. One step.

And then she sees the silver-haired man standing before her like a sceptre. Dead-still. A blade silver fluid in his fist. She kills the flame instinctively, side-stepping in the darkness. She feels Giovanni brush past. Pulls out her Beretta and steps back in the black. Nothing but the void, as she circles to her left. Not breathing.

There's a shuffle of shoes behind her.

And then a flashlight rays out, down the stone stairs, and then another dices the darkness from within the belly of the shelter.

Standing just two feet before her, Giovanni is captured in the light, with his blade about to slash down at her throat. His eyes staring at hers. Stunned like a trapped animal. The stiletto in his fist.

She fires at him, twice.

Giovanni spins back in a bouquet of blood.

A flashlight held in mid-air by a black invisible body rushes down the stairs at her. The other flashlight is coming at her from the bomb shelter. Robi aims and fires.

'No!' shouts a voice behind her. 'No, Roberta, police! No!'

'Fuck you!' she screams, turns, about to pull the trigger. A flash of purple-orange light comes from behind the flashlight, like the flash of a camera, and Robi is flung back into the damp wall. She slides down to the floor, smearing blood thick on the wall.

'Franco!' shouts Virdis, shining his flashlight at the man lying at the foot of the stairs. '*Franco!*' He shines his flashlight on Franco's face, but half if it is missing, pasted on the wall behind him. Virdis spins the beam onto Robi. She's shrivelled in the foetal position on the bottom two stairs.

Not moving.

Footsteps converge towards Virdis, running down the stairs, and he lifts his arms into the erratic torchlights spinning madly about the bomb shelter. The cops come to a halt, peering past Virdis at Robi, at Giovanni flat on his face with the stiletto still clasped in his fist. At Franco ...

Virdis shuffles through the line of cops and out into the street. A uniformed patrolman waves a cellular wildly at Virdis as soon as he gets out into the rain. 'Chief inspector, chief inspector, the *mayor*, sir!'

Virdis takes the phone with weary hands. Sits on the bonnet of his Volvo. Allowing the bitter rain to run down the collar of his shirt. He places the brick-like contraption on his ear and hears nothing.

'Other way, sir,' says the cop, motioning to the phone. Virdis' glare is enough for him to find something else to do, well away from Chief Inspector Virdis, who rights the phone and says, 'It's done. I'm bringing Santana in tonight.'

'What are you talking about?' asks the mayor, sounding as if he's on a submarine.

'We have him. Your recording, plus we just killed one of his—his fucking—'

'What recording?'

Virdis stares at the bomb shelter. The mayor's denial is certainly no surprise even to Virdis' weary mind. 'You didn't know?'

'Didn't know what?'

'Roberta Johnson contacted Santana this morning. They set up a meet, Santana was gonna pay a million bucks to ensure her silence. But Santana sent an emissary. Roberta was killed.'

'Emissary?'

'Giovanni Belladonna. Santana's right-hand man. Obviously, Santana sent him to eliminate—'

'That's impossible, Virdis.'

'What's impossible?'

'Santana left the country yesterday morning. He's attending a funeral in Chicago with our Minister of the Interior. He wasn't even *here* when you say he spoke to the girl.'

Virdis frowns. 'Sir, you told Franco Rinaldi—'

'Who?'

'Detective Franco Rinaldi, he's on my team. You spoke to him—'

'What the fuck are you on about? I've never spoken to this man.'

'Of course you have—'

'Listen to me, Virdis. Santana's corporation was being used for the importation and distribution of dope without his knowledge. The whole thing was orchestrated by Giovanni—'

'Belladonna,' completes Virdis with sudden insight. 'And he's dead.' Of course.

'That's it, Giuseppe, we got him.'

Virdis watches the paramedics hoist Roberta's corpse up the stairs, her one arm dangling over the side of the stretcher.

'—job well done, chief inspector,' says the mayor.

'After all the killing, after Onassio, and this *girl,* after, after—'

'Be grateful you caught him, Giuseppe. Think about it. *You* brought down King Coke—'

Virdis hurls the cellular into the night. Watches it explode in a technicolour spray of components.

It's over.

Virdis looks up at the sky. Rain washes his face. He welcomes it. Steps off to his Volvo and thinks, fuck it.

It's over. It's time to read his wife's letter.

ends

Joburg 1987